Heat slammed down across the desert like a smith's hammer on a glowing anvil.

Ahead of him, dim in the distance, Gereint saw the first high foothills that led up to the great mountains. As far as he could see, the hills were red with fiery sand. Heat shimmered across them.

Gereint stared at the hills for a long moment. Then he laughed—it was not much of a laugh, but he *meant* to laugh. He drank the rest of the water in the fourth skin in one draught. Then he threw the skin aside and strode forward, straight into the teeth of the sun.

That burst of defiance lasted only very few minutes. Then, from striding, Gereint found himself suddenly on his hands and knees, with no memory of falling. For a moment he thought he might simply lie down and let the heat finish killing him. But the desert was too profoundly inimical; he could not bring himself simply to give way to it. He crawled instead into the shadow of a narrow bladelike spire that pierced the hot air and collapsed its meager protection. Red heat beat up through him from the sand and closed down around him from the air, but he did not know it.

LAND OF THE BURNING SANDS

THE GRIFFIN MAGE TRILOGY: BOOK TWO

RACHEL NEUMEIER

www.orbitbooks.net

Copyright © 2010 by Rachel Neumeier
Excerpt from *Law of the Broken Earth* copyright © 2010 by Rachel Neumeier
All rights reserved. Except as permitted under the U.S. Copyright Act of 1976, no part of this publication may be reproduced, distributed, or transmitted in any form or by any means, or stored in a database or retrieval system, without the prior written permission of the publisher.

Book design by Giorgetta Bell McRee
Cover design by Lauren Panepinto

Orbit
Hachette Book Group
237 Park Avenue New York, NY 10017
Visit our website at www.orbitbooks.net

Orbit is an imprint of Hachette Book Group. The Orbit name and logo are trademarks of Little, Brown Book Group Limited.

Printed in the United States of America

First mass market edition: June 2010

10 9 8 7 6 5 4 3 2 1

This one is for my mother, from whom I absorbed a "feel" for grammar—so much easier than actually having to learn the rules!

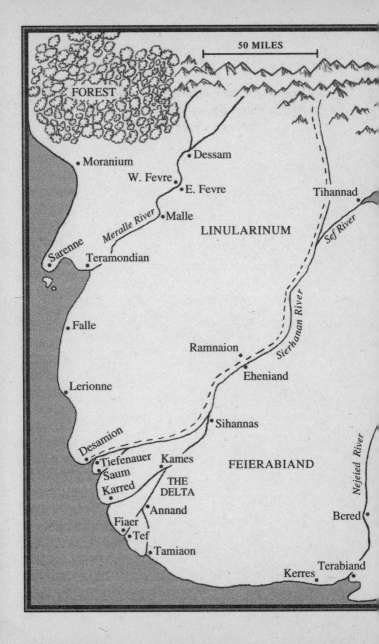

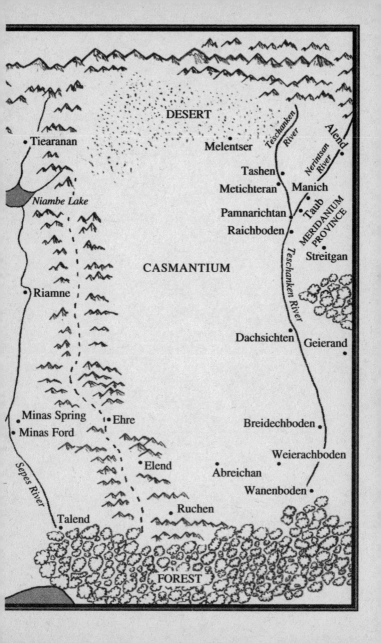

LAND OF THE
BURNING SANDS

CHAPTER 1

Gereint Enseichen sat on a narrow pallet in the lowest cellar of the Anteirden townhouse, waiting. He leaned against the rough stones of the wall, stretched his legs out before him, and listened to fierce sand-filled winds over his head pare the cobbles of the street down to bare earth. He could hear the savage wind, the scouring sand, faint crashes that marked the explosions of distant windows, the cracking of wooden beams, the collapse of stone walls: the destruction of the city under the ruthless wind and heat. Sometimes the very earth that surrounded him seemed to tremble in sympathy with the storm above.

Of course, the house's cellar was deep. Maybe Gereint only imagined he heard those sounds. Maybe he only imagined the occasional faint shaking of the earth. But if he went up the first flight of stairs to the upper cellar and then up the second flight to the door to the kitchens... If he did that, he would surely find the storm. Surely it had by now raked down from the north and fallen across Melentser. If it filled the world outside, it would be dangerous to go up those stairs.

Or if he imagined the faint sounds of destruction, if the storm hadn't yet arrived...it might be, for Gereint, more dangerous still.

Only if the storm had already come and destroyed Melentser and blown itself out would it be safe for him to leave the safety of the deep cellar. Gereint tilted his head, listening. Maybe the faint screaming of the wind, the raking hiss of blown sand, was his imagination. Maybe those sounds were not his imagination at all. Either way, he had no intention of going up those stairs. Not until he was *certain* the Fellesteden household was well away—and until he had given the storm ample time to arrive, rake across the city, and die.

According to Andreikan Warichteier's *Principia*, distance alone would break a *geas*. On the other hand, Pechorichen held, along with most other authorities, that only death could do that. How Warichteier had tested his idea was not clear, as no one *geas* bound could walk away from the man who "held the other end of the chain" unless he was given leave to go. But Gereint had not walked away from Perech Fellesteden. He had simply allowed Fellesteden to walk away from him.

If the *geas* actually broke, that would be best. If it merely became quiescent, that would do. Just so long as Gereint was not driven to follow the road south after his master, he should do very well. At the moment, he felt merely uneasy. He knew Fellesteden must be furious with him. But, sealed away beneath stone and earth, he was unable to hear his master's call, blind to the man's undoubted fury. The *geas* could not compel him to follow a man who was not *there*.

Or so Gereint fervently hoped.

The desert's coming had driven everyone in Melentser into chaotic retreat southward, on roads never meant to accommodate such a massive number of refugees. Or...probably not quite everyone. Gereint wondered how many others might be tucked away in cellars and wellhouses, waiting for the desert to drive the upstanding citizens of Melentser out of the city. The desperate, the stupid, the mad, those unfortunates both crippled and destitute: Probably few of her last inhabitants would survive Melentser's fall by more than a day or so.

Gereint counted himself among the desperate rather than the stupid or the mad, and hoped he would find no reason to change his mind. He had made good use of the scant days of preparation. No one had been able to keep careful count of supplies in those last days: Pilfering had been easy and nearly safe. Here in the cellar, he had a bottle of the Fellesteden's best wine, two rare books from the Fellesteden library, a change of clothing, decent boots a little loose in the ankle, a few coins, nine fat candles, two lanterns and four jars of oil, a twelve-hour sand timer, a bag of apples, some fresh bread and soft cheese, plenty of the hard cracker and dried beef that travelers carried, and six skins of clean water. He had not had time to make the waterskins himself, but these were the best he had been able to find. They should keep the water clean and cool; they wouldn't leak or spoil. They were for later. For the present, he had a small barrel, which had once held ale and that he had refilled with water before lugging it, with some difficulty, down to this cellar.

Aside from his own stolen supplies, there was nothing in this low cellar but empty racks where wine had been stored. It was a pity that all the racks were empty. The Anteirdens had been renowned for the quality of their wines. But they had left nothing behind when they closed their house, which they had done quickly: Berent Anteirden, head of the Anteirden household, was a decisive man and not inclined to risk his family by dithering. Unlike Perech Fellesteden, who had indeed dithered and let his own household's flight become...usefully chaotic.

Was he hearing the sound of sand scraping against stone overhead? Or was the sound merely in his mind? Gereint squinted up at the close-fitted stones of the ceiling and decided the sound was real. Probably.

To drive back the dark and his too ready imagination, he lit the second lantern as well as the first. This was profligate, but he had plenty of oil. He had made the lanterns himself and stolen only quality oil for them; the light was luxuriously clean and clear. There was nothing to do but wait for the dry storm to blow itself out. He did not intend to go up those stairs until enough time had passed to reasonably suspect it had. He picked up one of the books, Gestechan Wanastich's history of Meridanium, and let it fall open at random. Illuminations picked out in gold and powdered pearl glittered around the measured stanzas that marched down the page: *On this night, my friends, on this night of fire and iron / On this dark night of fire and rage / When we leave our wives weeping behind us / To play the game of death among the broken stones where the deadly wind cries*...

Gereint closed the book and set it aside. All his masters had been men of learning, or at least had wished to pass themselves off as such. Inclined toward old beautiful books even as a child, Gereint had learned early that a slave's best comfort and surest escape was to be found in black ink and painted illuminations, in philosophy and history and poetry. But perhaps not Wanastich's poetry, just at this moment when all his hope was bent on a more literal and far more dangerous kind of escape.

The other book was also a history, Berusent's great *Casmant Historica*. At least it contained no grim poetry, Berusent not being of a particularly dour temperament. Gereint picked it up, opened it to an account of the founding of Breidechboden, and read a few lines. But he found he could not concentrate. He put this book, too, aside, folded his arms across his chest, and stared at the ceiling.

How long *would* it take the storm of wind and sand to consume a city? A day, a night, and another day? That was how long Anteirch's account gave for the destruction of Sarachren. But then, Anteirch had fancied himself a poet. "A day, a night, and another day" was a poetical convention if Gereint had ever heard one. How long had it really taken? One day, three days, ten? Sarachren's destruction had happened too long ago, been recounted by too many unreliable historians. No one knew how long it would take for Melentser to disappear into the red desert. But if the storm took longer than three or four days to settle, Gereint would surely wish he'd stolen more food.

The sand timer ran down three times—counting off, as it happened, a day, a night, and another day—before Gereint lost patience and allowed himself to go up the first flight of stairs and open the heavy, close-fitted door that led to the upper cellar. He paused, then, listening. There was no sound at all. The air was different: not cool and moist. It was light and dry, with an unfamiliar scent to it. Like...hot iron, hot stone. Maybe. Or maybe that was his imagination again. But a haze of dust glittered and moved in the light of his lantern. That was not imagination.

He went up the second flight of stairs. Red dust had sifted under the kitchen door and down the steps. It gritted underfoot; it puffed into the air when he scuffed it with his foot. When he gripped the stair railing, his hand left pale prints in the dust. He touched the door. But then he merely stood there for a long, long moment. He told himself there was nothing to fear. He heard nothing, even when he pressed his ear to the door. The storm...probably the storm had subsided. And if that was so, then there was nothing to fear. No one would be in the kitchens. No one would be in the house. No one would be in the city—certainly no one important. Probably nothing would move in the broad streets of Melentser but wind and sand and one desperate man willing to risk losing his life in the desert if he could only lose the *geas* as well...Lifting his hand, Gereint rubbed his thumb across the brand on his face. The smooth scar of the brand still felt strange to his touch, though it had been there nearly half his life.

The door's brass knob was warm to the touch. Gereint turned it and pushed. The door did not budge. It was not locked: Gereint could feel the latch move. He shoved harder. To no avail.

He knew at once that sand had drifted across the door. Perhaps a lot of sand. Perhaps the kitchen was filled with it; perhaps the house was buried in it...Terror smelled like hot metal and hot stone: Fear lived in a handful of red dust. Gereint shoved frantically.

The door gave. Not much. But enough to suggest it could be forced open. Enough to let him push back panic, breathe deeply, stop fighting, and think.

The pressure was against the lower part of the door. He set his back against the stone wall of the stair landing and his feet against the door right at the base and pushed steadily.

The door opened a crack, heavily. Heat and light poured through the crack, and sand, and plenty of red dust. If there had been more than a few inches of sand on the other side of the door, Gereint would not have been able to open it. He couldn't quite block out this realization, though he tried. It was a well-made, sturdy door: Strong as he was, he probably would not have been able to break it. Clever fool: clever enough to hide in a nice, cool, secret death-trap…Anger as well as fear loaned him the strength to shove harder on the door, against the sand that had piled up against it.

The crack widened. Light and heat, dust and sand, and through it all that strange dry smell to the air, as though heat itself had a scent. Red sand and silence…He found the kitchen empty and silent when he finally had a gap wide enough to force himself through. The shutters on the windows were not merely broken, but missing. Splinters clung to the twisted brass hinges. The door that had led to the kitchen garden was missing as well. And the garden, itself: gone. Buried under sand, which had drifted much more deeply outside than in. Dust eddied in the corner where a white-barked birch had stood. No trace of the tree remained. Gereint could see the Fellesteden townhouse, but…ruined, nearly unrecognizable—half the roof and part of the wall broken, the brick deeply etched by blowing sand. The house looked a hundred years old. Two hundred.

Everything outside the house was drowned in heavy light and red sand.

By the angle of the sun, it was late afternoon. Gereint scooped sand away from the kitchen door and retreated back down into the cellars. It seemed to him that even the deeper cellar was drier and warmer now; that the smell of hot stone was perceptible even here. He shut the heavy cellar door, looked down at the red dust that had settled on the floor, and wondered how far the desert now extended.

His supplies...He had never thought himself generously supplied. But he had thought his supplies at least adequate. Now he thought of the powerful heat and red sand and tried not to doubt it.

That evening, as the powerful sun sank low in the west, Gereint sat in the shade of a broken wall, waiting for sundown and looking out across the ruins of Melentser. The sun was blood red and huge; its crimson light poured across broken stone and brick, across streets drifted with sand. Dust hazed the air, which smelled of hot stone and hot brass. Scattered narrow fingers of jagged red stone had grown somehow out of this new desert: a new inhuman architecture of twisted knife-edged towers. These strange cliffs were like nothing Gereint had ever seen. They pierced the streets, shattered townhouses, reached sharp fingers toward the sky. If one had torn its way out of the earth beneath the Anteirden house...But, though he flinched from the images that presented themselves to his mind, none had. Now the red towers cast long shadows across the shattered city.

Nothing moved among those towers but the creeping shadows and the drifting sand. And the griffins. A dozen or so were in sight at any given moment, though rarely close. But three of them passed overhead as the sky darkened, so near that Gereint imagined he could hear the harsh rush of the wind through the feathers of their wings. He stared upward, trying to stay very small and still against the dubious shelter of his wall. If the griffins saw him, they did not care: They flew straight as spears across the sky and vanished.

The griffins were larger than he had expected, and... different in other ways from the creatures he'd imagined, but he could not quite count off those differences in his mind. They looked to him like creatures made by some great metalsmith: feathers of bronze and copper, pelts of gold... Gereint had heard they bled garnets and rubies. He doubted this. How would anyone find that out? Stick one with a spear and wait around to watch it bleed? That did not seem like something one would be able to write an account of afterward.

Spreading shadows hid the red cliffs, the streets, the kitchen yard where once the garden had grown. Overhead, stars came out. The stars looked oddly hard and distant, but the constellations, thankfully, had not changed. And he thought there was enough light from the stars and the sliver of the moon to see his way, if he was careful.

Gereint stood up. His imagination populated the darkness around him with predatory griffins waiting to pounce like cats after a careless rabbit. But when he stepped cautiously away from the wall, he found nothing but sand and darkness.

He had already drunk as much water as he could from

the barrel. Now he picked up his travel sack, slung its strap across his shoulder, and walked out into the empty streets. He carried very little: the candles and a flint to light them, the travel food, one change of clothing and a handful of coins, and the six skins of water. More than he had truly owned for years.

The hot-brass smell of the desert seemed stronger now that he was moving. Heat pressed down from the unseen sky and hammered upward from the barely seen sand under his boots. He had read that the desert was cold at night. Though the furnace heat of the day had eased, this night was far from cold. The heat seemed to weigh down the air in his lungs and drag at his feet. The sand, drifted deep across the streets, was hard to walk through. Both the heat and the sand bothered him far more than he had expected.

He did not head south nor straight east toward the river. Those were the ways the people of Melentser had gone, and above all he did not want to walk up on the heels of any refugees from the city. He walked north and east instead, toward the unpeopled mountains. His greatest fear seemed unfounded: The *geas* did not stop him choosing his own direction. He could tell that it was still alive, but it was not active. He felt no pull from it at all.

Casmantium did not claim the country to the north, the mountains beyond the desert—no one claimed that land. Rugged and barren, snow capped and dragon haunted, men did not find enough of value in the great mountains to draw them into the far north. But a single determined man might make his way quietly through those mountains, meeting no men and disturbing no sleeping monsters, all two hundred miles or more to the

border Casmantium shared with Feierabiand. The cold
magecraft that shaped *geas* bonds was not a discipline of
gentle Feierabiand: When a *geas*-bound man crossed into
that other country, the *geas* should…not merely break.
It should vanish. It should be as though it had never
been set.

Or so Warichteier said, and Fenescheiren's *Analects*
agreed. Gereint was very interested in testing that claim.

Maps suggested that the foothills of the mountains
should be little more than forty miles from Melentser. On
a good road in fair weather, a strong man should be able
to walk that far in one night. Two at the outside. Across
trackless sand, through pounding heat…three, perhaps?
Four? Surely not more than four. How far did the desert
now extend around Melentser? All the way to those foothills? He had planned for each skin of water to last for
one whole night and day. Now, surrounded by the lingering heat, he suspected that they might not last so long.

While in the ruins of the city, he found it impossible
to walk a straight line for any distance: Not only did the
streets twist about, but sometimes they were blocked by
fallen rubble or by stark red cliffs. Then Gereint had to
pick his way through the fallen brick and timbers, or else
find a way around, or sometimes actually double back
and find a different route through the ruins of the city. He
could not go quickly even when the road was clear; there
was not enough light. Yet he did not dare light a candle
for fear of the attention its glow might draw.

So it took a long time to get out of Melentser; a long
time to clamber over and around one last pile of rubble
and find himself outside the city walls. A distance that
should have taken no more than two hours had required

three times that, and how long *were* the nights at this time of year? Not long, not yet. They were nowhere close to the lengthening nights of autumn. How quickly would the heat mount when the sun rose? Gereint studied the constellations once more, took a deep breath of the dry air, drank a mouthful of water, and walked into the desert.

The stars moved across the sky; the thin moon drew a high arc among them. The arrowhead in the constellation of the Bow showed Gereint true east. He set his course well north of east and walked fast. The night had never grown cool. There was a breeze, but it was hot and blew grit against his face. Sometimes he walked with his eyes closed. It was so dark that this made little difference.

Already tired, he found that the heat rising from the sand seemed to lay a glaze across his mind, so that he walked much of the time in a half-blind trance. Twisted pillars and tilted walls of stone sometimes barred his way. Twice, he almost walked straight into such a wall. Each time he was warned at the last moment by the heat radiating into the dark from the stone. Each time he fought himself alert, turned well out of his way to clear the barrier, and then looked for the Bow again. Usually the ground was level, but once, after Gereint had been walking for a long time, he stumbled over rough ground and fell to his knees; the shock woke him from a blank stupor and, blinking at the sky, he realized he had let himself turn west of north, straight into the deep desert. He had no idea how long he had been walking the wrong way.

Then he realized that he could see a tracery of rose gray in the east. And then he realized that he was carrying a waterskin in his hand, and that it was empty. It had not even lasted one entire night.

The sun rose quickly, surely peeking over the horizon more quickly than it would have in a more reasonable land. Its first strong rays ran across the desert sands and fell across Gereint, and as they did, he felt the *geas* bond to Perech Fellesteden fail. It snapped all at once, like the links of a chain finally parting under relentless strain. Gereint staggered. Stood still for a moment, incredulous joy running through him like fire.

Then the sun came fully above the horizon, and Gereint immediately discovered that he'd been wrong to believe the desert hot at night. Out here in the open, the power of the sun was overwhelming. Unimaginable. No wonder the sunlight had broken the *geas*; Gereint could well believe the sun's power might melt any ordinary human magic. Once well up in the sky, the sun seemed smaller and yet far more fierce than any sun he'd ever known; the sky was a strange metallic shade: not blue, not exactly white. The very light that blazed down around him was implacably hostile to men and all their works. Indeed, hostility was layered all through this desert. It was not an ordinary desert, but a country of fire and stone where nothing of the gentler earth was meant to live. The great poet Anweierchen had written, "The desert is a garden that blooms with time and silence." Gereint would not have called it a garden of any kind. It was a place of death, and it wanted him to die.

He had hoped he might be able to walk for some of the morning. But, faced with the hammer-fierce sun, he did not even try. He went instead to the nearest red cliff and flung himself down in its shade.

The day was unendurable. Gereint endured it only because he had no other option. As the sun moved through its slow arc, he moved with it, shifting around the great twisting pillar of stone to stay in its shade. But even in the shade, heat radiated from the sand underfoot and blazed from the stone. He could not lie down, for the heat from the ground drove him up; he sat instead and bowed his head against his knees. The sleep he managed was more like short periods of unconsciousness; the twin torments of heat and thirst woke him again and again.

He stayed as far from the stone as he could get and yet remain in its shade, but the short shadows of midday drove him within an arm's length of the cliff and then he thought he might simply bake like bread in an oven. The occasional breeze of the night was gone; the air hung heavy and still, very much as it must within an oven. If there were griffins, Gereint did not see them. He saw something else, once, or thought he did: a trio of long-necked animals, like deer, with pelts of gold and long black scimitar horns that flickered with fire. They ran lightly across the sand near him, flames blooming from the ground where their hooves struck the sand. As they came upon Gereint, the deer paused and turned their heads, gazing at him from huge molten eyes, as though utterly amazed to find a human man in their fiery desert. As well they might be, he supposed.

Then the deer startled, enormous ears tilting in response to some sound Gereint could not hear, and flung themselves away in long urgent leaps. They left behind only little tongues of fire dancing in their hoof prints.

But perhaps he only hallucinated the flames. Or the deer. The heat was surely sufficiently intense to create hallucinations. Though he would rather have seen a vision of a quiet lake where graceful willows trailed their leaves...

He could not eat. The thought of food nauseated him. But Gereint longed for water. His lips had already cracked and swollen. Berentser Gereimarn, poet and natural philosopher, had written that, in a desert, the best place to carry water was in the body; that if a man tried to ration his water, he would weaken himself while the water simply evaporated right from the waterskin and was lost entirely. Gereint wanted very badly to believe this. That would give him every reason to drink all the water in his second waterskin. But Gereimarn had been a better poet than philosopher: His assertions were often unreliable. And the thought of emptying yet another skin of water in his first day, of being trapped in the desert with no water left, was terrifying. Gereint measured the slow movement of the sun and allowed himself three mouthfuls every hour.

Even at midsummer, even in the desert, the sun did have to retreat eventually. Shadows lengthened. The hammering heat eased—not enough, never enough. But it eased. Gereint got to his feet before the sun was quite down and walked away from the stone that had, all day, both sheltered and threatened to kill him. He walked quickly, because now that the heat was not so desperately unendurable, what he really wanted to do was collapse into an exhausted sleep. But if he did that, if he did not use every possible hour for walking, he knew he would never reach the end of the desert.

How long had he estimated for a man to walk forty miles? Fifty, if he could not keep a straight course? He worked out the sums again laboriously in his head. He felt he was trying to think with a mind as thick and slow as molasses, but it helped him stay awake enough to keep his direction clear. He worked the sums a second time, doubting his conclusion, and then a third. How quickly was he walking? Not fast, not once his first burst of speed had been exhausted. Not four miles an hour. As fast as two? That would make it sixteen miles in eight hours. Sixteen? Yes, of course, sixteen. Or if he managed *three* miles in an hour, wouldn't that be...twenty-four miles? That would surely take him clear of the desert by dawn. Wait, *were* the nights eight hours long at this time of year? He should know the answer to that...Anyone would know that...He could not remember. If he could get to the mountains by morning...He had to. How fast was he walking?

Gereint stopped, sat down, and finished all the water in the second skin and half the water in the third. He made himself eat some of the cracker and dried beef. He had lived through one day in the desert; he doubted he would survive another. So he needed to walk fast and not let himself fall into a heat-induced trance, and to walk fast he needed strength.

He did feel stronger when he got back to his feet. He found the arrow's head in the Bow and set his direction. Then he counted his steps. He allowed himself a mouthful of water every two hundred steps. He counted in a rhythm to keep himself from slowing down. When he stumbled and caught himself and realized he'd once again been walking in a daze, he began to count by threes. Then by sevens. Then backward from five thousand, by elevens. He told himself that if he lost count, he'd have to start over and forfeit his mouthful of water. That self-imposed threat helped him keep alert.

He finished the third skin of water and began on the

fourth. He tried to suck on a pebble, but the pebbles of this desert neither felt nor tasted right in his mouth; they tasted of heat and hot copper and fire. He spat one out quickly, drank an extra mouthful of water, and tried to fix his thoughts on the northern mountains. There would be streams running down from the heights; it might be raining. He could hardly imagine rain.

It crossed his mind that it might be raining in the south. Perech Fellesteden had intended to take his family all the way south to the luxurious southern city of Abreichan: He had property there. Well, Fellesteden had property everywhere, but his holdings in Abreichan were among the largest.

If Gereint had gone with his master, he would be in the south. Maybe walking through the rain. But...he would still be with Perech Fellesteden.

Lifting a hand, Gereint traced the brand on his face with the ball of his thumb. Traced it again. Lowered his hand and lengthened his stride.

It occurred to him some time later that the ground was tending somewhat upward.

Then the sun sent its first deceptively gentle rose glow above the eastern horizon.

Gereint stopped and waited, straining his eyes for the first glimpse ahead of the mountains. He felt he was poised at the tip of a moment; that though the sun was rising, time was not actually passing; that the whole desert waited with him for the answer to the question of time and distance.

Then the sun rose, blazing. Heat slammed down across the desert like a smith's hammer on a glowing anvil. Ahead of him, dim in the distance, Gereint saw the first high foothills that led up to the great mountains. As far as he could see, the hills were red with fiery sand. Heat shimmered across them.

Gereint stared at the hills for a long moment. Then he laughed—it was not much of a laugh, but he *meant* to laugh. He drank the rest of the water in the fourth skin in one draught. Then he threw the skin aside and strode forward, straight into the teeth of the sun.

That burst of defiance lasted only very few minutes. Then, from striding, Gereint found himself suddenly on his hands and knees, with no memory of falling. For a moment he thought he might simply lie down and let the heat finish killing him. But the desert was too profoundly inimical; he could not bring himself simply to give way to it. He crawled instead into the shadow of a narrow bladelike spire that pierced the hot air and collapsed in its meager protection. Red heat beat up through him from the sand and closed down around him from the air, but he did not know it.

He woke in cool mist, surrounded by green light that filtered through branches dripping with water. A blanket guarded him from falling drops. A fire crackled an arm's length away, its tiny warmth a comfort rather than a threat. He was not thirsty. In fact, he felt a languid sense of well-being that at first was too foreign to recognize. Fragrant steam rose from a pot on the fire...Soup, he recognized eventually. The recognition drifted through the languor without urgency.

"Are you hungry?" a voice asked.

Gereint thought about this question. He did not quite know the answer, nor did it seem important. The voice was unfamiliar. A faint uneasiness made its way through the clinging vagueness.

"Can you sit up?" the voice asked him. "Come, now. Try."

Gereint did try, the uneasiness biting more sharply. He found himself weak, but less so than he had expected. A hand on his shoulder supported his effort...He turned his head, trying to focus his gaze on the owner of that hand. His vision faded oddly in and out.

"That will pass," the voice reassured him. "You need food; that'll get you back in proper order. Can you hold this mug? Try. Drink."

Gereint closed his eyes and sipped. It was a rich broth, thick with bits of meat, not beef...not mutton... venison, maybe. He drank the broth and found his attention sharpening, the languor receding. Strength seemed to pour outward from his belly through all his limbs. A recollection of the desert came back to him, the long walk and the final glimpse of the red desert going right up into the distant hills. The memory was vivid and yet seemed somehow long ago. It held little horror, and no terror.

Then he remembered the reason he had walked into the desert, and terror went through him like the crack of a whip. He put the mug down sharply—the handle broke off in his hand, he was dimly aware—and looked for his...benefactor.

The man wore the sort of good, tough, well-made clothing that any ordinarily prosperous man might wear for traveling, though the ring on his left hand looked more than ordinarily valuable. He was plump, round faced, older than Gereint...maybe in his fifties. Not tall. Not intimidating. He even looked kind, for what little that impression might be worth. But he was not meeting Gereint's eyes.

Then he did. And that was worse. There was a knowledge in that gaze that Gereint had desperately hoped he would never see again.

Gereint tossed the blanket back, got to his feet, and stared down at his own bare feet. His boots were gone. Fellesteden's little silver chains were no longer woven through the steel rings that pierced his ankles between bone and tendon. Instead, each ring was woven through by a neat little cord.

This was not exactly a surprise. Gereint had not needed to see those cords to feel the renewed bite of the *geas*. He lifted his gaze again, slowly.

The other man looked nervous, as a man might who was alone in the mountains with another, stronger man of dubious character and temper. But he also looked self-assured. He didn't seem wealthy enough to have owned *geas*-bound...servants. Even so, Gereint was sure the man knew exactly what he'd done with those cords.

Gereint made his voice soft. An easy, quiet voice. Not defiant, not angry, not frightened. Just...soft. Coaxing. "Let me go. You're kind...I can see that. There's no risk to you in letting me go. You don't even need to cut those cords. You can just tell me to walk away, not to come back. And I will. I promise you, that's all I want: a chance to walk away into the mountains..."

"Be quiet," said the man.

So he wasn't intimately familiar with the limits of the *geas* after all. That was, on the whole, rather more reassuring than not. Gereint did not point out his mistake, but obediently shut his mouth and waited.

"Kneel," ordered the man.

Gereint dropped immediately to his knees, not waiting for the bite of the *geas* to enforce the command. He bowed his head, though his new master hadn't commanded that. They had to try their power; it meant nothing. There was no reason to take it personally. It was what they did later that mattered, after they discovered they could do anything.

"All right," said the man. "Get up."

He sounded uneasy, which might be good... or otherwise. Some of the worst masters were the ones who felt guilty about the power they held over you. A man like this, prosperous but not noble, might well be one of that sort. Gereint got to his feet. Glancing covertly at his master, he said gently, "You don't need to do this, honored sir. It's not required. You can simply command me to walk away."

The man looked uncomfortable, but he shook his head. "I need you, you see. My—my companion died, in the desert. And then my poor burro... You were really much too heavy for her." He glanced regretfully at the pot simmering over the fire, a glance that suggested the final fate of the burro. "Everything was so much more difficult than I expected..."

Gereint could believe that, at least. He said softly, even knowing the effort was hopeless, "I'll help you with anything you need, sir. You saved my life, didn't you? You don't need the *geas*, I promise you. Or I'll help you now, and then, later, all you need to do is tell me to walk away..."

The man shook his head. "What did you do?" he asked abruptly.

"Nothing. I was not guilty," Gereint declared without hesitation. "I had powerful enemies, the judge made a mistake, I was condemned unjustly. Will you compound the injustice?"

Surprise gave way to disbelief and then to a kind of wry humor. "Yes, I recall Andreikan Warichteier says in his *Principia Magicoria* that the *geas* gives no control over the tongue, the eyes, or the thoughts. What did you really do?"

A first glance had definitely not suggested such perceptiveness. Nor had Gereint expected any random traveler to have read Warichteier's difficult and often abstruse *Principia*. He should have remembered that the man had known he could use a plain cord. Most people thought you needed the little silver chains mandated by custom. This man was more acute than he looked. Gereint let his face show something of his surprise and dismay and exclaimed without hesitation, "Nothing, honored sir! That *is* the truth."

The man tilted his head to one side, regarding Gereint with something that might almost have been sympathy. "I need your help," he declared. "And I won't release a dangerous criminal." He glanced around at the damp woods that surrounded them. "Even here, though I admit it seems unlikely you could do any harm here. You were in Melentser, I suppose? Where did you mean to go? Feierabiand? It's a long way. Even so…" His brows arched interrogatively.

There was no reason to deny it. Gereint shrugged. "Feierabiand, yes. But the desert was much worse than I'd expected. But why were you…?" He cut the question off short, bowing his head.

But the man did not seem to notice the impudence. "Collecting some things from a private residence. I see you brought a few books out with you, too." He gestured at Gereint's small pack, lying beside his own. Then he shook his head, apparently in wonder at Gereint's folly. Or maybe at his own. Said, with obvious pain and grief, "A few hours in, it was supposed to be; a few hours out. How difficult could that be?"

Gereint would have offered fervent agreement, only it wasn't his place.

The man sighed and glanced around at the woods, green and dripping even though the mist had cleared. Then he looked sharply at Gereint. "What's your name? How do you feel? You should be quite recovered. Are you?"

"Gereint," Gereint said. "Yes…master. I think so."

A second sharp look, this one distinctly uncomfortable. "I'm Eben Amnachudran. Call me by my name, please." He glanced around once more. "There's plenty of time left in the day. Put your boots on. Have another mug of soup. There's some cracker in a pouch by the fire. Have some of that if you like." He walked away, began putting things away in a good-quality traveler's pack.

Gereint put his boots on, binding the steel rings flat against his ankles with strips of cloth so they wouldn't chafe. He had another mug of soup and some of the hard cracker. He felt…well. Amazingly well. Too well. He wanted to ask the man…his master…he wanted to ask if he had done something, what he had done. But those questions might be dangerous, and anyway the answers were tolerably obvious. So his new master was a mage of some sort, and with at least a little skill in healing.

Likely he would not care to have Gereint asking about such things. Better to test his new master's temper with simpler questions.

Along with the ordinary pack, there were saddlebags. Four of them. Heavy, as though they'd been loaded with bricks. Gereint tried to picture the plump, soft-handed Amnachudran carrying even two of them for any distance, and failed. No wonder he'd brought a burro. And a companion. A friend, from the grief in his voice when he spoke of the man. Killed by the desert. That was certainly believable. The desert was visible from the woods: a straight line that cut across the hills. Behind that line was brilliant furnace heat blazing down on red sand and stone. On this side, trees dripping with moisture and a rain-fed stream racing its way down the mountainside across gray rocks. The stream ran straight into the desert and vanished; even the old streambed was barely discernable on the other side of the line. A long dimple in the sand, and then nothing.

"I think I can manage the pack and one of the saddlebags," Amnachudran said, coming briskly over to Gereint. "Do you think you can carry the other three?"

Gereint gave him a sidelong glance. "What if I said no?"

"I would tell you to try."

"I could probably carry all four."

"Try three for now." The plump man hefted the fourth, grunting, along with the two light packs. He glanced at the sky, heaved a resigned breath, and plodded away, east and south. Toward the Teschanken River, Gereint surmised. And then south along the river, toward Metichteran? Or across the river toward Tashen? He didn't ask. That was a good example of a question that patience would answer.

Three saddlebags, none of them made to sling properly from a man's back, were an awkward load. On the other hand, compared to walking unburdened through the griffins' terrible desert...there was no comparison. Even carrying three bags to Amnachudran's one, Gereint found he had to slow his stride to match his...master's. At first, he followed the other man. Then, seeing it made Amnachudran uncomfortable to have him at his back, he came up unbidden to walk beside him. The man gave him a grunt of acknowledgment and for a time they walked in silence. The woods dripped. Birds sang. Somewhere high overhead, a hawk cried. Gnats whined, but fortunately did not seem inclined to bite.

Amnachudran called a halt after about two hours. He dropped his saddlebag and the packs heavily to the ground beside another of the many little streams and stood for a moment with his hands braced on his knees. At last he straightened slowly, with a groan. He looked older now. The plump softness gave him a young sort of face, but Gereint revised his estimate of the man's true age upward.

Gereint dropped his three heavy bags beside the one. He wondered what was in them. Nothing that rattled or clanked or chimed. Unless it was packed so as not to rattle or clank or chime. Maybe he would find a chance to look through a bag later. Maybe Amnachudran would catch him at it. Maybe the things in those bags were secret and important, mages' things. Exactly the wrong kinds of things to be caught examining. He measured Amnachudran with a covert glance. Then he made a fire, found the small pot, filled it with water, and got out the packet of tea and a mug.

Amnachudran watched all this, frowning. "I didn't tell you to do that."

"I have to do everything you say." Gereint measured out tea. "That doesn't mean I can't do anything without your command. Do you not want tea...master? Ah, forgive me. Amnachudran, sir."

Amnachudran ignored this small provocation. He asked, "Why did you get out only one mug?"

Gereint was honestly surprised. He sat back on his heels, regarding the other man. "You expected me to get out two? That *would* be presumptuous."

"But you seem—" The other man stopped.

"Ah." Gereint felt a tug of reluctant amusement. He kept forgetting Amnachudran's perceptiveness. Or wanting to trust his kindness. Or even both. Worse than foolish: dangerous. And surprising. He said after a moment, "Yes, but carefully. Nothing quite so blatant as...ah... getting out two mugs."

"Get another out," said Amnachudran. He sat down on a rock beside the stream.

Gereint found the mug with the broken handle and measured out more tea.

"How long have you been...?"

Gereint didn't look up. "Nineteen years."

A short pause. Then, "How old are you?"

Gereint brought his master a mug, kneeling to hand it to him so he wouldn't loom over the smaller man. "Forty-two."

"Almost half your life...What *did* you do?"

"Murdered the governor of Breidechboden."

Amnachudran choked on a mouthful of tea, coughed, caught his breath, stared at Gereint, and at last laughed incredulously. "You didn't!"

"Well, no, I didn't," agreed Gereint. He went back to the fire, folded his hands around the other mug. Sipped, watching Amnachudran carefully over the edge of the mug. "I was caught plotting to assassinate the king himself, which he should have expected after he forbade public houses to serve ale after midnight. What does he expect young louts to get up to if they're thrown out on the streets while still sober enough to stagger?"

Amnachudran, undoubtedly remembering the uproar about that short-lived law, laughed again.

"No," Gereint conceded. "Not that either. I told you, I didn't do anything. I had the wrong enemies and not enough friends." Not enough friends and too many cousins, and too many of those had turned out to be among his enemies... He hadn't intended to speak truth to this man, and paused for a moment, hearing bitter truth echo unexpectedly in those last words.

Trying to shake off a sudden surge of bitterness—not a helpful emotion, for a slave—he said, just a little too harshly, "I'll carry these bags wherever you require. Please... once I have, let me go. You don't need to trust me. Do you think I'll stay anywhere in Casmantium?" He traced the brand on his face with one thumb. "Believe me, honored sir, my whole ambition would be to avoid meeting anyone at all until I was well into Feierabiand."

Amnachudran held up one finger. "You murdered someone." Another finger. "Or you raped a girl." He opened his hand again, shrugging. "Those are the two crimes for which a man is put under the *geas*. There aren't any others. I don't see how I can let you go. I don't think girls in Feierabiand ought to be raped, any more than the ones here."

Gereint said tightly, "I did not rape a girl."

"I'm glad to hear it. Whom did you murder?"

"I told you—"

"I don't believe you."

"Neither did anyone else," Gereint said tightly. "Why should you?" He swung away and stamped out the fire. He also picked up all four saddlebags, leaving only the two packs for Amnachudran.

"I can..." the other man began.

"Four balance better than three," Gereint snapped. He strode away, south and east.

They did make better time with Gereint carrying all the bags. He was too proud to let the pace slacken; an odd vanity, for a man who ought to have had every vestige of pride beaten out of him years ago. But there it was. He let Amnachudran call the halts, which the other man did every few hours. But he was glad to have them. Ten years ago, even five, he would not have needed those breaks. He had hoped, briefly, that he might grow old a free man in Feierabiand. Now that seemed unlikely.

A little before dusk, they came to the Teschanken. This far north, the river was narrow, quick, and cheerfully violent: It flung itself down from the great mountains and raced through the hills. Far below it would meet the Nerintsan and turn into the stately, broad river that watered the south.

"We'll follow the river south tomorrow," Amnachudran declared. He walked out onto the pebbly shore and stared downstream. "If we're where I think we are, we should cross it about noon, be home before supper—" He stopped suddenly.

A griffin flew past not a spearcast away, fast and straight, flinging itself through the air northward along the path of the river. The late sunlight blazed off it, striking ruddy gold and bronze highlights from its pelt and feathers. The light seemed somehow a far more brilliant light than seemed to fall across the rest of the world. The griffin's feathers seemed to slice the air like knives, its beak flashed like a blade, flickers of fire scattered from the wind of its wings. Gereint could not speak; Eben Amnachudran seemed struck as silent as he.

There was no time to be afraid, and, it appeared, no reason. The griffin did not seem to see them at all, though they stood so close to the path of its flight. Its eyes, fiery copper, were intent on its own course. Before they could breathe twice, it had flashed by and was gone. Though the sunset still painted the sky in carmine and violet, all the colors of sky and earth seemed somehow muted for its passing. The whole world seemed caught for a moment in a subdued quiet. Not a single bird rustled in the woods around them, and even the river seemed to run more quietly along its swift course.

At last, Amnachudran cleared his throat. "I believe that may have been one of the most terrifying things I have ever seen. Beautiful, but terrifying. But what was it doing on the wrong side of the border between fire and earth?"

"It was flying north," Gereint said tentatively. "Maybe it was trying to get back to the desert before full dark. Doesn't Beremnan Anweierchen write that griffins hate the dark and cling to the day, on the rare occasion that they venture into the country of earth?"

"But he doesn't explain why they ever do so venture,"

Amnachudran pointed out. "Besides, it would need to turn west of north to return to its desert. Though perhaps it intends to." Then he hesitated, turning to study Gereint. "*You've* read Anweierchen?"

The question shook Gereint out of the memory of fire. He shrugged, said shortly, "My old master had a good library," and set the saddlebags down in a row, then began to collect wood for a fire. The wood was drier here, at least. The swift-moving little river might yield something better than dried beef. He looked through Amnachudran's pack for hooks and line, with a careful eye on his new master in case the man resented his rummaging.

But Amnachudran did not seem to care. He watched Gereint for a moment and then said, "There aren't any hooks. We didn't think there would be much opportunity to use them."

Gereint nodded, picked up Amnachudran's knife, selected a bit of wood, and began to make a hook. He turned over the question before he asked it, but guessed Amnachudran wanted to talk about simple things, nothing to do with griffins or fire. So he asked, "We?"

The man's face tightened in grief, but he answered readily. "A friend. The man who owned the house that's now in the desert. He was older than I, but neither of us thought… It was his heart, I think. The desert was worse than we'd… We had reached Brerich's house, but I wasn't in the same room when he was stricken. If I had been, perhaps…"

That was not simple, after all. And it recalled the desert far too vividly. But Amnachudran seemed to wish to speak of his friend. So perhaps it was as well Gereint had asked, after all. He set the hook aside, found a length of cord, and delicately unraveled it to make a finer thread. He rolled the thread between his fingers as he worked, coaxing it toward strength and lightness, feeling it become supple under his touch. "I'm sorry about your friend," he said sincerely. "But how did you...If you don't mind, how did you find me?"

"Ah. That was luck. And poor little Fearn. You had one of your waterskins open, did you know? I think she smelled the water." Amnachudran, apparently not having much confidence in Gereint's efforts, dipped water out of the river, put the pot over the fire, and began to cut up dried beef. But he didn't order Gereint to stop making fishing line. Picking up where he'd left off, he added in a quiet voice, "But she couldn't carry both you and the bags. Even with me carrying two of the bags, she didn't quite..." His voice trailed off.

Gereint carefully tied the line he'd made to the hook. Tested his knot. Glanced up. "You could have left me there." He touched the brand on his face. "It would only have been the death of a murderer or rapist."

Amnachudran shrugged. "You were face down. I didn't see the brand at once. By the time I did see it, I knew you might live. Once I knew that, I couldn't leave you." He didn't ask, *Are you glad or sorry I saved your life?* But his eyes posed that question.

Gereint stared back at him for a moment in silence. He said at last, "That desert is not the place I would choose to leave my bones." Gathering up his line and hook, he went down to the river.

By full dark, the soup was boiling and two small fish were grilling over coals.

"I didn't think you'd catch any," Amnachudran admitted, turning one of the fish with a pair of twigs.

"I was lucky."

"That was a good hook. Nor would I have thought you could make decent line out of that cord."

"It's a knack." Gereint turned the other fish.

"You're a maker."

And Amnachudran was far too perceptive, and far too difficult to lie to. It hadn't been a question. Gereint said merely, not looking up, "It makes me a valuable slave, yes."

There was a pause. Then Amnachudran began uncomfortably, "How many...? That is, how many men...?"

This time, Gereint did glance up. "How many masters have I had? Is that what you would ask? Five, in all. Each worse than the last."

"Your family..." Amnachudran hesitated. "They couldn't protect you?"

"Protect a murderer?" Gereint asked bitterly. The older man looked down. Gereint, observing the flinch, paused, lowered his voice. "You could be the last of my masters. You saved my life: You might save it again in a different way..."

"Stop asking me for that," Amnachudran ordered in a low voice.

"You can't command my tongue," Gereint reminded him, waited a beat, and added, "Of course, you *could* order me to kneel and hold still, then beat me unconscious. Or at least until your arm was too tired to lift. You haven't got a whip, but"—he gestured at the woods around them—"there's plenty of springy wood. That would probably work. Shall I cut you a—"

"Be quiet!" Amnachudran commanded him, his tone much sharper.

"If you don't wish to own a *geas* slave, you could simply tell me to walk away—"

"You *want* me to lose my temper," Amnachudran said suddenly.

Gereint stopped.

The other man studied him. "Of course you do. Because you want to know what I'll do if I'm angry. You need to find out how far you can push me—and what will happen if you push me too far."

Gereint didn't try to deny this. He'd never had a master more intelligent than he was. It occurred to him now that Amnachudran might be the first.

For a long moment, the other man only continued to look at him. His plain, round face was difficult to read. He said at last, "Gereint. Get up."

Gereint got to his feet.

"Walk that way"—Amnachudran pointed into the woods—"fifty paces. Sit down with your back to the fire. Stay there till I call you. Go."

Gereint turned immediately and walked into the woods. Carefully, because it was dark under the trees. And chilly. He counted off fifty paces, found a rock, sat down. Wrapped his arms around himself for warmth. His imagination populated the darkness with wolves. Griffins—no, griffins would, like the one they'd seen, have headed for the desert as dusk fell. If it *had* been headed back to the desert. But surely it had been.

Dragons, then. Did dragons hunt by night? Would fire keep a dragon away or draw it? He knew there was almost no chance of dragons this far south, but he nevertheless half believed he heard some vast creature shift its weight away off in the dark.

Probably there was a better chance of wolves. Fire would definitely keep wolves away. Though not from fifty paces behind him. He tried to think about poetry instead of wolves. Gestechan Wanastich's measured cadences came to mind, unfortunately. Fire and the dark and women weeping: not what he wanted in his mind at this moment. And hadn't Wanastich actually written something about wolves? Ah, yes: the part of the Teranbichken epic with the snow and the black trees and the wolves' eyes glowing in a circle...Imagination was a curse, Gereint decided, and closed his own eyes. He knew perfectly well there were no wolves.

He wished he'd had a chance to eat that fish. He might have picked up a blanket, at least, if he'd been quick. Amnachudran might have let him keep it. He wondered whether the man meant to leave him out here all night. Probably not. Maybe. The command had been *sit*. Gereint would not be able to lie down. Though he probably would not have found a dry spot to stretch out, if he was going to be left out here all night, he was going to regret his inability to try.

Behind him, Amnachudran shouted his name.

Gereint jumped to his feet and, despite the darkness, walked back to the fire much more quickly than he had left it. Once he stepped out into the light, the idea of wolves seemed ridiculous. He walked more slowly back to the fire and stopped, facing his master.

"Well?" asked Amnachudran, looking shrewdly up at him.

Gereint dropped at once to his knees. "Pardon my insolent tongue, master—sorry. Forgive me, sir. I won't—"

"Stop it!" Amnachudran stopped, took a breath, and

continued more mildly: "I don't want you to, um. Grovel. What I was asking for was simply your *opinion*."

Taken aback—again!—Gereint asked cautiously, "May I get up?"

"Yes!" Amnachudran gestured toward the blanket on the other side of the fire. "Sit down, get warm, eat your fish. Tell me, are you going to stop prodding me for a reaction? Are you satisfied?"

Gereint settled by the fire, poked at the fish. Ate a bite. Amnachudran had boned the fish for him and had a mug of hot tea waiting along with the beef broth. Gereint had more than half expected his master to call him back to the fire. But this additional small kindness was so far outside anything he had expected that he did not even know what to feel about it.

He looked up, met the other man's eyes. "You asked for my opinion and whether I'm satisfied. Very well. You certainly haven't lost your temper. I'm satisfied you won't, or not easily. Or did you wish my opinion about the punishment itself? Very well: It was effective. I don't want you to do that again, for all you avoided brutality very neatly. Thank you for calling me back to the fire."

"What you said. About being made to kneel while someone beat you unconscious. Someone did that to you?"

Amnachudran might be a clever man. A perceptive man. But judging by his tone on that question, he was in some ways surprisingly innocent. Gereint controlled an impulse to laugh. He answered, with considerable restraint, "Oh, yes."

Amnachudran looked revolted. "I'd thought...You're right that I don't want a *geas* slave. Now less than ever.

I'd thought, once we get back to my home, I might find out your old master's name, send you—"

Cold struck through Gereint's body like death. There could not be many *geas*-bound men of his size and general description. Even if he refused to give Amnachudran his old master's name, the man could easily find it out. He put the mug of tea down, stood up, came back around the fire to where Amnachudran sat, and knelt. Put his palms flat on the ground. Bent to touch his forehead to the earth.

"Gereint—"

"I know you don't want me to grovel." Gereint straightened his back, looking the other man deliberately in the face. "My most recent master, now. He likes a man to grovel. I'm sure he was very angry when he realized he would have to leave me behind. He would be very grateful to you if you returned me to him. He's a powerful man; his patronage could probably be useful to you. Me...he would expect me to plead for mercy. He would expect me to eat the dirt in front of his boots. I would do that for you, except you wouldn't like it. If you were searching for an effective threat, you've found one. Don't send me back to him. Please, don't. Just tell me to walk—"

"Away into the mountains, I know—"

"—back to Melentser. I would rather that than go back into that man's house."

There was a pause.

"What did he do to you?" Amnachudran asked, his tone hushed.

Gereint said gently, "Eben Amnachudran. You're a decent man. You don't want to know."

This time the pause was longer.

Gereint bowed his head, drew a slow breath, let it out.

He didn't get to his feet, but said instead, "I know you won't free me. You've made that clear. I won't ask again. I'll ask this instead: What can I do to persuade you to keep me yourself? Not sell me, nor give me away, nor above all send me back to my old master?"

Amnachudran stared at him.

"You were right, of course: I have been pushing at you. I'll stop. I'll be respectful—I *can* be respectful. I'll call you by name, if you prefer. I won't grovel, since you don't like that. You can treat me as a hired man rather than a slave, if you wish. I can play that role. I can play any role that pleases you. You were right: I'm a maker. I could be useful to you—"

"Stop!" said Amnachudran, rather desperately.

Gereint shut his mouth. Rested his hands on his thighs, deliberately open and easy. Waited.

"What was it that you *did*?"

Gereint flinched, he hoped not noticeably. He began to speak, hesitated. Said at last, "If I tell you again I did nothing, you'll think I'm lying and be angry. I don't want that."

"Just tell me the truth!"

"You're waiting for me to lie to you. Are you so certain you would recognize truth, when you're listening for lies?"

Silence. Finally, Amnachudran made a disgusted gesture. "Eat your supper. Go to sleep. I'll think about your request...later. When we've gotten to my house."

The *geas* could compel Gereint to eat the rest of the fish and drink the tea. But even the *geas* couldn't force him to sleep, though it could make him lie quietly with his eyes closed.

*   *   *

The morning came watery and pale through the mist that rose from the river and the damp woods. There had been no sign of wolves or griffins or dragons. Or if there had been, it must have been in the small hours near dawn, when Gereint had finally slept a little.

Amnachudran had coaxed the fire back to life and made tea. He glanced up as Gereint got to his feet. "There's plenty of cracker. I'm sorry there's not time for you to catch more fish. But we should be home by evening."

Home. His, of course. Did he mean that it would be Gereint's home as well? Probably not. Gereint didn't ask. He went down to the river and washed his face and hands. Came back and began to roll up the blankets and stow away the little pot and other things. Ate a piece of cracker. Drank the tea. He couldn't tell what Amnachudran was thinking. If he was thinking about anything other than his home.

"I know you're much stronger than I am. But I think I could carry—" Amnachudran began.

"No, sir. That's not necessary. Just carry the packs," Gereint said. But respectfully. He inspected the straps on the saddlebags and spent a few minutes lengthening some and shortening the others. "We're crossing the river, are we? How waterproof are these bags? I brought some tallow candles. If you have a little oil, I can probably improve them."

"Thank you, Gereint. Yes. When we stop."

Gereint nodded, slung the straps over his shoulders, and straightened. The bags seemed to have grown heavier. He didn't let himself groan, but only glanced politely at the other man, waiting for him to lead the way.

The sun came out. The mist lifted. The river dashed cheerfully down the hill beside them. There was even a deer trail to follow. All in all, a pleasant morning. Gereint only wished he was alone, less burdened, and heading the other way.

On the other hand... on the other hand, he could be in Breidechboden. In Perech Fellesteden's house. Compared to that, Amnachudran's house, whatever it was like, would surely prove a perfect haven. Probably the man hadn't yet decided whether to grant Gereint's plea. Gereint glanced at him, a cautious sidelong glance. He did not want to annoy him. But he did not seem easy to annoy... Gereint asked, "Is it Tashen? Where your house is?"

"Near Tashen," Amnachudran agreed. "My house is out in the country, between the mountains and the city. Near the river, in fact. After the ford, we'll turn almost due east, walk fewer than ten miles. My house is at the base of some low hills, where a stream comes down year-round. It's easy country there, open and level, good for orchards and wheat and pasture. The apples are just beginning to ripen now. My wife loves apples; she's collected dozens of varieties..."

Gereint made an interested sound, listening with half an ear to descriptions of orchards and gardens and the new pond they'd just built and stocked with fish. Amnachudran was clearly wealthier than Gereint had guessed. And there was a wife. Gereint wondered whether she would object to the presence of a *geas*-bound servant. Would it be possible to win her over, make himself so immediately useful that she would object if her husband wanted to get rid of him?

But there were grown children, too, he gathered. With

children of their own, in and out of their grandparents' house. *Geas* bound or not, Amnachudran or his wife might reasonably hesitate to bring a murderer into the house where their grandchildren played. Or a rapist.

Gereint's thoughts tended darker and darker. He doubted he could persuade Amnachudran to release him, but the more he thought about it, the less likely it seemed that the man would keep him either. Even if he did not send him back to Fellesteden... If he sold him, what were the odds Gereint's next master would be kind? Kind men did not buy *geas* slaves.

What were the odds, if he was sold, that it would be to someone from the city? The court nobles and the lesser nobles, the rich men angling for power and influence... Those were the men who liked to own *geas*-bound slaves. He might very well be sold and re-sold until he found himself in Breidechboden after all. If he were sold to anyone in the king's city, Perech Fellesteden would almost certainly learn of it eventually.

Gereint was very silent by the time they reached the ford, about an hour past noon. The river was wider here, still fast but not deep. Rocks thrust up through the water. A man would not be able to walk from one bank to the other without getting his feet wet, but he might come closer to that than Gereint had expected. In the spring, the river might be impassable. But now, only one thirty-foot channel looked difficult, and even that did not look actually dangerous.

And on the other side, fewer than ten miles away, Amnachudran's house. Perhaps forty miles from Melentser as the falcon flies. It seemed both infinitely farther than that and, at the same time, hardly any distance at all.

Amnachudran stared at the river and grunted. "Could be worse. I thought it would be worse, in fact. That's lower than we'd usually see, even this time of year."

Gereint, not very interested, nodded politely.

"I'll make tea," Amnachudran said, "if you'll see what you can do about the saddlebags?"

Gereint got out two of the tallow candles and found Amnachudran's jar of oil. And the broken mug, since his master was using the pan for the tea. He melted the candles with the oil over low flames, rubbed the hot tallow between his palms, and nodded toward the first of the saddlebags. "It would be easier if they were empty."

Amnachudran opened the first bag without a word. It contained books. Maskeirien's eclogues, Teirenchoden's epic about the nineteenth war between Ceirinium and Feresdechodan. Histories and poetry, natural philosophy and political philosophy. Leather embossed with gold; fine heavy paper illuminated with dragons and griffins and storm eagles and slender sea creatures with the tails of fishes and the proud, fine-boned faces of men. Nothing common. Not a single volume that was not beautiful and rare and precious. They made the two books he'd stolen look almost common.

Gereint wondered why he had not guessed. Heavy and valuable, but not breakable; valuable for themselves and not merely for their market price. Exactly the sort of riches a man might risk the new desert to recover. Especially if he'd thought, *A few hours in and a few hours out, how difficult can it be?*

No wonder Amnachudran was willing to wait in order to enhance the waterproofing on the bags before he carried those books across the river. Gereint rubbed the

tallow across the leather. He gazed dreamily into the air
while he rubbed it in, thinking about waterproof leather,
about tight seams, about straps that closed tight and firm.
He tried not to let himself be distracted by the books
themselves, although he couldn't resist a glance or two
as Amnachudran unloaded the second bag.

"The oil won't stain the books?" Amnachudran asked.
He touched the first cautiously, inspected the tips of his
fingers.

"It might if someone else did this," Gereint answered.
"Not when I do it."

"A knack."

"It's a matter of knowing exactly what I want the oil to
do and not do. And yes, it's a knack."

Amnachudran grunted and, finding his fingers clean
and dry, began to replace the contents of the first bag and
unload the third. "Just how waterproof can you make
these?"

Gereint, massaging melted tallow into leather,
shrugged. "It would probably be better not to actually
drop a bag midriver."

Amnachudran grunted again and went to get the fourth
bag.

Midchannel, the river was chest deep. And very fast.
Gereint took his boots off and waded out cautiously, leaving the books behind while he tested the footing and the
strength of the current. He came out shaking his head.
"I don't like it… It's not too bad when you've got your
hands free and no weight to carry…"

"I have rope," Amnachudran offered.

They slung the rope from shore to shore; it just
reached. Then Gereint took the packs and his boots,

and Amnachudran's boots, across first. The technique seemed sound. He could brace an awkward weight on his shoulder with one hand and cling to the rope with his other. He took three bags across, one after another, while Amnachudran watched anxiously. Then he came back for the last, standing back to allow Amnachudran to precede him into the water.

"Be careful," Gereint warned him as they came to the deepest part of the channel. "Chest deep on me is—"

"Just about over my head. Yes, I know. Even so, it's the nearest thing to an easy crossing anywhere above the bridge at Metichteran. I admit, it looks easier when you're ahorse than it does when you're on foot."

Gereint shrugged. "Keep hold of the rope. I'll be right behind you."

Amnachudran went ahead of Gereint, hand over hand along the rope, gasping with cold and sputtering as the racing water dashed into his face. He made it to the first of the broad stones on the other side of the channel and began to pull himself out of the water.

Gereint, ten feet behind the older man, saw the log come spinning down the river just too late to shout a warning. It hit Amnachudran's legs with a *thud* Gereint could hear even from that distance, tearing the man away from the rope. He cried out, falling, but the cry was choked off as the water closed over his head; Gereint, appalled, saw him come back to the surface in time to smash against one stone and then another and then go under once more.

Gereint heaved the last saddlebag toward the rocks without watching to see where it landed and flung himself into the current. He fended off a rock with his hands, followed the rushing current by instinct and luck, glimpsed the log, hurled himself after it, found himself in a great sucking undertow, went down. Found cloth under his hands. An arm. Stone beneath: He kicked hard and broke into the air, rolled to drag Amnachudran up as well, slammed back first into stone. Cried out with pain and at the same time clutched for any handhold he could find. The current pinned them against the stone. Gereint got an arm around the other man's chest, dashed water out of his own face, and found pebbles rolling under his toes. The river was fierce, here, but not much more than shoulder deep. And he could see where another stone offered support against the current.

Amnachudran was limp. Gereint tightened his hold, got his feet against the rock that supported them, and lunged for the other stone. Made it, and now the water was only chest deep. He dug his toes into the river's rough bed, heaved Amnachudran up onto the stone, made his way around it to where the water was still shallower, grabbed the man's arm, dragged him across his shoulder, and slogged for the shore. Dropped him—not as gently as he'd meant—on a shallow shelf of pebbles and sand. Fell to his knees beside him and felt for a pulse in his throat. Found one. Rolled him over and pressed to get the water out of his lungs; made sure he was breathing on his own. And only then realized what he'd done.

Gereint climbed to his feet. Everything had happened so fast; too fast. He felt dizzy and ill. His back and hip hurt, his knee hurt with a deep ache that told him it was at least wrenched, maybe sprained. The palms of his hands were raw—how had that happened?

But Amnachudran had suffered much worse. But he

was still breathing, though the sound had a rattle to it that suggested water in the lungs. His pulse was rapid and thready with shock. There was a lump the size of a small egg above and behind his ear. Gereint thought one of his legs was probably broken.

Letting the other man drown hadn't occurred to Gereint fast enough. But now... an unconscious man could not command his help. Without care now, Amnachudran would probably die. Gereint stared down at him. He could not kick the man back into the river; even without the *geas* he didn't think he could have done that. But... he wouldn't have to do anything so active, would he?

The situation at this moment was too uncertain for the *geas* to bite hard. His master was too near death, maybe. Too deathly. Interesting word, "deathly." The *geas* seemed to accept it as nearly the same as "dead." Gereint was fairly certain he could simply walk away. His hip hurt; his knee hurt like fire. But it didn't seem to be sprained. He could walk well enough. He didn't even need a stick.

Judging from his previous experience, when Fellesteden had left him behind in Melentser, distance alone would suffice to keep the *geas* quiet. And now Gereint knew, as he hadn't then, that if he could step into direct desert sunlight, it would break the *geas*—and he could step back out immediately. He'd made a slight detour, yes. But the mountains still waited, and Feierabiand, and final freedom from the *geas*.

If Gereint walked away and, against all likelihood, Amnachudran did wake... well, then, he would be hurt and cold, with the chill of the night coming and no fire. It would not take wolves to kill a man left hurt and alone in the dark. He would die...alone and abandoned...fewer than ten miles from his home...Gereint cursed.

Then he heaved the smaller man up into his arms, grunting as his back and hip flared with pain. He limped back to clear ground near the saddlebags and put the man down there. Found out the blankets, and laid one out on the ground for a bed. Stripped away the wet clothing. A great spreading black bruise showed where ribs were probably broken. The leg was gashed as well as broken, but there wasn't much blood. Gereint bound up the gash and covered the injured man with the other blanket. Made a fire, afraid all the time that Amnachudran might wake after all. But he did not stir. Gereint glanced at the sun. Hours yet till dusk. And Amnachudran's breathing already sounded better. The pulse in his throat beat more strongly. If Gereint left him now, he might be all right. Though the leg...But surely his family was waiting for him. They must surely expect him to be on his way home. Someone would come down to the river soon to look for him.

Gereint went back to where he'd left the bags and packs. Absently collected the fourth saddlebag from the shallow water where it had fallen and put it with the others. The books it held were dry, he found. Then he looked at the book he held blankly, wondering why he'd bothered to check. He put it back and did up the straps.

He changed into dry clothing. Found his boots and put them on. Did not look back at Amnachudran. Most carefully did not look. If he looked, he might find himself compelled to go back to him. If he didn't look...If he fixed his mind firmly on the sky and the river and the sound the wind made in the leaves...why, then, he could swing a pack over his shoulder and walk away, upriver. He didn't look back.

The *geas* didn't stop him. He'd thought it might, at this last moment of abandonment: an act of defiance more active than merely letting Perech Fellesteden walk away from him had been. But the *geas* did not stop him. It wasn't gone. He knew by this that Amnachudran still lived. But it did not bite hard. An unconscious master, a master who was dying, was not something, perhaps, that the *geas* magic understood very well. He walked on.

Amnachudran was already too far away to call him back.

But Gereint hadn't even gone a mile when he saw the griffins. This time, there were three of them: one bronze and brown, one copper and gold, and one—the one leading—a hard, pure white, like the flames at the very heart of a fire. The air surrounding them was dense with light, so that Gereint had to squint against it to see them. It smelled of fire and hot brass; the air shimmered with heat.

As the other griffin had done, these were flying along the river—only these were heading south, downriver. Unlike that other griffin, these very clearly knew he was present: The white one tilted its head and looked down at him as it passed, a flashing sapphire glance of such hot contempt that Gereint swayed and took an involuntary step back. But they did not hesitate in their course or drop toward him, for which he was fervently grateful.

The griffins flew low, so low that their wingtips nearly brushed the topmost branches of the trees, so low that Gereint was gripped by a compelling illusion, as the last one soared past, that he might have touched its feathers if he'd reached out his hand. He wondered if those feathers could be as sharp edged and metallic as they seemed— probably not. But the light flashed off their beaks, and off talons as long as his fingers and as sharp as knives. It came to him, vividly, what those talons might do to a man...to a defenseless man, say, who had been left abandoned and injured on the riverbank...He shut his eyes, trying to close out the images his imagination suggested to him, as well as the too-brilliant light.

When he opened them again, the griffins were past, out of sight. The light was only ordinary sunlight, and the river and woodlands seemingly untroubled by any memory of fire.

The griffins surely would not stop to trouble Eben Amnachudran. They did not seem inclined to stop for any reason. The other one had not paid any attention to them; these three hadn't stopped to tear Gereint to pieces, though they'd clearly seen him. Why would they pause to kill a man who was, after all, already dying?

They wouldn't. Gereint was certain of it. Almost certain. He took a few steps along the river, northward.

Then he stopped again. What if the griffins passed Amnachudran by? They probably would not pause to kill him. The scholar had thought them beautiful as well as terrible. Maybe he was awake now. Maybe he would see them pass. Helpless as he was, he would be frightened. He would watch the griffins pass by—surely they would pass by. And then he would wait. And for what? How long would it take for the injured man to give up hope? How long might he linger, in pain and growing despair, until he finally died quietly there by that fire? While his wife and children and grandchildren waited for him not ten miles away?

Gereint could not put that image out of his mind. It was worse than imagining griffins tearing the scholar to ribbons. How long *would* it be before someone came down to the ford looking for the man? Who would it be: His wife? One of the grandchildren?

So it wasn't fear of the griffins that made Gereint turn back south. After all, if they wanted to kill Amnachudran, Gereint could never stop them, even if he was there. But the image of that kind, civilized, cultured man waiting in slowly dying hope, while the hours passed, maybe days, and no one came…that was what made Gereint turn back.

It took about a quarter of an hour to get back to the ford. Everything was exactly as Gereint had left it; there was no sign that griffins had stopped there. This was almost a shock, even though he had thought it unlikely that they would. Nor was Amnachudran awake. But he was still alive. Gereint stood for a moment, gazing down at him, and wondering if he wished the man had died. He did not know. But he knew he could not simply leave him a second time.

It took another quarter of an hour, maybe, to make a litter with green saplings and the blankets. Longer than seemed likely to get Amnachudran on the litter and the saddlebags arranged. Gereint discarded the packs, only tucking his own books into one of the saddlebags. He would not need tallow candles or a cooking pot now.

Then he picked up the stripped ends of the saplings and leaned into the weight.

His knee screamed as he took the weight. But the leg held. Blades of pain lanced down his back and stabbed into his hip, but he still thought nothing was actually broken. His hands hurt when he gripped the poles, though next to the knee and hip that seemed a minor distraction. Less than ten miles, Amnachudran had said. How much less? It had better be a lot less, Gereint thought grimly, or he would never manage it.

The ground might be easy compared to the high mountains, but soon enough Gereint doubted whether he'd manage this last leg of his journey after all. Merrich Berchandren had famously declared that the last mile of any journey was always the hardest. If the last mile was harder than the one he was currently traveling, Gereint did not look forward to it.

Now, though, rather than trying to coax the *geas* to sleep, he could actually use it. He pretended Amnachudran had ordered him to get him home. He imagined the man's pain-filled eyes and strained tone: *Gereint, get me home.* The *geas* couldn't really be fooled, but then, getting his badly injured master to his home *was* a desperately important service. There was no pretense about that. He glanced over his shoulder at Amnachudran's white face, thought hard of getting the man to shelter and safety, and felt the *geas* shiver awake at last and bite down hard. After that there was no question of stopping: Next to the compulsion of the *geas*, neither his hip nor his knee nor his bleeding palms mattered at all.

Gereint had been tall, big all through, all his life: He had been big for his age as a child and a boy and a youth, and once he'd got his growth he'd seldom met a stronger man. And much good it had done him. But his strength served him now. And hard-trained endurance. And sheer doggedness... The sun slid lower in the sky behind him. Shadows stretched out. The countryside opened out, patches of open meadows and woods replacing forest and then pastures replacing the woodlands. Gereint watched the shadows to keep his direction. He tried to remember to glance up sometimes, look for apple orchards and a house set against hills where a stream came down. He was thirsty...Thirst became a torment as soon as he thought of it. He had not thought to fill waterskins at the river. He put one foot in front of the other, though half his steps were short; he could no longer bend his right knee very well. But that was all right because the pain of his hip would have shortened his steps anyway.

Dusk, and shadows stretching out to cover the countryside, and no house with candles in its windows to light home a late traveler...He had missed the house. He knew he had missed it. Every little rough place in the ground made him stumble. He should just stop, wait for dawn. But he *couldn't* stop, not now, no matter how unreasonable pressing forward might be. Not until the last shreds of his strength had been spent and he just fell where he stood...He realized, dimly, that he was no longer going straight east, and for a long moment could not understand why. Then the breeze shifted, and he blinked. Apples. It was too dark now to see the trees, but he could smell the fruit on the gentle breeze. He lifted his head, turned his face toward that sweet fragrance...There was a light. There was a lantern, after all: a lantern in a high window, and beyond the light, dark rolling hills that cut across the starry sky.

Gereint made it through the orchard and right up to the gates of the house's yard. The gates were closed. He stood for some time, too dazed to understand why he had stopped. Then a voice called out from within the gate, and another voice answered. Gereint did not understand anything he heard, but he let go of the litter poles. His hands, cramped from hours of gripping, could not open. But he could hammer his fists against the gate. He could not form coherent words. But he could shout, hoarsely.

There were more voices, then. And the ringing sounds of boots against flagstones. And the scraping sound of wood against wood as the gates were unbarred. Lantern light spilled out as the gates were opened, and incomprehensible voices exclaimed. Gereint barely heard them. He was aware only of the *geas* relaxing within and around him. He did not even feel himself fall.

CHAPTER 2

Gereint dreamed of the hot iron. It traced a circle across his cheek, burning.

When the branding had actually happened, they had warned him against struggling. He might lose an eye, they warned, if the iron slipped. Gereint had been horrified by the threat. He had not fought them.

This time, he knew what the hot iron meant. He knew there were worse things than risking the loss of an eye. He fought desperately.

Weight pinned him. Hands gripped his arms, his shoulders, his body. Hands clamped around his head, holding him still no matter how he fought. The iron was slow, this time, tracing its deliberate path around its circle. Its path was agony, and the scar it left would be a torment forever, but he was held too tightly and could not stop them. He screamed...He had not screamed at the time, but he did this time, because he knew what kind of life the iron would leave him. And he screamed because he had nothing left but his voice; the *geas* would take his body and his hands, but it would leave his voice... Darkness and fire and the hot iron, and screaming in the dark...

Gereint jerked awake, shaking.

He was lying in a bed in a large, airy chamber with a pale-yellow ceiling and delicate yellow curtains fluttering at the window. He understood that almost at once. He was not in pain; he understood that almost as quickly. His face did not hurt. The iron had only been a dream; the branding was years in the past. But he dimly felt that he had been injured, that he should have been in some pain. He wasn't. He felt...well. Confused. But well.

His wrists were tied to the sides of the bed, and his ankles to tall ornate posts at its foot. Gereint realized this only gradually, when he tried to sit up. He did not immediately understand why he couldn't. Then he lifted his head as well as he could and squinted at the bonds, which were soft cloth. Nothing to cut or chafe. No wonder he hadn't understood at first that he was bound. He couldn't think why he should be tied to the bed...Well, he could think of one or two reasons a *geas* slave might be tied to a bed, but they seemed unlikely...Why unlikely? Ah. Eben Amnachudran. Some of the immediate past began to settle back into order. Yes. This was Amnachudran's house, surely. And those reasons did not seem very likely, if he was still *his* slave.

But he *was* bound...

Someone opened the door and came in. Gereint could not lift his head enough to see who it was. It occurred to him only too late that perhaps he might have been wiser to pretend to be asleep, but he did not think of that until the person made a little sound of surprise and hurried out again.

Gereint lowered his head back to the pillow and tried to think. It was hard. He felt strangely adrift. Thoughts came slowly and faded before he could quite grasp them...

The door opened again, and this time Amnachudran himself came in. He walked quickly to the head of the bed and stood frowning down at Gereint. His round, mild face did not seem meant for frowning. Gereint stared back at him in confusion, feeling the internal shift of the *geas*. Was the man angry? He had not meant to do anything to anger Amnachudran... Had he? But it must have been Amnachudran himself who had ordered him tied down... but the man could simply have commanded him to lie down and stay in the bed... Gereint looked away in confusion, feeling weak and somehow ashamed. He *was* weak, but he didn't understand the shame.

"How do you feel?" Amnachudran asked. He held up one hand. "How many fingers am I holding up? What's your name? What's *my* name?"

Gereint turned his head back, stared up at him. "I think I could manage... three out of four, maybe."

"Which one seems doubtful?"

"I feel... very odd."

The other man laughed, sounding relieved. He was no longer frowning. "Gereint..." he said, and shook his head.

"Why am I...?" Gereint moved his hands illustratively.

"You fought us. Very hard."

"The *geas* didn't stop me?"

"Nothing stopped you. You were out of your mind.

I don't think you recognized me. It was a lesson to me
about desperation and the limitations of the *geas*." Amnachudran produced a small knife and began to cut Gereint
loose, very carefully. The knife did not want to cut the
soft cloth. If Gereint had made the knife, it would have
done a much better job.

Gereint watched the knife. He watched the other man's
hand working carefully to cut the cloth bonds. He said
tentatively, "I was...you were...is my memory right?"

"I don't know. What do you think you remember?"

"Didn't you have a broken leg? Among other things."

"Among other things, yes." Amnachudran finished
cutting Gereint's hands free and stepped down to the
foot of the bed. "My wife is a skilled healer-mage; fortunately she is skilled especially with traumatic injuries.
I...um. I'm more of a specialist, myself." He finished
cutting Gereint's feet free, reached to a table by the bed,
and handed Gereint a small hand mirror. The kind a lady
would use, with an ornate brass frame and little birds
etched in the corners of the glass.

Gereint took it wonderingly. Looked in it, since that
was what his master clearly intended.

He almost did not recognize the face that looked
back at him. Oh, the *face* was the same: The forehead
with untidy hair falling across it; the wide cheekbones
were the same, the nose, the line of the jaw...but there
was no broad circular scar from the branding. Gereint
stared hard, not understanding what he was seeing. Or
not seeing. There was *nothing there*. He lifted a hand,
traced with his thumb the path of the brand. But he had
to trace it from memory: He could not find the smooth
raised scar by touch. He began to put the mirror down,

snatched it back upright and stared again. Tried to speak and found his throat closed—and besides, he had no idea what to say.

"I'll be, um. Around," Amnachudran said quickly. "Come find me when you, um. Feel up to it." He gestured rather randomly around the room. "There's food—be sure and eat something. I think the clothing should fit. Um—" He retreated.

For a little while, Gereint thought he might weep like a child, as Amnachudran had clearly feared. He didn't, in the end. He ate a piece of bread while standing in front of a full-length mirror, staring at his unmarked face. The *geas* rings still pierced his ankles, but he had known they must. The cords Amnachudran had used to bind him were still woven through those rings. He had known that, too. But the face...Did Amnachudran *know* what he had done?

The man was clever. And perceptive. And kind, with a depth of honest kindness Gereint had almost come to believe could not truly exist. At least, not for him. Gereint stared at his own face in the mirror and decided that Amnachudran had known *exactly* what he was doing.

Gereint touched the unblemished skin of his cheek and went to get another piece of bread. And some thin-sliced beef to layer on it. The food did help. He felt more solid and grounded every moment. The clarity of his thoughts showed him how vague and blurred he had been earlier. He thought he might need all the acuity he could own, soon. He went back to the mirror, chewing.

It was a lady's mirror, as the graceful table and pretty curtains were clearly the appointments of a lady's room.

He wondered whose bed he had awoken in. And whose clothing had been provided for him. Someone big: The shirt was only a little too tight across the shoulders, the sleeves only a little too short. It was a good shirt. All the clothing was good. Better than anything Gereint had worn for a long time.

There were boots. And cloth to bind around the *geas* rings so they would not chafe. Gereint put on the boots and went back again to the mirror. The man that looked back at him could have been any man. Could walk through any town and never collect a second glance, save for his size.

Gereint went to find Amnachudran. It wasn't difficult. A servant, clearly posted in the hallway to wait, led him down the hall. The servant wore good clothing. Brown and pale yellow. Livery, by the look of it. Yes, hadn't Amnachudran said that his wife was nobly born? Gereint thoughtfully followed the man.

Eben Amnachudran was waiting in a room that seemed both an office and a music room. A delicate, graceful ladies' spinet stood in pride of place; a tall floor harp occupied one corner. But a desk cluttered with papers sat at the other end of the room, and books as well as scrolls of musical scores were shelved along the walls. Amnachudran stood by the desk, sorting the fine books he'd brought back from the desert. The collection was even more impressive spread out like that.

A woman, not beautiful, but plump and comfortable, sat at the spinet. She was not facing the instrument, but one of her hands rested on the keys. She had struck a note: just one. The sound lingered in the air, clean and clear and beautiful.

Amnachudran turned as Gereint came in. He did not speak. His wife—or so Gereint surmised—turned her head and smiled: a surprisingly warm, unconstrained smile.

Gereint nodded to her, faced Amnachudran, and lifted one hand to sketch the brand that wasn't there. "I know thanks are inadequate. But I do thank you, sir. Most earnestly."

Amnachudran looked uncomfortable. "You still bear the *geas*—"

Gereint held up a hand to stop him. "You've made it possible for me to walk unrecognized anywhere among men. As long as I wear boots, no one will covet me or guess he ought to. No one will know I was condemned; no one will wonder what crime I committed. You've given me back a kind of privacy I never—" His voice failed. He did not let himself look away, but met the other man's eyes and said quietly, "And you know you have. You meant to do this. Don't make little of it. I would kiss your feet for what you have done. Willingly. Except you wouldn't like it."

Amnachudran shook his head. "You saved my life. Should I not even have noticed?"

"I'm *geas* bound," Gereint reminded him.

But Amnachudran surprised him again. "The *geas* can force a man to do a great many things, I'm sure. But it can't force him to leap instantly into a river to drag out a drowning fool, when he hasn't been ordered to do anything of the sort. Andreikan Warichteier spends three entire chapters detailing the uses and limitations of the *geas*."

"He gets most of it right," Gereint admitted. "As one

would expect from Warichteier. But you'd already saved my life."

Amnachudran replied patiently, "You didn't value your life. I valued mine very much."

The woman's mouth crooked. She leaned an elbow on the spinet, cupping her chin in her hand and regarding her husband with affection and humor.

Gereint glanced at her, bowed his head respectfully.

Amnachudran followed that glance. He said wryly, "You probably wondered why I had no men to help me. Why there was no one to meet me at the ford. It's complicated—"

"Not complicated in the least," murmured the woman, raising her eyebrows.

Amnachudran sighed. "Embarrassing, then." He said to Gereint, "This is, as you have surmised, my lady wife, Emre Tanshan. One of *those* Tanshans, yes. She married down, when she agreed to marry me."

Lady Emre lifted an eyebrow.

"What she is graciously not saying, among other things, is that I foolishly slipped away with just my friend, telling no one else, because I knew my wife would—quite reasonably—object to the whole venture."

"Just a few hours in and back out," said Gereint. "How difficult could that be?"

"Exactly." Amnachudran hesitated, then said. "You even brought the books. That surprised me."

"By the time I needed to abandon them, I wasn't thinking very clearly. But I'm glad they are safe." It was Gereint's turn to hesitate. He said slowly, watching the other man carefully, "You wouldn't have done this"—again, he ran a thumb across his unmarked cheek—"if you meant to send me back to my old master. Nor even if you'd just meant to sell me. I'm extremely grateful. But I wonder whether you do in fact mean to keep me. Or—or whether you might free me after all. I don't want to anger you, sir. I know I'm presuming on your kindness to me. I said I wouldn't ask again. But I beg you will permit me to ask just once more whether you might—"

It was Amnachudran's turn to hold up a hand. He said in a crisp, firm tone, "I won't sell you or give you away, whatever you tell me. I won't let anyone take you from me, either. You are safe here. Do you understand?" His tone gentled. "I would like to free you, in fact. I think I owe you that, and besides...well. But I will ask you one more time: What did you do?"

Gereint knew he shouldn't have been surprised. But he was. He felt badly off balance. Nothing in this house seemed to follow ordinary paths; all the things he would ordinarily do or say seemed...impossible.

He had never intended to answer that question. He had to answer it.

He did not dare lie to Amnachudran. He did not even *want* to lie to him, exactly. He wanted to turn the question aside, somehow. He couldn't do that, either.

Gereint braced himself. Tried to make himself meet the other man's eyes. Could not support the effort. He stared instead at the wall. Said, in his flattest tone, "When I was twenty, I married a lovely girl of good family. We were very happy. I thought we were. When I was twenty-three, I found her...with a man. A friend of mine, I thought. I picked up a chair, broke it to make a club. I meant to kill him. I swear I did not mean to kill her. I didn't hit her with the club. I slapped her." He stopped, glanced at Emre Tanshan. She did not look away, and after a moment Gereint bowed his head. "I knew my strength. I don't claim otherwise. Maybe I did mean to kill her. She died. So did he." He gazed down, then, at his hands. Closed them into fists. Opened them again. Made himself look up to meet Amnachudran's eyes. He couldn't read the other man's expression. "It's not a glamorous tale. Not exciting. It's common and stupid and petty and ugly."

"And true."

"Yes."

"Usually they don't bind a man under the *geas* for such an ... impulsive crime."

Gereint nodded. "Her father was an important man. So was his. I told you I had powerful enemies. That part was true. My own father was dead; my cousins could not—didn't care to—protect me." He cut that off, didn't explain that his cousin Gescheichan had been a rival for his wife, that he'd been young enough and stupid enough to find that amusing, until he'd found Gescheichan doing everything in his power to make sure Gereint was *geas* bound. None of his other cousins had tried to intercede. If his mother had been alive—if his sister had still been in Breidechboden and not far away in Abreichan—but no one had even tried to help him.

He drew a deep breath. Looked again into his master's face. Amnachudran's expression was hard to read. So was his wife's. Gereint said with some intensity, "It was nineteen years ago. When I was still young enough to believe a woman was worth dying for. Even then, I hope I wasn't stupid enough to believe any woman was worth ..." He touched his face. Traced the path of the iron. Repeated, "It was nineteen years ago."

"They're still dead," Lady Emre said quietly.

Gereint dropped his hand. He didn't look at the lady. But he said, "Yes, that's true." Then he drew a breath. Faced Amnachudran again. "I'm no longer that stupid boy. An impulsive crime, you said. It was that. I'm... about as far from impulsive, now, as any man you'll ever meet. Sir. Master." Promises about future behavior were pointless: Amnachudran was not a fool. Gereint said with low, passionate intensity, "You didn't ask to be my judge. I know that. I just...fell into your hands. But you could free me. No one else can. No one else will. Please free me."

"In fact..." Amnachudran began, but then stopped. He looked at his wife. She raised her eyebrows, but said nothing. Amnachudran nodded as though she had spoken. He turned back to Gereint, frowning.

Gereint bowed his head under that stern regard. He fought to clear all signs of recent emotion from his face. He was shaking; he couldn't help that. He tried desperately to recapture a proper slave's resignation—he would have done anything to be this man's slave when he'd belonged to Perech Fellesteden. The worse thing, the very worst, would be for Amnachudran to decide that, after all, he was too much trouble to keep...He tried to think of something to say, anything, to prevent that. It was important to remember that Eben Amnachudran was more intelligent than he was...

"Take off your boots," Amnachudran ordered.

For a long moment, Gereint did not believe he could have heard that command properly. The *geas* believed it, however. His body moved without conscious direction; he had his first boot off before he could actually believe the man had said those words. If Fellesteden had given that order—but if *Amnachudran* gave it, he meant to—he actually meant—Gereint fumbled off the second boot with clumsy hands and looked up, hardly breathing, in terror that he might have somehow misunderstood.

But Amnachudran had a knife out and was beckoning for Gereint to put his foot up on the edge of a chair. He cut the first cord. Gereint thought he could feel the strands part. The entire *geas* trembled, poised on the edge of that knife.

Then the other foot. The other cord. As quickly and easily as if it was any cord.

The *geas*, defanged, settled quietly to the back of Gereint's awareness to wait for a new master's claim. Gereint stared down at his feet, at the plain silver rings, at the bits of cord scattered on the floor.

Amnachudran went back behind his desk and put the knife away with fussy precision. His wife nodded in calm approval, rose to her feet, smiled at Gereint—he was far too stunned to smile back—and went out of the room.

Gereint put his boots back on, hiding the rings. Then he stood up, turned, and deliberately dropped to his knees.

Amnachudran looked up sharply.

"Tell me to get up," Gereint suggested.

Amnachudran half smiled. "Stand up!" he commanded.

"No," said Gereint, and laughed. "I didn't expect you to do it. I never for one moment thought you would do it! Ah!" He flung his head back in extravagant joy, lifting his hands. "Do you doubt you've repaid me for your life? Don't doubt it!"

Amnachudran did smile this time, but shook his head. "Gereint—"

"You won't regret it," Gereint promised him. "Not by anything I do."

"I trust that I won't. Please get up, as a kindness to me? Yes, thank you, much better," he added, smiling, as Gereint climbed once more to his feet. "What will you do now? Head for Feierabiand by the fastest road?"

"I suppose so. I hardly know."

"You need rest, more food, time to think. We have supper an hour after dusk. If you're still here, I'd like to talk to you then, yes?"

Gereint hadn't expected this. He didn't quite know what he'd expected. But he said, "If you wish me to stay, I'll stay. Or if there's something you want me to do, you can tell me now."

Amnachudran shook his head again. "I don't think so. No. You need to, um, accustom yourself to the idea that you can choose your own course. No. Go for a walk. That's a suggestion, not an order, yes? Do what you like. And if I see you at supper, good."

Gereint stared at him for a moment. "I have—it was—it's been—" He stopped. Turned without another word, since coherence was clearly beyond him at the moment, and went out.

He found a traveling pack in his room. A small hunting bow lay beside the pack, the kind meant for squirrels or birds. A dozen little arrows filled a small quiver. Gereint stood for a long moment, looking at the things. He didn't wonder who had brought him a traveler's kit: He knew it had been Amnachudran's wife.

He went quickly through the pack. A change of

clothing, a blanket, a belt knife, cord. Travel food. A small bag of meal. A little oil. Flints. Candles. He laid a fingertip against one of the arrowheads and nodded. Squirrel and rabbit.

At the bottom of the pack, he found the two books he'd brought away from Fellesteden's house. Gereint looked at those for a long moment. Then he put everything back in the pack except the knife. He slid the knife's sheath onto his belt, drew the knife, looked at it. Ran the tip of one finger down its length. Turned it over in his hand, trying the hilt. Touched its blade briefly to his lips.

It was a good knife. Meant for nothing more dramatic than cutting meat or cord, slicing apples or green wood, but well made. Gereint gave it a little shove, pushing it toward the balance a fighting knife ought to have. To really alter it, he'd need tools and a forge. But he could do a little just by letting the knife know his preference.

The frilly lady's bed looked inviting. Gereint ignored it. *Go for a walk*, Amnachudran had said. He'd meant, *Test your freedom*. It was, of course, a perceptive suggestion. Gereint slung the pack over his shoulder, hung the little bow and quiver in their places, and walked out of the room. Down the hall. Down some stairs. It was a big house...down the largest hall he could find. He passed servants, who nodded. A pair of shaven-headed men-at-arms in livery, with swords at their hips, who also nodded politely but turned to watch as he passed. Cold ran down Gereint's spine, prickled at the back of his neck. He forced himself not to look over his shoulder, and after a moment breathed again when he found that the men had not followed. He turned the corner and found the main door of the house in front of him. It led out into the courtyard, filled with people…hurrying about their business. Some of them glanced up at Gereint, a few with enough interest to make his skin prickle.

But the courtyard gates were open. No one stopped Gereint from walking through them. In the light, with a clear mind, he could see how the road unrolled gently south and west through a pleasant patchwork of orchards and pastures.

Gereint followed the road through the nearest orchard, nodding to the people he passed. He didn't look back. He picked two apples—no one objected; one woman even looked up with a grin and a wave—splashed across a stream, put a gentle hill between him and the orchard, and turned across country, heading north. Glanced at the sun for his direction, turned east, and came back to the house from the northeast, where the quiet hills offered conceal-ment. From this angle the house lay far below, a gracious presence at the heart of a gracious countryside. He found a decent rock to sit on and padded it with the blanket. He ate the apples and a strip of dried beef. Watched the house.

There was no unusual bustle that he could see. People moved around, going about the ordinary business of the day. A shepherd and two dogs brought in a small flock of sheep; a boy chased and caught a goose; women carried baskets of apples in from the orchard. No one hurried; no one seemed to feel any urgency about their chores. No one, as far as Gereint could tell, had followed him or tried to track him into the hills. There was no sign that the freedom Eben Amnachudran had offered had been any sort of deceit or trap.

The sun slid across the sky. Gereint dozed. Woke.

Read some of Berusent's *Historica*. Dozed again. At dusk he finally stood up and stretched. Folded up the blanket and put it back in his pack, along with the book. Picked his way down the hill alongside the little stream, skirted the new pond with its raw-clay bank, and came back to the courtyard gates. The gates were standing open. He went through them.

A man-at-arms posted by the gates moved in the dimness. Gereint stopped.

The man-at-arms looked Gereint up and down. Said, expressionless, "The honored Amnachudran said he's expecting you. I am to ask, do you wish the gates left open tonight?"

Gereint stared back at him. "Not if your custom is to close them."

The man-at-arms shrugged. He said, "There's a man to show you where to go."

There was in fact a servant woman, who looked Gereint up and down in quite a different manner than the man-at-arms had, smiling in appreciation of his height. Being looked at by a woman was an entirely different experience without the brand. The woman said cheerfully, "The family is dining in the little hall. I'll take you there. May I take your pack? I'll put it safe in your room…"

Gereint let her take it.

The little hall turned out to be a spacious room with a single table and long sideboard, appointed in rich wood and dark, quiet colors. The table was covered with dishes of sliced beef and bread, late carrots and early parsnips, beans with bits of crisp pork… Gereint's mouth watered, despite the apples he'd eaten earlier.

Amnachudran was at the head of the table. The

"family" consisted of Amnachudran, Lady Emre, a dark-bearded man of about thirty—one of their sons, Gereint assumed—and, at least tonight, no one else. The family evidently served itself; there were no servants in the room. The son glanced up at Gereint with friendly curiosity; Gereint guessed his father hadn't told him every detail of his recent adventures. Lady Emre smiled a welcome. Amnachudran himself smiled in welcome and what seemed relief. So the man had not been as confident of Gereint's return as he'd seemed. That was, in a way, reassuring.

An extra place was set at the table. Amnachudran gestured an invitation that was not merely kindness, Gereint understood. It *was* kindness; he didn't doubt the man's natural sympathy. But it was also a test, of sorts. Of whether he could use tableware like a civilized man? Or, no. More of whether he could put off a slave's manner and behave not merely like a civilized man but like a free man. He did not even know the answer to that question himself.

Gereint nodded to Emre Tanshan and again to the son, walked forward and took the offered chair. Lady Emre passed him a platter of beef; the son shifted a bowl of carrots to make room for it.

"Your day was pleasant?" Amnachudran asked politely.

"Very restful, honored sir," said Gereint. He took a slice of the beef and a few carrots.

"Take more beef," Lady Emre urged him. "One needs food after hard healing."

Gereint took another slice of beef, nodding polite thanks when Lady Emre handed him the bowl of beans, and said courteously, "You are yourself, like your husband, a healing mage, lady?" Yes, he remembered Amnachudran saying something like that...

Emre Tanshan waved a casual hand. "Oh, well...more or less."

"My lady wife is a true healing mage," Amnachudran explained. "She is the one who healed us both. Not like me at all; I couldn't have managed anything as difficult as your knee. I am, ah. More of a scholar than a practitioner, you understand? My skill lies with, hmm. With injuries that are...symbolic or...one might say, those that have a philosophical element."

Like scars from a *geas* brand, evidently. Gereint couldn't remember ever having heard of any such surgical specialty, but he nodded.

Amnachudran made a small, disparaging gesture. "Philosophically, I have some skill, I think. My practical ability...I removed the scar, but I didn't guess the procedure would cause you such terrible pain. And then it was too late to stop. I'm very sorry—"

Without even thinking about it, Gereint set his hands flat on the table and leaned forward. "Eben Amnachudran. I beg you will not apologize to me for anything."

The scholar stopped, reddening.

His son said earnestly, "But after you rescued my father from the river and dragged him all the way to our doorstep, I'd think it would be my father in your debt, honored sir, and not the other way 'round, whatever old and symbolic injury he eased for you."

The son wasn't much younger than Gereint himself. Standing, he would likely be taller than his father, broader in the shoulder, a good deal less plump. The shape of his face was his mother's, but his cheekbones were more prominent and his jaw more angular. His black hair was cropped very short, short enough to suggest he had recently shaved his head in the common soldier's style. His beard was also like a soldier's; maybe he had recently been with the army. Either way, his honest curiosity was hard to answer. Gereint said after a moment, "I suppose it's a debt that cuts both ways," and took some parsnips.

"Not from the account I heard," the young man declared enthusiastically. "Though I suppose we always feel our own debts most keenly. Still, it's a great service you did our household, honored sir; never doubt it."

Gereint felt his own face heat. He muttered, "You're kind to say so." He dipped a piece of bread in gravy and ate the bread to give himself an excuse to let the conversation go on without him.

"My eldest son, Sicheir," Amnachudran said to Gereint. "Sicheir is a more practical man than I. He is an engineer. He will be leaving for Dachsichten in the morning. The Arobern is gathering engineers there, you may know."

Gereint had not known, though he was grateful for the change of topic. He nodded. It made sense that the Arobern, King of Casmantium, would command his engineers to gather in Dachsichten, crossroads of the whole country. There, the great east-west road met the river road that ran the whole length of the country from north to south. Everything and everyone passed through Dachsichten.

"We're to head west from Dachsichten," Sicheir explained, as Gereint had already surmised. The young man leaned forward, speaking rapidly in his enthusiasm. "We are to widen and improve that rough little mountain

road from Ehre across the mountains into Feierabi-
and. It's part of the settlement the Arobern made with
the Safiad king. He"—meaning the Arobern, Gereint
understood—"wants a road a spear-cast wide, paved
with great stones, with bridges running straight across all
the chasms. It will be a great undertaking. We'll have to
lay down massive buttresses to support the road through
the mountain passes, and devise wholly new bridge
designs, and new methods of grading—there's never been
another road so ambitious in Casmantium, probably not
anywhere."

It surprised Gereint that the Arobern had gotten any
concessions at all out of the Feierabianden king, under
the circumstances. But that the Arobern would then
design a massive, hugely ambitious road—*that* wasn't
surprising. He nodded.

Eben Amnachudran cleared his throat. "You might go
west with Sicheir. If you wish. It's the long way 'round,
to be sure, going so far south before you head west—
I'd understand if you preferred to make your own way
through the mountains after all. But in these troubled
days a man puts himself at risk traveling alone. A good
many brigands have appeared, far more than usual—
preying on the refugees heading south from Melentser,
you know. Besides, a good road under your feet cuts
miles off the journey, as they say." He offered Gereint a
platter. "More bread?"

Eben Amnachudran came to find Gereint later, long
after the household had retired for the night, after even
most of the servants were abed. Gereint was still awake.
He was standing, fully dressed, in front of the long mirror in his room, studying his unmarked face and thinking

about the advice Merrich Berchandren suggested for travelers in his book on customs and courtesy. Among other recommendations, Berchandren suggested that "an uncertain guest might best speak quietly, smile frequently, and depart discreetly." The line did not make clear whether this advice was meant to apply when the guest or the situation was uncertain. Or, considering Berchandren's subtlety, both.

Gereint twitched when the knock came. But it was a quiet knock, the sort of circumspect rap that a man on the edge of sleep might ignore. Nothing aggressive or alarming. Gereint swung the door wide, found—of course—Amnachudran waiting there, and stepped back, inviting the scholar to enter with a gesture.

Amnachudran came in and stood for a moment, looking around. "This is my daughter's room," he commented. "I have four sons, but only one daughter; youngest of the lot. She hasn't stayed here for several years, but we keep the room for her—unless we have a guest, of course. It may perhaps be," the older man glanced around doubtfully, "a little feminine."

Gereint assured him solemnly that the room was the very essence of perfection, adding, "According to the precepts of Entechsan Terichsekiun, who declares for us that aesthetic perfection lies both in the flawless detail and the eye that appreciates it, and which of us would dare argue with the greatest of philosophers?"

Amnachudran laughed. "Any other philosopher, as I'm sure you know very well! But, you know, that you would quote Terichsekiun makes me wonder…My daughter lives in Breidechboden. Tehre. She's a maker, like you. Or, maybe not quite like you. She works on these, ah"—he gestured broadly—"these abstruse philosophical things. Nothing as practical as waterproof saddlebags. I may be something of a philosopher myself, if hardly in Terichsekiun's class, but I can't say I understand my daughter's work."

Gereint, wondering where Amnachudran was going with this digression, made a polite sound to show he was listening.

"Well, you see…I know my daughter's been searching for another maker who might help her do something or other. Someone intelligent and experienced, with a powerful, flexible gift. It's important to her, but she hasn't found anyone who suits her."

Gereint wanted to say, *You want me to go to* Breidechboden? *You do know there's no city I want to visit less?* Instead, he made another politely attentive sound, *Hmm*?

"Yes, well she *will* tell fools they're fools. I've advised her to keep her tongue behind her teeth, but she can't seem to. She's not precisely rude—well, she can be, I suppose. My wife says she would have an easier time of it if she were married, though I don't know…"

Gereint said *hmm* again. He could easily believe that any man a wealthy, well-born woman maker approached would take her unmarried status as an opportunity or a challenge. Especially if she told him he was a fool. Especially if she was pretty. If she followed after her mother, Tehre would be small and pretty and plump—the sort of girl a man might well take too lightly. Until she called him a fool and proved she was more intelligent than he was. Then he would be angry and embarrassed and probably twice a fool. That seemed likely enough.

He had known Amnachudran wanted something from him. This particular suggestion surprised him. The scholar wanted *Gereint* to go meet his *own cherished daughter* in, of all places, *Breidechboden*? He hesitated, trying to find a polite way to express his hesitation. A point-blank refusal would be churlish. He owed Amnachudran a great deal, not only for removing the brand, but also... In a way, he realized, he also owed the scholar for simply reminding Gereint that true, profound kindness existed, when, in Fellesteden's house, he'd come to doubt it. It was as though... as though Amnachudran's act had redeemed all his memories of kindness and compassion and generosity, limned all those memories with brilliance that cast years of horror into shadow.

That was what he owed Amnachudran. But... Breidechboden?

"Of course, I know you didn't intend to go to Breidechboden," Amnachudran said apologetically. "I'm sure you'd be concerned about meeting someone who might recognize you. But I also have a friend in the capital. A surgeon mage, a true master with the knife." He made a vague gesture. "There's—theoretically—a way to remove those, um, rings. They can't be cut, you know, except by the cold magecraft that made them. But any sufficiently skilled surgeon mage ought to be able to detach the tendon from the bone, do you see? Remove the rings whole, reattach the tendons..." He trailed off, caught by the intensity of Gereint's stillness.

Gereint did not speak. He couldn't have spoken to save his life. He only stared at Amnachudran.

The scholar dipped his head apologetically. "The difficult part is reattaching the tendons. If the surgeon isn't sufficiently skilled, the, um, patient would, well. You see."

Gereint did, vividly. Fellesteden had driven him to risk death in the desert. But not even to escape Fellesteden had Gereint ever considered crippling himself.

"I wouldn't dare attempt it," Amnachudran explained. "But my friend could manage that sort of surgical mage-craft." He hesitated and then added, "I'm fairly certain."

"Would he?" Gereint asked after a moment. "He would do that for me?" His tone had gone husky. He cleared his throat. It didn't help.

"Ah, well…I can't say that my friend has done any such surgery in the past." Amnachudran's tone implied that although he couldn't *say* it, it was true. "But I think it's possible he might be willing. As a favor to me, and for, ah, other reasons. I'd write a letter for you to take to him, of course. If you were willing to go to Breidechboden."

Gereint said nothing. Interfering with a *geas* was thoroughly illegal. But Amnachudran had already done it himself, and it seemed clear he knew very well that this friend of his had done the same and would be willing to do it again.

"You're a strongly gifted maker. Aren't you? Modesty aside?"

"Well," Gereint managed, still trying to wrap his mind around the possibility of true freedom, "Yes, but—"

"And if you did go to Breidechboden, you'd need a place to stay and a respectable person to vouch for you. Tehre could provide you with both of those. And," he gave Gereint a faintly apologetic, faintly defiant look, "Tehre really does seem to require the services of a really good maker, or so I gather from her most recent letter."

"Your daughter...you..."

Amnachudran tilted his head, regarding Gereint shrewdly. "Should I mistrust you? I don't assume my judgment is infallible. But as the Arobern's appointed judge for the district north of Tanshen, I've had a good deal of experience assessing men's characters, and so has my wife, and in this case we're both fairly confident—"

"You're a judge?" Gereint was startled, almost shocked. But...at the same time, perhaps that explained why the scholar had felt himself able to interfere with the *geas*. He didn't exactly have the right; no one had the right to interfere with a legally set *geas*. And in fact the king famously held any of his judges to stricter account for breaking any law than an ordinary man. But still...a judge might feel he *ought* to have that right.

Amnachudran looked at him, puzzled. "Yes, I petitioned for the position some years past. Having to run down to Tashen every time we wanted a judge was so inconvenient. Everyone seems to prefer to simply come to me. Ah—does it make a difference? I can't see why it should."

It did make a difference, if not to Amnachudran then to Gereint. In some strange way, Amnachudran's generosity seemed to negate that other, long-ago judge's harshness. Gereint didn't know how to put this feeling into words, however.

After a moment, the scholar shrugged. "Trustworthiness, like soundness of design, can only be proved in the test. If you choose to go to Breidechboden, I think we will both find our best hopes proved out. I've a letter of introduction for you." He took a stiff, leather envelope out of his belt pouch and held it out to Gereint. "The man's name isn't on it. I'll tell you his name. It's

Reichteier Andlauban. Anybody in Breidechboden could direct you to his house." He hesitated, studying Gereint. "You needn't decide right away. Or even before leaving this house, whether heading south or west or north."

Gereint had heard of Andlauban. Everybody had. If there were two better surgeon mages in all of Casmantium, there were not three. He said, a touch drily, "I think I can decide right away. I'll take your letter and go to Breidechboden. If your daughter will offer me a place to stay in the city, I'll take that, too, of course. I'm sure I'll find her work interesting."

Amnachudran gave Gereint a long, searching stare. "I'm not trying to coerce you," he said earnestly.

"Save perhaps with generosity."

Amnachudran gave a faintly surprised nod, perhaps not having quite realized this himself. "Yes, perhaps." He hesitated another moment, then merely nodded a good night and went out.

Gereint stared down at the envelope in his hand.

Andreikan Warichteier said that the cold magecraft that made the *geas* should break in Feierabiand, where no cold mages practiced their craft. He claimed that the gentle earth mages of the west forbade *geas* bonds to be imposed on any man, and laid down a powerful magic of breaking and loosing at the border to see their proscription was carried out. A contemporary and rival philosopher, Entechsan Terichsekiun, agreed that a *geas* could not be carried into Feierabiand, but argued that the limitation was a natural quality of the other kingdom. Feirlach Fenescheiren, not so widely read in the modern day, but a careful scholar whom Gereint had generally found reliable, disagreed with them both. Instead, he credited the

Safiad kings with the proscription of every kind of cold magecraft—and warned that the Safiads would regret that proscription if they ever found themselves opposing the desert of fire and silence, as Casmantium was always required to oppose it.

Of course, Berentser Gereimarn, writing a hundred years later than any of the three, said that was all nonsense and that nothing whatsoever prevented cold magecraft and all its sorcery from working perfectly in Feierabiand or Linularinum or any country, however far west one went. Gereimarn was not the most reliable of natural philosophers, but Pareirechan Lenfarnan said the same thing, and he had been a more careful scholar.

But every single philosopher Gereint had ever read agreed that if the *geas* rings could be removed, the *geas* would come off with them. And Reichteier Andlauban, with his skill in surgery and magecraft, could surely detach and reattach tendon from bone if any man could. Eben Amnachudran had clearly implied the man had done so in the past.

At last, Gereint opened the envelope and slipped out the folded letter within. It seemed to be exactly what it should be: a personal letter, asking—as a personal favor—for an unnamed man to provide an unnamed service to the bearer of the letter. There was a clear indication, reading behind the ink, that both men agreed a favor was owed—and that, in any case, the man asked was not likely to object to the particular service requested. Gereint put the letter back into its envelope. When he finally undressed and lay down on the bed, he kept the envelope under his hand, as though there were some risk it might vanish before dawn if not constantly guarded.

*   *   *

In the morning, an hour after dawn, Gereint found Lady Emre in the breakfast room before her husband. It was a small room, very feminine, with delicately carved furnishings all in pale colors. Emre Tanshan, at the head of the graceful breakfast table, looked very much at home in it. Gereint said, "Ah—you were aware—that is, your husband *did* tell you—"

Lady Emre smiled with uncomplicated satisfaction. "Oh, yes. My daughter will be so pleased if you can help her make sense of whatever it is she's trying to work out," she assured Gereint. She nodded graciously toward the chair across from hers. "Have some eggs. You're too thin, you know. I suggested, in fact, that Eben should ask you to go meet Tehre."

Gereint could not quite find an appropriate response to this. But he did fill his plate.

"My daughter will appreciate you, I think," Lady Emre continued comfortably. "Especially if you quote Entechsan Terichsekiun to her at frequent intervals. Have you read his *On the Strength of Materials* as well as his *Nomenclature*? She *will* quote all this natural philosophy about materials and structures and the compulsion of tension compared with the persuasion of compression, or perhaps it's the other way around. Have some of this apple cake."

The apple cake was heavy, moist with the sweet liquor the cook had drizzled over it, and redolent of summer. Gereint let himself be persuaded to have a second slice. He *had* read *Materials*, but he could not at the moment recall what Terichsekiun had had to say about tension and compression.

"Now, my son is, as you know, going south to Dachsichten. He'll travel with half a dozen men-at-arms. There's some risk on the road south, you know; not everyone from Melentser departed in good order. You might go with Sicheir as far as Dachsichten, if you chose. He does know all the good inns along the way, though you're not likely to get anything better than mutton stew or boiled beef until you reach Breidechboden, I suppose."

Gereint nodded noncommittally. He did not say that buying mutton stew or boiled beef in any inn, and eating it in the common room like any free man, was a luxury he hadn't dreamed of for nineteen years.

"Good morning," said the architect of his new freedom from the doorway. Eben Amnachudran gave his lady wife a fond smile and Gereint a searching look.

Gereint got to his feet with a deference ingrained by long habit, then flushed, unable for a confusing moment to tell whether he'd shown a guest's proper regard for his host or a slave's shameful obsequiousness to his master.

Amnachudran, with characteristic kindness, showed no sign of noticing Gereint's uncertainty. He said cheerfully, hefting a large pouch bound up with a leather thong, "I have several books I'm sending to Tehre; you can show them to any patrol officer who asks." He set the pouch on the table at Gereint's elbow.

Thus furnishing a legitimate reason for Gereint's presence in the capital; the city patrol routinely turned indigents away at the gate. Only travelers who could show either some means of support or proof of legitimate business in the city were welcome in Breidechboden.

"A copy of Garaneirdich's *The Properties of Materials* and Dachsechreier's *Making with Wood*," Amnachudran went on. "And a copy of Wareierchen's *Philosophy of Making*. She has that, but this copy has all the appendices, not just the first. I know you'll take great care of them. And I'm including a letter for Tehre, covering them. And explaining, ah—"

"Me," Gereint said, recovering his composure. He sat down again at the table, shifting the platter of apple cake and one of sausages toward Eben Amnachudran's place.

"Not in great detail," Amnachudran assured him, sitting down and regarding the cake with enthusiasm. "Emre, my dear—"

"Summer Gold apples, and that's the last of the berry liquor," Lady Emre answered. "Have a slice, and be sure to tell the cook how nicely the liquor sets off the apples; you know how he frets."

Amnachudran cut himself a generous slice, tasted it, and closed his eyes briefly in bliss. "Mmm. I'll be certain to reassure him. The last of the liquor, do you say? My dear, shouldn't the brambles be bearing soon? Let's remember to send the children berrying as soon as possible, yes? Now, Gereint, do you mean to travel with Sicheir as far as Dachsichten, or make your own way south?"

"I'd think travel between Tashen and Dachsichten must be a little hazardous just now, for a man on his own."

Amnachudran gave a serious nod. "It is, unfortunately. We really must do something soon about all the brigands. So you'll go with Sicheir, then? Good, then. I do hope you will find yourself able to work with my daughter."

Gereint let his mouth crook. "I'm sure it will be impossible for her to offend me."

Lady Emre smiled at him warmly, and Amnachudran

laughed. He waved his fork in the air. "'Three imperturbable things there be: the indifferent sky, the sums of mathematics, and a man too wise to be proud.' Though I always thought that *pride* was not quite the concept Teirenchoden wanted there."

"Vanity, perhaps," Lady Emre offered. Her wry glance Gereint's way suggested her suspicion that life had taught him the dispensability of vanity. Gereint lowered his eyes before her too-perceptive gaze.

"Very likely," agreed Amnachudran. He leaned back in his chair. "Now, Gereint, I have some coin for you; enough for you to get to Breidechboden and then through the gates. Breidechboden is not a kind city to the indigent; if you do any work for Tehre, make sure she remembers to pay you what it's worth."

"You've already been very generous—"

"'My friend, if I am too generous, I can only hope you will forgive me and believe I don't intend to compel you with the bonds of gratitude.'"

Gereint blinked. He said at last, "Banrichte Maskeirien. Some epic or other…"

"Yes, the Engeieresgen cycle; very good." Amnachudran paused. Then he said kindly, "I would not dare try to improve upon Maskeirien's words."

Gereint considered the older man. "If I am compelled by the bonds of gratitude, it is because I choose to be."

Amnachudran was silent for a moment. Then he stood up, came to Gereint, and laid two fingers on Gereint's cheek where the scar of the brand had been. "As long as I do not regret this. I think I can trust you for that."

"You can," Gereint promised him. He met Lady Emre's wry gaze, including her in that promise.

CHAPTER 3

Gereint traveled with Sicheir Amnachudran and half a dozen men-at-arms. From Amnachudran's house, it was twelve miles south to Tashen. Because they did not leave the scholar's house until noon and were not pressed by any need for haste, they stayed the night at an inn in the town. No one paid Gereint any attention: Travelers passing through Tashen were nothing worth comment, no doubt especially after the flood of refugees from Melentser had passed through. That perfect lack of interest was even more to be treasured than a comfortable bed.

From Tashen, it was only about fifteen miles south to Metichteran, all on a good road. There, the northernmost bridge across the Teschanken River led from East Metichteran to West Metichteran. Gereint looked down with interest at the bridge as they crossed the river.

This bridge had been built so that that Casmantium, invading Meridanium, could send half its army down from the north upon the Meridanian forces. Casmantian builders had flung the bridge across the river in a single night and a day, according to Sichan Meiregen's epic, and the Casmantian soldiers had come down upon the armies of Meridanium like reapers upon wheat. Meridanium had lost its king and its independence and had become merely one Casmantian province among many. Then, in the more peaceful era that followed, there had been time for towns to grow up and roads to be built...but nothing that had been built in the north had stood longer or more solidly than Metichteran's bridge. Though Gereint sincerely doubted any account that claimed a night and a day sufficient for its building, no matter how great the general or how gifted his builders. It was a very solid-looking bridge.

Then they headed south again through the low, rocky hills along the river road. Here the road was narrow and rough, and though there were obvious signs of large numbers of recent travelers, there were few now on the road. This was a stretch of farmless backcountry where brigands might well wait for vulnerable travelers, but theirs was too large a party to tempt any brigands who might have been watching the road. They passed other travelers, slow-moving refugees who had left Melentser only right at the deadline. Those travelers had also been warned about the brigands, clearly. Very few of them traveled in parties smaller than Sicheir's, and those that did looked decidedly anxious.

From Metichteran, they traveled thirty miles south along the Teschanken River to Pamnarichtan, where the swift little Nerintsan River came out of the hills to join the wider Teschanken. The inn at the confluence was not very impressive, but the confluence itself was a great sight. The upper Teschanken flowed clear and swift from the north, and the Nerintsan came down in a quick, cheerful dash from the steep hills, but the lower Teschanken that resulted from their joining was very different in character from either northern stretch of river. It was broad and deep, colored a rich brown with sediment, seemingly lazy but treacherous, its currents running in unexpected directions. No one would try to build a bridge across the South Teschanken, but there was a ferry to Raichboden, southernmost town in the once independent province of Meridanium. Riverboats appeared here where the Teschanken was navigable; inns were crowded with boat crews as well as accommodating travelers off the road.

"Can't we try a boat?" asked the youngest of the men-at-arms, Bechten, craning wistfully to look after one that floated past.

"Oh, to be sure. The price will be high with all those folk crowding south from Melentser. But you can sell your horse for passage and walk on your own legs from Dachsichten back home," one of his elders answered, not unkindly. "No, boy; the road's a good one and the weather's fine, so don't tempt the sky with a grumble, eh? Besides, see, the river's running low. You wouldn't think it, looking at the water here, but once they get farther down, those boats will be snagging up and pressing even their paying passengers to get them over the bars."

So they rode at an easy pace, and the weather held fair; they came to Dachsichten six days after leaving Eben Amnachudran's house.

Dachsichten collected important roads that ran from the north and the south and the west. It was not a pretty town, but it was crowded and busy; the roads around

Dachsichten thronged with respectable carters and farm wagons, with drovers and merchants' convoys, with the slow-moving wagons of families resettling from Melentser, and the carriages of the wealthy, and swift-horsed couriers.

"There won't be trouble with brigands from here," Sicheir commented to Gereint. He was standing on the tiny balcony of their room at the inn, looking out over the crowded city streets. It was not a good inn, but the only one they had found with rooms still to let: Many of the refugees from Melentser still lingered in Dachsichten while they decided where to go. Some would stay, probably. Especially the less well-to-do. Dachsichten was not a pretty town, but it was prosperous; folk looking for work might well find it here.

But it left the inns crowded. With Sicheir on the balcony, there wasn't room for Gereint to even set a foot on it. That was well enough; it was, no doubt, extremely unlikely that anyone from Melentser would happen to glance up and recognize him, but why take the chance?

"The men can all go back north in the morning, and we'll part company," Sicheir added. The young man looked over his shoulder at Gereint. "I'll be sorry for that. You've a good memory for the odd tale out of the histories. I see why my father thought you might work well with Tehre."

Gereint murmured something appropriate. He was distracted by a sudden desperate temptation to declare that he'd changed his mind, that Breidechboden was no longer his destination. He could head west to the pass at Ehre with Sicheir, test once and for all the notion that crossing the border would break the *geas* magic, avoid any possible encounter with any previous master or cousin or anyone else in Breidechboden who might recognize him.

Of course, if he did that, he would never find Reichteier Andlauban, never have the opportunity to ask the surgeon mage to remove the *geas* rings. Even if the *geas* itself broke crossing the border, Gereint knew that the physical presence of the rings would fret him for the rest of his life. He could endure that. There were far worse things than carrying merely the *symbol* of bondage. Even so... Gereint wanted the rings gone with an intensity that ached through all his bones.

And he had promised Amnachudran he would go to his daughter's house.

Gereint had spent years learning to disbelieve in the existence of true kindness. And then Eben Amnachudran and his family had effortlessly demonstrated that all the painful lessons he'd worked so hard to learn had been wrong. It had been as though the world had suddenly expanded before him, reclaiming all the generous width he remembered from his distant childhood. And Gereint had realized, gradually—was still realizing—that he'd spent all those years wanting nothing more than a reason to believe in that generosity. And Amnachudran had given him that reason.

So in the morning Gereint said nothing, but swung up on his borrowed horse and rode with Sicheir only so far as the western gate of Dachsichten. Then he left the younger man with a handclasp and a nod and rode south without looking back, through a pearly morning mist that drifted across the city and glittered on the slate roofs of the houses and cobblestones of the streets.

The mist turned into a cold rain before he even reached Dachsichten's southern gate, and then the rain stayed with him as he rode south. The road was too well made to go to sloppy mud; water simply beaded on its surface and ran away down its sloping edges. But the persistent rain got down the collar of his shirt and made the reins slippery in his hands, and he rode with his shoulders hunched and his head bowed. He tried not to take the rain as a sign of things to come.

The character of the countryside changed south of Dachsichten, becoming flatter and richer. Gereint rode now through a tight and tidy patchwork of fields and pastures and orchards, with woodlots few and much prized. The river rolled along on his left, the color of muddy slate, rain dimpling its surface. Boats with brightly painted trim slid past him, running downstream at a pace no horse could sustain. But as the man-at-arms had suggested, Gereint not infrequently saw one or another boat snagged up, the men of their crews cursing as they worked to free it.

There were few inns south of Dachsichten, but far more farms that offered travelers meals in their huge, busy kitchens, and the hospitality of a clean, hay-sweet barn or an extra room for those who wished to barter coin or labor for a night's comfortable rest. Gereint, disgusted by the continuing bad weather, halted early his first evening out from Dachsichten, when he came to a particularly pleasant-looking farm. He stayed there an entire extra day, watching the rain fall and setting his hands to small tasks of mending and making that had proven beyond the limited skill of local makers. He even borrowed the small portable forge the farmer owned and showed the farmer's twin sons, both moderately gifted, how to repair worn pots and skillets.

It occurred to Gereint for the first time that even bearing the *geas* rings, he might not need to go to Feierabiand to find a new life; that he might trade his skill as a maker for a place at almost any normal, peaceful farm and disappear from the sight of anyone who might wish to find him. Unless, of course, someone someday caught sight of the rings. Then that new life would vanish in a heartbeat... No. He set his face south when the rain finally stopped and went on.

The sun came out at last, and Gereint's horse strode out with a will in the clean air, happy with its rest and with the generous measure of grain the farmer's sons had measured out for it. The most common travelers on the road were now farmers with small dog-carts and teams of wagonners with six-horse teams of enormous horses. The carts were for local travel, but the wagons were heading, loaded, to Breidechboden, or returning empty to their farms.

It had been years since Gereint had lived in Breidechboden, and he had neither intended nor wished to return. Nevertheless, a strange feeling went through him when, two days later, he finally saw the Emnerechke Gates rise up before him: great stone pillars that marked the beginning of the city proper. It was foolish to feel he'd come home. Breidechboden was not, could never again be, his home. But even so, the feeling was there, surprising him with its intensity.

A wall had once run between each of the four hills that framed the city, encircling the valley that lay in their midst. That wall had been two spear-casts thick and six high, faced with stone and huge timbers from the heart of the great forest, heavy with builders' magic so that it would stand against even the most powerful siege engines.

Berusent described the great wall of Breidechboden in his *Historica,* when he described the founding of the capital. Tauchen Breidech, one of the early kings of the original, smaller Casmantium, had built this city on a base of seven wide roads linking eight concentric circles; the outermost circle comprised the wall and its famous gates. But successive iterations of war and conquest and peace and growth had thoroughly disguised the great king's original plan. The wall had been first absorbed into the widening city and finally, after a century or so, torn down completely. Its great stones had been incorporated into the innumerable tenements and apartments and private houses that now ascended the hills, rising rank above rank, pink and creamy gold in the soft morning light. Gereint wondered whether any of those residences might possibly prove impervious to siege engines, if a catapult happened to fire against them: Berusent had not commented on whether the builders' magic might have stayed in the stones and timbers when the walls were taken apart for their materials.

The Amnachudran townhouse was set on the lee side of Seven Son Hill, which lay to the right hand of the Emnerechke Gates. Gereint gave his name—not his real name, of course—and the townhouse address to the city patrol at the Gates, explained he was a maker, showed the patrol officer the books he carried, and at last gained the necessary month's pass to the city.

"Keep this pass with you at all times," the patrol officer told him. "You're from the north? Melentser would that

be? There's too many of you lot wanting into Breidechboden." His suspicious look made it clear that if not for
the books and the Amnachudran name, he'd have thought
Gereint might be looking not for work but for a big city
in which he could profitably beg or steal.

"I'm from Meridanium," Gereint lied, and added, in
order to show normal curiosity, "So a lot of Melentser
refugees have come here, then?"

"All of 'em, I sometimes think," the patrol officer said
sourly. "I suppose we can be grateful those cursed griffins didn't demand Tashen as well as Melentser, or we'd
be flooded to the gates. Even as it is, most days there're
shortages of bread and meat in the markets. You'll
move on, if you take my advice. Wanenboden might be
better."

Anywhere not here, was the clear subtext of that suggestion. Gereint said, "I'll likely be heading west."

"Good. But if you do decide to stay in Breidechboden,
apply for a permanent residence pass as soon as you
qualify. Clear? Go on, then." And he waved Gereint into
the city.

The public roads were wide near the Gates, the apartments tall and well built, faced with bright-painted
plaster. Only specially licensed wagons and carts were
allowed into Breidechboden between dawn and dusk,
so the streets offered plenty of room for people ahorse
or riding in sedan chairs or walking on their own feet.
Wagons and riders kept to the middle of each roadway;
pedestrians and sedan chairs traveled on raised pavement
walks that ran on each side of the streets, clear of the
refuse that littered the roadways. Gereint headed right,
toward Seven Son Hill.

The street led in an arc around the curve of the hill.
The apartment blocks here were less tall but considerably
finer, faced with white limestone and plaster painted to
resemble marble. Then these gave way in turn to private
houses with small walled gardens. Wealthy merchants
and men of business lived here. If one continued around
the circle, one would come eventually to the Hill of Iron,
where the king's palace rose up above the common city.

The lee side of Seven Son Hill—the side that faced
away from the center of Breidechboden—was a place
where the private houses were large and the gardens
generous. Here the facades were real marble, the doors
carved and polished, and the gates decorated with the
figures of dogs or horses or falcons or grotesques. The
public street was much cleaner, and the private walkways
that ran to each house were lined with tubs of flowers.

Tehre Amnachudran lived in one of these houses.
Gereint had known more or less what the Amnachudran
townhouse must be like when her father had told him
where she lived, but he was surprised again, studying it
now, at the family's wealth.

The house had leaping deer figures by its gate. More
deer held round porcelain lanterns on either side of its
walkway; at night, each stag must seem to carry a small
glowing moon between its antlers. Mosaic tiles ornamented the pillars that framed the heavy double doors
of carved oak. The house itself was faced with gray
marble and exotic porphyry; the windows that faced onto
the street were fitted with fine, expensive glass. Beside
the door, a bell cord of red silk led away into the inner
reaches of the house.

Gereint stood for a long moment, holding his horse's

reins and gazing at the bell cord. But if he meant to stay in Breidechboden at all, he needed a place to stay. And he trusted Eben Amnachudran. And he was, he acknowledged to himself, curious about Tehre Amnachudran Tanshan. So at last he reached out, gave the cord a strong pull, and heard the distant clangor of the bell—iron, by the sound of it, but with a mellowness to the note that was unusual for iron.

Rapid steps sounded, and the shutter in the center of the door swung open. A sweet-faced older woman gazed out at him with some surprise.

"A letter from Eben Amnachudran for his daughter," Gereint said quickly, before the woman could say anything about tradesmen not being welcome. He gave the woman the letter through the shutter, expecting her to tell him to wait and take it away to give to her mistress.

Instead, the woman gave him a long, assessing look, nodded, slipped the letter out of its leather envelope, and read it herself. Then she looked up again, this time smiling a welcome. The shutter swung closed and latched, and there was the sound of the bar being drawn away. Then the doors swung open and the woman smiled at him. "Honored sir—please be welcome," she said warmly. "My name is Fareine Reinarechtan; I have the honor to manage Lady Tehre's household. Loop your horse's reins over that stag's antlers; that's right. I'll have someone come at once to take it around to the stable. It's quite convenient, not a quarter-mile down the street, and I promise you the animal will be well cared for; everyone keeps their horses there. Come in, honored sir, and be welcome."

Gereint stepped through the door, bowing slightly. It

felt...very strange, coming into this house as a welcome guest, with a false name in that letter of introduction and the *geas* rings hidden by his boots. "Forgive me for intruding without warning. If a message had been sent ahead, it couldn't have come far before me. May I ask whether Lady Tehre Amnachudran Tanshan is at home?"

"She is, and I'm sure she'll welcome you, but if you will be good enough to wait, honored sir...I am afraid Lady Tehre does not like to be interrupted while she is working, but she will be down very soon, I am sure. Permit me to show you to the kitchen while I have a room prepared for you—Esmin! Such a long way you have come, all the way from the honored Eben Amnachudran's house?"

"I was very interested in Eben Amnachudran's description of his honored daughter's work, though he was not able to be very, ah, detailed. As I've business of my own in Breidechboden, the honored Eben Amnachudran was kind enough to provide me a letter of introduction."

"A fortunate moment for my lady, I am sure. Esmin! Where *is*—? Ah, Esmin, dear! Get a room ready for our honored guest, please, and mind you make certain there are plenty of towels by the water basin. Honored sir, Lady Tehre will be down very soon, I am sure..." Still producing a gentle flow of chatter, the woman led the way down the hall.

The reception hall was all red marble and porphyry, with fluted columns in the best southern style and mosaics on the walls. It gave way to massive vaulted rooms just as intimidating. Thankfully, the kitchen turned out to be much more approachable. It, too, was a vast room, but comfortable and friendly. Ovens lined one end and a huge table stood at the other, with a narrow stair leading down, Gereint surmised from the cold draft, to an ice cellar. There were two assistant cooks as well as the head cook, and a clutter of girls to do the scullery chores and run errands. To Gereint's faint surprise, the cook and both her assistants were women. Was all the household female?

The cook appeared to take Gereint's bony height as an amusing challenge. She was a placid, ample woman with small black eyes set in a broad moon-face. She jiggled when she laughed, which was often. The kitchen girls clearly adored her.

"I do like men who know how to eat," she remarked with approval, offering Gereint a second plate of sandwiches after he cleared the first with gratifying speed. "That'll put some bulk on those bones, so it will. And there are cakes to finish, plenty to have some now and leave some for the evening."

Gereint was pleased and a little surprised that the household staff did not seem to stand on ceremony: There must be a formal dining room somewhere but no one suggested eating there. He and the household staff alike sat around the big table to eat the sandwiches and stole slices of apple from the girl who was slicing fruit for pastries. The girl threatened to stab their hands, but laughed.

The second round of sandwiches vanished almost as quickly as the first, but there was still one untouched plate remaining when the kitchen door swung open once more. The household staff leaped up. Gereint got to his feet as well; the cook hissed sharply at one of the girls who was slower than he to take her cue. The girl flushed dark red and jumped up as well. Lady Tehre Amnachudran Tanshan swept in just as the girl made it up.

For a small woman, Lady Tehre managed to sweep very convincingly. On a first glance, she was very little like either of her parents. She was small breasted and narrow hipped, yet she did not look boyish, either. She had dark hair; not black like Sicheir, but dark like molasses, a rich brown with golden highlights. She wore it tucked up on her head in an untidy style that went beyond casual to thoughtless. It was lovely hair. Yet she was not actually pretty—or maybe she was, but she did not hold herself with the conscious awareness of a woman who knows she is pretty.

Tehre Amnachudran had nothing of her father's visible kindness or her mother's comfortable warmth. She looked...not precisely stern. But if she had been tall and stately, she might have possessed an intense, striking beauty that went beyond ordinary prettiness. Because she was small and delicate, she merely looked high-strung.

And, unlike her staff, she was not very welcoming of strangers. "A maker, do you say?" she said to Fareine, doubt clear in her tone. "I don't know—I haven't been—"

"Your honored father sent him," Fareine put in smoothly. "All the way from Meridanium." Gereint had given his name as Gereint Pecheran, which was one of the most common Meridanian names.

"Oh, did he?" Lady Tehre hesitated. "Well...well... let's go to my workroom, I suppose. Fareine—"

"I'll bring you something there," the older woman promised immediately.

"Good, good," Tehre said, but absently, very much as though she had not actually heard what Fareine said. She gave Gereint a mistrustful look, but waved for him to accompany her. "You're a maker? I'm working on this problem having to do with the elongation of cracks in large structures. Of course, when you're working with masonry, stone breaks when you subject it to remotely applied tension, I'm sure you know that, but what I can't see is how the cracks shift from slow, sporadic propagation to sudden catastrophic propagation. Do you work with masonry? Large structures?"

"I have." Not often, but Gereint did not say this. Women were often makers, but very seldom engineers, but Tehre Amnachudran certainly sounded more like an engineer than an ordinary maker.

The workroom proved to be a large, cluttered room on the main floor of the house, with wide windows that probably opened to the garden, though these were all tightly shuttered. Broad papers covered with delicate sketches in ink and charcoal were unrolled and pegged down on the tables—no wonder the windows were shuttered: Too strong a breeze would not be kind to those delicate papers. Expensive lamps shed an even, steady glow over the diagrams.

Edging closer to the table nearest the door, Gereint saw that one of the sketches was a detailed diagram, heavily notated, of some sort of mechanism with unfamiliar mathematical equations tucked around the edges. He frowned at the diagram, trying to make sense of it—it looked like someone had tried to design an extremely ornate bridge, a bridge with twin exterior galleries on either side, its galleries supported by pillars and connected to the bridge proper by high arches. The design might have made more sense to an engineer than it did to Gereint, who gave up on it after a moment and turned to studying Tehre Amnachudran instead of her mysterious diagram. Fareine edged past him and set plates of sandwiches and honey cakes carefully on the edge of one of the tables that was not entirely covered by sketches.

"You probably know that cracks don't usually run dangerously in bridges or walls or ships or things like that, until they suddenly do," Tehre said to Gereint, showing no sign of noticing the plates. She tapped one of the diagrams, where mathematical equations marched down the clear space of the margin. Gereint tilted his head, trying to read the equations, but they did not seem familiar.

Tehre said, "I think it's clear there's a critical length and once a crack reaches that length, it'll run catastrophically. You'd think that as the strength of a material increases, so the critical length would increase, but obviously that's not the way it happens, yes?" She spoke rapidly, her voice sharp and demanding—or not exactly demanding, but intense.

"Because anyone knows that some very strong materials like stone can tolerate hardly any kind of crack at all before they break under tension, which is why you can build with wrought iron under tension but you always put stone under compression, yes? So we really need to think of resistance to crack propagation as a property related not to strength exactly, but to the forcefulness of the blow it takes to fracture a piece of the material, do you see? What I think—" tapping the row of equations once more, she seemed suddenly to wonder whether Gereint was following this, and stopped, looking at him with doubt.

Gereint said, "I haven't worked extensively with bridges or walls, but I'd think that what you need most is proper definitions of qualities like 'strength' and 'forcefulness' and 'toughness' and 'brittleness' and 'flex-ibility.' And 'stretchability,' once you start thinking about metals, because once you start thinking about crack propagation through metal, it's probably 'stretchability' that allows for greater resistance to fracture, don't you think?"

Tehre gazed at Gereint as though actually seeing him for the first time. Her eyes, an unusual bronzy green, were large and striking in her delicate face.

Then she flipped open a large book on the nearest table, paged through it rapidly until she reached blank paper, and picked up a quill. "The length of a 'safe' crack in a structure must depend on the ratio of its 'brittleness' to the amount of tensile force applied to the material," she said, writing quickly. "No! Not the amount of ten-sile force *applied*, but the amount actually *absorbed* by the material. And so the critical length of a crack would actually be inversely proportional to the 'stretchability' of the material." She paused and blinked down at the book. "That seems counterintuitive. But isn't that right?"

Gereint said, "It follows, but it means you need a term for 'toughness' as well as one for 'stretchability.' One is more like resistance to fracture as a result of a blow, isn't it, and the other is more like resilience under tension. Or is that right?"

"I can see you two will do well," said Fareine. "But, Tehre, don't forget, you still need to eat one of these nice sandwiches."

"What?" Tehre turned to the old woman and stared at her for a moment before actually focusing on her. Then she laughed.

Gereint was surprised at that laugh. It was a nice laugh,

filled with affection and genuine amusement—at herself, at her own intensity and distractibility. It occurred to him that Tehre might well borrow a word like "distractibility" to mean "ability to slip under friction" or something of the sort, and he smiled.

"We'll go out to the garden, I suppose," Tehre suggested. "Fareine, is everything"—she waved her hands vaguely, still holding the quill—"in order?"

"Your guest is properly settled," Fareine assured her mistress. "Thank you, honored sir; if you could take these plates, I'll go fetch jugs of wine and water, shall I?" She handed over the sandwiches and cakes and bustled out again.

Gereint raised his eyebrows at Lady Tehre, meaning *Which way?*

"Through here," the lady said, swinging back a small door. She immediately went on, walking backward through the doorway into brilliant sunlight and catching herself with the automatic skill of long practice when she tripped over the step. "You're a maker, did Fareine say? Or an engineer?"

"A maker, primarily. But I was wondering the same about you, since you seemed to be thinking about building large structures..."

"Neither the one nor the other," the woman said, a little bitterly. She looked around, seemed to spot a nearby shaded bench as though it was the first time she'd ever seen it, and sat down. Gereint followed, offering her the plate of sandwiches again, since she seemed to have forgotten about it.

"Or maybe both," added Tehre, taking a sandwich and gazing thoughtfully down at it. She was still thinking about Gereint's question, evidently. He hadn't meant it to be so complicated. But the woman said absently, "A maker and a builder and an engineer and a philosopher..." She looked suddenly up at Gereint. "I'm trying to understand how things work. But some important concepts are"—she made a frustrated gesture with the sandwich—"missing. I'm sure if I just define my terms properly...You're quite right, by the way, that's the first thing that has to be done, but you have to work with the concepts before you see what you need names for..."

"I have business of my own in the city, so your father was kind enough to suggest you might wish to offer me a guest room while I'm here," Gereint said after a moment, as the lady did not seem inclined to go on with her thought.

"Yes, of course, if you like," Tehre said, but Gereint had the impression she hadn't really heard him.

"Are you going to eat that, or just wave it around? Meat is expensive since the refugees from Melentser started arriving, you know," Fareine added, returning with the promised jugs and a pair of goblets.

"Oh," said Tehre, and took a bite. But her attention remained on Gereint. No wonder she was so small, if she never ate anything without being prompted.

"Wine, honored sir?" Fareine poured for her lady and Gereint and for herself, a little wine and a good deal of water, and then settled on the end of Tehre's bench.

"What do you make?" Tehre asked Gereint abruptly.

"Small things, mostly. But all kinds of things. Knives and lanterns, belts and boots, pots and plates..."

The woman laughed, unexpectedly. It was the same laugh as before, quick and genuinely amused. "Not a specialist! All right. I'm mostly working philosophically right now—with the philosophy of stone and iron and wood, with the building materials of the world." She sighed. "It's hard to actually *practice* building large structures just to see how they'll break if you apply different kinds of stresses. Have you read Wareierchen?"

"Yes," Gereint said promptly. "And Dachsechreier's *Making with Wood*, and Garaneirdich's *The Properties of Materials*. What do you think of Terichsekiun?"

Tehre's small face lit up, giving her, at last, the misleading appearance of uncomplicated prettiness. "Oh, his *Strength of Materials* is so fascinating! It's so interesting that cast iron acts so much like stone, isn't it, and so different from wrought iron?" She took another bite of her sandwich and chewed absently, lost in thought.

"You seem to have been thinking about bridges," Gereint commented, and was entertained to see how Lady Tehre was instantly distracted. She jumped to her feet, set her sandwich aside half finished, said, "I'll show you; come look!" and started back toward the workroom.

Fareine, looking resigned, gathered the half-sandwich up in a cloth and followed her mistress. Gereint picked up the platter, since it didn't seem proper to simply leave it sitting on the bench, and followed them both.

The diagrams were very interesting. There were large, detailed drawings of bridge after bridge—short, flat, beam-supported bridges across narrow gullies; high-rising arches across streams; rope-supported plank bridges that looked extremely precarious. Some of the bridges were made of many small arches, some supported merely at either end.

"Are these all after real bridges?" Gereint asked,

leaning over a particularly unusual bridge made of open latticework in a single extremely long, flat arch. "This can't really be to scale?"

"Oh, it is, though! That one's from Linularinum—it crosses that river at Teramondian, you know, the Meralle? Terichsekiun referred to it and had a small drawing, but this one is more accurate and much more detailed. It cost a fortune, sending a man all the way to Linularinum to draw it for me, but it was worth it. See, this bridge has a span of a hundred fifty-nine feet, but a rise of only twenty-six feet. It's made of cast iron, so it's lighter than masonry would be, do you see? And that means it pushes sideways against its foundations much less than masonry would, which is why Terichsekiun says it works, but I'm not sure that's the whole answer." She bent intently over the diagram.

Gereint watched Tehre Amnachudran study one part of the diagram and then another and then absently pick up a quill and begin working out equations in the blank space along the edge of the paper, and wondered why she'd had such trouble finding other makers to work with her. She was obsessive, yes. But what she was trying to work out was very interesting. Surely any real maker would think so?

And, also... he clearly did not need to worry that this woman would prove very interested in who *he* was or where *he'd* come from. It hadn't even occurred to her to wonder. Ah. That might explain a great deal, after all. That lack of interest might well offend any man who believed all women ought to find him naturally fascinating.

Gereint merely found the lack of curiosity reassuring. Restful. He glanced at Fareine, who gave him a friendly smile and stayed in the background, possibly to run any errands her mistress thought of, but more likely as a guar-antor of respectability.

Tehre brought out a new diagram and pinned it open across the others. This one also showed a bridge, but not like the others. This one had chains suspended from two high, parallel semi-circular arches and a roadway of beams suspended from the chains.

"That's unusual," Gereint observed, examining the diagram. "Where's this one from?"

Tehre gave him a glance that had gone suddenly shy. "Oh, well...I made this one up. When I was thinking about the differences between cast iron and wrought iron and steel, and about the bridges they'll need to build when they run that road through the mountains. It's supposed to be a real road, you know, the kind that will gladden the Arobern's ambitious heart—four wagons abreast and all the fretwork to match." Despite her acerbic tone, she sounded like she would enjoy a chance to test out some new ideas in the building of a really fine road.

"Steel wire is what I'd like to use for this," Tehre added. "Only that would be much too expensive, of course. So I worked it out for wrought-iron chains. Only you'd have to have *very* good makers to make those chains and bolt them to the decking of the road—I designed that like the deck of a ship, in a way. I'd like to show you the kind of bolts I have in mind and see what you think—have you worked with wrought iron?"

"I've worked with everything," Gereint assured the woman.

"Have you? That's good," Tehre said absently. She looked around vaguely. Fareine came forward and put her half-full mug of watered wine in her hand. Tehre gazed at the older woman for a moment; then down at the mug she held with much the same air of vague surprise and sipped.

"You should eat the rest of your sandwich, too," Fareine said, offering it.

"I suppose." Tehre allowed the woman to press it on her.

"Cakes, honored sir?" Fareine offered him the other platter.

"Don't get honey on the diagrams!" Tehre exclaimed, and then, with sudden pleasure, "Oh, are there cakes? Thank you, Fareine, but mind the honey."

The older woman smiled patiently and passed around damp cloths to take care of the honey.

"So," Tehre said to Gereint, and then paused as though unsure how to proceed. Then she asked cautiously, as though it was a potentially dangerous question, "So have you worked on bridges before? Or the ways structures fail?"

"Not specifically," Gereint admitted. "It sounds interesting, though."

"Everything's interesting," Tehre responded. She didn't say it as though she was making a joke; there was nothing arch or sidelong or humorous in her tone. She just said it. *Everything's interesting*, exactly as though she meant precisely that. Then she added, more wistfully, "But I do think I'm missing something: some fundamental concept that would let me see more clearly how bridges and walls and ships and little mechanisms like bows and clocks and dumbwaiters all work. I think I'm missing something that would help explain bridges and crack propagation and,

and, I don't know. Why ropes break and stone shatters and metals bend." She ate a cake in two impatient bites, gazing moodily down at the diagram on the table.

"I've been mostly in the practical end of making," Gereint told her. "But I think you're asking good questions. You can tell me what you think about strength and cracks and resilience, and maybe I can help you come up with proper definitions of the qualities of materials. Why should Garaneirdich and Wareierchen and Terichsekiun have all the fun? Though maybe the first task is to clarify what all those great philosophers said and see how their terms match up to each other and the qualities you want to define."

Tehre gazed at Gereint with, possibly, the first real attention she'd paid him. "You've read all the philosophers? Yes, you have, haven't you? You'd understand what you read and summarize properly?"

She sounded doubtful on this last, as though, if put to the test, he'd possibly prove to be functionally illiterate. Gereint tried not to smile. He said gravely, "I think so, yes."

"Well, then. Well, then, if you could do that for me—exactly what you said—I have these equations I'm trying to work out—it would save me a great deal of time and then, you're right, maybe it would be easier to see what qualities are already defined and what Wareierchen and Terichsekiun might have missed—does that sound too arrogant?" she added, once again doubtful.

Gereint tried, again, not to smile. It was getting harder. "Not to me."

"All right. Good. Good! I'll show you my library, then. Or Fareine—Fareine! Would you show, ah…"

"Gereint Pecheran," Fareine reminded her.

Tehre blushed. "Of course!" she snapped. "Would you show our honored guest to the library? And get him anything he wants? Quills, paper, whatever? Thank you so much, Fareine; I don't know where I'd be without you. Honored Gereint, would you join me later, after I've had time to sort out these equations about cracks that run or stay? I think the thing to do after that, really, is set up the right kind of situation with masonry under tension and then see what we can get cracks to do..." She trailed off in thought.

"This way, honored sir, if you please," Fareine said to Gereint, and held a hand out to invite him to go before her.

"The honored lady doesn't mean to sound...That is to say..." the woman began, earnestly, as she guided him through the halls of the great house.

"Yes, that's plain." Gereint let himself smile at last, and then laugh. "She's not like anyone I have ever met. Not even like any maker I've ever met! She's working out *equations* about crack propagation? I don't recall even Terichsekiun explaining how to predict whether a particular crack will run instead of rest. That would be a very valuable contribution to the philosophy of materials and making, if she could do it."

"She'll do it. As you said, she might as well be an engineer as a maker: She thinks large-scale as often as small. And she really is a philosopher." Fareine, too, was smiling, as she registered Gereint's tone of amusement and approval. "Allow me to show you the library, honored sir, and then your suite. I hope you will be comfortable in this house. If you find any aspect of Amnachudran hospitality lacking, please bring the lack to my attention."

Not Tehre's, Gereint understood. He nodded.

The library was a good one, though very heavily biased toward natural philosophy and, to Gereint's mind, severely lacking in poetry. He laid out the books Eben Amnachudran had sent; then, after a moment's reflection, added the ones he'd stolen from Fellesteden to the library shelves. They went some little way toward remedying the basic lack of history and poetry—and they would be safe if anything happened to him. He tried not to imagine any of the things that phrase might encompass.

The household served the evening meal late, and more formally than Gereint had guessed from the sandwiches in the kitchen, though the dining room was at least not vastly oversized. Fareine attended with her mistress, of course, and so did one other young woman who Fareine introduced as Tehre's companion. Gereint gathered that she was a chaperone, meant to attend Tehre while Fareine saw to the business of running the household. From her shy manner, he guessed she'd just been elevated to her new position because of Gereint's arrival. Her name was Meierin. She was a little younger than Tehre, quiet voiced, pretty in an unassuming way. Gereint suspected that the girl was also stronger minded than she looked, if Fareine had chosen her for her mistress' protection.

The dinner was elaborate, the new cook showing her skills to her mistress' guest. Gereint made sure to comment on the dishes, which were all very good.

Tehre didn't seem to notice what she ate, except that when Gereint commented, she would blink, focus on the food for a moment, and say something like, "Oh, yes, very pretty," or "Why, this *is* a very nice way to have duck—do we have it this way often, Fareine?" Then she would go back to arguing with Gereint over the right way to define tensile strength. Gereint felt he was talking more during this one meal than he had in years, but neither Fareine nor Meierin could discuss makers' philosophy and Tehre was hard to redirect to more common topics.

"They say the griffin's desert is inimical to creatures of earth," Fareine commented at last, making a valiant effort to drag the conversation by main force to subjects other than tensile strength. "I gather you met the honored Amnachudran in the desert—what is it truly like?"

"Oh, yes, can you tell us about the desert?" Meierin asked eagerly, leaning forward.

"I wonder what is meant by 'inimical' in this context," Tehre said, diverted at last. "It would be interesting to visit the desert and examine its qualities." Then she blinked and asked, "But what was my father doing in the desert?"

"Collecting books from a private estate," Gereint explained.

"Oh, yes, that sounds like him."

"And Gereint met your father at the edge of the desert and helped your father when he met with an accident— it's all in the letter your honored father sent, Lady Tehre. The honored Gereint saved his life when your father met with an accident on his way home."

"Did you?" Tehre said, looking at Gereint in surprise. "Then we're all very much in your debt. What kind of accident?"

"A fall. Crossing the river. Anybody would have done the same." Gereint was uneasy at this close attention to his personal history.

Fareine shook his head. "That's not what the letter says." She turned to her mistress. "The honored Gereint dragged your father all the way home on a pole litter, collapsed as soon as the gates were opened, and raved in a delirium all that night and half the next day, for all Lady Emre could do."

A *delirium*. That was how Eben Amnachudran had explained the screaming to his household, of course. Gereint tried to keep his expression blank. Tehre was gazing at him with surprise and, for once, focused attention; Fareine with warm approval; Meierin with shy appreciation. Gereint said uncomfortably to Tehre, "Your honored father has been very kind to me."

"Apparently he had every reason to be," Tehre responded tartly. "But sending you to me wasn't kindness, I expect. Except maybe to me."

"I'm grateful for a comfortable place to stay in Breidechboden while I conduct my own business here." This was an open bid to change the subject, and Gereint expected an inquiry about what his business might be. He would then make something up or else evade answering, and with any luck they would be off this particular topic.

Instead, Tehre said, "Well, I shall certainly want to read that letter—but not now, if it makes you uncomfortable, Gereint. What have you found in the library? Sufficient?"

Gereint paused for a moment. Then he said, "Everything I could want, honored lady, except that I might like a copy of Teirenchoden's epic about the war between Ceirinium and Feresdechadren. Your honored father has a copy, but your library lacks one. And, come to that, a copy of Sichan Meiregen's epic about the later war between Meridanium and Casmantium. The one that describes the war in the fifth century, not the fourth. You have very little history in your library, and that *is* a lack because I'm sure the descriptions of the fortifications and the siege engines that breached them would interest you."

Tehre made a little *Hmm!* sound and looked at Fareine, who made a note. Then she said to Gereint, "I would like to hear more about the desert and how it differs from ordinary countryside—if you wish to describe it."

"That's an interesting question," Gereint answered at once. "The light, the air, even the dust is quite different in the desert."

"Oh?" There was no sign, now, that Tehre was in the least interested in how he had come to meet her father. She looked around vaguely. Gereint realized she was looking for a quill just as Fareine put one in her hand and laid out a little booklet of paper for her to write in. Tehre took the quill without seeming to notice how it came to be in her hand and leaned forward intently. "Different how?"

Gereint easily discovered where the surgeon mage Reichteier Andlauban lived, and went to his house the day after he'd arrived in Breidechboden. But Andlauban was not at home.

"I fear the honored surgeon has gone to Weierachboden," his doorkeeper said, his apologetic manner professionally sincere. "We anticipate his return within three or four days, honored sir. Surely no more than five days. Shall I give the honored surgeon your name? Have you a token to leave?"

Gereint shook his head and assured the doorkeeper that he'd return in a few days. Then he went back to Tehre's house. He was disappointed, of course. It had never occurred to him that he would venture into Breidechboden and then find so trivial a problem in his way. What if Andlauban wasn't back in three or four or five days? What if whatever business had taken him to Weierachboden took longer than that? Just how long was Gereint going to have linger in Breidechboden? And what were the odds that he'd happen across some old acquaintance, one of his old masters—more likely a servant from one of his masters' houses—worst of all, a cousin? Someone, anyone, who would recognize him? He could just imagine turning around a corner and finding himself face to face with one of his cousins: Brachan or Feir or Gescheichan. Possibly Brachan or Feir might hesitate, might not believe they could actually have recognized him. But Gescheichan would not doubt himself for an instant.

This thought brought the sweat out on Gereint's forehead and stretched all his nerves tight; he felt now that every step he made outside the Amnachudran townhouse was dangerous, and looked over his shoulder until he was back within its protection. But, though he kept his head down in the city and tried to be as inconspicuous as possible, he also made himself detour into an open-air market long enough to buy the appropriate materials, and that evening he made Tehre a scale model of a bow-style catapult. He used cypress and tendon and wire, and he used his own money—or, at least, some of the money Amnachudran had given him.

He met, so far as he could tell, no one he'd ever known.

Gereint demonstrated the model for Tehre the next morning. "But if you scale it directly up, the dimensions might not be quite right," he cautioned her.

"Yes, I know," Tehre answered absently, examining the mechanism with delight. "Masonry's the only type of structure you can almost always scale up directly." She paused to think about this. "I think when you direct loads through a mechanism like this," she concluded, touching the model catapult, "it probably matters how strong the tensions are, because how the materials take the loads probably changes with the scale. With masonry, it matters less—as long as you keep everything in your building or bridge under compression. Because you never reach the compressive load that could actually break the stone."

"Stone breaks," Gereint objected.

"Buildings break," Tehre corrected absently. "But not because of too much compression on the stone. Generally somebody made the wall too thin or not heavy enough and the line of compression gets outside the wall and the wall tips up and falls over. Hmm. You've made a strong draw, here." She wound back the catapult string and loaded a stone ball in the cup. Then she touched the trigger. The stone flew true, striking with a satisfyingly solid *thud* the target Gereint had set up in the garden.

Tehre crowed with glee like a child. "Wonderful! *Wonderful!* Oh, I ought to have been looking at siege engines all along! Would you mind if I broke this? I'd like to fire it unloaded and see how it fails. Not today!" she added at once, suddenly realizing how this might sound. "It's a splendid mechanism and I want to play with it for a few days first, but later—"

"I know you're interested in how structures fail,"

Gereint assured her. "I can make you another one—as many as you like."

"Oh, could you? Please do start another one, would you? Just tell Fareine what materials you need, if you don't want to go out into the city to order them yourself." Tehre loaded another stone and asked shyly, "Would you like to fire this one?" as though she didn't think Gereint's reluctance to leave the house, or the fact that she'd noticed it, was worth the least comment.

It was typical, Gereint thought, that Tehre both noticed something odd about him, something he was in fact trying to conceal, and at the same time didn't notice that it was odd. He suspected she simply thought most people were odd and didn't notice when someone was odd in an unusual way.

He thought no one else had noticed his fear of going into the city. Well, possibly Fareine; she was an observant woman. But by the household as a whole, Gereint found himself accepted as a normal and valued man for the first time in nineteen years.

Perhaps for this reason, Gereint liked everything about the house and household. He enjoyed the liveliness of the primarily female staff, enjoyed the friendly warmth of the kitchen and the staff—and they *were* friendly, right from the first, and only became more so. But Gereint didn't dare take any of the offers that came his way from several of the young women. Even if he would risk insulting Lady Tehre, he could hardly go to any woman while *geas* bound. But surely Andlauban would return soon... He touched the stiff leather envelope that contained Amnachudran's letter to the surgeon, drawing assurance from it.

The surgeon mage would soon return, and he'd agree to take out the *geas* rings, and then at last Gereint would be truly free to find a different course for his life . . . though he found, to his own surprise, that he would be sorry to leave Breidechboden if leaving meant losing the chance to see what odd bridges and complex mathematical philosophy Tehre Amnachudran might come up with.

But he *would* leave. The risk of being recognized by someone he'd once known was just too great.

But in the morning, Tehre found him before the sun was even properly up. Gereint had risen early. He was in the kitchen, cadging pastries stuffed with apples and golden raisins from the cook and letting the kitchen girls tease him about his early morning and what did that imply about his early nights and was he quite sure he was sleeping well? But they scattered, startled, when the mistress of the house came in.

Tehre looked as though she'd been up for hours, or even all night—but also as perfectly cheerful and rested as though she'd never missed a long night's sleep in her life. "Oh, Gereint, good!" she said. "Are those apple? Thank you," she added to the cook, accepting a fresh pastry. "Gereint, an important lord is coming to see me this morning. Did I tell you about that yesterday? Yes, I thought I forgot; Fareine must not have thought it was important to mention it to you, but I've decided I want to show off your catapult and then make it fail and explain about material failures. I think that's exactly the sort of demonstration that will impress this man. He has lots of property and wealth and I want him as a patron so he can represent me to the guilds. So do you mind? And I thought I could explain that you're the one who made the catapult; that ought to impress him and that would be good for you."

"Ah—" said Gereint, not very cogently. He found himself gripped by a senseless but powerful conviction that the intended patron was one of his cousins. Brachan or Feir or, worst of all, Gescheichan. But that was foolish. His cousins were men of wealth and property, but not one of them would be the least interested in bridges or material philosophy. He would not know this man—whoever the man was, he was not likely to know Gereint—especially after nineteen years.

"Good, then, come this way, I want to receive my new patron in my library." Tehre, nervous, seemed oblivious of Gereint's reluctance. "Cook, could you please provide some of these lovely pastries for my guest? That will surely make him decide to represent me." She said this last in a very matter-of-fact tone, clearly not realizing she was delivering a compliment. Catching Gereint's hand, she towed him out while the kitchen girls exploded with very quiet giggles behind them.

Gereint told himself, firmly, that the prospective patron would be someone he'd never met, someone who'd never heard of him. He even found that he looked forward to watching Tehre focus her formidable will on dragging this man into her plans. If the man was intelligent, he'd be delighted to represent her. If he was a fool, perhaps Gereint himself might help Tehre hook him, and thus repay something of the woman's kindness to him...

CHAPTER 4

The very last possibility that crossed Gereint's mind was that the prospective patron might turn out to be Perech Fellesteden. Fellesteden had intended to go to Abreichan—Gereint was *sure* his former master had intended to take his family to Abreichan. Yet he was here.

For a long, long moment after Fellesteden came into Tehre's library, Gereint could not move at all. Not to speak, not to run, not at all. He felt he had been struck to stone by some inimical magic, as though he literally *could not* move.

Fellesteden, clearly, was just as astonished. "*This* is a surprise," he said, but his tone, smooth and pleasant, indicated that it was one that pleased him very much. But he always sounded like that when he was most dangerous—when he intended to indulge himself at someone else's expense.

"You know one another?" Tehre said, but then she picked up some quality in Fellesteden's tone or in Gereint's silence and stopped, her eyes narrowing.

"Harboring fugitives, are you, honored lady?" Fellesteden said to her, though his eyes did not move from Gereint's. "Was it you who removed his brand? Or had it removed? Of course it was." He began to smile. "Did you think to gain a loyal servant whose special qualities might go unnoticed? How very clever of you." His eyes moved at last to meet Tehre's. "But I had heard that about you. That you are clever."

Gereint said, "She knows nothing about it." He measured the door behind Fellesteden and the men he had brought with him—Perech Fellesteden always traveled with a retinue. He had today. There was no hope of getting past them that way. And there was no other door to the room.

"Of course she does," Fellesteden said mildly. He was still smiling. "Is it coincidence you are here? I think not."

Gereint shifted back a step.

"Derich," Fellesteden said, and one of his men-at-arms came smartly forward, his hand going to the hilt of his sword.

Gereint knew Derich. And there were far too many men behind him. He stopped. Derich smiled—not a smooth, polite smile like his master's: The man-at-arms had very little interest in smooth courtesy. His head was shaved in the manner of a soldier, but Derich was not a soldier—as Gereint knew very well.

Tehre knew neither Fellesteden nor Derich. She said sharply, "Fareine! Go for the patrol."

"Derich," Fellesteden said gently, before the old woman could take so much as a single step, "be so good as to ensure that no one leaves this household until I give permission. If anyone should happen to wish to enter, that's another matter, and they are certainly welcome to come in."

"My lord," said Derich, and lifted a hand, grinning. Men moved. One took Fareine by the arm. She looked, white faced and helpless in his grasp, to Tehre for help.

"This is entirely illegal!" cried Tehre, outraged. Not yet frightened.

Fellesteden looked thoughtful. "An interesting question. I think it will prove otherwise. I do think so. Gereint..." He stood for a long moment, studying Gereint. "Let me see your feet," Fellesteden said to him at last.

Gereint did not move. It felt very strange not to move in response to that smooth voice. Not to feel the bite of compulsion. It was not a freedom he was likely to enjoy for much longer.

And it was in a very real sense an illusory freedom, because Fellesteden sighed and shook his head, just a little. It was the exact gesture a tired father might use toward a recalcitrant small boy. "Shall I have my men compel you?"

Without a word, Gereint bent and removed his boots. The *geas* rings piercing through the flesh between bone and tendon glinted coldly silver. Gereint did not look at Tehre Amnachudran. He did not meet anyone's eyes.

"Not bound, after all," observed Fellesteden. "I am surprised."

"I told you," Gereint said, and was mildly pleased and considerably astonished to find his voice steady. "The lady knows nothing of me other than that I am a maker." He forced himself to look straight into Fellesteden's face. "You have no business here, except with me."

"Oh, well," Fellesteden murmured, and paused. "Do you know," he said then, "I imagine that may even be the truth, or why else would you be free? But who else would believe it?" His gaze moved from Gereint's face to Tehre's. "Theft of a *geas*-bound servant...honored lady, I am shocked. Shocked. Interference with the brand of such an infamous person...clearly to disguise his *geas* for your own benefit...Anyone would be profoundly shocked. I believe that we might well come to an understanding on this matter. If you are indeed clever." He paused again.

Tehre's face had gone blank. Her eyes were fixed on Fellesteden's face, but she did not speak.

"Derich..." Fellesteden murmured. "Derich—let us be certain this house is secure. The honored Fareine will be so kind as to assist us, I am sure. Please remain here, honored lady. You might well take these few moments to consider your situation. We may hope that you do indeed deserve your reputation for cleverness. A practical cleverness will serve you much better, at this moment, than defiance." He gestured to his men and withdrew, shutting the door gently behind him.

Tehre, her small fists clenched in silent fury, glared at the door for a long moment. Then she transferred the glare to Gereint. "That man," she said in a tight voice, "that man is going to accuse me of having stolen you from him. No. You came here from my father's house. He's going to accuse *my father* of having stolen you."

"I'll deny it," Gereint promised her.

But Tehre shook her head. "What good will that do? No one will listen to anything *you* say! Lord Fellesteden is a powerful man—he has powerful friends, friends at court, that's why I wanted his patronage! Somebody

removed your brand, and then you turned up in my
house? It doesn't matter what you say—it barely matters what I say: If Perech Fellesteden brings accusations
against my family, everyone will believe him, not us!"

"I'm sorry—"

"That does very little good." Tehre stared at him for a
brief moment, her eyes intense with thought and anger.
She asked sharply, "Who *did* remove your brand?"

Gereint did not answer.

Tehre's lips compressed. She looked quickly around
the room, thinking. There was still only one door, and
Fellesteden's men would still be guarding it; outside,
Tehre's female household would be thoroughly overmatched by his retinue. "This is absolutely illegal!" Tehre
said furiously. And helplessly.

"Bind me," Gereint said suddenly, and when Tehre
swung around to stare at him, "Bind me yourself! Don't
wait for Fellesteden to do it! You can say—you can think
of something to tell any judge." Gereint paused, trying to
think what the woman might plausibly claim. "You can
say you bought me legally. You can say I was unbranded
when you bought me. You're too trusting of people: When
the man who sold me told you that the judge ordered my
face left unmarked, you believed him. I didn't contradict
him because I didn't want the brand renewed. Anybody
would believe *that*. Fellesteden will say I wasn't bound
when he found me in your house, but it's his word against
yours and I'll swear to any judge he's lying. I'll say anything you like; I'll *refrain* from saying anything you like.
But you have to stop Fellesteden from claiming me. If he
binds me—"

He didn't have to finish that thought. Tehre was

already searching through the library for anything that would do for the binding. There were no fine silver chains handy, but she clearly knew that one did not actually need the chains. But nothing like a fine cord seemed to be available, either. She stopped and bit her lip. "Where's an embroidery kit when you need one?" she asked the air. Then she blinked, reached up to her head, and pulled the pins out of her hair. It tumbled around her shoulders, dark and thick, glinting with gold.

"That won't be very strong—" Gereint began.

Tehre cut him off. "It will be for me. Anyway, do you see anything else handy to use?"

Gereint didn't. He closed his mouth.

"I don't know what's to stop him forcing me to release you again," Tehre said, her small fingers darting along the strands of dark hair, braiding, braiding, faster and faster, pulling more hairs from her head to lengthen the cord. Her eyes were fixed on her work and at least part of her mind had to be, but she also said, "What will stop him?" as though it was a real question and she really expected Gereint to answer it.

Gereint opened his mouth and shut it again. He had no idea. Then he said, knowing it was impossible, "No matter what he does, you'll have to persuade him you won't."

Tehre made a scornful little sound, but she glanced up only for a second and her racing fingers did not slow. She finished the first cord and began on a second.

Gereint moved to the door and listened carefully. It was easy to imagine that he heard rapid, triumphant steps ringing down the hall, coming toward the library door. He couldn't tell if he really heard such sounds or not. "Hurry," he urged Tehre.

The woman didn't dignify this with even a glance, far less an answer. But she finished the second cord with flying haste and beckoned urgently to Gereint, who crossed the room in four long strides, swung a second chair around beside Tehre's, and put his right foot up so she could reach the *geas* ring.

Tehre threaded the first cord she had made through the ring and tied it off with a neat little knot. She had seemed far more outraged than frightened when Fellesteden had threatened her, but she was more frightened than she looked: Her fingers trembled against his ankle.

Steps sounded outside the room, loud and definite and not at all the product of imagination. Gereint gritted his teeth against a desperate need to urge Tehre to *Hurry, hurry, hurry* and forced himself to stand perfectly still while she completed the first knot. There were voices outside, loud but indistinguishable, and he put his right foot on the floor and his left on the chair.

Tehre completed the second knot, and the *geas* woke, twisted tightly around Gereint's self-determination and will, and bit deep. He caught his breath in something that was not quite pain and grabbed the back of the chair to steady himself against what seemed almost a physical dizziness, although it was not actually physical at all.

Just at that moment, Derich opened the library door. He stepped aside for Perech Fellesteden to enter. Derich entered at Fellesteden's back; another of Fellesteden's retainers held Fareine by one arm. The woman looked older and far more helpless than she had ever seemed before.

Tehre stood up, crossed her arms across her small breasts, tilted her chin up, and glared at Fellesteden.

Gereint moved a step out from her side. He was not at all certain now what could possibly prevent Fellesteden from forcing Tehre to cut the cords she had just made. He had wanted her to bind him for his own protection—to do it herself before Fellesteden could—but now Fellesteden could simply threaten Fareine; he could threaten one woman of her household after another, and he wouldn't stop at threats; Tehre could not possibly resist him—

"Gereint," Tehre commanded, staring straight at Fellesteden, "kill him."

Gereint couldn't believe she had said that. Perech Fellesteden couldn't believe it. In fact, *no one* could believe it. For that first instant, everyone in the room was frozen in astonishment. Except for Gereint. Because he did not have to believe it. It did not matter that *he* was shocked or that he had never in his life killed anyone and probably would not have been able to do it on his own; the *geas* could not be astonished and did not accommodate delay.

Gereint's body moved in automatic *geas*-driven response to Tehre's command. He yielded to it instantly, let the *geas* drive his lunge forward, put his own will behind it, and rode it for strength and force and, most of all, speed.

The man holding Fareine had a knife drawn; Gereint hit him hard in the throat, caught his knife as he staggered, spun, plunged the knife into Fellesteden's side and ripped forward and up, ignored the man's gasping cry as he jerked the knife out, and pivoted as Derich, shouting wordlessly, moved at last. Gereint caught Derich's wrist in his other hand and struck viciously at the other man's chest, but Derich twisted away and snatched out his sword, and the *geas* was already dragging Gereint back around to make sure of Fellesteden, whatever threat Derich presented at his back—

Tehre hurled herself bodily against Derich and the two went down together in a flailing tangle. Gereint had no attention to spare for that struggle, all his focus was on Perech Fellesteden. The man was down on the floor, on his knees, one hand braced against the floor, the other hand pressed tightly against the wound Gereint had dealt him. He stared up, his face white, his mouth open, unable to catch his breath to speak.

Gereint felt no pity at all. But it would not have mattered. Fellesteden was still alive, so the *geas* was still a goad, still a source of speed and violence. Gereint jerked Fellesteden's head back by the hair, whipped the knife across his throat, and felt the compulsion of the *geas* relax as the life went out of his old master's eyes. He did not watch, but whirled, looking for Derich.

Derich was just getting to his feet, and Tehre as well, though much more slowly. Gereint faced Derich, horribly aware that the knife he still held was not a match for the other man's sword, that even if he'd had a sword of his own, he would not have been a match for Fellesteden's man. Derich knew it too. He stalked Gereint, smiling tightly, as he always smiled when about to murder or torture or inflict any sort of brutality. Gereint wondered if Tehre might give him another *Kill him* command, and whether that might help—

Fareine, her face set and white, stepped forward, swung the long bronze statue of a flying swan up by its neck, and brought the heavy base of the statue swinging down toward Derich's head. The man jerked to the side and the swan hit his shoulder and arm a glancing blow. Not his sword arm. He shouted—the cry sounded more furious than hurt—and swept his sword around in a vicious low cut that would gut the old woman like a fish. Fareine cowered from the sword, lifting the bronze swan in a hopeless gesture of defense.

Gereint flung the knife he held, using all his maker's skill to encourage it to fly straight and hard and hit point first. But he knew even as he threw the knife that it would not strike Derich in time to stop him cutting Fareine in half.

But Tehre flung her hands out, making a twisting motion as though wringing the neck of a hen, and when Derich's sword struck the bronze statue, it did not batter past the statue and slash into Fareine's body. It wasn't that Fareine was holding the statue firmly enough to block the sword. But when the sword struck the statue, it *shattered*. Metal splinters exploded across the room.

Fareine dropped the swan statue, crying out as some of the steel splinters struck her—Derich shouted too, in surprise if not in pain—so did Tehre, in sympathy perhaps, she was too far away to have been injured—Gereint's knife snapped into Derich's lower back with all the force and precision he might have put into ordinary practice with a straw target when making throwing knives.

This time, when Derich cried out, it was definitely in pain.

Gereint was already on him. One big hand snatched the neck of the bronze swan from Fareine. But when Gereint swung the statue up like a club and brought it down, he put a lot more force behind the blow than the old woman ever could have. And his aim was better. It took only one blow.

Then he looked at last for Fellesteden's other retainer. He found the man at once, fallen where he'd stood when Gereint had struck him in the throat. He was not moving. So Gereint had hit him hard enough the first time. And no other enemy was in the room. And Fellesteden was— yes, Gereint confirmed, staring at his old master's body. Perech Fellesteden was dead.

They were safe.

For the first instant after that realization, Gereint could not believe what had happened, what he had done, what any of them had done. He braced his hands on his knees, lowered his head, and tried to catch his breath.

Tehre said faintly, "That was . . . We are . . ." and stopped. She closed her eyes, breathing deeply. The room stank of blood and terror, and her pallor only deepened. She opened her eyes again quickly.

Gereint went to her and put a hand under her elbow. "There's no time to faint, yet," he told her urgently. "Though, earth and iron, you deserve to!" He turned his head. "How many men did Fellesteden bring with him? Do you know, Fareine? There's no knowing what they'll do, now their lord is dead—"

Fareine straightened her shoulders. "They'll leave," she declared. "They'll get out! That's what they'll do. Their master illegally invaded the house of the honored Lady Tehre Amnachudran Tanshan and threatened the lady and her household! The honored lady has every right to bring charges, serious charges, against Lord Fellesteden! Or his—his heirs and estate, I suppose." She glanced quickly at the bodies and away again. But then she drew herself up and, although she was still trembling, glared haughtily at Gereint.

"That's…one possible view," Gereint allowed. He, also, still felt sick and shaken, but he couldn't help but grin at Fareine's prim tone. "Especially if the city patrol was here to see to it. Do you think—?"

"They can be brought," Tehre promised. "Fareine, you can—no. I don't know how you could get out of the house. The rest of Fellesteden's men must be watching the doors." She rubbed her forehead, trying to think.

"How many are there? Do we know?" Gereint asked Fareine.

"About…about ten," the old woman said, but uncertainly. She glanced involuntarily at the man with the crushed throat and winced, but did not let herself recoil. "Or nine, I suppose. There are men in the kitchens, in Tehre's workroom, in the garden…He sent men everywhere…"

"The servant's hall?"

"Yes. I told you, they're everywhere—"

Gereint closed a big hand on the woman's shoulder and shook her, very gently. "Nine men can't be everywhere. The bedrooms?"

Fareine thought about this. "No," she said at last in a surprised tone. "I don't think so. Tehre's suite is just down the hall, you know, and it looks out over the front walk. And those iron lanterns make a good step down… Tehre used to sneak out that way, when she was just a bit of a girl and her family stayed here."

"You knew about that?" Tehre asked, astonished, and Fareine gave her a wry look.

Gereint longed to ask why Tehre had, as a girl, snuck out of her father's house. But probably that was not the most urgent question to ask at this moment. He began instead, "Ah…Fareine…"

"Young man, I'm not so old I can't manage a little climb like that," Fareine said with some asperity. "If you will make certain none of Fellesteden's brigands are in the hall, please?"

Gereint flexed his hands and looked for the knife… remembered it was in Derich's back and swallowed. He rubbed his palms on his thighs and glanced unhappily at the body. But he needed a weapon before he opened that door.

Though Fellesteden's other retainer ought to have— yes. A sword, still in its sheath. Much better than trying to pull a bloody knife out of a dead man. Much better. Gereint didn't try to get the sheath off the retainer's belt, but gingerly drew the sword and straightened again. The sword had decent balance, fit comfortably in his hand… ah. It was, he realized at last, one he'd made himself, as he'd made many of the swords and knives Fellesteden's men carried. The recognition carried a strange kind of reassurance with it, as though Gereint had unexpectedly found a friend at his side in an uncertain situation.

He shifted the sword in his grip, glanced over at Tehre. He knew very well that, sword or no, he was not a match for any of Fellesteden's thugs. But if there was no more than one man…If he could at least make the man hesitate…all he needed was to win enough time for Fareine to get out of the house and the day was won… "Maybe we should all go?" he said to Tehre.

The small woman lifted her head proudly. "I won't be chased out of my own house by thugs! And anyway," she added more practically, "if those men find their lord dead and want vengeance, I'm the only one whom they might hesitate to attack. I won't leave my household at their mercy. I can make them pause, at least, and all we need is for them to hesitate."

Gereint hated for her to remain in danger, but he also knew she was right. Taking a deep breath, he stepped past Fareine, flung open the library door, and stepped through with a bold, confident stride that might deceive one of Fellesteden's men, if not himself.

The hallway was deserted. Gereint let his breath out, extremely relieved.

"Tehre's bedroom is right down…" Fareine slipped past him and hurried twenty feet down the hall, cautiously opened a door, glanced into the room, looked back at Gereint, gave him an all's-well sign and a shooing gesture that obviously meant, *Get back to Tehre*. Then she slipped into the room and closed the door after her.

It seemed odd to let a woman, a matron who was no longer young, climb down from that window, risking danger from Fellesteden's men as well as simply from falling. But there was no other choice, and Fareine was right—he needed to get back to Tehre. If any of Fellesteden's thugs discovered what had happened to their lord…Well, maybe Tehre could make them pause and maybe she couldn't, but if not, he would have to try to hold them himself until the patrol arrived.

In the library, Tehre was sitting in a chair she had pulled around to face the door, carefully angling it so she could also more or less avoid looking at the bodies. She was rubbing her face with both hands, but she glanced up when Gereint came in. Her face was tight with strain and weariness. When she saw he was alone, she nodded and pressed her hands over her eyes.

Gereint laid the sword aside on a table and came forward.

"Fareine?" Tehre asked without looking up, in a small, tight voice, before Gereint could speak.

"Well away. There was no sign of any of Fellesteden's men. It shouldn't take the patrol long to arrive. With luck, before Fellesteden's thugs find out what's happened."

She nodded, lowered her hands, and glanced vaguely around the room. But her glance snagged on Fellesteden's body and stopped there. "He would have ruined us," she said after a moment, as though answering an accusation.

Gereint was not going to argue. "He would certainly have tried."

"Huh. Well, now he won't." But Tehre seemed to be unable to look away from the body. Gereint moved forward to lay a hand on her shoulder, and she flinched and jerked her gaze up at last, her breath coming sharp and quick. But after a moment she said, in a tone that only shook a little, "Lord Fellesteden threatened me, threatened my household—he intended theft and violence. He intended it from the first, in complete disregard of the king's law—he probably quarreled with my father in the north—thus he brought so many men." She glanced sharply up to meet Gereint's eyes. "Will the city patrol believe that? Will a judge?"

"When your enemy is dead, honored lady, you are free to offer any story that pleases you. It seems to me that one is somewhat plausible." Gereint paused. Then he said, "But here's a better story, if you will permit me. I've never encountered your father. I met your brother in Dachsichten. He suggested I come to you because he knew that you were looking for a maker to assist you in your work. He wrote you a letter representing me to you; your father never wrote a word to you about me. I came here for reasons of my own; you had no idea I was *geas* bound and can't imagine who might have removed my brand. Fellesteden recognized me. He never intended anything against your household; he merely recognized me and wished to reclaim his lost property. In a madness of rage and despair, I managed to kill him and both these other men. All the fault is mine. You and your household are merely witnesses. You summoned the patrol to protect yourself against me, not against Fellesteden's remaining men."

All of Tehre's formidable attention was now fixed on Gereint. She said nothing.

"It's a plausible tale. Fellesteden's remaining men will hardly object—they may even believe that tale *themselves*, if you tell it properly. You'd need to write immediately to your father and brother so neither of them contradicts this, um, adjusted version of events. And of course," he gestured awkwardly down toward his own feet, "you will need to cut those cords."

The woman began to speak, clearly a protest, from the rigid shake of her head.

Gereint interrupted her. "No, listen, Tehre. They can't do anything to me that hasn't already been done, do you see? But if I was bound under your control when I killed them, then *you* are responsible and I merely your weapon. If a judge finds against you—if he *does*, Tehre, and the precedent is all against you, believe me that I know—if you are found to have done murder, Tehre, *you* could be *geas* bound. Nothing would be worse, do you understand? And there is *no reason* for you to risk it!"

"My father removed your brand. Isn't that true?"

Gereint shook his head emphatically. "I will never say so. If anyone makes that suggestion, I will deny it. Tehre, the patrol will surely come very soon. Your cords—there's no time to hesitate—cut them, Tehre!"

"I can't leave you to take all the blame on yourself!"

"You can. Don't be foolish. Of course you can! You must! Do you want everyone asking about your father? They won't stop with you, Tehre! They'll ask why your father sent you a *geas*-bound slave with an unmarked face, and you won't like the answers they think of—"

A man's deep voice rang out somewhere in the house, barely audible. It might be one of Fellesteden's men. But Gereint thought it was probably the patrol.

Tehre's eyes widened with alarm. "I—" she began.

"Let me take the blame! It doesn't make any difference to me! I can't get away now anyway!" It occurred to Gereint that he might have earlier, if he'd managed to persuade Tehre to cut the binding cords quickly enough. Grab his boots and out the window right after Fareine—too late, too late, the opportunity had been fleeting and was gone. He tried not to think about it, but said urgently, "Cut me loose, Tehre! Hurry!"

Her eyes were wide and shocked, but her small mouth firmed with decision. She said quickly, "I'll petition—whom does one petition? Never mind: I'll find out and I'll buy your bond properly. I won't abandon you, Gereint, do you hear?"

"I would...I would be very grateful," Gereint admitted. He tried not to depend on the promise: Maybe Tehre would find herself or her family coming under too much suspicion if she tried to buy his bond. Maybe she would simply change her mind. He would have no recourse if she did. He gazed down at her for a moment. Those bronze-green eyes met his with utter conviction and he thought, surprising himself, *No, she will keep any promise she makes*.

He was surprised by his own confidence: no one was bound by a promise made to a *geas* slave. But even so, he thought *Tehre* would be. And was even more deeply surprised at how important that seemed—that he should trust her, that even when he would not dare approach anyone he'd once known, neither family nor friend, there should still be someone he trusted in the world. And it had happened so quickly, and he had hardly even noticed—not really allowed himself to notice.

But everything he'd argued was still true. He stepped toward the woman, turning so she could reach the *geas* rings.

Tehre didn't need a knife to cut the cords she'd made herself. She'd woven strength and resilience into them, but when she touched them, the knots she'd tied in them came undone and all the braiding unraveled. The cords simply fell to pieces. Gereint stared down at the unidentifiable wisps of hair, feeling the *geas* once more release its grip and subside to the back of his awareness. This time, he had no hope that this freedom would last.

Boots rang authoritatively in the hall outside the library.

Gereint stepped quickly away from Tehre and tried to look like the sort of desperate criminal who might have killed three men in a wild fit of terror and rage. This was not very difficult. It was harder to imagine why he would still be here in this room—maybe he had been struck insensible in the struggle and had only just recovered—he caught up the sword, tossed it on the floor by a chair, went quickly to one knee and braced one hand on the chair's carved seat as though trying just this moment to haul himself to his feet.

Tehre stared at him, then sank back into her own chair. She looked tiny, young, feminine, fragile, and perfectly helpless. Putting a hand to her face as though dazed, she stared vaguely at the door.

The next moment a big man in the livery of the Breidechboden patrol flung the door wide. He stood a moment in the doorway, filling it: as broad in the shoulder as Gereint, though nothing like so tall. His eyes went quickly from Gereint to the sword discarded on the floor nearby, to Perech Fellesteden's body, and at last to Tehre Amnachudran. His mouth tightened. He stepped into the room, gesturing to his men.

Gereint flung himself to his feet, staggering, just in time for two more men of the city patrol to rush forward and grab his arms. Fareine, who had followed the men into the room, started to protest; Tehre said, cutting the older woman off before she could manage even one word, "Patrol captain! Please send your men to secure my house and ensure that my people are safe. I had better accompany them. I'm afraid there has been a great deal of confusion."

"Honored lady, I see there has," said the captain, shaking his head—not doubt, Gereint saw, but simply amazement. He gestured to his men, and they led Gereint toward the door. He did not fight them. Nor did he try to turn for a last glance at Tehre. He simply bowed his head and went where the men took him.

*   *   *

Six days in a windowless stone cell provided plenty of
time to think of fifty better ways he might have handled
a sudden confrontation with his previous *geas* master.
The best of them involved avoiding the confrontation
altogether. Gereint reviewed in painful detail his decision
to come south at all, his decision to stay on the southern
road from Dachsichten rather than turn west, his fatal
acquiescence when Tehre had suggested he meet her new
patron.

If he had chosen differently at any of those moments,
he might have gone to Feierabiand as planned. He might
even be in Feierabiand right this moment, rather than
sitting here on the cold stone floor, watching occasional
slivers of light creep across the floor as guards carried
lanterns past in the hall.

Gereint spent some of his time chipping carefully
at the stone of the door with the buckle of his belt. He
thought about what Tehre had said about cracks and
masonry, and he thought of how she had made Fellesteden's sword shatter—an astonishing act of unmaking,
the very antithesis of making. If he could do that...he
would do more than break the door: He would shatter this
whole prison, pull all its walls down around him. But no
matter how he tried, he could not find any way to coax
the scratches he made to run through the stone and break
it to pieces.

In moments of hope, Gereint thought he might eventually be brought out of the cell and led up into the light
to find that Tehre Amnachudran had indeed purchased
his bond. He remembered thinking, *She will keep any
promise she makes*, and though the original conviction of

that thought was lacking, he still hoped, sometimes, that it might prove true.

But in other moments, Gereint was certain Tehre would be furious that he had deceived her, furious with her father, too. Though she had not seemed angry. But she might find herself and her family endangered by too close interest—she would realize that she had to avoid, by whatever means, any suggestion that her father had sent Gereint to her house, or that her father might have been the one to interfere with the *geas* brand. Either way, she would not want to further any connection between herself and Gereint. She would not intervene for him.

He could learn nothing from his guards about any legal proceedings against Tehre—or any legal proceedings she might have initiated herself—or anything having to do with his own eventual disposition. The door was heavy and always shut; the guards slid plates through a gap below the door twice a day. Gereint could hear them outside his cell. But they hardly spoke to one another; they never answered him when he called to them through the door. Anything might be happening. Tehre's family might be ruined; he would not know. His own auction might be underway and he would not know.

At first, Gereint expected to be brought before a judge and questioned about Fellesteden's death, about his own presence in Tehre's house, about his unmarked face and his reason for coming to Breidechboden. That might still happen. But it had not happened yet. He no longer knew whether to expect it. More than likely, some judge had already heard the evidence and made some decision without finding any need to question Gereint. He wondered what it might have been.

And at first he waited every day for men to come with the hot iron and restore his *geas* brand. He could imagine the iron vividly: He knew exactly the path it would trace across his face, the fiery agony of the branding. The angry scar it would leave, impossible to obscure, setting him aside once more from the world of free men.

This dread intensified over the first days and then ebbed as no iron appeared. In some ways, that surprised him more than the silence and the waiting.

On the afternoon of the sixth day, he heard the guards in the hall early—far too early for supper. So he was not surprised when he heard the bolts draw back and the door was hauled effortfully open.

He got to his feet and stood facing the door, thinking of the hot iron. He knew he would fight if they brought that in—though fighting could win him nothing, he would fight anyway—he knew exactly how it would be to be pinned down and held still while the iron came down against his face. Swallowing hard, he stared at the open door.

But no iron appeared, no pot of glowing coals. The guards brought only chains.

If he was chained, he would not be able to fight, whatever they did to him. He submitted to the chains anyway, seeing no immediate threat and, after all, no choice.

They brought him out of the cell and into a hall that, dim as it was, seemed bright after the more profound darkness of the cell. They brought him up a flight of stairs and along a hall, to a lantern-lit room with a basin of cold water and a bar of coarse soap. So his bond had been sold, Gereint surmised. Someone wealthy and important had bought him, and the director of the prison did not want to offend this person by handing over a filthy prisoner. The only question that concerned Gereint was—was that person Tehre Amnachudran? He set his teeth against the desire to ask; the guards probably did not know and certainly would not answer.

The guards took the chains off and waited while Gereint washed. They offered neither abuse nor even comment; they were utterly indifferent and did not even speak to each other. Gereint put on the new clothing they gave him. It was plain, but not as rough or cheap as he had expected. Gereint took the quality of the clothing as another sign, if he had needed one, that whoever had bought Gereint's bond was important or wealthy. Or most likely both. There were no boots, of course, but the guards gave him sandals. Gereint put them on and waited to see where the guards would bring him next.

The guards put the chains back on and led him again into the hallway, then up another flight of stairs to a better part of the prison. Here there were, at last, windows set in the walls. The golden light of late afternoon slanted through the windows and lay in long bars across the floors. Gereint's eyes watered in the brilliance. He blinked, bowing his head, and went without protest or question where the guards took him.

They took him to a richly appointed room that hardly seemed to belong in the same building as the windowless cell. Here there was at last a man wearing the heavy gold chain of a judge, and a clerk with a large book open before him and a quill in his hand, and a third man who was less easy to place. This was a small man. Small all through: not much taller than a child. But he was not young. It was hard to guess his age: He might have been fifty or sixty, or seventy, or older still. His hair was white as frost, worn long, caught back at the nape of his neck in a style almost aggressively nonmilitary. He had ice-gray eyes and fine, straight bones, elegant hands and an inscrutable smile.

It was easier to guess the small man's rank than his age, for he was well and expensively dressed; the workmanship of his sapphire rings was very fine. This was not merely a gentleman, Gereint thought, nor merely some petty lord. He was more than likely a court noble. He wondered if he'd ever known this man before...before, but certainly he was memorable, and Gereint could not remember ever having met a man like this one.

He looked at Gereint as a man might look at a horse he had purchased; as a captain might look at a man who had been transferred into his company; as an appointed judge might look at a prisoner. With that kind of deliberate detachment. Gereint met his eyes for just an instant and then, allowing sense to beat down pride, bowed his head. He watched the lord covertly through lowered lashes. So this man had purchased his bond—and where, then, was Tehre? The depth of his anger and sense of betrayal at her absence shook him. He discovered only at that moment how deeply he had depended on Tehre Amnachudran to keep her promise and buy his bond. He made himself stand quietly, with a slave's practiced passivity, showing nothing of the rage that shook him.

"Well, my lord?" said the judge. Expectantly, as though this was the end of a discussion and not the beginning.

"I think he may do," said the lord, cool and judicious. "I will take him, certainly, and we shall see." He turned his head toward the clerk, who offered him a small wooden box.

"I imagine my lord does not require instruction in the use of the *geas* chains," said the judge, in the tone of a man making a small jest.

"I believe not," agreed the small lord. His voice was smooth and light. It was impossible to read anything of his disposition from that voice. He took the box from the clerk, opened it, and spilled a pair of fine silver chains into his palm. Then he looked at Gereint and beckoned. The crook of one finger: *Come here*, as to a dog.

Gereint moved stiffly forward and stood still, his face blank, his shoulders aching from the awkward posture enforced by the manacles, and waited while the lord fixed the first chain in place and then the second. The *geas*, coiled patiently at the back of his mind, shifted with the first chain, then woke and sank sharp fangs into his will with the second. Gereint let his breath out. The rage that had shaken him a moment earlier died; fear leaped up in its place and immediately burned away, leaving nothing. He felt as though his heart had turned to ash. He looked into his new master's face as the lord straightened, but without much interest.

For a moment, the lord merely stared back at him. Then he said, "Gereint Enseichen. Kneel."

No hesitation was possible, but Gereint did not try to hesitate. Dropping to his knees, he bowed his head and said in his most passive slave's tone, "Master."

"So that's done, then, my lord," said the judge, satisfied. "Do you wish my staff to brand him for you?"

Fear was not entirely dead after all. Gereint tensed, but he did not look up. He knew at once he should have expected this: Of course they would wait until he was *geas* bound and could be ordered not to fight. So much easier for everyone. Except, of course, the man who must submit to the brand and could not even struggle against it...

"That will not be necessary," said the white-haired lord.

"As you wish, my lord. You are, of course, aware that by law a *geas*-bound man must be branded—"

"I am aware," repeated the lord, his smooth tone unreadable. "I will see to it myself. If you would be so good as to have your men remove the manacles. Thank you so much, honored Mereirnchan. You have been most helpful. Gereint"—as the chains fell away—"get up and come with me."

Gereint got obediently to his feet and walked behind his new master. Out of the room, out of the prison, to a very fine carriage, with two liveried servants waiting and four beautifully matched white horses to draw it. One of the servants placed a step in the street for the lord, who needed it to reach the high sill of the carriage door; Gereint ducked his head low as he followed.

The lord was already seated, looking perfectly relaxed, on the forward-facing seat. He gestured to Gereint to take the seat opposite.

Gereint might have said something—anything. He knew he should test his new master's patience, the limits of his temper. But he could not, at this moment, find the courage or resolve to do it. He said nothing.

The prison was hardly in the best part of the city. But they quickly left the area of narrow streets and shabby tenements, passed through neighborhoods where the roads were wider and lined with more substantial marble-faced apartments and small shops, and came to a district of private houses with small walled gardens—Seven Son Hill, Gereint realized, but they were on the city side of the hill now and not the lee side where the Amnachudran house lay.

They followed the curve of the road and the houses grew larger still, the gardens larger and more elaborate. The river, contained here between banks of white limestone and bridged with elaborate bridges of stone and iron, ran beside the road. The river should have been beautiful, but now the water was low, surprisingly low, lower than Gereint remembered ever seeing it. The water, unpleasantly thick and greenish, moved sluggishly between stone banks gritty with silt. In some places it seemed one might not need a bridge to cross the river, if one had not minded wading in the green water.

Public buildings with columns of porphyry or green-streaked white marble and statues of marble and gilded bronze appeared on the other side of the street, which widened until it resembled a parade ground more than a thoroughfare. They had come to the Hill of Iron and now took the main road that spiraled around it toward the king's palace. Porticoes and fountains, ornate columns and high-buttressed towers...They were approaching the palace itself. Gereint had guessed correctly: His new master was plainly a court noble.

The carriage drew up at last, and one of the servants leaped down from the driver's bench and hurried to place the step and open the door. The white-haired lord motioned for Gereint to get out first. Gereint obeyed, glancing around as he emerged from the carriage. They had come to a wide courtyard bordered on two sides by gardens; behind them the graceful street wound back down the hill into the city. Before them, a colonnade of flying buttresses three times Gereint's height shaded great doors of gilded bronze that stood open in a wall of white marble and fluted columns.

The lord did not seem to notice this magnificence. He beckoned to Gereint and walked briskly toward the gilded doors.

From him, a gesture had the force of a spoken command. Gereint followed.

Once through the doors, there was a high-arched hallway with mosaics on the walls and priceless Linularinan rugs on the marble floor. Statues of gold and marble stood on plinths, and a pair of golden fishes leapt in a marble fountain, water cascading down their jeweled scales and splashing in the pool below.

They came to an antechamber paneled with carved and polished cedar, hung with sapphire curtains, and lit by round porcelain lamps. Men-at-arms in blue and white livery saluted the lord and stood aside, noticing Gereint only with flickering covert glances.

The antechamber opened into a graceful receiving hall graced with an intricate mosaic floor and a single huge painting. The painting was of a battle—immediately recognizable; Terechtekun's victory over General Lord Perestechen Enkiustich of Meridanium, at the White Cliffs. It must be Ferichtelun's famous painting; undoubtedly it was the original, but Gereint's new master did not slow, so Gereint could not pause to look at it.

The receiving hall gave onto a long hall with a polished marble floor and wide glass windows. The lord proceeded, without pausing, to the end of the hall and went through a carved door; Gereint, following as though leashed, found that they had come to a library or a study or an office, or perhaps all three. By contrast with the rest of the apartment, this room was almost plain. The rugs on the floor were of high quality, but they were simply blue, without pattern or decoration. The furniture was similarly good but plain, with a minimum of carving. The windows were paned with expensive glass and curtained with heavy sapphire draperies.

Between the windows, paintings on the walls showed different views of Breidechboden. The city was pictured in every season, but the perspective was always from high above, as though the artist had stood in the highest tower of the city in order to paint them. Gereint could see that the same skilled artist was responsible for all the paintings, but Gereint did not recognize either the paintings or the hand. Underneath the paintings, the walls were lined with shelves of books and scrolls. Three tables stood in the room, each stacked with papers and more books.

Here the lord turned at last and stood, his hand resting lightly on the surface of one of the tables, regarding Gereint with impenetrable calm. He asked, "Do you know who I am?"

Gereint stared back at the lord, completely unable to guess what his new master might be thinking. "Forgive me, master; no. I have been gone from Breidechboden for a long time."

" 'My lord' will do. I know you have. Your bond has never been held by men of Breidechboden. Most recently, you belonged to Perech Fellesteden for eight years. For most of that time, Lord Fellesteden maintained his primary household in Melentser." The lord's smooth voice, like his calm face, gave nothing away: neither offense nor amusement nor satisfaction. He added without emphasis, "I am Beguchren Teshrichten."

Gereint blinked. He said after a moment, "The cold mage. The *king's* mage. I should have recognized—" He stopped.

The fine mouth crooked in wry humor. "You would be surprised how few men recognize me, despite the river of gossip that floods through this city. Men expect the Arobern's own mage to be taller, I suppose. But, yes. I am the king's mage. The last of his mages, now."

"What—?" Gereint began, then remembered he had no right to ask, collected himself, and stopped, reaching after the hard-won impassivity he'd learned, years ago, to wear as a mask.

But the white-haired mage did not seem offended. He was smiling, a small uninterpretable smile. "What do I want with you? Either nothing or a great deal. Let us find out which. Kneel, please, and look at me, Gereint."

Gereint obeyed immediately, of course; he did not have time to wonder about the command until he was already down. But when he looked up, he found his gaze unexpectedly caught and held by the compelling ice-pale eyes of the mage. Beguchren Teshrichten stepped forward, rested one hand on Gereint's face, and sent his mind probing suddenly past the slave's blankness that Gereint showed him, through the surprise and anger and fear beneath, slicing into memory and laying bare the privacy of mind that was the only privacy a slave could own.

At first, Gereint was too shocked to resist this intrusion. Images rose through his mind, memories that he had not called up for years, the past washing across his awareness like a tide: Memories he had learned to put away when

he had become a slave, recalled now by an inquisitive
awareness that was not his own. His mother's face came
before his eye; his sister's. His cousin Gescheichan's, first
as a smiling narrow-faced boy and then, for a flashing
moment, as a man, his expression closed and hostile.

Gereint remembered the thin, bony hands of his first
tutor, setting before him a massive leather-bound volume
of poetry...It had been one of Teirenchoden's epics, the
words marching across the fine vellum in a fine, strong
hand, the pages illuminated with gold leaf and delicate
washes of color from the illustrator's brush. He had loved
the dusty smell of it, the heavy feel of the pages...His-
tory and poetry had opened up before him in that volume,
though he had not been able to read it, not then. Nor had
he known how desperately important such books would
be in maintaining his sanity, later in his life. He had been
seven...He stirred, trying clumsily to close his mind's
eye to that memory, fighting the intrusion that opened his
mind to that foreign, knife-edged awareness.

The mage's mind shifted, eased away, turned, sliced
inward once more. Gereint remembered running through
the rain on a summer night, running to reach the shelter
of an open door. Lightning had flared around him; thun-
der had rolled down deserted streets, no one else being
fool enough to brave the storm. He had been young and
strong and innocent of any knowledge that life might
hold storms worse than those loosed from a dark summer
sky. There had been a girl waiting in the doorway, laughing at him because he had run through the rain to come to
her. He had reached out to seize her hands and lightning
blazed behind him, lit the whole city with dazzling light,
and he met her beautiful eyes and laughed with joy.

That memory tried to shift and turn, tried to become another memory. *"No!"* Gereint said, but he could not tell whether he cried the word aloud or only in the silence of his mind. He fought the intrusion determinedly, blindly. But the mage's mind was too powerful to fight; it cut into his with a relentless skill he could not resist; he could not stop the probing curiosity. But he found a way to let his memories become fluid instead. When the mage tried to reach after them, he let the past flow away like water, impossible to grasp or hold.

Then the mage lifted his hand and Gereint found himself, dizzyingly, back in the study, kneeling on the thick blue rug. The frost-haired mage was gazing down at him with sympathy, but without apology. Gereint panted as though he'd been running or fighting. He supposed he had been, in a way. He did not know what to say, what to do. He was shaking. His expression was probably far too easy to read. He dropped his eyes, though it was a wrenching effort to look away from the mage, as it would have been hard to look away from an unpredictable coiled serpent or crouching wolf.

The king's mage said, his tone perfectly matter-of-fact, "As it happens, I have need of a gifted maker, a maker with certain predispositions and skills. I am prepared to be generous to such a man, if he offers me loyal service."

Gereint, still trembling with reaction, had to suppress a startling and extremely unwise desire to laugh or curse or weep, or perhaps all three. He had no right to demand, or even request, any answer or justification from his master. So he set his teeth hard against any question, bowing his head.

"The *geas* compels obedience," the Arobern's mage murmured. "Dedicated skill, however, is more difficult to compel. As you know better than most, I imagine, Gereint Enseichen." He paused, then said gently, "Look at me."

Gereint had no choice but to meet his eyes, though he looked up with trepidation. But this time the mage's ice-pale eyes met his without effect. The mage's expression, he found, was utterly unreadable. "If you give me such service, I am prepared to be generous," he said.

"Of course I will serve my lord to the best of my ability," Gereint said smoothly, managing the smoothness only because he'd had years of practice keeping everything out of his voice.

"If you do, I am prepared to free you." The mage made a small gesture, indicating the rings that pierced Gereint's ankles. "You seem to have found yourself unable to remove those. I could remove them easily. Legality is not a concern. The Arobern would grant me your freedom, if I asked." He paused to study Gereint's expression, and once more smiled his small, inscrutable smile at what he saw.

Of everything the king's mage might have said, this was perhaps the least expected. Gereint felt as though he had been struck through by a spear, save that there was no pain. But he felt, oddly, as though he was waiting for pain to strike suddenly outward from an unfelt wound.

"Well?" Beguchren Teshrichten asked at last. "Is this a reward that would interest you?"

"You know it is," Gereint whispered. He did not know whether to believe the mage. But he knew he wanted to believe him. "For the hope of that reward...I will serve you, my lord, as well as I can."

The small, fine mouth quirked with unexpected humor. "Better than you served your previous master, I hope. Tell me…who removed the brand from your face? Or conspired to have it removed? One of your cousins? A friend? Tehre Amnachudran? That's been suggested, though the proposed motive seems thin to me."

Caught by surprise, Gereint hesitated. Then he said with practiced conviction, "A man in Dachsichten. A surgeon who dislikes *geas* magic on principle and for whom I did a small service. I could give you the name he told me, but I doubt it was his right one."

There was a brief pause. Then the king's mage said, "Gereint, you are lying to me. What surprises me is that you would believe you might do so successfully."

Gereint had not actually expected the mage to be deceived. But he had hoped a smooth, fairly plausible tale might serve—at least that the lord mage might not care to pursue the question. Seeing this hope fail, he bowed his head and said nothing.

"Gereint?" Beguchren asked, with deliberate patience. "Do you not wish to earn your freedom? You will not do so with lies. Tell me the truth."

"I…it was…" Gereint took a breath. He began again, "My lord, the truth is, I cannot answer that question. I am willing to serve you, my lord, very willing, but I beg you will not ask me."

The king's mage regarded him steadily. "But I do ask you, Gereint."

"My lord…" Gereint tried to catch his breath and balance against what seemed suddenly treacherous footing. "My lord, you ask for my loyalty. What would it be worth if I betrayed so easily the loyalty I owe elsewhere?"

The mage crossed his arms across his chest, tilted his head to the side, and answered quietly, "But *I* will have your service. It is not acceptable to me that you should owe loyalty elsewhere. Did one of your cousins help you? Brachan? Gescheichan?"

Gereint laughed bitterly at the suggestion, then realized if he'd only thought more quickly, he might have cast suspicion toward his cousins and away from Tehre and her father—then was at once disturbed that the idea of doing so even occurred to him. And twice disturbed to know he'd have done just that if he'd thought it might work.

He found his hands closed into fists and forced them open. He tried to think. It occurred to him that the entire offer the king's mage had made him might be false; that the offer of freedom might be merely a ploy to find out the answer to the question he had asked. This immediately seemed likely—and then, after another instant, extremely unlikely: Why should the *king's own mage* stoop to trickery when he could open a man's mind like a book and read the memories hidden there, never mind drawing upon the compulsion of the *geas*? But the next moment, the possibility again seemed very real. He could not decide.

Gereint looked at his master's face, found the calm impassivity completely impenetrable, and took a hard breath. "If you want my dedicated service, you will have to accept my silence on this one question," he said at last. "Maybe you can take it from my mind; I don't know. But I'll try to prevent you. I will not answer willingly."

Their eyes met and held. Gereint waited for the mage's mind to slice into his, but it did not happen.

"While I would prefer your willing service," Beguchren Teshrichten said at last, "your absolute submission will be adequate. Punishment as well as reward is within my authority. Do you understand?"

Gereint understood *that* very well. He said nothing.

"Do you believe you can withhold any answer I would demand? You have no protection whatsoever against anything I might choose to do to you," Beguchren reminded Gereint, unnecessarily.

Gereint stared silently back at him, taking refuge in a slave's practiced impassivity. It was the only refuge available to him.

"Strip," the mage commanded him. "And wait here for me." He turned his back and left the room.

Gereint had never imagined he would have reason to be grateful to Perech Fellesteden for anything. But he found he was grateful now for the hard lessons in endurance he had learned at Fellesteden's hands. He knew how to accept humiliation, how to believe that all things pass, how to flatten his awareness so that he did not think even a moment ahead—so that he barely thought even of the moment as it actually passed.

What he could not believe was that the king's mage had first lifted him so high and then cast him so far down—no. No. He had done it to himself. Nothing the mage had said had ever been real, and an experienced slave should have known it was not real. Beguchren Teshrichten had never intended to free him. Only to hold out the hope of freedom...Gereint folded his clothing neatly across a nearby chair and turned to face the mage as the mage returned.

Beguchren carried a branding iron in one hand and a

riding whip in the other. Next to the iron, the whip seemed almost innocent. Gereint tried not to stare at the iron. He fixed his gaze instead on one of the paintings: a scene that showed the south side of the Hill of Iron in the afternoon of a mellow autumn day. The white marble of the king's palace seemed, in that golden light, to have been poured out of honey; the gilded rooftops on the towers seemed to be made out of flame. It was a beautiful painting, full of warmth and peace; a surprising piece, perhaps, to find in the dwelling of a cold mage.

"Gereint," Beguchren said softly. His voice was still soft, but it carried all the implacable cold the painting denied.

Gereint looked at him, he hoped, steadily. Everything depended on the next moments: If he yielded now to the mage's demands, then they would both know he would always yield before any threat. But if he held fast, he might persuade the mage that he could not be broken. That belief might set the terms of this new servitude into a more tolerable path. If anything could. Gereint stared at the mage with flat defiance and said nothing at all.

But the white-haired mage's air of calm assurance was chilling. Beguchren laid both iron and whip on a table and faced Gereint. "I will set the brand back on your face, give you this whip, and send you, naked, to the bottom of Wide Hill. I will command you to tell any passersby that you are being punished for impudence and defiance and that your master invites them to punish you as they choose." The mage paused. He touched the iron with a fingertip, and its circular head first frosted and then smoked with a cold as frightening as any coal-red glow.

"Or you may simply obey me," added Beguchren, after

a silence long enough to allow Gereint to contemplate the threatened punishment. "Do as I command and I will forget your defiance. Serve me well, and I will restore your freedom." Another pause. "Well?" he asked at last.

Wide Hill encompassed the worst areas of Breidechboden. Gereint could well imagine the reaction of the rough denizens of that area to such an invitation. He knew he had probably paled. But he did not let his expression change. In a way, he was even glad of the brutal threat, because he was far too angry now to capitulate. He said harshly, "You had better send retainers of yours to be sure I survive your punishment, *master*. We can both imagine, I'm sure, the creativity of the men who will find your invitation amusing."

Beguchren began, sounding mildly exasperated, "Gereint—"

Gereint stepped forward, picked up the iron by its wooden handle, and held it out to his master. "You had better phrase your command carefully when you send me down to Wide Hill. Or I swear I will kill the first baseborn dog-livered coward who touches me."

There was a silence. The mage did not move to take the iron.

"Perech Fellesteden owned me for *eight years*," Gereint said with contained fury. "Do you think there is anything of degradation I do not know? Do what you will: I have been trained to endure and I will yield *nothing*."

Beguchren Teshrichten took the iron from Gereint and laid it once again aside on the table, where the vicious cold of its head scored the polished wood as a flame might. The mage smoothed the mark out of the wood with the tip of a finger, studied Gereint for a moment longer, and then said, his tone absolutely uninflected, "Come with me. You will not need to dress."

It would have taken Gereint an instant to recover from the surprise of this apparent admission of defeat and follow the mage, except for the compulsion of the *geas*, which did not allow hesitation.

This time, his master led Gereint to a starkly plain, windowless room that contained only a table cluttered with the obscure paraphernalia of a mage and a narrow thin-mattressed cot. Beguchren picked up and contemplated an iron flask. He appeared utterly unconcerned about Gereint. Gereint, for his part, stood in the doorway and tried not to speculate about the things on the table or wonder why there was a cot in this room.

Beguchren poured a generous measure of pale green liquid from the flask into a earthenware cup, turned, and held the cup out to Gereint. "Drink this," he commanded. "And sit down there." He indicated the cot.

Gereint took the cup and tossed the green liquid back like cheap ale. It tasted like herbs and winter ice, like new-mown hay and hoarfrost. The taste was not unpleasant, but nothing in the taste was familiar or identifiable, and the liquid chilled his tongue and throat unpleasantly. Gereint gave the cup back to the mage and sat down on the cot. He waited to see what would happen. He wanted to ask, but would not give his new master the satisfaction of knowing he was frightened.

Dizziness rose up through Gereint like a mist, spreading from his belly outward along all his limbs, rising last to his head. He seemed to taste the drink again and swallowed heavily against a sudden nausea, which at least did not grow worse. The dizziness did, however. He closed his eyes against it. He knew he should lie down, but he was no longer certain exactly where the cot was. He felt around uncertainly, searching for its edges. But his fingers felt distant and...strange, like they belonged to someone else very far away...A small, strong hand closed on his arm, and he let himself be led downward, though in a way it seemed he was rising and not falling. Cold green mist poured through Gereint, carrying his mind upward as it rose to the clouds...He was very cold...and then nothing was left but green mist.

CHAPTER 5

Gereint woke in a large, heavy bed hung with sky-blue curtains. The mattress was soft. That was what he knew first. The mattress was soft and there were plenty of down-stuffed pillows. The curtains that surrounded the bed turned the light to a softly luminous blue. The ceiling was white plaster. Gereint gazed at it, trying to think. The sounds of birds singing came to him, muffled by the curtains. The delicate liquid songs of finches and sparrows...So it was morning.

He felt...very strange. Light, in a way that had nothing to do with his actual weight. As though he had laid down some great burden in the night. But he could not remember anything of the night that had led him to this room and this bed. He tried to think back further but could not remember the previous evening either. Yet he did not think he had been ill, certainly not so ill that he should not remember the past day. He frowned at the ceiling, pushed himself slowly to sit up, and put aside the bed curtains.

The room beyond the bed was all ivory and rose and blue, gentle in the soft morning light. There was a painting on the far wall: The artist had painted Seven Son Hill at dawn in the springtime, from above, as though he had captured the view of a finch or a sparrow.

Memory rose through Gereint like mist. His breath caught. He shut his eyes and pressed a hand across his face, at once terrified and violently furious. All the horror of the previous days flooded through him, utterly unexpected. He thought he might shout; he thought he might weep. He held perfectly still, pressing his hands across his eyes, and waited, shaking, for the storm to pass.

It did pass, eventually. The room was quiet except for the songs of the birds. He might have been the only one awake in all the house, in all the court entire, except for the birds.

The shaking eased at last. Gereint took hold of the bedpost and got to his feet. He was naked. But if the king's mage had done anything to him while he was unconscious, he could not tell it. He felt normal. Except for that odd lightness, so that he wondered whether, if he leaped down from the window of this room, he might float down to the gardens below as gently as a down feather from his pillow. This was not an unpleasant feeling. But it was unusual and uncomfortable because he almost thought he should recognize the feeling, only he did not.

There was a jug of water, a wide brass basin, and a small pile of folded clothing on a table next to the bed. The room was not large. It contained little save for the bed and the table and a small writing desk. There was paper on the desk and a quill and a bottle of ink. The ink was sapphire blue.

Gereint poured water into the basin and washed his face. He put on the clothing. It was not blue and white nor any other livery, but plain brown and tan. But the material was good, and the clothing fit.

There were no boots, but house sandals sat under the table. Gereint picked them up and sat down at the desk to put them on. And stopped. He sat still for a long time, staring down.

The silver *geas* rings were gone. Not merely the little chains Beguchren Teshrichten had threaded through them: the rings themselves. Gone entirely. Nothing but small scarred holes interrupted the smooth skin between tendon and bone. When Gereint tentatively reached down to touch his ankles where the rings had been, he felt the holes. But the rings themselves were *gone*.

Gereint had felt only joy and gratitude when Eben Amnachudran had removed the brand from his face. He did not know what he felt now.

There were servants outside the blue room: a broom-wielding woman in servant's drab brown and, more to the point, a man in livery waiting outside the door. The man, who addressed Gereint as "honored sir," guided him through halls and up stairs and along a pillared gallery open to the weather, and at last through an intricately carved portico into an antechamber hung with blue and violet and decorated with mosaics of birds and trees. All of this was clearly part of the palace; all of it was clearly designed to impress and overwhelm.

It made Gereint angry—he was ready to be angry, he found. To be *furious*. Everything in this place was meant to manipulate, to make a man feel small and subservient—and that meant everything was of a piece, because everything here had been a manipulation, right from the beginning—and for what unguessable purpose? Beguchren Teshrichten needed Gereint, clearly. And had deliberately put him through all that farce of bait and threat, and for what? For what?

The liveried man gestured respectfully that Gereint should wait in the antechamber and himself went through a curtained doorway. Gereint did not wait, but followed on his heels.

"My lord—" the man was saying to the frost-haired mage.

The mage himself was sitting on the edge of an enormous desk, looking rather like a child who had made himself at home in his father's study. A man sized to fit the desk was lounging in a chair to one side of the room, but Gereint barely looked at him. He had no attention to spare for anyone but the mage.

Beguchren Teshrichten had been running the long feather of a quill pen absently through his fingers. He did not seem to be paying very much attention to the liveried man, but he looked up sharply when Gereint came in, waved the man silent, and hopped down off the desk to face Gereint. He was not smiling, but his calm seriousness was just as inscrutable as his smile. He said to the man, in a tone of polite dismissal, "Thank you, Terechen," and the man darted an unsettled look at Gereint and went away.

Gereint had just enough self-command to wait for the liveried man to leave. Then he took two steps forward and said through his teeth, "The man who took away the scar of the brand did it for kindness. And why did you do *this*?" He gestured sharply downward. "Not for kindness, is it? What is this but payment for service—and for *what* service? What was that game with the threats and the iron? What do you *want* from me?—Not that it matters: if you think I'm interested in playing your game, you're badly mistaken, *my lord*."

The mage did not answer, but impassively looked aside from Gereint's angry stare, laying the feather quill carefully down on the desk.

The other man, however, stood up and set his fists on his hips. "What?" he demanded. He was not quite as tall as Gereint, but broader all through, and his voice matched his big frame: deep and guttural. That deep voice was especially harsh now, with annoyance and also with an odd kind of disdain. "You object to payment, do you?" he went on, glowering at Gereint. "What, do you find the payment is not sufficient? Is it base coin? What service would you have refused for this coin? Would you wish to specify? Well?"

Taken aback by this unexpected rebuke, Gereint stared at the big man. He had assumed Beguchren Teshrichten was master in this place; now he did not know. This man was heavyset and powerful, but his air of authority went beyond his size. He looked like a soldier: black hair cropped short on his head, thick beard close-trimmed to outline an aggressive jaw. His features were strong, even heavy, but his eyes snapped with energy and outrage.

It was the outrage that finally prompted Gereint's belated recognition: There was authority in that guttural voice, but the anger was also clearly the ire of an offended friend. Beguchren Teshrichten, as everyone knew, was the *king's* mage. This... this was the king. Brechen Glansent

Arobern. *The* Arobern, himself. As soon as the possibility occurred to Gereint, he was sure it was true.

"Well?" repeated the king, still scowling.

Gereint, appalled, took a breath and tried to think what response he could make.

"Forgive him, my king: He is justifiably both angry and frightened," Beguchren Teshrichten cut in. His light voice was as smooth and unreadable as ever. "Under the circumstances, I would be amazed at equanimity. If I'm not offended, why should you be?" The mage came a step toward Gereint and added to him, "My actions were unpardonable, but may I ask you nevertheless to pardon them?"

Gereint stared at him, still unable to respond.

The king shook his head, looking only slightly mollified. "What Beguchren does not say is that he was following my orders." He pointed a heavy finger at a chair near Gereint. "Sit down and listen."

Gereint sank into the indicated chair.

"You were to be returned to Perech Fellesteden's heirs," the king told him grimly. "Only Lady Tehre Amnachudran came to me and told me a story that interested me. Beguchren has an urgent need for a strong maker. I told Beguchren he could have you. I said: How useful, the man is already *geas* bound! But Beguchren said if he could have free loyalty instead of bound obedience, that would suit him better. So I told him to try your loyalty and courage. I said, prove both or be satisfied with the *geas*. That was my order, do you understand?" He paused.

Evidently satisfied by the quality of Gereint's silence, the king then went on: "So you are here, free. And I have no use for these, unless I think of another use, do you understand?" He picked up a pair of small silver rings from a side table and threw them down on the polished desk so that they rang like bells.

Gereint had not noticed the rings until the king picked them up, and flinched involuntarily as they rolled and chimed on the desk. He knew what threat the king was making with that gesture—then he realized, belatedly, what threat the king might *actually* be making and could not stop himself from flinching a second time.

"So," the king said, giving him a hard stare, "you serve my friend Beguchren as he requires, and I will let *you* choose how to dispose of those, do you understand me, Gereint Enseichen? You may melt them down or throw them in the river, what you wish. That is the coin *I* offer—but if you will not serve my mage, I will think of something else to do with them. Do you understand?"

Gereint began to say "yes," found his mouth too dry to speak, and swallowed. At last he managed to whisper, "I understand."

"I think you do," the king said. "Beguchren, tell me later what you decide. But soon. Yes?"

The mage inclined his head a minute degree. "Of course."

"Hah. Of course you will," said the king. He gave his mage a short nod, and Gereint one last scowl, and went out.

"He is not so harsh as he pretends," Beguchren said, wryly apologetic. "Gereint Enseichen, I did not wish to, as you say, play a game of threats and the iron with you, and I ask your pardon."

Gereint did not answer. He was not sure he *could*

answer. He felt as though he'd battered down a door and stormed through, only to find he had stepped over a cliff. As though he were still falling, even now.

"You're very angry," the mage observed. "And— understandably—very frightened." He turned and went to a sideboard, poured wine from a carafe into a silver cup, topped the cup up with water, came back, and held the cup out to Gereint.

Gereint took it silently and held it, not drinking.

"I have no doubt you've swallowed a great deal of anger and fear in your life," said the mage. He leaned his hip against the edge of the desk, barely tall enough to do so, and tilted his head, meeting Gereint's eyes. His manner was more assured than many a court noble's; indeed, his manner was entirely unlike the usual arrogance of an ordinary court noble; the white-haired mage seemed to combine assurance with an unusual, wry matter-of-factness. He added softly, "I'm glad you trust me enough to show your anger to me. The Arobern was wrong to admonish you for it."

Gereint put his cup down on the arm of his chair hard enough that the watered wine nearly sloshed over the rim and started to get to his feet, then changed his mind and sank back. He demanded harshly, "What do you want from me? What did you *do* to me?"

"I did nothing, or nearly nothing," the mage said gently. "Truly, Gereint. I went into your mind, but you know what I saw there. You have a specific sort of gift: not merely strong, but peculiarly, mmm, flexible, and flexible in particular ways. Did you know?" He paused, but when Gereint did not answer, he went on. "Your gift is suitable, I believe, for my need. I needed to know whether that was so. So I went into your mind, into the private memories you hold. That is why you are so angry. But I had no choice. Gereint Enseichen, I ask your pardon."

For the third time. Gereint was beginning to feel that continued refusal might merely be churlish. He managed a curt nod.

Beguchren bowed his head a little, despite the ill grace of that nod. "Good. Thank you. You say the man who removed your brand did it for kindness; you claimed a man in Dachsichten did it for principle. Will you believe, at least, that if I did not act from kindness, I might have done so from principle?"

"Cold magecraft is what fashions the *geas* rings!"

"My principles are not entirely consistent, I admit." The mage paused, then added softly, "But I was glad to free you, Gereint."

Gereint stared at him wordlessly. If he had spoken, he knew he would say too much, so he said nothing.

"It's true I act from my need. But what I need from you, you must give willingly. Perhaps time will lay a foundation for trust to grow. There will be at least a little time. I will be going north tomorrow. You will go with me. I will expect you at the Emnerechke Gates at dawn."

It did not escape Gereint that the mage still had not said what it actually *was* he needed from him. Clearly, he was not going to. He did not ask again, but said instead, "You'll expect me, will you?"

The pale-eyed mage tilted his head. "Shall I not? I know you are capable of gratitude. You might belong now to Lord Fellesteden's heirs; what do you owe me that you are here"—a slight downward gesture with two fingers—"and free?"

Gereint set his jaw.

"And beyond any consideration of debt and gratitude…
I need your help," the mage added softly. "I do not wish to
sound overly dramatic, Gereint Enseichen, but as it happens, we have encountered some difficulty in the north.
There are no more mages now, you know. Only I. I am in
need of a maker with a strong gift, a certain kind of gift;
the kind I believe you possess. A man possessed of both
courage and integrity; a man"—and this time the slight,
wry gesture compared his own height to Gereint's—
"who is physically strong. So…I shall expect you at the
Emnerechke Gates at dawn. Shall I?"

Gereint wanted, for no reason he understood, to say
"Yes." He wanted to bow his head dutifully and agree.
He set himself hard against any such acquiescence and
said nothing.

"Then, though you may wish to take your leave elsewhere in the city, I shall expect you at the gates at dawn,"
concluded the mage imperturbably, exactly as though he
had agreed.

It was a dismissal as well as a command. Gereint
got to his feet, turned his back on the king's mage, and
walked out.

Fareine opened the door of Tehre Amnachudran's house
when Gereint knocked. Her smile held surprise and
delight; her glance downward toward Gereint's feet
seemed perfectly involuntary.

Gereint was still wearing the sandals he had been
given. He obligingly turned one foot so the woman could
see his ankle. "Legally," he added. As he said it, it came
home to him, almost for the first time, that this was true.

Legally free, as he had never truly expected to be again in his life. It should have been a realization of powerful joy. Perhaps it would be, eventually. But he remembered the Arobern throwing the silver *geas* rings down on the desk and declaring, *I have no use for these, unless I think of another use*. He said, "I need to speak to Tehre."

"Of course. The honored lady's in the library. You are most welcome! She has been very worried for you." Fareine stepped back and swung the door wide.

Tehre Amnachudran was sitting at the library's largest table, surrounded by heavy books and scrolls, most of them open. A sheaf of blank papers lay at her elbow and she was holding a long quill in one fine-boned hand. Gereint did not expect her to notice any intrusion, but she looked up sharply when the door opened. Then her small face lit with an unconsidered smile and she jumped to her feet. "Gereint!"

Gereint turned his foot to show her, too, his ankle. "They tell me I have you to thank for this," he said. Not directly, but Tehre had clearly forged the first link of that chain and hammered it into shape. "You went to the *king*?"

"Well, I had to," Tehre said simply. "They said you would go to Lord Fellesteden's heirs; they said I couldn't even petition to buy you. So I had to go to the Arobern. No one else can overrule a judge, you know." Then she stood still for a moment, her formidable attention focused on him. "He said he would give you to Beguchren Teshrichten. Did he?" And, deeply suspicious, "Are you all right?"

"He did," Gereint answered. "And I don't know. But I'm free of the *geas*, and that's not something I ever expected. What did you tell the Arobern? You told him the truth? That was foolish—"

"I had to," Tehre repeated, surprised. "Not quite *all* the truth—not the part I've only guessed at myself." She meant she had carefully left out any speculations about just who might have removed Gereint's brand. "But most of the truth, yes. How else could I persuade him to listen to me? It worked: He believed me about Fellesteden, you know. He said he needed a man who could be loyal. I told him you would do very well."

"He might have put *you* under the *geas*—"

"But he didn't."

Gereint didn't say, *He still might*. He thought again of the Arobern's heavy voice declaring, *I have no use for these, unless I think of another use*. He said harshly, "You should never have gone to him!"

"But I did," Tehre said reasonably, "and it's done. And the Arobern freed you, so everything is fine. I didn't tell him my father interfered with your brand, you know. Only that you didn't have it when you came to my door." She gave a little nod, as though to add, *So that's all right*, and turned back toward the table. "As you suggested, I've been working on synthesizing our current understanding of the philosophy of materials—"

Gereint was sure she had been.

"It's slow work," Tehre added, staring down at the piled and scattered books with a dissatisfied expression. "It takes me away from actually working on the mathematics— I think I'm close to formulating a useful equation about the velocity of propagation in a crack once it actually starts to run, and here I am looking up what other makers and philosophers have said about things that are only obliquely related." The woman began idly sketching parabolas down the margin of a book, fitting tangent lines to them as she went. She added, "I would greatly prefer to have you do this for me," and turned her head to give Gereint an intent look.

"I am to go north in the morning," Gereint told her. "With Beguchren Teshrichten." He was surprised at the regret this statement caused him: He had not realized that he did, in fact, want simply to say "yes," and take the quill out of Tehre's hand.

"Oh!" said Tehre. She paused, her eyes narrowing. "How far north? Tashen?"

She meant, *Anywhere near my family's house?* Gereint opened a hand in a gesture of uncertainty. "I don't know. So you had better write your father, if you haven't already."

"Oh, I have. I will again. You came to tell me that? Thank you, Gereint. That may be important, if you—and the lord mage—should go so far." Tehre paused. Then asked, "Why north? What does the king's mage want with you?"

Gereint shrugged ignorance. "I would tell you if I knew. There's evidently some trouble in the north. With the new desert, I suppose. I don't know what or why the lord mage thinks I'd be useful to his hand in dealing with it."

"Trouble. Huh. In the north, but you don't know what it comprises." Tehre glanced down at her sketches, then back up at Gereint. "I wonder what this 'trouble' is, and how close it's come to my parents' house. Maybe... hmm. Maybe... there are all those refugees, and Fereine says they say the desert pursued them south. I wonder how large the new desert actually is?"

"Larger than one would think necessary to encompass Melentser," Gereint said, a little too quickly for a man who was supposed to be from some town in Meridanium and not from Melentser at all. He added, "Or so I've heard."

Tehre nodded, looking thoughtful. "I wonder if it's still growing? Beyond the agreed bounds? It could be very hard on the north if the desert presses too close to the towns. And on the south if any more people have to leave the north. The prices of everything are already high, even with only the people of Melentser forced to leave their homes." Her eyes were dark with worry. "My family...Well, but Beguchren Teshrichten is very powerful. I suppose he will be able to settle this 'trouble,' whatever it is."

Gereint, remembering the mage's hooded eyes and inscrutable smile, thought this was probably true. "But in any case, I wished to see you, honored lady, to thank you for interceding for me. And, yes, to ask whether you'd sent a letter to your father, and urge you to send another. And...that is, if you don't find it an imposition, I find I would rather leave Breidechboden from the house of a friend."

"Of course." Tehre sounded faintly surprised, but she looked pleased. "If you're not leaving until tomorrow morning, you can help me break your catapult. I thought you would miss that; I'm glad you'll be here for it. I want to see if I can slow the fracturing process enough to let me really study how the materials break. Do you think you can help me with that? You've probably tried to slow down something that was in the process of breaking, haven't you?"

"Carriage wheels, and an axle once."

"Perfect!" Tehre declared, and headed for the garden, abandoning the books without a backward look.

Gereint gazed after her for a moment, smiling. The woman's focus on work was...soothing. Comfortable, in a way he couldn't really put into words. He could feel knots of tension in his neck and back relaxing. He didn't know what he thought about Beguchren; he barely knew what he thought of his freedom, such as it was—but he knew he was glad to find Tehre Amnachudran absolutely unchanged. He knew that whatever lay to the north, he would be glad to think of her in this house, breaking mechanisms and developing equations to describe how they fractured.

CHAPTER 6

Tehre did not know what she thought of Gereint's going north with Beguchren Teshrichten, but she knew she was glad he was going north as a free man. Or, if not free, at least no more bound than anyone subject to circumstance and the ordinary pressure a powerful man could bring to bear. On the other hand, that was surely compulsion enough. But it was much better than being *geas* bound to whatever brute was the heir of Perech Fellesteden. She was quite sure that, whoever the heir might be, he was a brute. What other sort of heir could a man such as Lord Fellesteden possibly have engendered?

Gereint left her house well before dawn. Fareine woke Tehre, as she had asked, and Tehre flung on the simple dress she'd laid out ready, pinned her hair up, and ran down to the main door to bid him a proper farewell. He had said, *I would rather leave Breidechboden from the house of a friend.* It had been important to him. So he had come here. To tell her about the king's mage and urge her to write her father—of course. But also because it had been important to him to have the house of a *friend* behind him when he left the city. He evidently had no family—or no family to whom he could go. Tehre had found herself shaken by pity at the idea that Gereint had been abandoned by his family. Whatever he had done. No matter what *she* might do, she knew *her* family would never close their house to her.

So she met Gereint at her door to bid him farewell, as a friend would do. He was surprised and, she thought, touched. Tehre wished him luck and fair weather, as she might have wished any friend going out on the road from under her roof.

The tall man tilted his head and quirked an eyebrow at her. "I'm sorry I didn't have the chance to build you a whole series of catapults."

So was Tehre. She nodded wistfully. "I'll break other things, I suppose," she said, and he chuckled, though she hadn't meant to say anything funny. But she didn't mind. Gereint laughed at her in a way that made it seem that he was inviting her to share the joke.

"You do that," he told her. "Thank you, Tehre. Fareine." He nodded to them in a way that made it plain he was sorry to leave. Then he left.

"Beguchren Teshrichten," Tehre said thoughtfully, looking out at the dim street after he was gone. "And 'trouble' in the north."

"Tehre?"

"Nothing. I just wonder…nothing, Fareine." Tehre shut the door on the faint pearly light of the false dawn and went back to her room to dress properly.

*   *   *

The Arobern's palace was an exercise in the builders' craft: ornamented nearly, but not quite, to the point of absurdity. As a child, Tehre had loved the sheer extravagant excess of it; even now, she loved the pinnacles and great statues that lined the tops of the walls—especially the shorter walls, of course. She understood now, as she had not as a child, that the higher walls had enough extra weight of their own that they did not need the weight of statues to stabilize them against the sideways thrust of the slanted roofs. But the statues were nice in their own right, and the stonecarvers had no doubt enjoyed making them.

Tehre's carriage passed a long colonnade where the columns, otherwise simple, had been painted purple and crimson—except where they had been gilded—and through a marble gate topped by a short, thick architrave. A straight stone lintel such as an architrave was not, of course, structurally stable. This one had cracked exactly as one might have expected: twice symmetrically on the upper surface and once, in the middle, on the lower, thus turning itself into a much more stable three-hinged arch.

Tehre would simply have suggested constructing an arch in the first place, but it was interesting to think about the way the stone had responded to the stresses it had found unacceptable. An interesting example of why one needed to consider the tensile stresses and thrust lines that bore on any given point within a structure; it was hardly coincidence that the straight lintel had cracked at those precise three points; those were the hinge points of the "arch" ring, of course. There should be a way to represent the relationship of the tensile stresses and the

resulting thrust lines to the thickness of the stones used
in the construction... One might let thrust t represent the
ratio between the strength of the thrust at a given location within the structure and the cross-sectional area of
that location, and that might let one calculate... Oh, had
they arrived?

Tehre blinked and gazed out the window; it seemed the
trip had gone rather quickly. She wished she had paper
and a quill to note down her thoughts about architraves
and thrust lines and the forces at work on the stone. She
even glanced around the carriage vaguely, as though she
might find such supplies on the seat beside her. Of course,
there was nothing so useful in the carriage, on the seat,
or elsewhere. She ought to put a box of writing things in
all her carriages... She had thought of that before, but she
never remembered.

The carriage had drawn up before a massive set of
gilded brass doors and her driver hopped off his seat and
came around to place a step for Tehre. "Will the honored
lady wish me to wait?" he asked.

"No," Tehre said absently, studying the doors. "No,
I don't know how long I'll be. I'll get a public carriage
home." She wondered if anyone would mind if she exam-
ined the door hinges. Hinges on doors that size must be
under a great deal of tension. Stresses in metal were very
interesting. They would probably fail by shearing, if they
failed... She decided reluctantly that she probably should
not take time to look at door hinges, no matter how interesting, and simply walked through the doors.

There were men-at-arms in the Arobern's livery, and
a quite exalted chamberlain. Tehre had met the chamberlain previously; he nodded to her and smiled and said

a lot of polite things that all meant, *You'll have to wait while I see if the king wants to disarrange his complicated schedule for you.* Tehre allowed him to guide her to an antechamber to wait. It was, at least, a particularly nice antechamber, with chairs that were comfortable as well as expensive and windows that let in plenty of light and air. The chamberlain hadn't forgotten that, on her previous visit, the Arobern had indeed been pleased to see her.

Only one other person was in the antechamber: a man Tehre didn't know at all. He didn't seem to have any attendants or servants... Well, Tehre hadn't brought even Fareine with her, so neither did she, and what did that prove? The man was tall, though not anything like as tall as Gereint. But there was something else about him she was not quite able to identify.

Then the man rose politely to nod to her and murmur a courteous acknowledgment, and Tehre realized that he was not Casmantian.

How interesting. Probably he was Feierabianden; at least, there were very good reasons a Feierabianden lord might be here in the Arobern's palace, and Tehre did not know of any reason a lord from Linularinum would be.

Tehre wished now she had let Fareine accompany her; she did not know how to speak to a foreign lord. Tehre never really knew what to say to anyone. She always seemed to make some perfectly obvious comment that nevertheless offended somebody. Fareine always knew what to say to everybody. Only Fareine was sometimes not willing to be very direct, and this morning Tehre had wanted nothing else but to get at once to the point, or why else bother coming back to the palace?

Well, but surely it was not polite to sit and pretend she was the only person in the room. Tehre said carefully, in the Terheien she had learned as a girl and had not spoken since, "My name is Tehre Amnachudran Tanshan." Exactly like a schoolroom lesson. "Be welcome to Casmantium and to Breidechboden. What is your name, lord?"

The lord of Feierabiand smiled, no doubt recognizing the careful, rote statements and question. He answered in strongly accented Prechen, "Lady Tehre Amnachudran Tanshan, I am Bertaud son of Boudan, Lord of the Delta and servant of Iaor Daveien Behanad Safiad."

He was careful and slow with her name, which lilted strangely across his tongue. On the other hand, the unfamiliar Feierabianden names sounded like they belonged in his mouth; Tehre could never have pronounced them as he did. It occurred to her that language was a making; words were like the bricks in a wall and syntax the mortar that joined them together. Pronunciation was like style; the maker's signature. She smiled.

"You are a court lady?" the foreign lord asked her. "Forgive me that I do not know your name…"

"No," Tehre said, surprised. "I am…" What was the word in Terheien? "A maker," she said in Prechen, because she could not remember the Terheien.

"A maker," said Lord Bertaud, and obligingly repeated the term in Terheien. "The makers and builders of Casmantium are famous even in Feierabiand."

"Yes," Tehre said, happy to strike familiar ground. "Andreikan Warichteier says in his *Principia*, 'Casmantium for making, Feierabiand for calling, Linularinum for law.'" Only she could not recall the Terheien for "law" and had to use the Prechen. She gazed at the foreign lord curiously. "Do you call? What is it like, to call?"

"Call?" he repeated, shaking his head to show he did not understand her. He repeated the word in Prechen: "Call? To call out, is this the term?"

"Oh—yes. But I mean 'calling.' Those who call, mmm." Tehre searched for the word for "animal," could not find it, and said carefully, "Dogs, horses, mice. So?" She was amused that she remembered the Terheien for "mice."

But the Feierabianden lord frowned and gave a terse shake of his head. "No. I do not call."

And she had angered him by asking. Maybe he was ashamed he could not call, if, as Warichteier had implied, almost everyone in Feierabiand could. Tehre did not know whether she should apologize. She had been pleased to meet a man who might call; she had never met anyone who could tell her about that sort of magic, so different from making. At least, she assumed it was very different. An interesting question: Maybe the experience was similar, though the expression of the gift was dissimilar? But she was sorry to have offended the foreign lord. She did not know exactly what she should apologize for, so it seemed safer to say nothing. Probably she should not have spoken to the Feierabianden lord at all…

But he said, seeming sorry to have frowned at her, "What do you…ah, make?"

"Oh…" Tehre was pleased the lord was not irretrievably offended after all. She wondered how to explain the philosophy of making in a language she barely spoke well enough to say, *My name is Tehre, what is your name?* But she tried to explain. "I think about making. You understand?

I study...how to make. How, ah, how things..." She did not know the words for "break" or "fail."

But Lord Bertaud was nodding. "You study. Like a mage."

"A little like a mage," Tehre agreed, though she was doubtful about the comparison. Perhaps in Feierabiand the mages were all also scholars. Mages did study things, she supposed. Magical things. She wondered whether there was a philosophy of magic passed along among mages, as there were philosophies of natural materials, and if so what it might comprise.

"And you—"

But the lord's question was cut off because the chamberlain came back just then. Tehre was almost sorry for that; the Feierabianden lord was interesting, even if he did not have the gift of calling.

"My lord, the Arobern will see you at once," the chamberlain said to Lord Bertaud, in Terheien much better than Tehre's. "But," he added to Tehre in Prechen, "I am sorry, Lady Tehre, the Arobern does not have time to see you now and asks that you make an appointment for an audience at a later time. Perhaps in ten days?"

"But—" Tehre protested. It had not occurred to her that the Arobern would refuse to see her. She might have gone to see Beguchren Teshrichten himself, if she had gone the previous day. She saw now that she should have done it that way, although it was the Arobern and not his mage she wanted most to see. But the mage might have made time to see her. But now it was too late. She said unhappily, "But..." But then did not know what to say after that. If the king would not see her...She looked doubtfully at the chamberlain.

"I did give him your name, Lady Tehre," the chamberlain said gently.

Lord Bertaud had been watching her face. "Perhaps the lady will walk with me," he said suddenly. "I am not..." He hunted for a word and guessed, "hurry?"

"My lord," began the chamberlain.

The Feierabianden lord looked sternly at the chamberlain. "I would, ah. Glad. Ah, I would *be* glad, if the lady would walk with me. I do not mind to wait. The king will not..." He hesitated and used the Terheien word, "Protest."

He sounded very certain of that last. Tehre realized—she should have realized it at once—that Lord Bertaud was very probably a representative and agent of the king of Feierabiand. Yes, of course, he'd said, *a servant of Iaor Something Something Safiad.* Iaor Safiad was the Feierabianden king, Tehre was almost sure. Certainly it was some Safiad or other.

And after the summer just past, no doubt the Safiad's trusted representative could say, *The king will not protest,* and be quite confident. Everyone knew, though no one said in so many words, that the Safiad king had comprehensively defeated the Arobern's plan to annex part of Feierabiand—that the improvements to the western road across the mountains were a gesture of magnanimity from the victor toward his defeated opponent. That the Arobern had been required to send his little son as hostage to the Safiad court. Tehre wondered suddenly whether this Lord Bertaud had been responsible for arranging that as well. It seemed very likely.

She said, not glancing at the chamberlain, "I am grateful for your kindness, Lord Bertaud," and smiled at the dutiful schoolroom phrase. But she *was* grateful, even if it was merely a whim born of the foreigner's wish to show a glint of steel beneath his polite court manners.

"I am glad to help," the lord answered graciously, and offered her his arm in a gesture just short of flirtatious. Perhaps that was the ordinary court manner in Feierabiand.

Tehre smiled again, took the lord's arm, and allowed him to guide her out of the antechamber just as though he knew where in the Arobern's palace he was going. The chamberlain, suppressing a just-audible sigh, hurried to get round in front of them so he could actually show them where to go.

Brechen Glansent Arobern was a big, aggressive man; black bearded, his hair cropped very short in the manner of a soldier. He affected a soldier's style, but if it was an affectation, everyone nevertheless agreed that he was a dangerous man to meet on the field of battle. It was a matter of common astonishment that the Feierabianden king had defeated him—but then, everyone knew the Arobern's defeat had not exactly come about on any ordinary field of battle. It was said that the Feierabianden king had allied with the griffins, and generally agreed that he would come to regret that dangerous alliance.

But the heavy gold chain the Arobern wore around his throat was not a soldier's ornament, and the contained restless power of his presence went well past the simple physical charisma of even the most impressive of soldiers. When he scowled at the Feierabianden lord, the whole room seemed to hum with the power of his displeasure; when he transferred that scowl to Tehre, she felt that disapproval as almost a physical force. She tipped her chin up and tried not to blink in dismay. The king had not been like this before; but then, when she had previously come to see him, she had not come in defiance of his command or in the company of a representative of the Feierabianden king. She tried not to look nervous.

"Forgive the lady," Lord Bertaud said, fairly smoothly, considering his awkward Prechen. "She said she wished to see you. I said I did not mind to wait." He offered a small, deferential bow.

The Arobern turned his thunderous scowl back to the foreign lord...Then surprised Tehre with a deep, amused chuckle. The humor might have had a hard edge to it, but it did not seem forced. "Well," he said to Tehre. "If you wish so strongly to see me, perhaps I should make time, hah? As my guest promises that he is patient." He beckoned to her and turned aside, leading her to the other end of the room where they could speak in semi-privacy.

It was a large room, but thankfully not one of the great halls with porphyry pillars and marble floors and high, vaulted, echoing ceilings. This was a quieter room, one with thick rugs and comfortable furniture, the sort of room where the Arobern might well prefer to conduct actual business rather than stylized audiences. He waved her to a chair, dropping heavily into another.

Tehre perched on the edge of the indicated chair and tried nervously to decide whether the king was actually annoyed with her or not. She could not tell.

"Well?" the Arobern said. "I am grateful you led my attention to Gereint Enseichen, and so I am willing to be patient. But if you have encountered difficulties with

Lord Fellesteden's heirs, that is a matter for the city patrol or for any of my judges, not for me. Or you wish to sue his estate for damages? That, too, is a matter for a judge and not for me."

"Of course," Tehre said, surprised. "That is, Lord King, I didn't come about Lord Fellesteden at all. I wanted to ask about Beguchren Teshrichten, and whom would I ask except you, since he left the city at dawn? I wondered what the trouble in the north is, and what the lord mage wanted of my friend Gereint. He freed him, I know. But I don't understand why, and I wonder if he imposed a different kind of bond when he took away the *geas*?" She paused and looked carefully at the Arobern. Tehre knew she sometimes mistook the effect of something she said, but if the king was angry, she couldn't see it. He only gazed at her, patiently neutral.

Tehre went on, "If your honored mage wanted a maker, well, there are many fine makers in Breidechboden. I'm a maker myself, and not the least skilled of all makers, though I know it's not modest to say so, but it's true. But I don't remember hearing that the Lord Mage Beguchren Teshrichten was seeking a maker, so he didn't just say so and ask for makers to apply to him, did he?

"And you told me you needed a man who was—who had a great capacity for loyalty. That was what you said. But what you meant was that *Beguchren Teshrichten* needed a maker who had that capacity, and for some reason he preferred a maker who was *geas* bound even though the first thing he did was take away the *geas*. I think that's odd. I've tried and tried to think what the lord mage might have had in mind when he chose Gereint, only I can't.

"And then they went north. So there's something important to do in the north, something to do with the griffins and the new desert because why else would you send your mage? And it's a problem, or there's a problem associated with it, or the lord mage expects to have problems when he tries to do it or solve it or handle it. And Gereint's a good maker, but I don't know if I would look for a maker on the grounds of *a great capacity for loyalty* if I had a problem with *making* in mind: I would look for the *best and strongest* maker, whoever that might be. But Gereint came from the north, didn't he? He said Meridanium, but I wonder if maybe it wasn't really Melentser? So I'm worried that *making* isn't exactly what the lord mage had in mind when he specifically wanted *Gereint* to go north with him—"

The Arobern lifted a hand, stopping Tehre. He said, sounding a little amused, "You are very direct, Lady Tehre."

"People say that," Tehre admitted. "Sometimes people get angry. If I've made you angry, I'm sorry. I didn't mean to. I don't understand how anybody ever gets anything said or done if they aren't willing to say what they mean. My family is in the north, you know, and if there's trouble there, I'm worried for them." She added belatedly, "Lord King."

"Lady Tehre, I am not angry with you," the Arobern said mildly. "You are right in this respect: There is a problem in the north." He watched Tehre narrowly. "It is not your concern, however. It is not a matter for makers or builders, you understand? It is a matter for mages. And as you say, I have only one mage, now."

"But Gereint—"

"The man is your friend, you say? Yet you have known him only for days, and not even by his right name, is that not true?"

"Even so," Tehre said, she hoped with dignity. She knew she had flushed. It was true she had not known Gereint's right name until the king had used it himself, but she hoped she had not given this away somehow. She said firmly, "I don't have many friends, Lord King. But when Gereint *Enseichen* needed the house of a friend to go to, he came to my house."

"I understand what you say." The king leaned back in his chair, looking at Tehre. "Lady Tehre, I understand your concerns. I promise you, so far as I am aware, your family, however far north they may be, is not in immediate danger. If danger arrives at the doorstep of your family's house, I think it will not come so swiftly that they and all their household cannot retreat before it."

"But..." said Tehre, but then did not know what to say. She blinked, trying to rid herself of the image of her father's house surrounded by sand and red stone.

"I have considered carefully," the Arobern said firmly, "and I am satisfied to leave matters as they stand."

"Oh." Tehre tried to think. She began uncertainly, "But—"

"No," said the Arobern, holding up a hand to stop her. "Let your friend go north. Let my mage see to this problem, as I have sent him to do. Attend to your own house, Lady Tehre." He got to his feet and stood looking down at her.

After a moment, Tehre realized that this was actually a command. She rose quickly. "Lord King—"

"No," said the Arobern. Patiently. But with enough

firmness that she knew she could not protest again. He added, "Lady Tehre, I see that you, too, have a great capacity for loyalty. I admire this. But, no. Go home. When there is news of practical importance from the north, you will hear it, I promise you."

Tehre hesitated. Then, as there was nothing else she could do, she bowed. "Lord King."

"And another time," the king said, showing a glint of iron under the patience, "I hope you will be content to wait for a proper appointment, Lady Tehre."

Tehre caught back several things that occurred to her to say. Her mother would have been amazed. Instead of saying anything at all, she bowed again, lower, in apology, backed away three steps, bowed once more, and retreated. Not in very good order, she knew.

Go home. Like she was a child. Or, she admitted to herself, perhaps merely like she was subject to the commands of her king. That was harder to protest. If the Arobern had ordered her to go home without talking to her at all, that would not actually have been surprising. He *had* been patient.

She was angry anyway. She was both angry and frustrated when she left the palace and told a servant to hail a public carriage for her. But the anger faded as the carriage rattled through the streets of the city, and by the time she stepped down and waved at the driver to go around to the kitchen door for payment, she was no longer angry at all. But she was still intensely frustrated.

"Tehre…" Fareine brought her a plate of apple pastries in the library, since she had not eaten breakfast.

Tehre picked one up, put it down, and asked, "Fareine, do we have a map of the north somewhere?"

Fareine regarded Tehre uneasily. "Several, I should think. But—"

"Would you get one for me, please?"

"What did you find out about Gereint? Or the lord mage? Isn't that what you went to find out?"

"Yes. Nothing." Tehre tapped her fingers on the polished surface of the table. "I saw the Arobern—"

"You went to the king? Again? Tehre, you're going to offend him, doing that!"

"Yes, maybe. Anyway, it didn't help."

"You couldn't speak to him?" Fareine sounded as though she suspected such a failure might have been a good thing.

"I talked to him," Tehre corrected. "He wouldn't talk to me." She was silent for a moment, contemplating the pattern of that encounter. "I might have said too much, too openly," she concluded. "But he said far too little. Fareine, would you please get me a map?"

"If I won't, I suppose you'll get one yourself. So I suppose I will. If you'll eat a pastry for me."

"Oh..." Tehre picked the pastry up again and bit into it. The apples were nothing like as good as the ones from her mother's orchards. She ate the pastry anyway, brushing crumbs absently off the table onto the floor, ignoring Fareine's little sound of protest. "What?" she said impatiently. "Do you want me to get grease spots on the scroll?"

"No," sighed Fareine. "I'll get a girl to come sweep."

"Yes, please," Tehre agreed absently, and set the plate with the remaining pastries on one edge of the map to hold it open. Then she studied it. It was really more a map of the northeastern province of Meridanium. The

Terintsan River formed the western border of Meridanium, small towns scattered along its length until it
joined the Teschanken in the confluence at Pamnarichtan.
Well to the north and west, at the edge of the map, lay
Melentser.

Or that was where Melentser *had* lain. Tehre supposed
it had all gone to desert now. She wondered how long the
city would last under the pressure of sun and scouring
sand-laden winds. Would all the tall buildings, so proudly
raised over the years by builders and engineers, merely
wear away? That might take a long time. Or would the
desert somehow destroy the remnants of the human city
quickly? And if so, how?

And why did Beguchren Teshrichten want to go north
toward that desert? And why did he need a maker to
go with him? Not just a maker, but one from the north,
maybe from Melentser, a man who might have actually
seen the desert come to the city. Yes, Gereint had probably used the coming of the desert to get away from Lord
Fellesteden; that seemed logical. But did the cold mage
specifically want a man who had been in Melentser, or a
man who had been *geas* bound? Or both?

Too many questions, and no way to answer any of
them. Tehre sighed.

"You—" Fareine began, but stopped.

"I think…" Tehre began. "I think—"

But one of her other women interrupted her. She came
quietly to the door, waiting for attention.

"Yes?" Tehre asked the woman.

"A visitor, my lady," murmured the woman apologetically. All the household knew Tehre did not like visitors.

Tehre nodded, developing and discarding half a dozen

quick guesses about who might have come—Gereint again, not likely; a servant from the king, more possible but still unlikely; her brother? A messenger from her parents? Oh, probably a representative from Lord Fellesteden's heir; now *that* seemed likely. If unwelcome. Tehre tried to think of a highly regarded judge in Breidechboden to whom she might appeal, if there was going to be trouble from that direction after all...

But the woman said instead, "A foreign lord, honored lady: a Lord Bertaud. He didn't give his other name..."

"They don't," Tehre agreed, blinking in surprise. "In Feierabiand, they say Somebody son of Somebody. Or daughter, I suppose." But she was not thinking about this interesting difference in customs. She was thinking about the Feierabianden lord she had met in the Arobern's palace. He had been kind to her...or interested in her, or more likely her business with the king...She said, "I will see him, of course. In, well..." She looked questioningly at Fareine.

"Your reception room has half a disassembled catapult in it," Fareine murmured.

"My workroom?"

"Not suitable. It had better be here, I suppose. Let me get this plate—is the floor clean? Honored lady, you need to go put your hair up."

"It is up..."

"It's coming down," Fareine said inflexibly. "Go put it up properly. I'll go myself to welcome our guest. Does he speak Prechen? Well, at least that's in his favor..." She went out.

Tehre ran up to her room, took one surprised look in her mirror, tried to tuck recalcitrant strands of her hair back where they belonged, gave up, took down the whole mass, and began impatiently to put it up again. Luckily Meierin arrived to help.

"Fareine says your green dress is fine," the girl told Tehre. "But she said to remind you that you can't wear gold in your own house; where are your copper earrings? Oh, never mind, here we go," and she collected earrings and bangles of fine twisted copper wire and helped Tehre put them on. "I've never seen a Feierabianden lord," she remarked wistfully, stepping back to look Tehre quickly up and down and add one last copper pin to help hold her hair in place.

Tehre laughed. "Bring a plate of cakes in a few minutes."

"Thank you!" said Meierin, smiling back, and ducked out to run down to the kitchen.

Tehre left her room with a good deal of stately care to avoid losing any pins, descended the stairs, and entered the library once more.

Lord Bertaud...son of Boudan, was that right? Such strange names, so soft in the mouth. Tehre smiled and inclined her head and limited herself to, "Lord Bertaud. Welcome." That should be safe...

The Feierabianden lord had been standing by the table, gazing thoughtfully down at the map that was still laid out there. But he looked up when Tehre came in, took a step forward, and bowed very correctly. "Lady Tehre Amnachudran Tanshan," he said, careful on the rolling syllables of her name. It sounded very exotic on his tongue. He went on in Prechen: "I, ah...intrude, not?"

"No, no," Tehre assured him in Terheien. "Welcome. I, mmm, I am glad you visit." She did not remember the

Terheien for "visit," but he seemed to understand the Prechen. "Do you sit, honored lord? I mean, mmm…"

"Will you," the lord reminded her. "*Will* you sit. Yes.
I thank you."

Tehre nodded, grateful for the prompt. She said ruefully, "*Will* you. Yes. Thank you. I should have study
harder with my, my…teacher, when I am a girl. *Was* a
girl."

"Yes," Lord Bertaud agreed, smiling. "I, the same. I
speak Prechen for day, for week, but still not good."

"Well. Not *well*. Good is…the cakes." She gestured
to the plate Meierin brought in and silently offered
around. "The cakes are *good*. You speak Prechen *well*.
You see?"

"Yes. Though I think I do not speak well," added the
Feierabianden lord. He smiled at Meierin and took a
cake. Meierin blushed, returned his smile, and backed
away, bumping into one of the chairs as she retreated.

"Just leave the plate," Fareine said, casting a tolerant
glance at the girl and waving a brisk dismissal. "Go on,
go on, my dear, before you drop those." She took the
plate herself and set it on a small table where their guest
could reach it.

"You come, why?" Tehre asked, and gave Fareine a
puzzled glance when the older woman rolled her eyes.

Whatever objection Fareine found in the simple question, Lord Bertaud seemed not to mind it. He glanced
down, frowning, but Tehre could see he was only trying
to find the words he wanted.

Lord Bertaud said at last, "I hear a little of what you
say to, ah, the Arobern. I hear a little of what he say to
you. 'Trouble in the north,' you say. 'Griffins, desert,' you

say. The mage, the king's mage, Beguchren Teshrichten, he goes north, is that so? There is a problem there, where the desert is. Melentser. I ask the Arobern." He made a small, frustrated gesture. "He say, 'Do not worry, not your problem.' But I think of the griffins in Feierabiand this summer, and I do worry. I wonder, what problem? I wonder, what does the king's mage do in the north? I think maybe you know because your friend go with the mage, is that not so? So I come here to ask. Do you understand?"

Tehre thought she did. "The griffins brought their desert into Feierabiand, is that not so? But they were on your side, everyone knows that; in the end, they came in on your side against us and that's why your people could defeat our king—" She realized suddenly, partly from Fareine's expression, both that she was speaking rapidly in Prechen and that this last statement might be taken as an insult to Feierabiand. She stopped.

But Lord Bertaud only nodded and said, "Yes. That is true."

Well, no wonder he was worried. And if this Feierabianden lord had been involved in all those events during the summer, no wonder the king did not want to tell him anything important. The memory of that defeat must burn like fire to a proud king such as the Arobern.

It occurred to Tehre, belatedly, that perhaps she should not say more to Lord Bertaud when her own king had already rebuffed him. But, then, she really could not tell him anything; she did not *know* anything. She explained, this time careful to speak Terheien, "I wonder also. I ask many question also. I do not know. My lord king the Arobern, he says, yes, there is a problem. But he does not tell me what." She echoed the lord's earlier gesture of frustration. "I do not know."

"Ah." Lord Bertaud looked down for a moment. Then he looked over at the map on the table. "That?"

"Oh…" Tehre did not know quite what to say.

The lord got to his feet, went to the table, bent his head over the map for a long moment. He traced the crooked line of the Teschanken River with the tip of his finger. Tapped a spot in the far north, hard against the mountains. "Here," he said. "Melentser. Is that so?"

"Yes…"

"Yes." The lord turned from the map, crossed his arms over his chest, and regarded Tehre for a long moment. "You go north?"

Tehre, startled, began to say "no." But then, returning that earnest gaze, she did not deny it after all.

"You must be joking," said Fareine, gazing at her in total exasperation. "Except you never joke. *Tehre…*"

"I think," Tehre said slowly, in Terheien, not looking away from Lord Bertaud. "I think…maybe I go north." And, to Fareine, "Hush, Fareine! I can certainly go visit my parents, can't I? That's perfectly respectable, and I want to *know* what's happening in the north, not just sit here and worry! Don't you? And I'm a very broadly skilled maker, you know, much more so than Gereint. Maybe the king believes he has to have a man to deal with whatever is wrong; maybe Beguchren Teshrichten, for whatever reason, believes Gereint is just the right man, but maybe they both ought to consider their options a little more widely, do you think?"

Fareine, who had opened her mouth, looked faintly nonplussed and shut it again.

"Surely you wouldn't think I just wanted to chase north after a…a…" Tehre glanced quickly at the foreign lord and instead of *lover* finished with a far more obscure word: "Swain." She let the tartness of her tone suggest what she thought of this suggestion.

Fareine blushed, but she said stubbornly, "Tehre, dear, traveling with a foreigner? Meaning no offense to the honored lord, but your reputation isn't something to toss aside into the street—think of your honored father and lady mother!"

"There's no reason for anyone to think anything of my reputation one way or the other," Tehre said crisply. "As you know perfectly well. If anyone even notices anything I do, and why would they? But if I decide to visit my parents and then choose to travel in company with a respectable and honorable foreign lord who also happens to be going north, that's just good sense and why ever would anybody think twice about it?"

From Fareine's expression, she would have liked to argue with this, but she couldn't quite manage it. But she said, "Aside from 'everybody,' you might give a thought to what the *Arobern* might think! You're used to being cleverer than most people, but he's not a fool, Tehre."

Tehre paused. This was harder to answer. At last she merely shrugged. To the foreigner, she said again, "I think maybe I go north. My…" She could not remember the Terheien for "parents." "My father and mother live here." She touched the map. "I think maybe I go, ah, see my mother. One day, two, maybe. Then I go. But the…" "path," "street," "trail," what was the word for "road"? "The way is, ah, it is not safe. I find other person to go with. Yes?"

Lord Bertaud nodded. The swift exchange with Fareine

had been too fast for him, but he understood her slow Terheien well enough, however clumsy. It was the satisfied sort of nod that said, *I knew I was right.* He said, "I go north. You, me, is that so?"

"Yes," Tehre said, satisfied. "You are kind to offer."

"The Arobern—" Fareine began, herself far from satisfied.

But Lord Bertaud only shook his head and held up a hand, smiling at the old woman. He said to Tehre, but also to Fareine, "I do not ask leave to come and go." He smiled at Tehre, not a cheerful smile, but somehow confident and grim and sad all at once. "But I do not, ah. Speak well. I do not...I am from Feierabiand, anyone can see. It would be good to go with a person from Casmantium. You go north, I go north, is better, yes?"

Tehre met the foreign lord's eyes. She tapped the map again, north of Tashen, where her father's house lay. "You, mmm...You might come and will be, mmm, my mother's guest?"

Lord Bertaud looked at the map, and then carefully at Tehre. "Generous, you. Yes. I come."

Tehre remembered very clearly the Arobern telling her, *Go home.* "I," she said firmly, "also do not ask leave to come and go."

CHAPTER 7

When Gereint left Tehre's house, in the dark before dawn, he headed down the street with a long stride as though he knew exactly where he was going. But, though he had not admitted it to Tehre, he was actually struggling with a dilemma. Because the Emnerechke Gates were not the only gates that led out of the city. There was still the other road, the one that ran west toward Feierabiand.

Trouble in the north; yes, that was interesting. But then, an intelligent man would not necessarily rush *toward* trouble. If the *king's own mage* was heading north, how crucial could Gereint's presence be? All this *I need a maker* aside…there were no few strongly gifted, highly skilled makers in Breidechboden. Some of them must surely suit Beguchren's need, whatever that might be. If Gereint did not appear at the Emnerechke Gates at dawn, Beguchren Teshrichten could invite or compel one of them. Or a dozen. Earth and iron, the king's mage could probably march every maker from the city into the far north in one long *parade* if he chose. They'd probably feel it an *honor*. Gereint did not even want to know why the king's mage had found *him* so uniquely suitable for whatever purpose he had in mind. Though probably he was going to find out.

But when he came to the cross street, he paused. He looked for a while down one cobbled avenue, where chilly wisps of morning mist drifted pearl white in the lamp light of the streets, hiding the farther reaches of the city from view. Then down the other way, equally veiled in dim light and mist. North? Or west? If he went west, how far would he get before he found Beguchren Teshrichten waiting for him? The man was, after all, a mage. Gereint could easily visualize his inscrutable smile as Gereint came around some bend in the road and found him standing there, waiting.

Though he would more likely be sitting in the court-yard of some pleasant inn, sipping ale while he waited. Or an expensive vintage of wine, more likely. And he might not be smiling, if Gereint tried to run for Feierabiand.

Gereint also thought of the *geas* rings chiming down out of the Arobern's hand: *I shall find something else to do with these, do you understand?* The threat frightened and angered him in nearly equal measure. He might chal-lenge the king's mage. But he was afraid to try the king's own temper.

And he had told Eben Amnachudran, *You will not regret this by anything I do.* He had promised him, prom-ised Tehre. *No harm will come to you because of me.* Had he not said that to each of them? Promises like that were meant to be like stone, like earth: solid and endur-ing. Had he made his to be merely like the morning mist, dissolving at the first glint of sunlight? He stood for a moment longer, staring away to the west.

But then he turned, reluctantly, to the north.

The streets in this part of Breidechboden were wide, well cobbled, lit by glimmering lamps whose silvery light echoed the moon. The lamps shed their light across the facades of beautifully appointed houses and across the wrought-iron gates that guarded them. Many of the gate posts were topped with figures that rose out of the drifting mist, startling and vivid—grotesques with badger bodies and bat faces, or mastiff dogs, or slim falcons. The figures announced family and affiliation to any knowledgeable visitor. Gereint knew some of them: The bat-faced grotesques marked the house of some scion of the Pamnarech family, and the mastiff dogs indicated an affiliation with the noble Wachsen house...Gereint passed them by, feeling oddly homesick for the leaping deer that marked the Amnachudran townhouse.

No one else was out upon the streets. Gentlefolk were all abed, even their servants not yet stirring. Bakers might be already sliding loaves into their ovens and carters were certainly bringing produce to the market stalls, but there were no shops here. Yet somehow Gereint did not feel either obtrusive or out of place in this solitude. He walked quickly through the dim streets, his head up, listening to the sound of his own sandals on the cobbles. His own footsteps seemed very nearly the only sound in all the city.

The great houses of the nobility and the wealthy eased imperceptibly into the apartment blocks of the moderately well-to-do. Late carts and wagons were audible in the near distance; several wagons passed Gereint as he came to the part of the city that held shops and markets as well as apartments.

The first shutters clattered open in one of the apartments near at hand and a woman leaned out, peering at the morning with an expression of weary surprise, as though she'd never seen the gray predawn streets before in her life. Her eyebrows went up when she saw Gereint. She gave him an unenthusiastic but companionable nod, one person up too early to someone else up even earlier, but withdrew back into her apartment without waiting for him to return her nod.

The Twin Daughters glimmered near one horn of the crescent moon, almost lost in the pearl-and-lavender dawn, and then the sun rose behind Gereint and both the moon and the late stars were lost in its strengthening light. The sunlight struck off the east-facing walls of apartments and tenements and shops, turned plaster to ivory and brick to amber, gilded the damp cobbles, and outlined the heavy stone pillars of the Emnerechke Gates in fire.

Breidechboden rose up the hills behind him. High cirrus clouds stretched out in feathery peach and pink above the hills. The distant city, clean and silent in this moment between night and day, was all rose-washed ivory where the early light fell across it, or lavender and slate and pearl gray where the shadows of the hills still lingered. To his right, the open road led north through fields gone late-summer gold with ripening grain.

A fancy carriage with gold-scrolled doors and high narrow wheels, matching coppery chestnuts with braided manes standing before it, waited just inside the Emnerechke Gates, catching the eye with its stillness as well as its ornate decoration. The common carts and wagons made their way around the carriage, its fineness preventing their drivers from any display of annoyance more overt than a roll of their eyes.

Did Beguchren Teshrichten reject simplicity and plainness on principle? Though Gereint supposed it was at least possible the carriage belonged to some other lord... but he knew it belonged to the king's mage. He walked slowly toward it.

Not at all to his surprise, the driver set the brake, twisted the reins of the horse around the post, and jumped down to open the door for him as he came up. From within the carriage, Beguchren Teshrichten, his expression blandly uncommunicative, turned to give Gereint a little nod and gestured toward the bench beside him.

Gereint stepped up into the carriage, ducking his head under the low roof, and somewhat uneasily took the indicated seat. He would have preferred to sit farther away from the mage, but the carriage was a small one. Even so, Gereint felt the presumption of sharing the lord mage's bench. He sat as far toward the window as he could and said nothing. The driver picked up the reins and started the horses moving at an easy trot, weaving among the farmer's wagons and easily outpacing the common outbound traffic as they left the crowds behind.

"Good morning," Beguchren said, in exactly the polite tone he might have used to an honored guest in his own house. The little mage was as finely dressed as he had been the previous day: lace at his wrists and gold thread on his shirt, tiny pearls beading the cuffs of his high-heeled boots, and, on three fingers of his left hand, those delicate sapphire rings. He might have been heading across the city to attend a court function rather than departing Breidechboden for a long journey north.

Gereint asked, after a moment, "Do you always travel in such little state, lord mage? Just a driver, and no other servants or men-at-arms? You don't precisely fear brigands, I gather. No doubt for any number of excellent reasons."

"Just so," agreed Beguchren, smiling slightly. "But, Gereint, please call me by my name."

Gereint looked away, out the window of the carriage. Watched the scattered buildings on the outskirts of Breidechboden give way to low golden hills, the last of the morning mist burning off in the sunlight. At last he turned back at the mage, "Lord mage, why are we going north? And how far north, and where precisely? Melentser? Why did you go to such trouble to bring me—me, especially, with you? What are you doing, and what is my part in it?"

There was a long, thoughtful silence. Beguchren said eventually, "I need a maker. Not merely any maker with a reasonably strong gift. A man who has been *geas* bound for many years…I expect such a man to have gained, shall we say, certain predispositions and inclinations. Qualities that matter more than mere strength."

Gereint said drily, "Oh, yes: a capacity for loyalty?"

To his surprise, the mage laughed. "Hardly. No. That's a quality any man may either develop or not, I imagine, but I would hardly expect servitude to enhance it. No," Beguchren said, seriously now, "I mean, among other qualities, endurance. An ability to smother strong emotion. I might say, self-abrogation."

It was Gereint's turn for silence. A slave might certainly

develop all those qualities. But he was not at all certain he wished to know why the mage valued them. He asked at last, abandoning for the moment that line of inquiry, "How far north are you going?"

"We," Beguchren said gently. "How far north are *we* going? And we are going all the way, Gereint. To the place where the country of earth gives way to the country of fire."

"Melentser?"

"Perhaps."

"What if I refuse? What if I get down out of your fine carriage and walk away?"

"Walk away," suggested the mage, still gently, "and find out."

Gereint did not move. He said, testing carefully, "I'd find you in my mind, would I, compelling my direction?"

The mage's silver eyes glinted. "No. No, Gereint. That's one promise I believe I may safely offer you: I won't go into your mind again."

Gereint considered this. As promises went, that one seemed less solidly based than some. He allowed his tone to take on more of an edge, "Do you think I should trust you, lord mage? You asked me what I owe you, but I hardly know why you asked. It's clear enough what answer you think I should make. You believe I should do your bidding and walk at your heel like a dog."

Beguchren, refusing to be drawn, answered only, "Do you trust me, Gereint?"

Gereint was uneasily aware that, though there was no honest reason it should be true, the answer might be "yes." He said, "No, my lord."

"Perhaps you will learn to."

They had passed out of the immediate vicinity of Breidechboden. This far south, there were few woodlands, and those were cultivated as carefully as wheat fields, but for wood and game. The polite, civilized countryside rolled out endlessly green and fertile, blocked into neat fields and pastures and orchards. Sometimes beside the road and sometimes well away to the east flowed the Teschanken, riverboats running with the current down toward Breidechboden or hauled by teams of oxen back up toward Dachsichten.

More traffic passed north and south on the road: fancy high-wheeled carriages of men of property; plain coaches for ordinary travelers; riders in company or alone—everyone knew there was no risk of brigands between Breidechboden and Dachsichten. Gereint suspected there were more travelers than usual, northern folk uneasy at the new desert, trickling south in families or small groups. He remembered the patrol officer at the gates saying, *Wanenboden might be better*, and wondered if any southern city was actually going to welcome displaced or nervous northerners.

"The river runs low this year," Beguchren murmured. "You see how all the boats are small, with short keels and shallow drafts."

Gereint glanced at him, surprised. But the mage did not seem inclined toward further comment. When Gereint did not answer, silence fell once more.

They changed horses at a posting house along the river, trading the chestnuts for a pair of flashy bays with white feet and white faces. Beguchren permitted a short rest in the courtyard of the posting house while his driver assisted in leading the chestnuts away and then bringing up the bays to harness in their places. Beef pies appeared from the posting house, and good wine. Gereint, studying the horses, asked, "Do you *own* any plain horses, my lord?"

Beguchren appeared honestly surprised. "Why should one not enjoy beauty in everything, if possible?" he asked reasonably. "And they are fast, sturdy animals. We will trade horses once more today; I don't intend to stop for the night until we are well on the other side of Dachsichten. I hope to reach Pamnarichtan by tomorrow night—though I realize that requires an optimistic estimate of our pace. We will see what we can do to press on a little."

Gereint debated inwardly another moment, but finally asked, "My lord...why such haste? And why now? If the...the trouble earlier this summer created this problem, then why delay in Breidechboden while the days stretched out toward autumn?"

"We did not realize at once what we...that a problem had arisen. Then we took some time to consider what we might do."

"We?"

"The Arobern and his brothers and I, and others. We moved swiftly enough, Gereint, once we decided what direction to take. But whether it was fortune or fate that set you in my hand at the moment I needed you, even I cannot say."

Gereint guessed that whoever might have been involved in considering what they might do, the king and his mage had been the ones who had decided. He asked, "What do you want from me? What part do you mean for me to play?"

Beguchren gazed down at the table between his hands, so that it seemed he did not intend to answer at all. But at last he looked up, meeting Gereint's eyes. "When we reach the country of fire, I will answer all your questions."

Gereint stood up from the table, turned his back, and walked away.

The bays were harnessed, the remnants of the pies cleared away, the driver back on his high perch…and Beguchren had entered the carriage. Which did not move. The horses shifted restively, tossing their heads, impatient to go now that they were harnessed and ready. The driver held them. He did not look toward Gereint, who had stopped in the shade of the courtyard wall and now waited, arms crossed and jaw set, to see what Beguchren would do.

The answer appeared to be: nothing. The carriage waited. The posting house gate stayed open. The driver held the horses in place, though they mouthed the bits and showed something of a desire to jig sideways. Beguchren did not even look out the carriage window.

Not letting himself think about what he was doing, not letting himself consider whether he was making a decision or merely a test, Gereint swung about and walked away from the posting house, heading west. He clambered straight over a rail fence and strode across the pasture that bordered the road, ignoring the cattle that grazed in the distance. It didn't occur to him that there might be a bull until he was across the fence and then he would have looked foolish if he'd turned back. So he went on. The bright sunlit day seemed to close around him like walls, for all he could see the wide spaces of the pasture.

He needed to understand the king's mage. Just as Tehre tested the limits of structures in order to understand them, Gereint thought, a sharp defiance of Beguchren's intentions might reveal far more than quiet compliance ever could.

Even so, Gereint felt a strangely powerful sense of guilt as he lengthened his stride. *What do you owe me?* the silver-eyed mage had asked him, but neither of them had answered that question. Gereint was answering it now: nothing. But he knew that answer was false—

—the rough ground under his feet slid sideways. He staggered, took a quick step to catch his balance; his foot came down on the packed earth of the road rather than on the pasture grasses. The sun had abruptly shifted its place in the sky, shadows lay out at an odd angle; his head swam with the confusion of direction and place. The gates of the posting house stood near at hand, and by the gates, the fancy carriage with its matched bays. The driver was staring at him. The posting house staff had left their tasks and clustered by the gate, also staring.

But there was no movement at the carriage window. Having brought Gereint back to the posting house, Beguchren seemed perfectly content to wait all day for him to come back to the carriage.

If Beguchren wanted to compel obedience, why take away the *geas*? And if there was all this need for haste, why was he so patient now? Why not twist the world about and drop Gereint directly into his carriage? Or the both of them straight into place at the edge of the desert?

"Earth and ice," Gereint muttered. The philosopher Beremnan Anweierchen had written, *Obedience is a*

*quality a man imposes on himself; if it is imposed from
without, it is not obedience, but compulsion.* Anweierchen,
Gereint concluded, hadn't known what he was talking
about. All this pressing to get on, fresh horses waiting at
posting houses and this *Pamnarichtan by tomorrow night*
haste. And now Beguchren was willing to simply sit all
afternoon in that quiet carriage?

Finally, Gereint crossed to the carriage with long,
impatient strides, jerked the door open, stepped up to
the bench, and flung himself onto the seat. But when
Beguchren looked at him, he glanced down with a slave's
bland, submissive deference and murmured, "I beg you
will forgive the delay, my lord."

A trace of color actually rose in Beguchren's face.
"Gereint..." the mage began, then stopped and instead
leaned forward to tap the back of the driver's seat. The
driver eased the reins, and the horses, glad to be moving
at last, leaped forward in a canter rather than the customary collected trot.

Beguchren tried to catch himself against the jolt, but
he was flung first hard backward and then forward by
the lunging start of the horses. Gereint had no such difficulty; he put a foot against the opposite wall, closed a
hand on the edge of the window, and, without thinking,
put out his other arm and first caught the smaller man and
then braced him until the motion of the carriage steadied.
Then, embarrassed at both the familiarity and the very
automaticity of the response, he let go and drew away to
the farthest extent of the carriage.

The mage might also have been embarrassed. He
straightened his sleeve fussily, concentrating on that. He
said, not quite glancing up, "Thank you, Gereint."

Gereint barely looked at him, but answered in his most colorless tone, "Of course, lord mage."

Beguchren hesitated, began to speak, stopped, and finally said nothing. Silence stretched uncomfortably between them. Gereint could not decide whether he was satisfied or ashamed to have achieved this silence. He hoped the mage felt as uncomfortable with it as he did.

And perhaps he did, for he began at last, "Gereint..."

Gereint refused to look at him.

Beguchren sighed. He asked, "Should I have left you bound? Would you have been more comfortable under the compulsion of the *geas*? I might have left you bound right to the last. But I wished you to choose freely to come with me."

"As long as I don't choose freely to go my own way?"

"Just so."

Gereint shook his head, baffled. He should have been angry as well as baffled, but anger seemed to run out of him like water from a cracked fountain; he could not hold to it. "When you won't permit me to use the freedom you gave me, you can't expect an avowal of gratitude!"

"I don't."

"What do you *want* from me?" Gereint demanded.

Beguchren sighed. Nodded out the window. "At the moment, only your company on a pleasant, if long, day's journey."

Gereint set his jaw...then laughed suddenly. The argument seemed too ridiculous to keep up, when the mage continually slid sideways and left Gereint arguing alone. He said, "One day's journey and another, and soon enough we *will* be looking out into the country of fire. And you'll tell me then."

"I will."

Gereint only shook his head.

They traded the bays for young, energetic dappled grays at the next posting house, this time with less of a pause. As promised, they reached Dachsichten before dark and passed through the bustling town without stopping. Even the grays were long past any desire to run; the driver let them fall into a steady walk. Gereint asked no questions about when they might stop.

An hour north of Dachsichten, as dusk silvered the sky and the earliest stars glimmered into view, the carriage slowed, turned off the road, bumped gently across a grassy verge, and came to a halt beside a large pavilion of blue and ivory cloth, with orange and gold ribbons braided down its front, and more ribbons, bound to its roof, rippling in the breeze that came off the river. A fire leaped cheerfully before the pavilion; round white lanterns hung from poles on either side of its door. By their light, Gereint could make out half a dozen smaller tents around and behind the pavilion, blue and pink and flame yellow.

Men in the royal livery came to take the tired horses; another man, this one in the mage's own blue and ivory, appeared at the doorway of the carriage, placing a step and murmuring deferential welcome. Beguchren allowed the man to take his arm and assist him in stepping down. The mage, now that Gereint came to look at him carefully, looked drawn and weary. He turned at once toward the fire and pavilion.

Gereint stepped down from the carriage without assistance and walked aside, working off the stiffness of travel while watching the servants whisk around. He'd been surprised the lord mage had been content to rest overnight out in the open rather than in a proper inn. Now he wondered why he hadn't guessed what sort of arrangements had been made. Little effort had been spared; he could glimpse a low table within the pavilion and the silver glint of warming dishes.

Beguchren went into the pavilion and settled at the table; almost immediately one of the servants came over to Gereint with a formal invitation to dine with the lord mage. He followed the man to the pavilion without a word, ducked under the graceful awning, and settled on a cushion laid on the floor in lieu of a chair. There were other cushions and bolsters laid out and screens of fine cloth to block the rear of the pavilion into private rooms.

Gereint glanced around at the pavilion and the crowded table. "Luxurious."

Beguchren smiled. He took the cover off one warming dish and another, revealing plates of venison in gravy and quail in cream. Passing the quail toward Gereint, he said, "I didn't expect this, in fact. I asked for a simple tent and a change of horses. But the Arobern knew where I intended to stop, and it pleases him to make generous gestures toward his servants."

Gereint could not think of anything to say to this. His only experience of the king had not led him to expect generosity. Though, then, he was not precisely one of the king's servants. Or certainly not the way Beguchren Teshrichten was. He said at last, trying to mend his tone, "You have served the king...for a long time, I think?"

Beguchren inclined his head. "All his life. Though... at times less well than I might have wished."

Gereint guessed that the cold mage was thinking now

of the summer, of the griffins and the disastrous foray
into Feierabiand that had surely led now to this second
foray. Whatever its purpose. He might have asked again,
but he knew Beguchren would not answer. He might have
asked anyway, offered one little cut and another against
the man's temper... but he found, strangely, that he had
no heart for that game. He asked instead, simply, "How
far do you intend to go tomorrow? You're still thinking
of traveling all the way to the confluence of the two rivers, staying the night in Pamnarichtan? That must be fifty
miles from here, surely, for all we pressed hard today:
another long, hard day. Have you arranged for fresh
horses all along the river road, then?"

Beguchren glanced up thoughtfully, meeting Gereint's
eyes with a strange kind of appreciation that suggested he
had noticed Gereint's restraint. "I would like to get all the
way to Pamnarichtan, yes. But we will not be changing
horses, so I think we will likely not make it quite so far."
Also because of the earlier delay Gereint had caused, he
did not say. "Likely we will stop at Raichboden."

They would not actually stop at Raichboden itself. The
town was fifteen miles south of Pamnarichtan, but east of
the river; it was the southernmost town in the province
of Meridanium, for which the river was the border. But
there were a few amenities surrounding the ferry landing
on this side of the Teschanken, including a decent inn to
serve all the overoptimistic travelers who found the road
north stretching out longer than they'd hoped.

"We should reach Pamnarichtan by midmorning the
next day, I imagine," Beguchren added. "Then I think
we will go up toward Metichteran, cross the river on that
impressive bridge Metichteran boasts, and then simply

continue north toward Tashen. We can stop in Tashen. And from Tashen, we will simply ride north and west until we strike the edge of the desert."

Gereint nodded, keeping his expression bland with a slave's hard-earned skill. Eben Amnachudran's house was north of Tashen and east of the river. How likely were they, realistically, to stop there? Likely enough, he concluded. And if Lord Mage Beguchren Teshrichten found that Amnachudran knew Gereint and heard that story about Gereint bringing the master of the house back on a litter, how long would it take him to guess just who must have removed the *geas* brand? Not long, was the obvious answer. Gereint wondered whether Tehre's letter had yet arrived at her father's house, and what Eben Amnachudran might have made of it. He said nothing.

"I will ask you to be patient," the mage said quietly, mistaking Gereint's silence. "I know you are still angry with me. But we will come to the country of fire soon. So I ask you to be patient and bear with my reticence only a little longer."

Gereint met his eyes and, after a calculated pause, nodded a second time. But when he went aside to his private tent, he lay awake for a long time, thinking about the road north.

In the morning, Gereint half expected the Arobern's servants to pack up all the finery and ride along with Beguchren's carriage. But they only served an elaborate, if swift, breakfast while fresh horses were brought out. The horses were black mares with white feet and white stars on their foreheads and dark blue ribbons braided into their manes and tails. And, to Gereint's surprise, this time the horses were saddled and bridled rather than harnessed to the carriage. He looked at Beguchren, raising his eyebrows as he noticed that the mage was dressed this morning in clothing that, while still expensive and fine, was much more practical for traveling. Though there was still a little lace here and there, and he still wore those sapphire rings.

"As you said," the mage answered that look, "the roads in the north are not as good." He gave the carriage a look of regret and took another cheese-filled roll from the generous basket provided.

The roads were perfectly all right until north of Pamnarichtan, but Gereint did not challenge this putative explanation. He was not surprised when Beguchren took the reins of the first horse and gestured for the man to give the other horse's reins to Gereint; he was not surprised when not a single servant or man-at-arms mounted a horse to accompany them. He didn't *understand* it, but he wasn't surprised.

Beguchren, Gereint noticed, rode as though he'd been suckled on mare's milk, as the saying went. Well, perhaps that wasn't surprising. Any nobly born boy would be taught to ride young, and this was something a small and delicate boy might do as well as his larger brothers and cousins. If he'd had brothers and cousins. It seemed likely; most noble families were large.

He found he could, surprisingly easily, imagine the little lord as a boy. He'd learned that bland, inscrutable smile in boyhood, Gereint guessed, to hide what he felt when every other boy was bigger and stronger and, probably, treated their little cousin with contempt. Or worse, with casual disregard. Gereint was surprised by the strength of the sympathy he felt for that long-vanished boy.

They rode beside the river most of the day. They seldom spoke—Gereint had nothing to say if he couldn't
ask questions, and Beguchren seemed content with the
silence. The river spoke, filling what might have been
an uncomfortable quiet with continuous rippling babble
as it ran through reeds and across its pebbly bed. It ran
low, revealing shelves of gravel and sand abandoned by
the retreat of the water. Dragonflies perched on the reeds
and darted like jeweled needles over the brown water; a
kingfisher dove from the overhanging branch of a tree
in a dash of sapphire no less pure than the stones on the
mage's rings, and broke the water into glittering spray
where it struck after a minnow. The flatboats stayed far
out from the banks, keeping to the middle of the channel.
There were no keelboats; the water had drawn too far
from the bank where the oxen would have leaned into
their collars to haul the boats upriver.

There were few other travelers on the road. Those that
they passed were mostly going south, and mostly traveling in large parties. These met Beguchren and Gereint
with curious stares, but drew aside to yield a respectful
right-of-way; Beguchren was, despite his lack of a proper
entourage, still very obviously an important lord. It
occurred to Gereint that the small mage was deliberately
substituting a blatant display of wealth for the physical
size and strength he lacked. Once he thought of this, it
seemed obvious, even inevitable. But then he caught a
sardonic glint in the mage's eyes and was no longer sure
the explanation was anything so obvious, after all.

"Pamnarichtan and Raichboden, Manich and Streitgan
have all sent men to patrol the road," one man-at-arms
told them, turning away from his own company to ride

beside them for a few minutes. "In fact, all the northern towns are contributing; well, except for Tashen. You know how Tashen is: They're not personally having trouble, so what do they care? All the towns of Meridanium province, I should say, plus Pamnarichtan. We're all agreed we're tired of the brigands." He shook his head. "I don't know what's been worse, the dregs of Melentser who saw opportunity in their own city's misfortune, or the straggling refugees who put off the southward journey and made themselves into prey. Well, we're clearing them out—pushing the stragglers on south and hanging the scum who've turned to brigandage—but I wouldn't say it's exactly safe to ride along here just yet with only one retainer." He gave Beguchren a respectful nod. "Begging your pardon for my forwardness to say so, lord."

Gereint didn't comment on the man's taking him for Beguchren's retainer; in too many ways it was an uncomfortably accurate assessment. He gave the mage a sidelong glance, waiting to see how he would respond.

"I thank you for your concern," Beguchren answered in a mild, assured tone. "I have carefully considered this risk, and I am satisfied with my decision to proceed as I am. But I am glad to know that the northern towns are undertaking a permanent solution to the problem. Tell me, if you will, has the Arobern sent assistance from the south?"

The man-at-arms eyed the mage with sharp interest and deepening respect. "Lord, not so as I know."

"An oversight, I believe," Beguchren murmured. "In these unsettled times, perhaps unsurprising. Still, the cost of dealing with these brigands clearly arises from the resettlement of the people of Melentser, and as such the governors of the northern towns are entitled to reimbursement for some portion of their expenses incurred in the effort. Whose man are you? Geiestich? Warach?"

"Lord...my name is Gentrich Feiranlach, and I ordinarily command the southern cohort of the Raichboden patrol."

"Geiestich's man, then," said Beguchren, naming the governor of Raichboden. He produced—from the air, as far as Gereint could see—one of the intricately carved purple-dyed bone tokens that marked the authority of a king's man. He gave this to the man-at-arms. "Take this to Geiestich and tell him I suggested he apply for proper reimbursement. If he sends this token with his request, I think it will be met with favor."

The man-at-arms clearly thought so too, from the depth of his bow as he accepted the token. "Lord. Thank you, lord, and I know my lord the governor will be grateful. I beg you will permit me to lend you a reasonable number of men for the remainder of your journey, lord. The north would be ashamed if harm came to a servant of the king in our lands—"

"Thank you," Beguchren said patiently. "But I assure you, I have considered the risk, and I am satisfied with my decision to proceed."

The man-at-arms hesitated for a long moment. Then he bowed once more, accepting this dismissal, and reined his horse around, lifting it into a canter to catch up with his company.

"He thinks you're one of the Arobern's personal agents," Gereint commented watching the man go.

Beguchren gave Gereint one of his most inscrutable looks. "I am. Why else would I have that token?"

Gereint had no answer for this. He asked instead, "Why not accept the offered escort, at least? Surely brigands would at least slow you down a little."

"Us," the little mage said patiently. "Slow *us* down, Gereint. No, that possibility doesn't unduly concern me. If brigands are drawn toward convenient prey, why not let them come to us? It's easier than tracking them down, and a good deal better than letting them find truly vulnerable travelers to attack, don't you think?"

Gereint stared at the mage in surprise. "You're using yourself as *bait*?" This hadn't occurred to him.

"It's perfectly safe," Beguchren said, nevertheless sounding a little apologetic. "Or, at least, nearly."

"I don't doubt it." Gereint stared at him for a moment longer. The mage looked exactly the same: small and neat handed, fastidious and vain, weary with the day's travel. But he had changed shape yet again in Gereint's eyes.

They did not make it within sight of Pamnarichtan before dusk. They had not even made it within sight of the Raichboden ferry landing, though Gereint thought they must be getting close at least to that. He thought Beguchren might turn off the road to find a campsite, but the mage did not even seem to notice the dwindling light. They rode between the river on one side and, on the other, a dense scrubby woodland that seemed to Gereint to make excellent cover for brigands. Beguchren did not, of course, seem concerned about the possibility. For all Gereint knew, the mage agreed with him about the possibility of brigands, but thought it an advantage rather than a drawback.

The sun slid lower and lower in the sky, sinking behind

the woods that crowded the riverbank. Narrow fingers of golden light pierced through the tangled branches and stretched themselves across the road. The river turned from green to opaque gold as the angle of the sun shifted, and then to dusky blue. Yet, though he allowed his horse to fall into a gentle amble, Beguchren still did not suggest they halt.

Gereint hesitated. Then nudged his mare up beside Beguchren's and asked at last, "We're not stopping?"

Beguchren didn't even turn his head. "I do think we can at least come up to Raichboden before full dark, don't you?"

Indeed, no. Gereint shrugged and said instead, "All right. We'll press on to the inn at the ferry landing: fine. Then we'll go through Pamnarichtan by midmorning tomorrow, I suppose; reach Metichteran sometime in the afternoon, be in Tashen by supper time. Unless I decide to settle on the riverbank at Raichboden and fish instead."

There was a pause. Then Beguchren, turning his head at last, asked softly, "Do you think you're likely to do that?"

Gereint gazed at the ears of his mare. He did not look up. He didn't want to see Beguchren's unbreakable composure—but, if he had managed to disturb that composure, he didn't want to see that either. "You won't tell me what you want me to do for you until we reach the desert. But will you tell me *why* you won't tell me now?"

There was no response.

"You won't. You think if you tell me now, I'd turn this pretty black mare and ride back down the river road as fast as she can take me, though after a day as long as this,

I don't suppose that's all that fast. I don't know why the possibility concerns you, since you can use magecraft to hold me. Do you simply not want to put yourself to the trouble?"

"Gereint—"

Gereint looked over at the mage at last, a hard stare. "What will you do, my lord mage, if I fight you? You can turn the road about on me, but what if I simply sit on the riverbank and refuse to take a step? What then? Wait patiently until the season turns and the snow comes down? I hardly think so. So what would you do?"

Begurchren checked his mare, twisted in the saddle to give Gereint his full attention, and leaned on the pommel, frowning. "Gereint...please don't fight me."

"You put that as a request, but it's a threat." Gereint, perforce, had brought his horse to a halt as well. It mouthed the bit uncomfortably, and he found he was gripping the reins too tightly. He made his hands relax, with an effort.

"Not at all," Beguchren said mildly.

"A warning, then. Or will you tell me it's an appeal?"

"That's closer."

"Which?" But there was no response to that. Gereint shook his head. "You wanted a man 'with a great capacity for loyalty.' But why? It isn't loyalty you're after from me. You said you don't want the forced obedience of the *geas*. But that's exactly what you do want—only without the *geas*."

"No. It's true that that's what I have now. But it's not what I want."

The urge to say *Yes, all right, I'm sure it will be fine. Don't bother yourself about it* was amazingly strong.

Gereint shuddered with the effort to control that urge. For half a shaved copper coin, he would have whirled his horse around and ridden away—heading anywhere. Except such an attempt would not work. And he could not even bring himself to wish it would. "Are you doing this to me? Stop it!"

"I can't. I'm not precisely doing it." Beguchren paused, stroking his mare's neck as it fidgeted. He went on after a moment: "You're feeling the pull of a natural affinity. In a way, it's similar to the *geas*. I'm sure you feel the likeness. That's one reason it disturbs you. But this, unlike the *geas*, you can overrule, if you wish. You're overruling it now."

Gereint shook his head, trying not only to understand what the mage was saying but also to clear his mind. This wasn't at all like the *geas*; Beguchren was wrong about that. It was more like an inexplicable impulse, despite everything, toward trust. "Is this why you wanted this slow journey together, just you and me? To let this 'affinity' develop?"

"What does Andreikan Warichteier say in his *Principia* about the relationship between mages and their students? About how men become mages?"

Faced with these academic questions, Gereint found himself steadying—and knew Beguchren had asked them for that purpose—and couldn't even resent him for it, though he wanted to. Or felt that he ought to want to. He said, "Less than I wish he had, now. I'm not any kind of mage or potential mage—"

"How do you know?"

Gereint said, as quietly as the mage but with so much intensity that he might have shouted, "If you're so powerful, then whatever I am, skilled maker or poor excuse for a mage, *what do you need me for?*"

"I'll tell you once we reach—"

"The country of fire! Yes, so you say! You'll tell me, it will be something terrible, I'll refuse, and you'll force me to do it anyway—"

Beguchren held up a hand, shaking his head. "No, Gereint, there you are wrong, I promise you. What I will need you to do for me is nothing I or anyone else can force you to do. Or the *geas* would have sufficed."

Gereint controlled, barely, an impulse to fling himself down from the saddle and stride away into the woods. His hands were shaking, he found, and he closed them hard around the reins to hide the fact. He said tightly, "Why did you free me? To coax me to trust you? Did you think that likely to work?"

"Under these circumstances? No."

Gereint waited. But Beguchren did not explain, only started his horse moving again, gently, upriver. Gereint's mare followed without any signal from him.

Gereint shook his head. He said grimly, "Warichteier says that like calls to like, and that there's a natural affinity between mages and natural creatures of earth. You seem to believe I might be some sort of mage. I hope you haven't set all your hopes on that. I'm only a maker. But I'll stop fighting you. All right? I won't fight you, my lord mage. I'll go north as far as you wish, as fast as you wish. But I don't believe for a moment you don't intend to force me to fit your need. Whatever that may be."

Beguchren hesitated, his eyes on his mare's neck. He began to speak, then stopped, hunting for words. At last he lifted his gaze and began, "Gereint, necessity can bind a man more tightly than any *geas*. Magecraft," said Beguchren, "like any magic, is a natural quality. Warichteier was half right, but only half. A mage is...a point of focus in the world. A point where forces balance and pivot. Any mage is like that, though earth and fire mages balance different and opposing forces. When we study, what we learn is to notice what we're doing to the world and, hmm, how to bend in the right direction the pull we always exert, do you see? For all his learning, Warichteier was not a mage and he did not really understand magecraft. That is why his commentary on the subject is so opaque and not altogether accurate."

"A cold mage—"

"We say 'cold mage' when in a sense we mean merely 'a mage trained to oppose fire.' But if an earth mage develops his...inclination...to oppose fire, he gives up certain kinds of power in order to emphasize certain other kinds. Do you understand?"

Gereint didn't, but didn't like to say so, lest Beguchren realize he was speaking almost freely and stop.

"To be sure," Beguchren added, "an ordinary earth mage must give up certain kinds of, hmm, power as well. Whereas a gifted maker such as yourself is not any sort of mage: A gift is different in kind from magecraft. However—" He lifted a hand—to gesture, to demonstrate something, it was not clear. Because a short little hunting arrow flicked through the air not a hair's width from the mage's fingers and disappeared with a wicked little hiss into the dark river, and two more sank, humming, into the earth at their horses' feet.

Gereint would not have thought there was enough light left for shooting. Clearly there was. Mouth dry and heart pounding, he checked his horse. Beguchren had drawn up as well, peering into the dusky woods with no great alarm so far as Gereint could see. Another arrow whipped past in front of them. Gereint lifted his hands to show they were empty and muttered under his breath, "I thought this was *perfectly safe*?"

"It is," Beguchren replied seriously. "Or nearly. Shh. Don't frighten them away." As Gereint wondered how exactly either of them could possibly frighten away a troop of brigands—frown sternly at them?—the smaller man also held his empty hands out in token of surrender.

Gereint said grimly, "If that first one was a warning shot, it came remarkably close to hitting you—and if they just want to stay under cover and shoot us both, I don't know what's stopping them—"

"They might intend to take me as a hostage," suggested Beguchren. He didn't sound overly concerned about the prospect. "Perhaps someone among them has realized that they might send to my family to demand a rich ransom."

Gereint stared at him. "You believe they'll think that far ahead, with the men-at-arms of all the northern towns beating through the woods for them? I hope you have some way to protect us besides depending on the reluctance of murderous dog-livered cutthroat brigands to shoot us out of hand."

Beguchren gave him a look.

"Well, you haven't been very quick to show it, if you do!"

"Gereint, I should think you, of all men, had learned patience?"

"You might think so," Gereint muttered, and saw Beguchren's mouth twitch toward a smile. If the brigands hidden in the woods saw that smile, he thought, then if they had a thimbleful of sense among them, they'd sneak away from this camp as quietly as they'd come and not stop running till they hit the edge of the desert...Maybe they had. There was certainly no sound from the woods, and no more arrows. "Where *are* they?" he asked again.

"I think..." murmured Beguchren. "Yes, I rather think they are coming out now."

This was true. The brigands had finally decided that their quarry were truly at bay, and were slowly coming out into the moonlight. One, and then another, and then a third—all with bows—another, armed more simply with a club. A fifth man, and a sixth. "Not eager to close in, though," observed Gereint.

"You probably frighten them."

Gereint almost laughed. "Bows?" he reminded the smaller man.

"I don't suppose they'd have turned to brigandage if they were brave men—" But Beguchren fell silent as the men finally began to approach. There were eight altogether. Only three had bows—though three were certainly enough. The rest carried clubs. To Gereint, they looked alarmingly ready to use those clubs. Even eager. They looked warily at Gereint, but their glowers were directed toward Beguchren.

"It's my size," the mage murmured. "A certain sort of man resents wealth in a man smaller than he is. If you were the one wearing the rings, they'd still be planning to kill you, but they wouldn't feel they had to break all your bones first."

Gereint gave the smaller man an incredulous glance. "Of course they would. They resent me just for being bigger than they are, whether or not I'm wearing a lot of sapphires. I hope you have something in mind other than appealing to their generous natures."

"Do you think that's all of them?"

"All who are going to come out, at least."

Beguchren nodded. "I think so, too."

The leader of the brigands, a man nearly as broad across the shoulders as Gereint, hefted his club. He had a mean look to him, like a scared dog that nevertheless meant to bite. If he intended to take Beguchren as a hostage and let Gereint go in order to collect a ransom, it wasn't apparent at the moment. He looked a lot more like he meant to beat them both to death himself. He looked them over, then said, in a growling, contemptuous tone, "Where'd you hide the rest of it?"

Beguchren shook his head in gentle puzzlement. "The rest of—?"

The man gestured again with his club. "Those rings can't be all you've got. You're stupid, but you can't be *that* stupid. Everybody knows to hide their money." He flicked the club back and forth mockingly. "Get down off that horse, little dog-lord, and tell me where you put it. In the saddle cloth? The saddle? Huh?"

"I guess they're not thinking about hostages," Gereint murmured, glancing down at the mage. "If you're going to do something, now might be a good—" He stopped.

Beguchren had reached out across the distance that separated his horse from Gereint's and taken hold of Gereint's arm. He gripped hard, not as though he sought support, but more as though he needed to mark Gereint's position. He was gazing at nothing, his expression abstracted. After a moment, both the packed earth of the road and the black river that had been all but hidden in the dusk began to shimmer with a pale, cold radiance like moonlight through winter fog. The air chilled, as though the seasons had suddenly shifted forward straight to winter, passing through the rest of summer and all of autumn in an eye-blink. The pale light grew steadily brighter, though no warmer.

Most of the brigands simply gaped. Two of them started to edge back toward the woods, but they stopped before they had retreated more than a few steps.

Like moonlight, the cold light of the stones was gentle to the eyes. Though it was bright enough to cast shadows, Gereint did not need to squint through the light to glance at Beguchren's face. The mage looked perfectly calm and quite unmoved. The pearly radiance filled the whole road between river and woods. Like moonlight, the cold magelight stripped color from the world it revealed. The white feet of the horses gleamed like lanterns in the cool light; they sidled and backed, but did not panic. Gereint would have liked to panic himself, but did not dare. He reached out quickly to catch Beguchren's reins, afraid of what might happen if the two horses moved apart and the mage lost his hold on Gereint's arm. The tangled branches and leaves of the woods were black and dense; the river, rimed with ice at its near edge, glinted an almost metallic silver.

The brigands did not fall. They were dead where they stood. Frost sparkled on their faces and hair; their eyes were wide open and unblinking. Their skin was white as ice; their clothing stiff and glittering. The cold shattered their clubs and bows; the wood broke with clean, crisp snaps. The dangling bowstrings cast back the light as though they had been made of silver wire.

Gereint sat very still. Beguchren still gripped his arm; he did not want to find out what would happen to him or to his horse if the mage let go. The pale light was ebbing at last, washing slowly down out of the air like fog, sinking into the earth and water. It left frost behind, spangling the ground like a fine diamond net. The cold eased as the world remembered summer warmth; the natural moonlight, now alone, seemed pallid and weak.

Beguchren drew a deep, slow breath and let go of Gereint's arm.

Gereint immediately backed his mare half a dozen steps. He was shuddering, not entirely with the lingering cold.

Beguchren blinked, shook his head, breathed sharply, and straightened his shoulders. Then he gave Gereint a sharp look, seeming for the first time to realize Gereint's horror. "What I did was swifter and kinder than hanging."

Gereint took a breath, but stopped without speaking. Took another breath and let it out again, still without saying a word. He looked around at the eight dead brigands. As he stared, the first one fell at last—stiffly, as a rigid board might fall, not limply like a shot deer. Then the second. Gereint tried not to flinch at the heavy thudding sounds as first one man and then the other hit the ground. The horses pricked their ears forward in nervous curiosity at this strange human behavior. When they shifted and stepped, their hooves left dark prints in the frost.

Gereint made himself meet the mage's eyes once more. He said at last, "You're one of the king's agents. So you had the right."

Beguchren inclined his head. "Anyone has both the right and the duty to clear the road of brigandage if he can. But, yes, the Arobern specifically asked me to assist local efforts as I found the chance." He paused. Then he said gently, "I think we can get to Raichboden yet this evening. I don't think we would be comfortable camping along the river in the dark."

"No," Gereint agreed grimly, and put his horse into a trot, slightly too fast a pace for the dim light, but it seemed as glad as he to leave the icy brigands to thaw behind them. He did not even want to think about the dreams he might have this night—if he dreamed; he doubted he would sleep at all and probably that was just as well. He glanced involuntarily over his shoulder as a third brigand fell, with a ringing, crystalline crash, behind them.

They found the inn at the Raichboden ferry no more than a mile farther north. The ferry was not at the landing but tied up at the dock on the town side of the river. Or not actually *at* the dock; the water level was so low that the ferry had simply been run up on exposed mud flats near the dock and tied up there. Fortunately, the inn on their side of the river was a good one, and well accustomed to late-arriving travelers. It had a small but decent private room, with two clean beds and, best of all, a bath basin already filled with steaming water. Beguchren provided the soap. The soap was smooth textured and rose scented, exactly the sort of soap Gereint would have expected the

mage to carry if he'd thought about it. He almost wanted
to laugh. He would have laughed if he'd been trying to
use this fine soap to scrub grease off pots, rather than
the memory of death off his body. He was glad to use
the bath first, while the king's mage arranged for men
to go back down the road in the morning to collect the
bodies for a proper, if symbolic, hanging. Beguchren also
arranged for broth and bread, neither of which Gereint
thought he could stomach.

"A little broth, at least," Beguchren said quietly. "You
need something."

Gereint accepted a mug, though he merely turned
it around in his hands rather than sipping. He couldn't
decide whether the rich, meaty smell was appetizing or
nauseating.

Beguchren said softly, "It's not precisely honorable, I
know—"

"It's not a sport," Gereint said grimly. "Or a hunt. Do
you think I don't know that?"

"Of course you do."

"I'm surprised you couldn't just whistle for them to
come crouching trustingly to your feet like dogs, and then
freeze them solid with your magelight—"

"Gereint!" Beguchren set down his own mug so
sharply the broth spilled onto the table. "Please don't
mistake brigands like that for men like yourself. There's
not one of them, gifted or not, who hadn't turned his back
on *any* kind of trust. You know that is true."

Gereint made no answer.

The mage went on more gently, "Nothing could have
saved them, even any among them who might somehow
have retained some trace of decent human sensibility. If

taken by men-at-arms, they would all have been held for hanging. Would that have been kinder?"

Gereint bowed his head a little.

"Can you eat something? Will you let me—" Beguchren paused. Then he went on, but with an odd note of constraint in his light, smooth voice: "Will you permit me to ease your rest tonight? If you wish, I can ensure that you do not dream. Will you take my word that I would do nothing but give you dreamless sleep?"

Gereint looked over at the mage. He could see that Beguchren expected him to refuse and guessed as well that, surprisingly, he might be hurt by the refusal. He said finally, "I'd take your word. But I think even men such as those are worth one or two bad dreams."

Beguchren gazed at him for a moment. Then he nodded. "So long as you can rest a little. It will be a long day tomorrow; almost as long as today. I'd like to get at least to Tashen tomorrow, if we can. Past Tashen, if possible."

"Past Tashen" was very likely to mean right into Amnachudran's lands, if Beguchren insisted on going upriver on the east side of the Teschanken. One more worry to run through Gereint's dreams. He didn't let his expression change, but merely nodded and said, "And then the day after, the desert." He didn't say, *And then you can end all this mystery and tell me at last what you mean to do in the griffin's country.* But he didn't need to. Beguchren bowed his head in agreement.

Gereint stood up and glanced inquiringly from one small narrow bed to the other.

"Whichever you like," said Beguchren.

Gereint nodded. He didn't, under the circumstances, wish the mage a pleasant night.

CHAPTER 8

Immediately outside Breidechboden, the road that led west toward the ornate and wealthy city of Abreichan widened enough for four carriages to travel abreast. Indeed, for the entire distance between Breidechboden and Abreichan, the road was that wide. And for that whole distance, it was paved with great flat stones quarried from the local hills and lined with tall plinths topped with grim-faced stone soldiers chiseled roughly out of granite. This road was always guarded, those carved soldiers proclaimed. Travelers journeyed under the protection of the Arobern kings. Brigandage might from time to time be a concern in the wilder north, but here in the broad, rich lands of the south, that protection was constant and powerful. Only after a traveler passed west of Abreichan and pressed on toward the little mountain towns of the far west did that protection become less reliable. After the Arobern completed the planned improvements to the mountain road, that might well change: the king would not want brigandage to soil his new road.

Tehre wished they were actually traveling west. She had never even been so far as Weierachboden, far less Abreichan, which everyone knew rivaled Breidechboden in splendor and ostentation. But even more than she wished to see the cities of the western plains, she longed to go all the way to Ehre and watch the builders and engineers of Casmantium go about the business of flinging their great road through the mountain passes to Feierabiand. The engineers would be carving their new road out of the sides of the mountains, bracing narrow paths that overhung desperate precipices, building buttresses to make a level road where nothing level had ever existed, bridging steep-sided chasms with arches and architraves and, possibly, hanging bridges with wrought-iron chains...Tehre had not even realized, until she turned her face to the west and put Breidechboden at her back, how much she would have loved to take this road *all* the way.

But they were only taking the western road to encourage casual observers to think that Lord Bertaud was heading back to Ehre; he might not ask the Arobern for leave to come and go, but then neither was he inclined to throw open defiance in the king's face. Nor, once she thought about it, was Tehre.

Lord Bertaud had brought a small entourage, as Tehre ought to have guessed he would. A foreign lord was hardly likely to travel anywhere in Casmantium alone. He'd brought a couple of men-at-arms and a driver and a servant. They were his own people, Feierabianden. Not one of them had more than a word or two of Prechen; no wonder Lord Bertaud had wanted Tehre's company for this journey.

Nor, of course, could Tehre travel alone amid strangers. She hadn't initially thought of this, a failure of sensibility about which Fareine had found a great deal to say. Fareine herself had not come; someone needed to supervise the household, and she was too frail in these years to travel quickly or easily, and after all this was not *really* a leisurely journey home. Or at least, in the event, it might prove to be something other than a leisurely journey home.

So Meierin had come. The girl had never been out of Breidechboden and was eager to travel, and Tehre liked her—and, more important, Fareine approved of her.

"She is a responsible child, and she has some sense," Fareine had told Tehre. "And she's young enough to think long days of travel are an *adventure*." The old woman had shaken her head in wistful regret for her own past youth, when she, too, had longed for travel and perhaps even for adventure.

Lord Bertaud's carriage was a good one, well built, but plain...He probably had a fancy one to show off his consequence. This one was much better for quiet travel. And comfortable. The seats were broad and well cushioned, and leather cushioned the windowsills below sheer curtains that let in light while keeping out dust. There was enough room on both the front and rear benches to allow three people to sit together—even four, if they were slender or friendly. Certainly there was ample room for Tehre and Meierin to sit facing forward, Lord Bertaud having courteously taken the backward-facing bench. Tehre gazed out to the west. The early sun struck the distant stones of the road to gold; it unrolled, gleaming, through all that gentle country toward Weierachboden, and she wished again they were going west.

Meierin touched Tehre's sleeve, and she became aware that Lord Bertaud had said something to her. She blushed with embarrassment, having no idea what he had said. Meierin could only shrug helplessly; the girl did not speak Terheien, of course, and probably also had some difficulty understanding the foreigner's accented Prechen.

"I beg your pardon?" Tehre said—then realized she'd spoken in Prechen and paused, searching for a similar phrase in Terheien.

But, "No," said Lord Bertaud, and borrowed her own phrase: "I beg your pardon, Lady Tehre; I did not mean to, ah." Looking frustrated, he said something in Terheien, then added in Prechen, "You were thinking. I did not mean to bother."

"It doesn't matter at all," Tehre answered quickly, then groped for the proper phrase in Terheien. But Lord Bertaud was nodding politely, so apparently he had understood. Tehre wondered how to explain that she was always drifting into abstraction and that if Lord Bertaud worried about interrupting her thoughts he would never be able to speak to her at all. Though she had to concentrate, to speak Terheien. If one took language as a *made* thing, words and syntax and the thought behind both, then did that imply that makers ought to be able to work with language somehow? Well, Linularinan legists did, in a way, though as a tool rather than as a product.

Gereint would have been the perfect person with whom to discuss this idea: He'd know if one or another of the great philosophers had already considered it. In fact, he'd probably know if a minor, obscure philosopher had. Or a poet. Maybe especially a poet...She wondered where he was at this moment, and whether he might be discussing some peculiar philosophical idea with Beguchren Teshrichten. She blinked and sighed, gazing out the window through the sheer curtain, finding that they were passing now through the villages and sprawling farms that lined the western road. Soon they would find some little country road that would lead them around to the north...

"Lady Tehre," Meierin said, in that patient tone that meant Tehre had forgotten something. Tehre blinked at her. The girl said, "Lord Bertaud wanted to show you..." and her voice trailed off as Tehre exclaimed in dismay.

She turned to the Feierabianden lord. "I always distract," she said apologetically. "Please forgive." She concentrated on her Terheien and asked carefully, "What do you have?"

Lord Bertaud showed her the small map he had brought, turning it so Tehre could see it. "Where?" he wondered.

Tehre leaned forward, studying the map with interest. It wasn't detailed enough to show the little roads around Breidechboden; it showed only the great cities and largest towns. And the river, of course, for it was the Teschanken that gave life and prosperity to southern Casmantium.

Tehre braced a hand on the seat against the mild jolting of the carriage. "Here," she explained, showing the foreign lord their approximate location. "We go here. This way. Around to the north, to the river road. Then to Dachsichten."

"Dachsichten," repeated Lord Bertaud, trying out the name. His tongue gave it a strange, soft pronunciation, more like "Dashenten." He looked at Tehre, eyebrows rising, half smiling at his own incorrect pronunciation.

"Dachsichten," Tehre told him, enunciating the name slowly and carefully, emphasizing the breaks in the word. "Dachsichten." Impatient with leaning awkwardly forward, she moved to sit next to the foreigner, bending to avoid knocking her head into the low roof of the carriage and catching awkwardly at the window as the vehicle jolted.

Lord Bertaud, eyebrows lifting with surprise, nevertheless caught her hand to steady her as she changed seats.

She dropped onto the seat next to him and began to point out the towns on the map, starting in the southwest of Casmantium and working her way east and north. She pronounced each one carefully and slowly, pausing to let Lord Bertaud try each word before she went on to the next. "Ruchen. Abreichan. Weierachboden. Wanenboden. Breidechboden. Dachsichten. Geierand—that is, mmm, close? Close to Terheien, yes?"

"Yes," Lord Bertaud agreed, looking grateful that one of the names, at least, came easily to his tongue. "The rest, no." He shook his head in rueful dismay over the other names. "So hard to say! There should be a way to learn easy. More easy?"

"More easily," Tehre told him, and wondered whether, if one treated words as materials and languages as mechanisms...and syntax as joints...hmm. When constructing a mechanism, the trick was to see it, hold it whole in the mind while one's hands worked with the materials. The maker's clear and focused intention was what set quality into a made thing. What would the equivalent of that focused intention be if one was working with something intangible like language? She asked suddenly, "Feierabianden places? Names?"

Lord Bertaud gave her a puzzled look.

"Give—say—Feierabianden names?" Tehre wondered how she could put her request more clearly, but after a moment, he seemed to decipher her meaning.

"Terabiand," he said obediently. "Bered, Talend, Nejeied, Sepes, Niambe, Sierhanan, Sihannas, Annand, Tamiaon—"

Tehre held up her hand, stopping his recital so she could think. Words and syntax, yes, but also something else. She didn't quite mean "pronunciation." Style, one might say. Like the style of the palace in Breidechboden, all massive stonework and flying buttresses and architraves, those last built stubbornly straight although anyone could see they would crack; that aggressive, heavy style was entirely different from the graceful and modest wooden buildings of the forested north. Hmm. Words and syntax and style...One would not express these abstractions with mathematical equations, but perhaps one might find a way to express the components of a language in some relatively precise way. Hmm...

Tehre blinked back to awareness of the carriage with Meierin touching her hand, and realized they were no longer moving. They had stopped. She gave the girl a raised-eyebrow look of inquiry.

"There is a farmhouse here," Meierin explained, not quite hiding a smile. "It is after noon? You must want something to eat?" It was plain Meierin had received firm instructions from Fareine about feeding Tehre.

"There is a house here where they sell food," added Lord Bertaud, sounding a little apologetic about it. "If you wish, we stop here for a little while?"

His inflection suggested that this halt was up to Tehre, that they might simply go on if she preferred, but after all, it was his carriage. Besides, now that she thought of it, Tehre *was* hungry. She allowed Lord Bertaud to help her and then Meierin out of the carriage, turning to gaze curiously at the farmhouse with its trestle tables and long benches. Clearly a lot of travelers passed this way, and the farmer—or his wife—had decided to make the most of the convenient road that ran so close to their house. Theirs was not the only carriage that had stopped here for a midday break. The tables were already loaded with dishes, drawing in travelers with enticing smells of roasting meat and baking bread.

"Did you pay the women here?" she asked Lord Bertaud.

"You are my, ah, my..."

Guests, Tehre presumed he meant. "Not at all," she corrected him. "I am glad to travel in, ah, in your protect, Lord Bertaud, but you are *my* guest." She shifted gratefully back to Prechen. "Meierin, pay the woman. Remember the honor of my family and be generous." There *had* to be a better way to learn a language than all that fumbling for half-known words...She wandered toward the table, wondering if there was roasted chicken.

There was roasted chicken. And beef pies. And eggs baked in pastry. No wonder so many people stopped here. Tehre nibbled thoughtfully at a bit of chicken, set her plate aside, and said to Lord Bertaud, "Say for me a, mmm, a story. Yes?"

The foreigner smiled uncertainly. "A story?"

"Of your travel? Or a story for children? Any story. Say first in Prechen and then in Terheien. Yes? Please?"

Lord Bertaud tilted his head, still uncertain and also curious. "Same story? In Prechen and Terheien?" Smiling, he made a comment in Terheien that was too quick for Tehre to catch but was probably something like, *"Well, I suppose we both need the practice, don't we?"*

He told a children's story about three foxes and a rabbit. He told each bit of it first in flowing, graceful Terheien and then in halting Prechen. The story took the rest of the midday break and a little longer than they had probably meant to stop, but Lord Bertaud was too easy-natured to break off once the farmwife's children and several of the travelers drifted over to listen.

"But the third fox wasn't clever, really," protested one of the children after the story ended. "He was just lucky. The rabbit was the clever one, really."

"The rabbit was a little too clever for her own good, don't you think? Like quite a number of little rabbits," said her father, a carter, smiling. He gave Lord Bertaud a little bow, swinging his daughter up to his broad shoulder to carry her back to his cart. "Thank you, honored sir. Well told, may I say so?"

Tehre barely heard the other travelers murmur similar comments. She was trying to frame words in her mind, as she might have placed bricks in a wall or stitches in a tapestry. They were harder to work with than bricks or thread. Or perhaps it was the nebulous nature of the framework into which she was attempting to set them.

She was not really aware of re-entering the carriage or of the jolt and sway as they turned back onto the road.

After a time, Meierin said something she didn't pay any attention to. Finally Lord Bertaud leaned forward and said questioningly, "Lady Tehre?"

Him, Tehre noticed. He had all of Terheien ready on his tongue and in his mind: a river of words, an *ocean* of language. She could feel it in him, almost as though it had physical weight and was drawn by powerful tides. Tehre offered him her hand.

He took it, a little hesitantly. Tehre closed both her own small hands firmly around his broad one, and built a great wall between them. She built it of words, Terheien on his side and Prechen on hers. She defined the wall as a dam between one language and the other. Then she opened a sluice gate in the dam and locked it in place. Then she opened her eyes—realizing for the first time that she'd closed them—let her breath out, and said ruefully, "The hard part is that you have to get the whole thing in place at once, don't you, or it won't hold at all, and you have to put in the sluice at the same exact time you're building the dam or you won't get it in right. I think I got it right. *Did* I get it right?" She looked inquiringly at Lord Bertaud.

He was staring at her, astonished. "You—what did you do?"

"Am I speaking Terheien?"

"Yes!"

"Then I did get it right." Satisfied, Tehre glanced around for writing materials. Then, frustrated, she sighed and cast her hands upward. "Meierin, this is so provoking! Will you remember to find some quills and paper? I know I won't remember. Oh, I beg your pardon, am I still speaking in Terheien? Here, let me…" She built a language sluice for the girl as well. It was easier this time because she could use the wall she'd already made, but she longed for a quill and paper to help organize her ideas about the building of insubstantial structures. Hadn't Brugent Wareierchen said something about mathematics being a kind of making? Was that at all the same as language being a making?

Gereint would know—she wished Gereint was here; she wished she could show him what she'd made and find out what he thought about it—maybe he could think of a way to make it more generalizable...or get around the problem of needing somebody to hold each language in place on either side of the wall...It would be nice if you didn't actually have to have someone who knew Terheien at hand in order to build this sort of structure, but at the moment she couldn't see any way around that... She said, "Make a note, Meierin, would you? I want to look up what Wareierchen said about law and magic, and whether he said anything about language as an abstract making when he was writing about law. I can look that up in my father's library. Don't let me forget about that."

Meierin nodded, her eyes still wide and stunned. "Are you—are you speaking in Terheien?" She turned to Lord Bertaud. "Honored lord, is she—*is* my lady speaking in, in Terheien?"

"You are both speaking Terheien," the lord said, shaking his head. He didn't glare at Tehre, exactly, but clearly he wanted to. "Am I speaking Prechen?"

Tehre was embarrassed. "If we all keep forgetting which language we're speaking, I'll try to think of a way to make it easier, but I think an ability to keep track will come with practice."

"Lady Tehre—" The Feierabianden stopped, shook his head again, and said, "I believed you to be a maker. But I think, esteemed lady, you must instead be a mage? I did not realize—"

"I'm not precisely a mage," Tehre said, surprised. "It's just as well: Mages are so impractical, you know." Then she wondered which language she was speaking and concentrated on listening to the sound of her own words. She went on slowly, barely paying attention to what she was actually saying: "And they sacrifice so much of their natural character as they develop their magecraft, don't they?" She was still speaking Terheien. She repeated the sentence in Prechen, carefully. She tried, experimentally, to mentally order a lecture on the sort of stresses that fracture wood as opposed to steel, concentrating on the shape of her sentences...In fact, the way she framed ideas seemed to shift a little depending on which language she let come to her tongue. That was unexpected. She should try poetry. That should offer interesting insights about the nature of language. "Lord Bertaud, do you know any poetry?"

"I'm frightened to admit to any knowledge of anything whatsoever," murmured the foreigner, his eyebrows rising. "Esteemed mage, I don't understand how you did this, but I—"

Tehre shook her head quickly. "I'm not a mage, truly. Haven't you been listening? A mage is a...a focal point for power, you know? Or so Warichteier says, and I suppose he's right, he is about most things, I believe. I'm not like that."

Lord Bertaud raised his eyebrows. "Aren't you? I suppose a Casmantian maker understands the difference between making and magecraft..." But his tone was faintly doubtful.

Tehre shrugged impatiently. "I just think about things. Though I didn't know I...I've never actually thought about language before. It's interesting what you can do, isn't it, if you think about language the right way?" She considered pronunciation. "I suppose...No, that doesn't make sense. Or maybe...no. Hmm." Perhaps pronunciation had to do with capturing the style of a language... "I *do* wish I had a proper quill and some paper," she said, with sudden, intense impatience. "I can't think properly without a decent quill in my hand."

"I will find for you the very best paper and quills available in Dachsichten," Lord Bertaud promised her. "If you wish me to tell you another story, lady, believe me, you have only to ask."

Tehre laughed. But she hoped he remembered his promise to find writing materials. Or that Meierin did. She already knew she would probably be distracted somehow and forget.

In the event, Tehre was indeed distracted from any possible concerns about feather quills and good paper long before they arrived at Dachsichten. Because that very evening, they saw their first griffin.

The griffin was flying fast, low above the river, heading south. They saw it shortly before dusk, after they had stopped for the evening. No inn being convenient, they had simply camped beside the river, though with the supplies Lord Bertaud's retainers carried, this did not present much hardship. The campsite was a pretty one; three other parties had stopped in it as well, so there were tents scattered like a field of red and blue flowers all across the campsite. Lord Bertaud had set up his tents so they overlooked the river.

Tonight the sunset had piled up in rich purple and gold in the west; heavy golden light lanced through breaks in the towering clouds and set the river alight with reflected glory, poured across the rolling fields on the other side of the river, and turned every stalk of ripening grain to rich gold.

In this light, the griffin, too, looked like it had been fashioned by some tremendously skilled craftsmaster. The long feathers of its wings might have been made of black iron and red copper, its lion pelt of the smoldering coals that glow at the heart of a fire. Its savage beak and talons flashed like metal. The sun threw its shadow out across the river, but its shadow was made of light, of fire, and was not a real shadow at all. Tehre thought it looked altogether beautiful, but almost more like a clockwork mechanism than a living creature; she was half inclined to look for the cords that suspended it from the sky.

The griffin was soaring like a great eagle, wings stretched out wide and still, seeming to rest suspended in the air. Its motionlessness added to the illusion that it was not really alive. It looked a little, Tehre thought, like a butterfly in amber, for the light that surrounded it seemed richer and heavier and somehow more concentrated than the sunlight that fell across fields and road and river. It did not seem to notice them; it did not seem to notice anything. It was moving fast, its fierce eagle's glare fixed on the river before it. But then, as the griffin whipped past the campsite, it suddenly turned its head and looked with swift intensity at the travelers who, frozen with astonishment, stared back at it. Its eyes were black and fierce and utterly unreadable. Tehre wondered what it saw and whether to it they looked like they were not quite like living creatures.

Then it was past, gone. The sun dipped below the distant horizon. It was suddenly, comprehensively, dark. For a long moment, despite the light of the half-dozen campfires various travelers had lit, it seemed that the griffin had carried all the light of the world away with it.

There was a long, fraught silence. Then a sudden babble of voices, everyone in the campsite speaking at once, asking one another what they'd seen and what it meant and had it really been a griffin and what did that mean and would it come back and what would it do if it did return? Everyone in Lord Bertaud's camp was asking the same questions, too. Except, Tehre saw, for the lord himself. The foreigner was not paying any attention to anyone else. His expression was set and blank, as unreadable as the griffin's. He was standing perfectly still, staring steadily downriver after the griffin.

CHAPTER 9

Just at dawn, Beguchren led Gereint out to the inn's small, empty courtyard and stood watching with bland patience as their horses were saddled and brought out. None of the inn's few other guests was up quite yet, though the inn staff were stirring about their morning tasks. A girl, bringing fresh loaves back to the inn from some local baker, timidly came over to offer them a loaf. She didn't dare speak to Beguchren, but gave the warm bread to Gereint, along with a shy smile. And the inn-keeper himself came out of the stable along with the boys who led Beguchren's black mares, having personally assured that the horses would be ready no matter the early hour. Probably that story about the dead brigands they'd left a few miles south had assured attentive service. Though, at that, Beguchren's imperturbable calm and expensive rings might have been enough.

So they left the ferry landing almost as they had entered it, in pale, shadowy light. The river was still all but invisible in the dimness, just perceptible as a black smooth ribbon and a ripple of sound. The fat crescent of the moon still stood overhead, with the Twin Daughters glimmering by one of its sharp tips.

That was the moment when they saw their first griffins. It had never occurred to Gereint that the griffins would leave their desert to venture this far into the country of men. But he saw at once that Beguchren was not surprised.

There were five griffins. They were flying high, so high they might almost have looked like eagles, except somehow they didn't look anything like eagles. Even at this distance, the sunlight struck off them as though they were made of gold and copper and bronze, but that wasn't why they caught the eye. There was something else, something about the way the sky glinted and changed above them, something about the way the wind itself almost seemed to glitter as it tangled in the feathers of their wings. They flew as geese fly in the fall: in a narrow spearhead formation. They traveled in a long curving arc that carried them from the southwest away to the east and north. They could not be coming from their desert, not from the southwest. But if they were returning to it, then they were strangely far east, and heading more easterly still.

Gereint stared after the griffins until they vanished into the far reaches of the distance and then pulled his gaze, with some effort, from the sky and turned to Beguchren.

The mage was not looking at him. He was gazing steadily into the sky after the griffins. His expression was as blandly inscrutable as ever, but his mouth was set and there was a tightness around his eyes that suggested he was not quite as calm as he appeared. His grip on his mare's reins was so tight his knuckles were white. As Gereint watched, he loosened his hold on the reins and set one hand on the pommel of his saddle instead, seemingly for balance, or possibly support, for then he leaned forward and bowed his head over the mare's neck as though suddenly gripped by weakness.

"Are you well?" Gereint asked tentatively.

Beguchren did not look up. "Of course."

Gereint paused. Then he said tentatively, "I'm surprised to see them this far south. Or this far east."

The mage straightened in his saddle, put his shoulders back, lifted his head, and said, "Yes." His tone was perfectly neutral. He did not glance at Gereint, but stared straight down the road between the ears of his horse.

Gereint had thought he might ask again, given the sighting, whether the mage might tell him why they were going north. Perhaps seeing griffins would count as coming to the desert? But something in Beguchren's blank neutrality made him hesitate, and the moment passed. He said instead, "It should be possible, as you suggested, to reach Pamnarichtan this morning and Metichteran sometime this afternoon."

Beguchren took a breath. Then another. He managed a slight smile, giving Gereint a sideways look. "You don't wish to go fishing?"

"No," Gereint said slowly. "Or even if I had, not after seeing the griffins. Somehow this doesn't seem like a morning for fishing." He concentrated, in fact, on keeping his own tone as neutral as Beguchren's. It wasn't as easy as the mage made it seem.

Yet somehow Gereint felt, for the first time, truly

easy about his decision to continue north, as though it was truly *his* decision, unconstrained by the mage's subtle—and not-so-subtle—compulsion. But was it the griffin sighting that had made the difference? Or some indefinable alteration in the mage's manner? Something else entirely?

But Beguchren said only, "Good," turned his mare's head to the north, and nudged her into a trot.

Gereint followed, wondering whether he was right to hear more than one meaning in that simple word. He tried not to look away into the woods beside the road or imagine that the occasional snap of a branch in the woods along the road revealed the approach of more brigands. He knew Beguchren had been right, that every decent traveler did have the duty to put down brigands if he could—but he did not want to see the king's mage bring that frozen light glimmering out of earth and water a second time.

But the woods were quiet.

Gereint tried not to think about riding along this road in the other direction, with Sicheir and the rest, on the way to Breidechboden and freedom. That ride had been wound about with uncertainty and worries. Despite remembering all of them perfectly clearly, that journey seemed, in memory, one of the more pleasant interludes in his life, and Tehre's house at the end of it a haven of peace.

What would Tehre be doing this morning? Breaking something, undoubtedly. Some small ordinary household object, or a catapult somebody had made for her— somebody else, and how foolish to be jealous of that unknown and hypothetical maker—or a wagon or carriage or who knew what. Maybe a model bridge. Maybe she'd persuaded the Arobern to let her have a large building to tear down. Gereint thought of the way Tehre had made Derich's sword shatter upon striking the bronze swan and wished he could watch her bring down a building. What kind of minor stress might she use to make stone shear and shatter? It would be fascinating, he was sure. And impressive.

The road was very quiet. Only birds sang, not with the urgency of spring, but with a desultory chirp here and there. Other than the sluggish river to their right, only squirrels moved, running along the occasional branch or darting across the road. Probably the odd rustle back in the woods was a squirrel. Or a deer. Almost certainly none of the rustles signaled the presence of brigands or wolves or anything in the least alarming. Gereint wondered what Beguchren would do if a brigand in the woods tried to shoot them from hiding, then tried hard not to wonder about any such question. He did not really want to know.

For all his comments about pressing the pace, the mage had let his mare fall into a gentle walk. He rode with the reins loose and his head bowed. Maybe he, also, was concentrating on the sounds from the woods?

They rode into Pamnarichtan about four hours after leaving Raichboden. The horses, sensible creatures, pricked up their ears and tried determinedly to head for the hay and grain scents of the stable at the southernmost inn, which overlooked the confluence where the Nerintsan ran into the Teschanken.

Gereint reluctantly held his mare and the packhorse from leaving the road. He looked at Beguchren. "We don't *have* to stop here you think it's urgent to get on."

"No, we'll rest here. And get something to eat. If we don't, I imagine we'll wish we had long before we reach Metichteran." Beguchren let his horse turn toward the stable.

Beguchren sounded as calm and unruffled as ever, but Gereint saw that the mage was holding the reins with one hand and bracing himself unobtrusively against the pommel of his saddle with his other, much as he had immediately after the griffins had passed. He watched him narrowly, surprised. Just how hard had it been on him to do what he had done to those brigands? But Beguchren had seemed all right afterward...

Gereint let his horse follow the mage's mare, then nudged it into a slightly faster pace so he would reach the inn's stableyard first. Swinging quickly down from his saddle, he came around into position to offer Beguchren a steadying hand and his bent knee as a stepping block.

Beguchren looked slightly taken aback, which for him was like an exclamation of surprise. For a moment he only looked down at Gereint. But he did not order him out of the way or make a point of dismounting without help. He merely said at last, "Thank you, Gereint," and accepted the offered assistance.

Gereint kept his arm under Beguchren's hand for a long moment, until he felt that the smaller man was steady on his feet. The inn's stable boys came out to get the horses. Gereint told them, "Go ahead and untack them and rub them down. Give them some grain. My lord will be here an hour or more and he'll want them rested."

"Honored sir," murmured the boys, with covert, fascinated glances that measured the difference in size between Gereint and Beguchren. But the white-haired man was so obviously a lord that they were respectful and quick and didn't whisper to each other until they were out of sight.

"There's a table in the shade," Gereint said, nodding to it. It was also the closest table. "I'll tell them to bring something to eat as well as tea, shall I?"

"Yes." Beguchren lifted his hand deliberately from Gereint's arm. "Thank you," he repeated calmly, and walked quite steadily to the table. But he gripped both the edge of the table and the arm of the chair to brace himself before he sat down.

"Tea," Gereint told the inn staff. He spoke briskly and casually, as though he had no doubt whatsoever that service would be instant and respectful—exactly the way an important lord's retainer would speak. "With honey and milk. Wine, whatever you have that's good. Sweet rolls—you have sweet rolls? Good. Sliced beef and eggs. Quickly, now, you understand?"

"Honored sir," murmured the women, and vanished to see to it.

Gereint went back to the table and leaned against the shading oak, his arms crossed. He found he was frowning and tried to smooth out his expression.

"You needn't look quite so worried," Beguchren murmured. He'd tilted his head back against the headboard of his chair and closed his eyes, so how he could know whether Gereint looked worried or impatient or irritated or anything was a question. His face was tight-drawn, the bones sharply prominent under the skin. He looked much older than he had in Breidechboden: Gereint would now have believed him to be in his sixties or even his seventies, and he wondered again how old the mage actually was.

"Is it what happened last night?" Gereint asked him. "I thought you seemed well enough after—after. But I was, um, I don't know if I would have noticed anything, ah, subtle."

Beguchren did not answer. Gereint found himself frowning once more and tried again to make his expression bland. The women brought tea, glazed rolls still warm from the ovens, and assurances that beef and eggs and bread were on the way. Beguchren opened his eyes and lifted his head when the women came up to the table, but he made no move to serve himself. It might have been a lord's arrogance, but Gereint, suspecting that the mage's hands might shake if he tried anything as demanding as pouring out tea, poured it himself without comment. He added two spoonfuls of honey and a little milk and handed the cup across the table. Beguchren, looking mildly amused, took the cup—in both hands, Gereint noted—and drank half of it at once, like medicine. The cup rattled in its saucer as he put it down.

"Why didn't you say something?" Gereint asked him. "Too stubborn?"

Beguchren shrugged, a minimal gesture. "By the time I realized the difficulty, we'd come so close to Pamnarichtan it seemed foolish to stop short." He'd folded his hands in his lap, waiting perhaps to regain enough strength to drink the rest of the tea.

"Was it the magecraft last night?" Gereint asked again. "Or is it just"—he did not want to say *a weakness*—"something that happens?" he finished.

A slight pause. Then Beguchren shook his head. "Not the magecraft. The proximity of the griffins this morning."

Gereint thought about this. Then he stood up to help

the women from the inn lay out platters of beef and bread, eggs, sausages, and fried apples. Beguchren ignored this activity with a lordly disdain for noticing servants, which was, Gereint suspected, actually a way of disguising that he could not lift a platter himself. Once the women had gone, he filled a plate for Beguchren first and set it across the table in easy reach, then one for himself.

Beguchren took a sweet roll and ate it slowly. Then a bit of beef and an egg. He lifted his eyebrows at Gereint. "Did you order everything in the kitchens? There's far too much."

"For you, maybe." Gereint filled his own plate a second time. "The griffins did this to you. Just flying past, a quarter-mile away? And you want to go up to their desert, do you, and find them in it?"

"Gereint..." Beguchren began, then shook his head, smiling with rueful humor. His hands had steadied at last. He said, "It's a consequence of the events in Feierabiand, I believe. The griffins expended a great deal of power there. I was...overpowered, I suppose."

And the rest of Casmantium's cold mages had been killed. Gereint had heard that. Because they had been less powerful than Beguchren Teshrichten? Because Beguchren had been with the king? Or because Beguchren had simply been lucky? Or for some other reason entirely?

Gereint wondered just what the battle between the griffins and the cold mages had entailed, and exactly how thoroughly the griffins had won it. Then he wondered whether he really wanted to know.

"The effects seem both more wide ranging and more lingering than I might have wished," Beguchren added, a touch of apology in his tone.

And might get worse if they encountered more griffins? Or encountered them more closely? Gereint remembered how profoundly inimical he had found the desert. And Beguchren was a cold mage: far more opposed to the desert than any man with a mere gift for making. The two philosophers Gereint respected most, Andrieikan Warichteier and Beremnan Anweierchen, both agreed that opposition to the griffin's fire was the entire purpose and character of cold magecraft.

Beguchren had said they would go north *all the way*. But if a handful of griffins passing a quarter-mile away had strained him to the end of his strength, what would stepping into their desert do to him? Gereint said, "You should have a carriage. Why did you leave yours behind in the south?"

Beguchren shook his head, a small, surprisingly gentle gesture. "I did not wish to risk a servant of mine. Irechen has been my driver for many years."

Gereint thought of and dismissed several obvious rejoinders. In the end, he said merely, "You might have asked me to drive. I wouldn't want to try six-in-hand, but I could certainly have managed a little rig like that."

Beguchren's eyebrows rose. He said after a moment, "I suppose I could have done. I didn't think of it."

Gereint leaned back in his chair, trying not to laugh. He kept his expression sober with an effort.

"Well," Beguchren said, a little nettled, "the roads north of Metichteran, as you have said, are not so good. And you know we will not be able to take horses into the desert. We will leave them, at the end, and go up on foot."

"Well, I suppose I can carry you, if necessary."

A flicker of offense in the pale eyes was followed almost at once by a glint of wry humor. "I suppose you could. If it became necessary. I don't believe that's likely."

Gereint didn't comment on this optimism. Beguchren *had* said he'd wanted a maker who was physically strong. Gereint had not asked why. He did not press the mage now, only split a sausage and laid it across a slice of bread. Then he asked instead, "You still wish to try to ride on to Metichteran today? It's, what, twenty miles, a little more?" By himself, and given Beguchren's tall black mare, Gereint was confident he could ride that far in five or six hours. He could *walk* it almost that fast, if he needed to. But Beguchren? He did not want to force the mage to admit to an incapacity he likely found shameful. But neither did he want to see him collapse halfway to Metichteran.

"I'll be well enough in an hour," Beguchren answered, mildly enough.

Gereint tried not to look doubtful.

Beguchren peeled and sliced an egg, layering the slices fastidiously across a piece of bread. He murmured, not looking up from this task, "I might ask the inn to wrap up some of this excellent breakfast."

"Including plenty of sweet rolls," Gereint surmised. "And cakes of sugar. Yes. I'll arrange it, lord mage."

The mage looked up at that, frowning. Not about the sugar. "Gereint—"

Gereint held up a hand. "Nobody here would understand it if I called you by name, lord mage." Nor would he regardless, but he did not say so.

"Nor will you," Beguchren said, echoing this unspoken thought. But he made a small, dismissive gesture with two fingers. "Never mind. Yes, Gereint, please acquire some more sugar. As I am sure you recall, I would like to reach not merely Metichteran by this afternoon, but Tashen by this evening."

This seemed wildly optimistic to Gereint. He didn't say this, either, but merely stood up and went to see about wrapping up a packet of food. With plenty of sugar.

The horses, happy with their rest and the sweetened grain the stable boys had given them, were inclined to stride out briskly. Gereint kept a wary eye on Beguchren, but the little mage showed no sign, now, of exhaustion or collapse. He was quiet, but then he was constitutionally quiet, so Gereint had long since concluded. Even if he had been surrounded by his own retainers or friends... did he *have* friends? Other than the Arobern, who could not be precisely a *friend*... It occurred to Gereint for the first time that he knew nothing at all about the mage: earth and iron, the man might even be married, though it was hard to imagine so reserved and inscrutable a man with a wife, or children or even parents or brothers of his own blood. Nor could he imagine invading that impenetrable reserve with questions.

But even if surrounded by friends, Gereint could not believe that Beguchren Teshrichten was ever precisely demonstrative. And Gereint himself, if not precisely an enemy—nor precisely a servant, nor precisely a prisoner— was certainly not a friend.

The country between Pamnarichtan and Metichteran was rougher than Gereint had remembered. Nor had he made sufficient allowance for the way the road climbed far more often than it ran level. Coming the other way, they had gone mostly downhill. Now, riding constantly uphill, they could not press the horses faster than an easy walk. There were more stones and snags, too. A fine carriage would have had a slow and difficult passage; even a farmer's wagon would be prone to broken wheels and axles. Gereint guessed that most carters and such who regularly used this road were probably makers, the sort sufficiently gifted that they could coax a breaking wagon to last from one town to the next. Perhaps Beguchren's leaving his carriage behind had been more reasonable than he'd first thought.

Gereint's own mare began to cast a shoe; he felt two of the nails start to shear and the rest to bend, and caught the metal with his wish that it hold, hold, hold. The nails held. Gereint didn't mention the problem. If he could coax the shoe to last to Metichteran, any smith could replace it; if it didn't, there wouldn't be anything to do but lead the mare and walk himself. He wondered what Tehre Amnachudran would think of shearing nails. Probably she would rather let them shear and watch how they broke. But probably she could brush a thumb over them and set them back into place without benefit of a smith, if it occurred to her to bother. He smiled, imagining the casual, distracted manner in which she would do such a small, difficult task.

The woods crowded close to the road here, and on their other side the river was narrower and swifter than below the confluence, and beyond the river the woods stretched out again, impenetrably dense and green. The woods might have hidden any number of brigands or wolves or mountain cats or dragons, but Gereint did not glimpse anything more dangerous than a squirrel. Occasionally a large animal thudded away into the woods, unseen. Each time, Gereint glanced at Beguchren. Each time, the mage, his expression unvaryingly bland, shook his head.

"How do you know?" Gereint asked him, the third time this happened.

Beguchren shrugged, a minimal gesture that barely lifted his shoulders. "I know."

Gereint shook his head, not in disbelief, but in surprise. "We look so harmless. I'd accost us, if I were a brigand. They can't all have been cleared out."

"The cleverer ones may have headed west, as Meridanium has begun clearing these roads near its border. Or even south, to see if they can get honest work now that robbing travelers has become more dangerous. Or—" But Beguchren paused and then finished, "Or simple luck may be keeping them out of our way."

Gereint wondered how he'd meant to finish that sentence. But he said only, "Luck for them."

Beguchren only shrugged a second time, dismissing any possible concern about brigands. Or wolves or mountain cats, probably. Even he might have paused if a dragon had come out of the woods, though. Not that one would this close to the towns of men.

There were no boats at all on the river now. Even in the spring floods, the channel here was dangerous: changeable and filled with snags. Now, in late summer, the river had narrowed to a swift slender ribbon, barely more than a creek, that raced down only the deep center of its exposed, rocky bed. Gereint guessed, as the morning passed and the road grew rougher, that it would take a good deal longer than five or six hours to reach Metichteran.

They saw no more griffins. Though the way the woods closed off any decent view of the sky, fifty griffins might have flown past half a mile away and been completely invisible to travelers on the road. But then, probably, Beguchren would know they were there. Probably he *would* collapse if griffins came near. Gereint watched him warily. But the mage showed no sign of difficulty. During the occasional break for sweet wine or a bite of bread or a cup of hot tea, he dismounted and moved with only a little more than ordinary stiffness. So far as Gereint could tell.

They passed the occasional party heading south. No one was traveling in a really large company, but no one was traveling in a group of less than half a dozen, either, and everyone was armed at least with crossbows. None of them were men of rank, and no one ventured more than a respectful nod to Beguchren. Gereint might have stopped one or another to ask for news, but he kept an eye toward Beguchren, and when the mage did not pause, neither did he.

They rode into Metichteran in late afternoon, seven hours after leaving Pamnarichtan. It had been a market day, clearly: The streets were busy with farmers packing up their surplus to cart back to their farms, or bargaining with the most frugal of the townsfolk for the last bushels of bruised apples or spotty turnips. The famous bridge across the Teschanken was busy, too, though the water level was low enough that children were picking their way right across the river's bed. Gereint gazed down at the fitted stones of the bridge's arch as they crossed. It seemed to him that the hooves of the horses rang against history as much as against stone. Blood and battle and years mortared the stones. He wondered suddenly whether they might be riding into a tale themselves; perhaps some traveler in some distant year would look down at this bridge and think, *Beguchren Teshrichten crossed the river here to do battle against the country of fire*...He hoped not. He hoped, fervently, that nothing that happened would be exciting enough to remember in tale or poem.

The yard of the inn in East Metichteran was even busier than the streets had been. Surprisingly busy, indeed, as it could not yet be time for the supper crowd...Indeed, no one was yet ordering supper. The townsfolk and the lingering farmers were instead gathered around the inn's tables, drinking ale and talking animatedly.

Gereint swung down from his mare and wordlessly moved to assist Beguchren down from his: abnormally weakened or not, that was a tall horse for a small man to ride, and mounting blocks were not really high enough for him.

Beguchren accepted his assistance equally wordlessly, allowed Gereint to take his reins, and stood for a moment, gazing with narrow interest at the gathering around the tables.

"The inn staff must be over there, too," Gereint commented. He considered, briefly, taking the horses into the stables himself. Then, looking thoughtfully at the tables and the chairs and the jugs of ale, he reconsidered. He whistled instead, loud and sharp.

A startled silence fell across the inn yard. Beguchren gave him a dry look. Gereint only shrugged. "What's the point of traveling with a court noble if one doesn't put rank to use?" he murmured, and lifted an eyebrow pointedly at the cluster of youngsters he guessed were the stable boys. He'd guessed correctly, from the way they jumped up and hurried forward.

"Sorry, sorry, honored lord," muttered a fat, balding man, clearly the innkeeper, assessing Lord Mage Beguchren Teshrichten's horse and clothing and manner with an expert eye. "We're all distracted just now, honored lord, but just let me show you and your man to our best table—we *do* set the best table in Metichteran, I promise you—just this way, if you will permit me—"

"Distracted?" Beguchren inquired, in his most neutral tone.

"From the sightings! Griffins, honored lord, all this afternoon!" The fat man's broad gesture sketched their path, from west and south to the northeast. "Four or five at a time, honored lord, and we've never seen griffins down this far south before, not even before, well, I mean to say, not even when there were a gracious plenty over yonder." This time his vague gesture toward the north-west indicated, by implication, the original sweep of the griffins' desert prior to their claiming of Melentser.

"I see," said Beguchren, still at his most neutral. He allowed the innkeeper to evict a crowd from a table under a big oak near the inn's door and pull the chair at its head out for him. "How many altogether, would you say?"

"Forty, fifty all told! Not that we could say whether they were forty different griffins, you know, honored lord, or the same ones circling about. Penach, he's my oldest boy, he said he thought it was the same ones each time, but how even young eyes could see so clearly I don't know. You won't want ale, honored lord: let me send for wine—our best—local, of course, but it's accounted fair enough by our guests—" He turned and waved sharply to a hovering girl, who darted away into the inn.

"And tea," Gereint said firmly. He pulled a chair out for himself and sank into it with a sigh. It wasn't a particularly well-made chair, unfortunately. Not very comfortable for a man who'd been in a saddle all day. Maybe Beguchren's chair was better. He glanced at the mage, trying to assess his general condition.

"I'm quite well," Beguchren assured him, in a mild tone that Gereint did not trust at all.

Gereint raised his eyebrows at the mage. He said to the innkeeper, "And something to eat. Bread with butter and honey. Or berry preserves."

"Of course, of course, honored sir," said the innkeeper hurriedly, and waved again to the girl, who'd hurried back with the wine, a pitcher of water, and—no doubt—the inn's best silver goblets. The man himself, perspiring in the late-summer heat, seemed disinclined to dash back and forth himself. He glanced nervously at Beguchren, who poured a little wine into his goblet, topped it up with water, and sipped. There was no way to tell from the mage's manner or expression what he thought of the inn's best local wine.

It actually wasn't bad, was Gereint's own estimation, when he tried it. For a locally produced northern wine. Not up to the quality one expected in the south, of course. Perech Fellesteden would probably have dumped it out of his goblet onto the inn's yard and might have made the innkeeper lick it up from the dirt, but Fellesteden had been much inclined to dramatic gestures, and why was Gereint thinking of his old master at all? Ah. Because he was thinking of Melentser, and the griffins flying among the red sharp-edged spires they had raised among the ruined buildings of the town. He closed his eyes for a breath, opened them, and looked deliberately at Beguchren.

"Perfectly acceptable," the lord mage told the innkeeper gravely. And to Gereint, "There is no need to hover. I have taken precautions."

"Precautions, is it? Here comes the bread. I trust you'll do me the favor of eating a slice or two, with plenty of honey. My lord."

"Yes, an additional precaution is perhaps not out of order," Beguchren said, with a barely perceptible glint of humor. He added to the innkeeper, who was looking baffled and worried, "When did the griffins last pass over the town? Can you estimate?"

"Yes, well, yes, that is to say, I suppose it was an hour or so ago, honored lord. Doesn't that seem right to you?" the innkeeper appealed to the girl, who was laying out plates of sliced bread and crocks of honey and blackberry preserves. The girl looked startled at being addressed, but agreed that this was about right.

"I do believe," Beguchren said to Gereint, "that it would be wisest to go on to Tashen today."

Gereint made no comment until the innkeeper and the girl had both bustled away. Then he said, "That wasn't an easy ride we've already had today. It's so important to travel another fifteen miles or so?"

"The road from East Metichteran to Tashen is better, I believe."

"It is. Even so… What does it mean, my lord mage, that the griffins are flying over Metichteran? Does it matter whether it's the same ones over and over, or different ones each time?"

"Gereint—"

"Don't trouble yourself, my lord. Pretend I never asked." But Gereint kept his tone mild. He spread a piece of bread with the berry preserves and ate it thoughtfully. "Fifteen miles. However good the road, the horses are tired. That's four, five, six hours? We won't manage it before nightfall."

"I can make a light."

"Ah. Will it continue to light our way after you've collapsed?"

Beguchren put down the slice of bread he'd been holding and regarded Gereint for a moment. "You know, you used to be afraid of me."

"I've given up reminding myself I ought to be afraid of you. My lord."

Beguchren gave him an unreadable smile. "Good."

"I suppose I can tie you to your horse, if you fall off."

"I suppose you can. I think we will arrange for fresh horses here. And perhaps we will leave the packs here. We will not need them in Tashen."

"I think we should take them. In case we stop a mile short of Tashen. You should eat that, my lord. And you should rest while I arrange for a change of horses."

Beguchren gave a little wave of his hand, conceding all these points with a casual air Gereint did not trust at all. But the mage only smiled blandly even when Gereint gave him a look of pointed suspicion. Giving up, Gereint, got to his feet and looked around to find the innkeeper. He would inquire about horses that might be for sale, and about the cost to board the black mares...Maybe he should ask Beguchren to let him show the token; that should guarantee the horses would be well cared for...

He turned back to ask about the token. Thus, he was looking straight at Beguchren when the little mage suddenly
folded bonelessly forward across the table.

Gereint took one long stride back toward the table.
Then a horse, not one of Beguchren's, suddenly reared,
screaming. Gereint spun on his heel, startled, as boys
flung themselves at its head. They grabbed for its bridle,
but the horse reared again, tore itself loose, and raced out
of the inn's yard, hooves thudding dully on the packed
earth. Gereint stared after it. But a flurry of exclamations
all across the inn's yard made him look sharply around,
and then at last, following the direction of others' gazes,
up. He stopped, transfixed.

Three griffins cut across the cloud-streaked sky, glittering like bronze spear points in the late afternoon sun.
They flew barely high enough to clear the trees and the
taller buildings of the town. A great silence had fallen.
Gereint could actually hear the rustle of the wind through
the griffins' wings. The sound was more like stiff cloth
flapping in a hard wind than like the gentler rustling he
would have imagined.

He could see every long feather of those wings, even
pick out the smaller individual feathers of the griffins'
chests and forelegs. Each feather looked like it had been
beaten out by a metalsmith and then separately traced
with gold by a jeweler; the griffin's lion pelts blazed like
pure gold. The light flashed across their beaks and talons
as across metal. Gereint guessed those talons were nearly
as long as a man's fingers, curved and wickedly sharp; he
was struck by a distressingly vivid image of what talons
like those might do to a man if a griffin struck him.

Something about the afternoon light had become

strange. It took a moment for Gereint's mind to catch up
to his eyes, but at last he understood that the light seemed
fiercer and more brilliant around the griffins; each one
was limned with it, every feather outlined by it. The sunlight itself seemed to radiate from the griffins as much as
from the low sun. And the light that fell across Metichteran was suddenly heavier, deeper, hotter than any light
should be, even in late summer. Not quite like the brutal
sunlight of the desert, but close, closer than anything
Gereint had ever wanted to experience again. The sky
beyond the griffins had gone strange, pale, harsh... The
very sky seemed to glint like metal. The wind carried the
scents of dry stone and hot brass.

The griffins did not look to either side; their flight was
arrow straight. They flew from the southwest toward the
northeast. Though it seemed to take a long time for them
to pass over the town, it could not have taken more than
a moment. Then they were gone. The light that lay across
the inn's yard eased once more into normal afternoon
sunlight, and the breeze that came across the town from
the hills was cool and scented with pine, as well as the
normal horse-and-cooking smells of the town.

The silent stillness that had gripped the town ended
suddenly, and exclamations and shouts and questions
once again filled the air. Men scattered in all directions,
or clustered in groups and leaned forward in furious
debate about what had just happened and what they
should do about it. Stable boys went after the frightened
horse, and the fat innkeeper sank, trembling visibly, into a
broad chair and mopped his forehead with his apron.

Gereint stared at the innkeeper for an instant, then
abruptly, with a shock, remembered Beguchren. Cursing

under his breath, he spun back toward the table. The little mage was lying half across the table and half across the bench. His hands were limp, his eyes closed, his breathing shallow and quick, his face very pale.

Gereint reached Beguchren's side in two hurried steps and caught him, barely in time, from sliding off the bench onto the ground. He had commented, not very seriously, about being able to carry the smaller man. He had not expected to need to. But now he picked him up in his arms, finding his weight a negligible burden. But then he only stood for a moment, uncertain. But, however urgently Beguchren had wanted to press on, Gereint could see only one option now. He went over to the innkeeper, who was still sitting limply on his wide chair, staring up with wide, worried eyes into the empty sky. Gereint had to clear his throat loudly to get his attention. But then the fat man brought his wide stare down at last to ground level, took in Gereint and his burden, flinched, and clambered hastily and clumsily to his feet.

"My lord is ill," Gereint stated, as though this was not abundantly obvious. "He will need your best room. A good room, at least, if your best is taken. Whatever is quickest." He emphasized the last word with a flattening of his tone and a direct stare.

"Of course, of course, yes, honored sir, we've plenty of room, all our rooms are good, if you could just bring the honored lord this way—" the innkeeper said, all in one breath. He gave Gereint a beseeching look, perhaps imagining that his staff would be expected to nurse an important but delicate lordling and be blamed if anything went wrong—or perhaps imagining the lord might actually *die* in his inn, and envisioning the recriminations that might follow. Gereint fancied he could see those exact thoughts arise, full formed, in the fat innkeeper's mind. The man asked with clear trepidation, leading Gereint up a flight of stairs, "Is the honored lord *very* ill, do you know, honored sir?"

"I think not," Gereint assured him. "I will care for him myself, honored innkeeper." He glanced at the room the innkeeper showed him, approved it with a brief nod, and added, with conscious hauteur, "Have someone bring broth and tea. And a crock of honey. And soft bread, with something off the spit for me, when you have it ready. Have my lord's horses carefully tended. One of them has a loose shoe. Get a smith to check them all. And don't let the saddlebags sit out in the stable, have them brought here! Is that all clear?"

"Absolutely clear, honored sir," muttered the innkeeper, and hastily backed out of the room before Gereint could make any further, possibly more difficult, demands.

Gereint laid Beguchren down on the bed—the linens appeared clean, at least, and he saw no immediate sign of bugs. Then he stood back and just looked at him for a moment. Then laid the back of his hand against the mage's forehead. Limp and pale and cool, and Gereint was no healer. He could hardly coax the man toward strength and health as he would coax nails to hold or wood to resist splintering. Though Tehre might have managed something. Tehre would probably treat healing magic as a kind of making. In fact, if she treated *everything* as a kind of making, that might go a long way toward explaining why she was so *broadly* gifted.

But he still had no idea how to handle any kind of healing himself. But then, if his guess was good, Beguchren might need nothing but rest and food. Until the next time a griffin flew overhead, to be sure.

Gereint pulled off Beguchren's boots and, as it seemed far too great a liberty to do more, settled for tucking a blanket around his slight form. The blanket was a light, soft wool, better than anyone had a right to expect in a common inn. Perhaps the innkeeper hadn't exaggerated so terribly when he claimed his rooms were good. A boy brought the saddlebags, and then the girl arrived in a flurry, too shy to look at Gereint. She blushed and stammered as she told Gereint, in a whisper, that supper would be served beginning in an hour, but she would bring him the first meat that was ready. She was obviously trying not to even glance at Beguchren as she laid out an earthenware pot of broth, a plate of bread, a crock of honey, and the tea things.

Gereint thanked her gravely and let her escape. The room was close and hot in the summer evening, but it was a comfortable, natural warmth, nothing like the inimical heat carried on the wind from the griffins' wings. Was Beguchren already looking a little less pale? Might there be a little tension in the small hands that lay so quietly on the blanket? Gereint fancied there might be—unless he was simply imagining what he wanted to see. He studied the man's breathing and was sure his breaths were deeper and more relaxed, no longer the rapid shallow breaths of shock and weakness.

Beguchren opened his eyes. Blinked. A faint, puzzled crease appeared between his eyebrows.

"Easy," Gereint murmured. "We're at the inn at Metichteran. We're staying here overnight after all. We'll hire a carriage or something in the morning."

A faint smile curved Beguchren's mouth. "Is that the plan?"

"It is now. Have some tea." He let Beguchren hold the cup himself, but kept his own hand ready to steady it if necessary. The mage managed to raise the cup successfully, but his hand shook badly as he tried to lower it again; Gereint closed his fingers around the cup and Beguchren's smaller hand and guided the cup down to the tray on the bed table. Beguchren seemed not to notice this assistance. Gereint certainly made no comment about it.

"I'll be well enough in the morning," the mage murmured.

"Unless the griffins fly over again."

"Yes," Beguchren said, in an absent tone. "I shall have to do something about that."

Gereint waited, but the mage did not seem inclined to unfold any specifics about this "something" he might do. Gereint said after a moment, "There's broth and bread. With honey."

Again, a slight smile. Not inscrutable at all, Gereint found: that smile contained a rueful, self-deprecating humor; a strict, bitter pride as well as an awareness of the foolishness of pride; a faint, barely visible echo of the effort necessary to put it down. When had he become able to read the little lord's smile?

"I'm not actually ill," Beguchren said mildly. "I believe I will be able to handle something more fortifying than broth."

Gereint didn't argue. He only handed Beguchren a mug of broth, watching to see that he could hold it steady. He wanted to ask what the mage meant to do about the griffins, or about his own weakness. Instead, he drew

the room's only chair around so he could both see out
the window and keep an eye on the resting mage. There
was a good deal of movement through the inn yard, and
voices, raised in worried argument, came clearly through
the window—too clearly, but though Gereint did not want
Beguchren disturbed, he did not want to shut out the light
and air, either.

The low sunlight slanted through the window and lay
across the floor and the foot of the bed. It was perfectly
ordinary sunlight. Gereint found it hard to recall, now,
exactly how the light that had blazed around the griffins had
differed from this homey light. He frowned out the window,
watching the sinking sun layer the sky with carmine and
gold...There was no sign of any griffin in the air. A hawk
turned far above, but the sky above it was an ordinary sky,
and the light that surrounded it ordinary light.

If Beguchren was awake, he was doing a very good
imitation of a man asleep. Gereint left him alone. The
voices rising from the inn's yard faded as—if Gereint's
nose did not deceive him—supper began to be served and
folk retired to the common room and to the tables at the
edge of the yard to eat. The girl, true to her word, brought
meat up to Beguchren's room—beef, of course, in this
hilly country, and more bread, and sweet roasted turnips
and onions. With a small stack of the wide, rimmed plates
used to serve someone in bed. Gereint nodded in appreciation of her thoughtfulness and, to encourage more of the
same, found a coin for her in Beguchren's belt pouch.

Beguchren did not move through any of the coming and
going. Gereint did not disturb him. He ate most of the food
himself, setting a little aside under an upended plate to keep
warm in case the mage might actually want it later. The

broth had cooled. Despite the close warmth of the room, he asked the girl to bring a brazier and to put the pot of broth and the covered plate over the coals to keep warm.

Outside, the sun sank slowly behind the hills. Its last light came scattering through the branches of nearby trees and across the rooftops of the town. The moon, fatly gibbous, stood above the highest rooftop. Above Metichteran, the wide sky was empty of everything but high, delicate clouds; the hawk had gone to its roost. The first stars came glimmering into the violet-streaked sky, and dusk closed across the world as the sun set at last. Gereint got up to close the shutters and light the oil lamp that hung in a corner of the room.

Across the room, Beguchren stirred, opened his eyes, and sat up.

Gereint was so startled he nearly knocked the lamp off its chain. The mage looked far better now than he had earlier; Gereint didn't think it was merely the ruddy light of the lamp that lent him color. He glanced around with something that, if not energy, seemed at least alertness. "Is there food?"

"Broth? Beef?"

"Both, if you please. Is there more honey?"

"Nearly a full crock." Gereint poured broth into one of the clean cups and carried it to the bedside. This time, the mage seemed to have no difficulty lifting or steadying the cup. Gereint said, not quite a question, "You seem much improved."

Beguchren glanced up at him. "There won't be griffins over Metichteran at night."

"Ah. Yes, I recall some minor philosopher...Who was it? Lachkeir Anteirch? Anyway, one philosopher or another said something about 'the absence of fire between dusk and dawn.' Does that mean you are less pressed by the griffins' presence now? Or that you are less, ah..." He hesitated, trying to frame his question.

"Less pressed by the effort to keep them away from the country of men? Both." Beguchren finished the cup of broth and looked inquiringly at the covered plate on the brazier.

"A moment..." Gereint tried, not altogether successfully, not to burn his fingers transferring the beef and turnips onto a plate cool enough to touch. He brought this plate to the mage, watched for a moment to be sure Beguchren could handle it, then went to spread honey on slices of bread and arrange these on a second plate. He asked, "*Were* you keeping them away from Metichteran?"

There was a short pause as Beguchren visibly searched for words. "I was reinforcing the...earthiness of this country. You recall how a mage focuses power. Hmm. Or bends and balances the forces that exist in the world; that might be more a more accurate way to put it."

Gereint nodded, not mentioning that this did not seem an overwhelmingly clear description of magecraft to him.

"The nature of earth is antithetical to the nature of fire. I, hmm. Brought out that quality a little more strongly in all the countryside around Metichteran. This should have made any griffins currently in the vicinity very uncomfortable indeed. You didn't see any after those this afternoon." The mage sounded very certain.

"No," Gereint agreed.

"No. They retreated to their own country."

"Huh." Gereint thought about this. "All of them?"

"They aren't mages. I believe—I hope—there is only one true mage left among the griffins, and he is not here."

Or Beguchren would know, presumably. Gereint lifted his eyebrows. "If he should come here?"

"I do not believe the griffin mage will challenge me here. In the country of earth, I am generally stronger than any mage of fire, whatever his provenance."

There were too many qualifiers in this statement to give Gereint much confidence. He asked, "Is it not difficult, doing, ah, this? You were already weary, surely?"

A wry smile. "The brief answer is that it is much easier to make earth more itself than to press against an intrusion of fire into earth. I will rest tonight, in this comfortable bed you insisted on procuring for me, and in the morning, I promise you, I will be strong enough to travel."

"Then you are still determined to go north." Gereint tried to keep his deep skepticism about this course out of his voice.

"Gereint...someone must."

Gereint thought about the griffins spending all the previous day flying in a vast circle, passing over Metichteran over and over. And over other nearby towns and villages? That northeast course of theirs might well take them over Tashen. He thought about the way the sky and sunlight had changed as the griffins crossed the sky, how the wind from their wings had smelled of hot stone and metal. He thought of the twisted, sharp-edged towers of red stone that had cut through the earth in Melentser, shattering streets and buildings; of the sand that had drifted through the streets and into the empty houses.

The mages of Casmantium...especially the cold

mages…had dedicated their strength for hundreds of years to keeping the griffins and their desert out of Casmantium proper. And Beguchren was the last of the cold mages. The picture that came to mind, now, given those two statements, was…decidedly troubling. Gereint said abruptly, "What does the Arobern expect you to do here? Alone?"

Beguchren met his eyes. The small mage was no longer smiling. "I'm not alone, Gereint. You're here with me."

Gereint wanted to snarl in frustration and stomp in circles. He suppressed this immediate reaction, paused. Asked at last, "What *is* it you expect from me?"

For a beat and a second beat, Beguchren regarded him in silence. But he did not look away. And rather than putting Gereint off with the customary promise or threat— *I'll tell you when we reach the edge of the desert*—he said at last, "One creates…or I believe it is possible that one might create…a new mage, full-formed, from a sufficiently gifted maker. If the maker is willing to, hmm, reshape himself according to a new pattern."

Gereint didn't move.

"The process would inevitably involve a remaking of, as it were, the self," Beguchren added, his tone becoming…not precisely apologetic. Nor precisely defensive. But perhaps…almost diffident.

"That's the part you can't compel," Gereint observed, after a moment to consider the idea. "Not to say, the part that made you think of, what was the term? Self-abnegation?" He paused again, then added, "I thought gifts such as making were thoroughly distinct from the true power of magecraft?"

"They are. That's why the self of the maker requires

to be remade. I did say Warichteier was, shall we say, not entirely correct in his conclusions regarding magecraft. Or correct in not entirely the right ways." It was the mage's turn to pause. This time the pause lengthened uncomfortably. He asked at last, "Gereint, should I have told you at once? Or, indeed, now? I hoped you might come to trust me a little on the road. But I know it's a kind of little death I ask of you."

Gereint moved his shoulders uncomfortably, a small motion that was not quite a shrug. "Are you asking for an analysis of the quality of your...building materials? Or your tactics?"

Despite the deliberate lightness of his tone, Beguchren didn't smile. "Both, I suppose."

"If you'd put me off again, I would have been angry. I'm glad you told me at last. And I'm glad to know. The other...how should I possibly estimate? I'm not a mage; I have only the faintest notion of what magecraft entails; I've never studied any of—whatever mages study."

"I have," Beguchren said mildly. "You're a strongly gifted maker, but there are other makers with strong gifts. But it's not your ability that concerns me. It's your willingness, which I can and must estimate. So. Will you come with me now to the edge of the desert?"

Gereint could see that the mage expected him to say "yes." He asked instead, deliberately, "Will you permit me a choice?"

Beguchren did not look away. His ice-pale eyes were steady on Gereint's. "Certainly. As long as you make the correct choice."

Gereint didn't quite laugh, but wry humor crooked his mouth. "Oh, indeed. And what is it you intend to do, there at the boundary between fire and earth, once I make your correct choice? No, don't tell me: It depends on what I do."

"Of course."

"I'm only one man. I don't understand why you didn't require half the makers in Casmantium to accompany you. I don't believe one man can make so great a difference as you imply. Certainly not, well, me. What possible difference can I make, even if I do everything exactly as you ask?"

Beguchren hesitated, then answered, "I did say that your power, as such, is not my concern. I must ask you to trust me that it will suffice. If I had brought half the makers in Casmantium with me, they would only have tangled their intentions and strength with one another and with mine."

"Um," Gereint said noncommittally. He half wanted to challenge this as an evasion, but he feared he understood the mage all too well. But he also feared Beguchren was simply wrong about what was and was not possible to make. Or remake. The idea of recasting a maker into a mage seemed perfectly demented. He lifted his own hands, studied them as he opened and closed his fingers. He could feel his own gift in his hands, solid and familiar. He had no idea what it would feel like to *pull on the world* or *balance opposing forces* or whatever Beguchren had said mages did.

Even if Gereint was willing to try, and found this "remaking of the self" possible, it was hard to believe it would make any substantial difference to any contest between Beguchren and the griffins' mage—and if he understood what Beguchren was not quite saying, that was what the cold mage expected. Or what he was aiming to provoke.

But he also felt, obscurely but with conviction, that it would be wrong to turn aside before he and Beguchren reached the edge of the griffins' desert and at least looked out upon that country of fire. After coming so far, after the cold mage had expended such effort, arguing over this last step of the journey seemed simply wrong. Whether the mage offered compulsion or merely asked for Gereint's cooperation.

He said, in a deliberately casual tone, "You'd never reach the desert alone, would you? So I suppose I must go at least so far."

Beguchren inclined his head in quiet thanks, exactly as though he had merely asked for cooperation and never thought of compelling anything at all.

Metichteran and Tashen had grown up from simple villages at nearly the same time, once the constant warfare between Casmantium and Meridanium had finally given way to the peace created by the decisive victory of Casmantium. Tashen had grown into the largest city of the north: a small bastion of, to Gereint's mind, rather self-conscious culture. Metichteran, Tashen's gateway to the south, had cheerfully settled for becoming a comfortable town of farmers and tradesmen. Gereint much preferred Metichteran, though Perech Fellesteden had generally lingered only in Tashen during his occasional journeys from Melentser to the southern cities or back.

The road between the two towns was quite good, if worn and weather beaten. The edges of the stones had been rounded by time. Some of them had cracked right across during the long northern winters; mosses grew in those cracks and along the edges of the road. But not a single stone was so broken it needed to be replaced, nor did the mosses grow far enough out from the cracks to make the road slippery. The builder's magic that had been set deeply into this road did more than cause the stones to resist weathering. The horses' hooves sounded just a little muffled on the close-fitted stones, for the builders had set sure-footedness upon their road to protect horses from slips and falls.

North of Metichteran, the forest thinned out to pretty woodlands, and then to fields and pastures that spread off to the east and north. The land gradually shifted from gently rolling to frankly hilly, with scrub woodland left to occupy the steeper slopes. Enormous trees spread out their broad branches to shade old farmhouses that had probably been built before the conquest of Meridanium. Here and there, a small apple orchard was tucked close to a house. The scent of apples was sweet on the breeze.

Low stone walls delineated the edges of the farms and pastures. The hardy little northern cattle grazed in the pastures; in the fields, wheat and barley, already going golden with autumn, glowed with a color that would have looked rich if Gereint had not compared it to the colors of griffins. He looked for griffins now, keeping a wary eye on the sky. But he saw nothing besides a single vulture, its wings slanted upward in the characteristic angle, gliding in its slow circle on the high thermals.

"Are you doing something to keep the griffins away?" he asked Beguchren, breaking the silence that had grown up between them. It was not a tense silence, more a sign of a mutual abstraction. They both had a good many things to think about, Gereint supposed. He wondered if the mage's thoughts were as circular and uncomfortable as his own.

Beguchren glanced up. He had seemed much stronger this morning, much more himself, but now his gaze was blank and unfocused. Gereint was momentarily alarmed; he had not realized the mage was so weak—he leaned forward, ready to try to catch the small man if he slumped out of the saddle—but then Beguchren blinked and Gereint settled again, warily, as awareness seeped back into the mage's expression.

Beguchren moved his shoulders, not quite a shrug, answering the question Gereint had, in that moment of alarm, almost forgotten he'd asked. "Not precisely. Not now. I'm drawing the deep magic of earth after us as we ride; it is set so deeply in this road, it takes only a touch to wake it. Roads *are* boundaries; they can easily be persuaded to, ah, bound. That hardly counts as 'doing' anything."

"Ah."

"Mostly I'm simply…listening. But I hear nothing. There are no incursions out of the desert, not this morning. I think the griffins are become cautious, now they know I am here."

"Um."

Beguchren smiled. "They do know, I assure you. And they know I am coming to them. I think they will wait. They will not wish to challenge me while I am in the country of earth. Certainly not while I have such an old and powerful road under me."

"They're afraid of you." Gereint didn't quite let this turn into a question.

"I hope they are."

"Um." Gereint hoped that, too.

The silence fell again, but now Beguchren seemed more inclined to remain aware of the road and the countryside. He glanced after the flash of a redbird in the woodlands, gazed admiringly at a huge chestnut tree standing by the road, raised an eyebrow at a stocky black dog that stood alertly near a small herd of tawny cattle to watch them pass. The mage was, Gereint realized, enjoying the ride. Only it was more than that. Beguchren looked about himself with exactly the air of an elderly man who, traveling, suspects that he is on the last journey of his life: as though he had set himself to enjoy the countryside as much as possible. As though he were making his farewells to the world through which he traveled.

Or so it seemed to Gereint. He didn't like it. But neither could he think of a way to comment. At last, simply to break a silence he, if not the mage, now found a little too fraught, he asked, "Will we stop in Tashen?"

Beguchren glanced up, mildly surprised. "No, no. No, we'll go straight through and continue on north. We may yet find the desert's edge today."

The mage sounded neither dismayed nor enthused about the prospect. Gereint knew which reaction seemed more natural to *him*. He half wanted to ask about magecraft and the maker's gift and what it meant to *remake the self*. But he also wanted, much more strongly, to ignore the whole question. He said nothing. Beguchren ran his hand absently over his mare's neck and watched a covey of quail dart along the edge of a pasture where a dozen ponies grazed.

They reached Tashen midmorning and, as Beguchren had said, barely halted. The streets seemed abnormally quiet, the courtyard of the governor's mansion abnormally crowded. Gereint suspected, uneasily, that he knew the reason for both aberrations. No matter how the people of Tashen prided themselves on their refined sophistication, he was afraid they had seen things over the past days that had pressed them beyond their ability to pretend nonchalance.

They paused only long enough to buy half a dozen meat pastries from an ornate stall in the beautifully laid out open market near the northern edge of the city. Gereint asked the pastry vendor about griffins, and then found it hard to get away again because the woman was so eager to talk. Griffins thick as sparrows, to hear her tell it; and the past three dawns with a sun that came up huge and hot-gold, and dusks where it only sank late and with seeming reluctance behind blood-red hills. "And there's a nasty red dust in the air, gets into everything," she told Gereint earnestly. "Hard to roll out pastry with dust mixed right in with the flour on the board! You're all right, though, honored sir: Today is better than yesterday or the day before. Those should be good pastries. Everyone knows I make the best ones in Tashen."

Gereint nodded gravely. "Then we'll take a couple extra." He added a bag of apples to his purchase for good measure.

"You watch yourselves!" the vendor called after them. "Stands to reason it's worse the farther north you go, and besides, my cousin brings me these apples from a northern estate out that way and he says there's worse than dust out that way. The governor should do something about it, that's what I say!"

She did not suggest anything the governor might do, but perhaps, Gereint reflected, it was comforting just to

tell herself that someone might be able to "do something"
if he only decided to trouble himself.

It still lacked an hour or more to noon when they left
Tashen behind and headed out on the much more narrow
road that ran north, parallel to the river but far to the east
of it, into the hills. Gereint passed a share of the apples
to Beguchren. They ate them as they rode and fed the
cores to the horses. Neither of them mentioned red dust
or crimson sunsets.

Barely two hours after noon, they came around a slow
curve in the road and found themselves riding toward a
large sprawling house at the base of low hills, with wheat
tawny in the fields and apples ripening in the orchards.

Gereint took a long breath and let it out again. He only
hoped, fervently, that at least one of Tehre's letters had
made it to this house far in advance of his own arrival in
company with the king's mage.

CHAPTER 10

Dachsichten was an important town; really a small city. It served as a waystation for nearly all the traffic flowing from south to north or back again, and it linked the river traffic with the first of the great roads that led out into the great plains of southern Casmantium. So it was an important town, and likely to grow more important still if the Arobern's plans to increase trade with Feierabiand came to fruition. Any goods that came down from the north would certainly pass through Dachsichten on their way south and west.

Tehre had traveled through Dachsichten many times, but she had never liked the town. It seemed too conscious of its own mercantile importance, too inclined toward bustle and business at the expense of grace and artistry. Its buildings were mostly of brick, because bricks could be made cheaply from the lowland clay deposited over the ages all along the wandering path of the river. Perhaps using bricks rather than stone or timber made sense. But the color of the clay was an unpleasant harsh yellow. And the buildings were steep roofed and sharp cornered, a style Tehre had never liked; and they were too tall and too crowded along the streets even in the wealthiest part of the city. Dachsichten was simply, inarguably, ugly.

"It is very different from Breidechboden, is it not?" said Lord Bertaud.

" 'Haste in building always leads to regrets,' " Tehre quoted, and added, "Aesthetic regrets, if not regrets because of unsound construction. There was no *need* to crowd Dachsichten like this, and I'm sure even this brick could be made more attractive with better design. The northern towns are far more beautiful, Lord Bertaud. Especially Tashen."

"Your family lives there?"

"Near there. I shall be pleased to show my home to you, Lord Bertaud."

"Honored lady, I shall look forward to it," the lord answered with automatic grace, but the smile had faded. He still gazed out at Dachsichten, but Tehre supposed his thoughts had gone back to something else, something difficult.

"But we'll stay the night here?" Meierin asked hopefully. She leaned forward, peering out at the narrow streets and ugly yellow buildings. "Can't we, honored lady? It's almost late enough we ought to stop, and wouldn't you like to sit in the inn's common room and watch the people? Look, those ladies have such interesting embroidery on their bodices—"

Tehre was not very interested in embroidery, but suspected from the abbreviation of the bodices in question that the ladies in question might not be, well, ladies.

Though obviously they were wealthy. But she smiled at
Meierin. "We do, usually. There's an inn at the northern
edge of town where we normally stop. As you say, it's
almost late enough we ought to stop, anyway."

The inn was large, clean, and well appointed. Tehre
had stayed in it several times and expected all this. Its
common room was pleasant enough, she supposed. Its
ceiling had interesting beam architecture.

But what she had not expected was to find her brother
in that common room when she came down for supper.

Lord Bertaud was not yet in evidence. But her brother,
Sicheir, had already laid claim to a long table to one side.
He did not look surprised in the least to see his sister, but
only stood up and politely drew her chair out for her.

Tehre cast her gaze upward. "Fareine wrote more letters than just to my father, I surmise. Sicheir—"

"Tehre." Her brother came to take her hands, giving her
an anxious up-and-down glance. "Fareine wrote, yes. You
should have sent me word yourself. Are you well? Are
you sure? I think I got a tolerably complete account—is
it true the Arobern didn't seem inclined to blame you, us?
It *is* still true that Lord Fellesteden's heirs aren't trying
to charge you legally somehow? Did you leave someone
looking out for our interests in Breidechboden, besides
the estimable Fareine?"

"Fareine will contact a good legist if there's difficulty,"
Tehre assured him. "The Arobern already ruled against
Lord Fellesteden's estate when he gave Gereint to his
mage, so the precedent is set our way. Maybe the heirs
are glad he's gone: He was a terrible man. Fareine must
have told you what he tried to do."

"And I'm very glad she did," Sicheir said firmly,

drawing her toward the table. "Come sit down, do, and give me a more complete account. I think perhaps you were wise to leave the city, though I don't want anyone thinking our family would run from a threat or entanglement. I thought of going to Breidechboden myself, taking up residence, being a visible presence." A solid, aggressive, male presence, he did not say. But that's what he meant.

Tehre glared at him. "*I* could have stayed just as well. I didn't leave Breidechboden because I was afraid of Fellesteden's heirs!"

"Of course not," said her brother, meaning that maybe she should have. "Though you should have sent for me. Tell me everything, will you? And about this foreign lord—especially about the foreign lord. What's he want in the north, do you even know? Or at least, what reason did he give you? You've no reason to trust a word he said, you know, foreign as he is! You know, the Arobern may not be very happy with you agreeing to escort this Feierabianden lord into the north—likely he's a spy, did you think of that?"

Tehre blinked. "He can't be. Spies sneak, don't they? They're unobtrusive, you know, they get into things and you never know it. Lord Bertaud is about as conspicuous as anybody could be. He can't sneak about, how could he? Anybody can see he's foreign!"

"Tehre, sometimes a spy doesn't have to tiptoe. This man—"

"He belongs to the Safiad. It's no secret; everybody knows it. Anyway, it doesn't make any sense, him leaving Breidechboden for the north, except just for the reason he said, because he wants to see what problem there is with the griffins. It's only natural he'd want to know about that, don't you think?"

"And only natural the Arobern wouldn't care to have him strolling up north to look, especially if there's something to see—"

"He said plainly the Arobern can't tell him where to come or go—"

"All the more reason not to be seen in his company, when he waves his untouchable defiance at the Arobern! Tehre, you've got to leave him. I'm here now. I brought a few men with me, we don't need the foreigner's men, least of all do we need *them*! We'll go back to Breidechboden, or if you insist we can go on north, but just you and I and our people, decidedly not in some foreign lord's dubious company!"

Tehre hesitated. In a way, this even made sense. But she said slowly, "It's obvious why he wanted to travel with me. He made no secret of that, you know. The company of a Casmantian, especially a Casmantian lady, eases his way through our country. I told him I would travel with him, Sicheir. I told him he could visit our father's house. I can't now say I changed my mind—"

"Of course you can!"

"—and just leave him on the road. It wouldn't be right!"

"Tehre..."

"And it's *not necessary*. You're far too concerned about appearances, but I don't think anything looks as bad as you think. Sicheir, maybe you'd better tell me now what you've heard. Just what did Fareine put in that letter?"

The problem, as Tehre knew perfectly well, was that if she stamped her foot and cried, *I can take care of myself*, she would look like a child. If she went cold and angry, she would look like a wicked-tempered harridan, and moreover would seem to distrust her brother. Yet, though she could not shout or even complain, if she was sweet and reasonable and said anything like *Well, I'm glad you're here* to her brother, that would make it seem that she agreed Fareine had been right to send for Sicheir, which she did *not*.

She rubbed her forehead, wondering if there might still be time to turn away the headache she felt coming on if she asked the inn staff for willowbark tea immediately. "Fareine pulled you away from your work—the work of a lifetime, and what if the Arobern's administrators won't permit you to come back? Sicheir, you walked away from the Arobern's new road; are you going to be able to go back to it? Tell me you haven't lost your chance to work on it—"

"I told the court administrator overseeing the work that I needed to see to urgent family business. He understood. Tehre—"

But Sicheir did not have an opportunity to finish his thought. At that moment, Lord Bertaud himself came down the stairs into the common room, paused for a moment, located Tehre, and noted Sicheir's presence. The expression fell off his face instantly, replaced by the courteous, empty smile of an experienced courtier suddenly dropped into uncertain circumstances. He made his way across the room, weaving between the tables, nodded to Tehre, and turned that blank smile to Sicheir.

Tehre said, "Lord Bertaud, may I present to you my brother, Sicheir Amnachudran? Sicheir is an engineer and a builder; if you have any questions about the new road,

you should ask him. Sicheir, this is Lord Bertaud—" She
should say, *son of Somebody*, but what was the name he'd
given her? Some soft-sounding Feierabianden name; she
couldn't remember. She said instead, "Of Feierabiand,
one of the Safiad's close advisors." Well, he hadn't said
so, but he must be, for the king of Feierabiand to send
him here. She finished, "The Safiad sent him to oversee
the construction of the new road, so if you have any
thoughts about that, I'm sure he'd be glad to hear them."

"To be sure," the foreign lord said smoothly. He
answered Sicheir's respectful bow with a little nod of his
own and added, "The road is a great undertaking. I have
studied the plans carefully. Only the engineers of Casmantium could build such a structure. But perhaps you
could explain to me the difference between an engineer
and a builder?"

Sicheir blinked, startled and disarmed by this interest.
"Well, lord, the distinction is clear enough. An engineer
understands the theory of building, but a builder has the
gift of making. Engineers might direct the new construction, but it's builders you want to actually lay their hands
on the stone and iron. You have makers in Feierabiand, of
course. Some, surely, must become builders?"

"But not like yours. It seems to me the new road will
come to rival any structure ever built by the hands of men.
The plans for the bridges and the buttressed roads are
quite extraordinary."

"You're kind to say so, lord. If I may observe, you
speak Prechen very well."

"Ah—" Lord Bertaud glanced at Tehre, who did not
want to try to describe her insight about language as a
made structure and therefore merely gazed back with

bland, innocent eyes. "Ah," murmured the foreign lord again. "Thank you. Ah, forgive me—"

"One would say, 'honored sir,'" Sicheir explained, apparently understanding the dilemma, which Tehre had not. "My sister has her title from our mother and her family—the title of nobility passes only from mother to daughter in a morganatic marriage such as our parents'. It's different in Feierabiand, I believe."

Lord Bertaud gave an ambiguous little tip of the head and made a polite little gesture of invitation, meaning they should all sit. "You are my guests," he declared. "No, please permit me the indulgence. Tell me about the road and the experience of building, honored Sicheir. What is your part in this great project? Have you been involved with anything comparable in the past?"

Tehre sat back and watched as her brother was, despite his concerns and suspicions and more than half against his will, drawn out into a companionable discussion of the Arobern's road. She had not precisely seen Lord Bertaud as a real court noble; he seemed too direct, too little pretentious. Now she saw that he was indeed an experienced courtier. Was charm, too, possibly a sort of making? Not even as structured as language, far less than a proper structure of stone or wood. What would the components of a courtier's charm be? Come to that, what exactly would the finished structure be? Maybe the analogy would not stretch quite so far...Then, as Sicheir began to sketch the first of the great bridges that would span a wide chasm, she dismissed the question and leaned forward.

"Is that to scale? Then it's all wrong. Masonry's too heavy for that width," she commented. "You have to have too much rise for that run. It could be done if you had a series of arches, but you can't put in a series if there's too much fall under the bridge, and I'm sure there is. No, Sicheir, not only will this design be very difficult to build, it'll be thoroughly unsound. Who designed this?"

"Tirechkeir."

"Yes, it's just like Emnon Tirechkeir to design something that looks like a radical departure but that really draws on a long tradition of design that doesn't actually apply to the situation at hand. The first problem is a wrong choice of materials. I really don't think masonry is the proper material to span such a long distance."

"It's available. We can get any quantity of good stone out of those mountains. That's a big asset, Tehre."

"However easy it is to get, it's far too heavy for this use. You'll never get it anchored properly, or if you do, it'll be because it's too steep to be practical." Tehre looked around absently for paper. Someone pushed a whole stack of good-quality draftsman's paper across the table to her—oh, Lord Bertaud, how clever of him to see what she wanted—she took the quill out of her brother's hand and began to sketch. "Now something like this would be much lighter and far easier to build. See, you can make *very* steep arches, as long as you hang the bridge *from* the arches rather than making the arches the footing of the actual bridge itself. You'd cast these arches of iron, you can do that in Ehre, there's no need to try to do it in place. Then just lift them into place from either side. Then use wrought-iron chains and suspend a timber bridge from the arches—"

Sicheir picked up the sketch and stared at it.

"It will work," Tehre insisted. "The theory is perfectly

sound. Just because no one's used this kind of structure before doesn't mean it's not sound. Here, look, let me show you how the mathematics work out. I know the mathematics can be misleading, there's something missing from our understanding of the equations..." She tapped the quill absently against her lips, thinking about missing quantities and concepts.

Sicheir interrupted her abstraction with practiced emphasis. "Oh, I believe you. It's not that I don't believe you. Tehre, you ought to come back to Ehre with me; you should help me present this to Prince Bestreieten himself." He saw her baffled expression and said patiently, "The Arobern's brother is overseeing the whole project, Tehre, you knew that, surely! He'd be interested in this—and if no one else has ever built a bridge this way, he'll only be more interested: He knows very well his brother would love to have special, unique bridges for his road. If you come—"

"I can't," Tehre said, surprised. "You know I'm going north." She paused, her eyes narrowing. "You *do* know I'm going north. Sicheir, that isn't kind, pretending you want me to come to Ehre when really you simply don't want me going north with Lord Bertaud."

Everyone stopped, looking at the foreign lord.

Lord Bertaud leaned back in his chair, tilted his head quizzically to one side, and regarded Sicheir with raised-eyebrow curiosity.

Sicheir flushed. So did Tehre, realizing for the first time that she had, once again, managed to say something desperately tactless. She should have let Fareine come after all; Fareine would have known how to interrupt her, or what to say now to smooth the moment...

"Honored lady, your honored brother undoubtedly *did* come find you to ask your advice about the bridges," Meierin said in her quiet little voice. "It will be much harder for him to ask you about things like this," she tapped the sketches they'd been drawing, "once you are so far away in your father's house."

Then the girl turned gracefully to Lord Bertaud and went on, sweetly reasonable, "Of course the honored Sicheir Amnachudran is grateful for your offer to escort Lady Tehre to her father's house, Lord Bertaud. It was so kind of you. You've seen how skilled a maker the honored lady is; perhaps you will be kind again and forgive the honored Sicheir his attempt to persuade his honored sister to go west with him now? Of course"—with an understanding nod for Tehre—"she will not go. You should know"—with a reproving look at Sicheir—"that when Lady Tehre says she means to visit your honored parents, she will not change her mind for anything."

Tehre stared at the girl. "You sound just like Fareine!"

Meierin lowered her eyes modestly. "Thank you, honored lady. I hope I have profited from the honored Fareine's instruction."

"I thought—" Tehre began, then stopped. She said instead, warmly, "Fareine did tell me you were sensible." Then she turned to glare at her brother. "And I thought *you* were sensible, too! I want to know what's going on in the north. Don't *you* want to know?" She flung up her hands at Sicheir's blank look. "*What* did Fareine write in that letter?"

Sicheir hesitated, his gaze sliding sideways toward the foreign lord.

"Never mind," Meierin said before the pause could grow awkward. She patted Tehre's hand urgently. "You can discuss the letters with your honored brother *later*, honored lady."

"There's no need for haste," Sicheir seconded. He rapped the table firmly to summon the inn's staff. "We'll have supper—Lord Bertaud, won't you permit me the privilege?"

Tehre rested her elbow on the table, set her chin on her palm, and stopped listening to the polite argument about who was whose guest. She thought instead about time and travel and uncertainty, and who knew what about everything. Or anything.

After some time, she put her spoon down, only then realizing that supper had been served and that she had been eating it. It was a thick barley soup with beef and carrots, a very northern dish that reminded Tehre, once she noticed it, of her home. She suddenly longed for home, for her mother's voice calling cheerfully down the polished halls, for her father's quick interest in building and materials and making and, really, everything...She thought of the griffin they had seen, the way the late sunlight had struck across the metallic feathers of its wings and turned its lion pelt to ruddy gold. The fierce unhuman stare it had turned their way.

Then she thought of that griffin flying above her father's lands and house. For some reason she did not understand, the image made her shudder with dread. Looking up at her brother, she said, "You need to come north with us, Sicheir."

A startled silence fell. Tehre looked from Sicheir to Lord Bertaud. They both looked equally baffled.

"Yes, Tehre," Sicheir said at last. "We were just agreeing that might be as well."

Tehre flushed. "Oh, were you?" She had missed this. "But your work?"

Sicheir only shrugged. "Family comes first. I'll send some of your drawings back to Prince Bestreieten with a suggestion that he consider something like it."

"Oh." Tehre thought about this. "Tell him, tell them all, that the drawings are yours. The administrators are much more likely to try the design if all their pet builders think it's yours and not mine."

"Tehre—"

"Later, after the bridges are built, you can tell them the design is mine. There's nothing they can do about it then. I want to see this," she tapped her rough sketch with the tips of two fingers, "built and raised and carrying proper loads. Don't you?"

Sicheir gave a conceding little flip of his hand, frowning. "Maybe you'll agree to go west with me later."

Lord Bertaud slid the sketch across the table and studied it with interest. "Most unusual."

"I got the idea from a Linularinan bridge," Tehre explained. "And from thinking about ways to actually *use* really steep arches."

"I wish to see this design put to a practical test," the foreign lord declared, and raised his eyebrows at Sicheir.

"Huh." Sicheir sat back in his chair, looking extremely thoughtful. "Yes. That might do."

Baffled, Tehre looked from one of them to the other. If Fareine had been here, she would have asked her later what they meant. But Fareine was not here. She glanced at Meierin. To her surprise, the girl was nodding and looking pleased. She leaned toward Tehre and whispered, "It's how Lord Bertaud will explain why you agreed to guide him into the north: He promised you patronage and you knew he would be a very powerful patron, at least for a little while, until everyone can see your bridges are the best. Everyone will understand this explanation. It'll prevent all sorts of, you know. Other questions."

"Oh." Tehre tried to decide whether this actually made sense but gave up almost at once. Materials and mathematics were far more straightforward than deciphering what people thought. They so seldom seemed to think at all, really, which was probably part of the problem. "Well, if you think so," she added, and, as everyone now seemed contented to go north, went back to sketching bridges. But even while structures of iron and stone flowed out of her quill, griffins continued to fly through the back of her mind.

But they did not go north in the morning. Tehre stayed up for a long time, sketching by candlelight. She found griffins creeping into her sketches, flying above and through and below the cliffs and chasms and bridges that flowed out of her quill. The fierceness of the mountains she drew and the fierceness of the griffins informed each other, so that sometimes when she meant to draw a jagged cliff edge she instead found herself tracing the savage line of a beak or the clean-edged sweep of wing or the taut curve of muscle beneath a lion's pelt.

When she blew out the candles and made her way through the darkness to the bed she was sharing with Meierin, the glint of fire seemed to linger just out of sight, caught in a griffin's fierce eye. When she finally slept, she dreamed of griffins soaring in high spirals over

Breidechboden, fire falling from the wind from their wings... She murmured in her sleep, half waking in the dark.

"Lady... you're dreaming," Meierin whispered back, sleepily, reaching to pat her arm. "Go back to sleep."

"Where are we?" Tehre asked her, her eyes still filled with dreams of fire, glad to have the practical, sensible girl to ask.

"Dachsichten. Remember? The inn in Dachsichten."

"Oh," Tehre said vaguely, not really remembering but willing to trust Meierin's word for it. She closed her eyes again and dropped her head back to the pillow, and if she dreamed again after that, she did not remember.

In the morning, Tehre felt exactly as though she'd stayed up too late and had too many strange dreams. Her eyes felt gritty, and the incipient headache she'd ignored the previous night had shifted to the back of her skull and settled in to stay. She wanted a long bath, several cups of hot astringent tea, and to go back to bed in her own room. What she had was a cold basin to wash her face in, a wrinkled travel dress, and a long, rough carriage ride to occupy the whole day. She sighed. There should at least be tea.

She and Meierin washed their faces in the cold water, helped one another dress, came out into the hall, and found the doors of Sicheir's room already standing open. Sicheir was sitting on the bed in his room, studying the sketch of the suspended bridge Tehre had drawn for him and frowning. He jumped up when Tehre peered around the edge of his door.

"You're up! Good!" he said, impatiently, as though she had slept very late.

"It's hardly past dawn," Tehre protested. "If you'd wanted a very early start, you might have said so. Who knows if Lord Bertaud is even awake yet?"

Meierin slipped past Sicheir's room to rap gently on Lord Bertaud's door. The lord opened it after a moment. He looked, Tehre thought, exactly like she felt: tired and headachy and like his rest had been troubled by unusual dreams. His smile was really more a grimace. "Lady Tehre," he said. His eyes went to Sicheir and he hesitated for a moment, then looked back at her. "I am concerned about the griffin we saw; I am concerned about what may be happening in the north of your country," he said baldly. "We must talk."

"Yes," said Tehre, more certain than ever that he, too, had dreamed of griffins and fire. "But, please, over *tea*."

But when they came down to the common room, they found the innkeeper, harried and sweating lightly, coming to meet them. With a worried jerk of his head, he indicated the finest of his tables, the one set back away from the heat of the kitchens and closest to the wide east window. The pale dawn light lay across that table and the tea things and sliced bread it held, and across the bony face and deep-set eyes of a man who sat there, waiting for them.

The man rose as they stared at him. He was clad in good-quality traveling clothes of leather and undyed linen, much too plain for a merchant but much too good for any simple tradesman or farmer. He was tall, lanky, his hands bare of rings, his face lined with weather and experience. He looked tired, as though he'd ridden through the night and only just arrived at the inn. Tehre had never seen him before in her life. She looked questioningly at her brother, at Lord Bertaud. Both men looked as puzzled as she felt.

Then the man reached into the collar of his plain shirt and took out a fine gold chain, on which hung, pendent, a carved bone disk that had been dyed purple.

Tehre stood frozen, and felt Meierin and her brother go as suddenly still beside her. Lord Bertaud, puzzled, glanced from each of them to the others. A wariness came into his eyes, and the politely neutral courtier's expression came down across his face. He drew a breath, but he did not speak, waiting instead for Tehre or Sicheir to give him a lead he could follow. Tehre would have been happy if she'd had an idea about what lead to give.

The man let the token fall against his shirt in plain sight and came forward a step. "Tehre Amnachudran Tanshan?" he asked her. His eyes moved to Lord Bertaud. "Lord Bertaud, son of Boudan?"

"Yes," Tehre admitted, her mouth dry. Lord Bertaud lifted an eyebrow and inclined his head. If he felt in the least nervous, his courtier's mask hid it so well Tehre could not tell.

The man bowed his head a little and then asked Sicheir, "And you, honored sir?"

"I—" Sicheir cleared her throat. "Sicheir Amnachudran, my lord. This lady's brother."

"Of course," the man murmured, neither surprised nor, apparently, curious about Sicheir's presence. He turned back to Tehre. "Lady Tehre, I am Detreir Enteirich. My master, Brechen Glansent Arobern, sends me to you to proclaim his desire that you attend him at once in Breidechboden. Will you come?"

It had never crossed Tehre's mind that the king would

actually care that she had ignored his wishes and instead
headed north; it was so small a defiance, and she so
unimportant, it seemed incredible he had even noticed.
And instead he had not only noticed but cared enough
to send one of his own agents after her...She wondered
whether the agent had tracked them through the back
roads around the capital, or whether he'd simply come
straight to Dachsichten...Her family always did stay at
this inn when they traveled either north or south. It had
not occurred to her to stay anywhere else. She could only
say, helplessly, "Of course."

Detreir Enteirich bowed acknowledgment. Then,
straightening, he turned to Lord Bertaud. "My lord," he
said gravely, "my royal master acknowledges that he cannot
require your attendance. However, he requests your presence at his court. He bids me say to you: As you were so
kind as to escort Lady Tehre north, he hopes your kindness
will not permit you to abandon her as she returns south."

Lord Bertaud flushed, slowly. His jaw set, the neutral courier's manner falling away like the mask it was.
"Does he say that?" He paused, clearly on the edge of
continuing: *Well, you can tell your royal master*. But he
didn't say it. He glanced at Tehre, hesitated, and said to
her instead of addressing the king's agent, "Lady Tehre, I
would be honored if you would permit me to escort you
wherever you wish to go."

Tehre nodded gratefully. If the king was angry enough
to send one of his agents after her, she thought she might
be very happy to have the Feierabianden lord ready to
speak for her before the throne.

"I'm coming, too," Sicheir said sharply, just a little
too quickly.

The agent turned his head to gaze at Sicheir. "Yes," he said, and paused, studying the other man. Then he continued, "I believe that would be wise. I am permitted, if not required, to inform you that Casnerach Fellesteden has brought a legal action against Lady Tehre and against your family, in regard to the death of his uncle, Perech Fellesteden."

There was a small, frozen pause. Sicheir drew a breath, looked once at Tehre, and let it out without speaking. Then he said, "We'll want to begin legal proceedings against Casnerach Fellesteden and against the Fellesteden estate."

"Of course," agreed the agent. "That is why I suggested you return to the capital. I think—personally, you understand—that you would be very wise to return to Breidechboden and address your legal affairs." He glanced at each of them in turn and added to Tehre, "I am instructed to make all reasonable haste. A brief delay for tea and breakfast seems reasonable. But, Lady Tehre, I must ask you to accommodate my necessity."

"Yes," she said numbly.

The agent bowed again, politely, and strolled out to the courtyard to wait for them.

Tehre blinked, swallowed, and said at last, "Meierin— tell the innkeeper we will want plenty of tea, will you?" and walked over to the table where the Arobern's agent had been sitting.

"How can you be so calm?" Sicheir demanded, taking a long stride to get in front of her, gripping her arm to make her stop and face him. "Tehre—"

"You're shouting," Tehre observed. "People will look." It wasn't quite true, and the common room was still nearly empty, but it made her brother stop and think, and it got him to let her go. Tehre pulled out a chair and dropped into it, feeling that she might still be dreaming—she would have preferred to dream of griffins and a fiery wind rather than think about what had just happened. She thought she might never have woken into a less welcoming morning. She would have gladly pulled the inn down on itself, brick by ugly yellow brick, if it would have hurried the staff with the tea. Instead, she rested her elbows on the table and laced her fingers over her eyes. The headache reverberated at the back of her skull.

"Tehre—" her brother began again.

Tehre interrupted without looking up. "Do you think the stable boys have our horses ready? And Lord Bertaud's carriage? Are all our people up?"

Sicheir paused. "I'll go see to it," he said tightly, and strode out.

Lord Bertaud put a cup of tea in front of Tehre—hot and bitterly astringent; he must have watched to see how she liked it. He pulled out a chair of his own. The echoes of hurried men drifted through the inn, so Tehre assumed Sicheir must have roused out all the retainers and guards and servants. She wanted to run in circles, shrieking. She slid her hands back over her eyes instead.

"If I may ask," Lord Bertaud said quietly beside her. "Who is this man? Not a court lord, surely?"

Tehre dropped her hands to the rough surface of the table, looked at her tea for a moment, then picked up the cup at last and sipped. The astringent liquid seemed both to clear her mouth of the cottony feel of too restless a night and her mind of the shock that had met them along with the dawn. She put the cup back down, looked at the

Feierabianden lord, and sighed. "A king's agent," she explained. "He speaks with the king's voice; orders from him are as binding as commands from the king himself. I think—I think the Arobern must *really* have meant it when he told me to go home. But who ever would have expected—?"

"I think perhaps your king is angry with me, not with you," Lord Bertaud said. He gave her an inquiring glance. "Do you think? He can't command me to return, so he commands you and offers a slight against my honor if I refuse to accompany you. Well, we shall see." His eyes, over the rim of his own cup, were shadowed and grim. "You might have done better to go north on your own, Lady Tehre. I am sorry—"

Tehre shook her head. "If Fellesteden's heirs are moving against me, against my family, somebody had better be there to counter them. Though Sicheir—if the Arobern is angry with me, though I hope you are right about that, but if he is, then *Sicheir* is the one who should answer whatever charges have been made." She was silent for a moment, thinking about that. Then she added, "I'm sorry the Arobern is using me to compel you to return." And angry, she found. She was even more angry than frightened. The king's sending an agent after her somehow solidified her conviction that whatever was wrong in the north was *terribly* wrong. The king ought to have told her what it was, he ought to have *sent* her north, did he really think she would only stumble over her skirts and get in the way of his mage?

"Ah," Lord Bertaud said softly. After a moment, he added, "Lady Tehre...I confess I feel a great urgency to go north."

Tehre began to say, *Oh, you, too?* But then she put one puzzling observation together with another and said instead, "Oh, because of the griffin we saw flying over the river?"

An unconsidered gesture from the Feierabianden lord nearly tipped over his cup; he steadied it hastily and gave Tehre an unsettled look.

Tehre had no idea whether she should apologize, or, if so, for what. It seemed obvious that Lord Bertaud had, or felt he had, some connection or understanding with the griffins. Probably he did. The Feierabianden king had reached his accommodation with the griffins *somehow*. She slanted a curious look at the foreign lord. His manner was bland, his expression neutral, his eyes hiding...what, she wondered. What had Lord Bertaud's role actually *been* in the brief, ferocious struggle in Feierabiand in the early summer?

She did not ask that. She asked instead, "What does it mean that we saw a griffin so far south? Why do you need to go north?"

Lord Bertaud's mouth tightened. He did not answer.

Tehre tapped the table restlessly with the tips of her fingers. "You said you would escort me south. I could free you from that promise—"

"Lady—"

"But if you could tell me why you need to go north, maybe I could see whether I, too, should go north. Even in despite of my king's command." She tilted her head back, meeting the foreigner's eyes with direct inquiry. "Do *you* know what the trouble *is* in the north?"

"No," the Feierabianden lord admitted in a low voice. "But I think it may be worse than even your king suspects.

I have—" He paused, then shrugged and said simply, "I have a suspicion about this."

"A suspicion," Tehre repeated. She eyed the foreigner. "A suspicion, is it?"

But then Sicheir came back in, and after him the king's agent, and there was no more chance to speak privately.

CHAPTER 11

Eben Amnachudran's house looked exactly as homey and comfortable as Gereint recalled. The big house sprawled amid the wide scattering of stables and smoking sheds and other outbuildings. The wheat was not yet quite ready for harvesting, but a scattering of women and men worked in the neat gardens or collected fruit from the orchards of apple and pear trees that surrounded the house. Cattle grazed in generous pastures. Nearer the road, a boy and four dogs watched over a flock of tall black-faced goats with tawny coats and soft, floppy ears.

Gereint, keeping his expression blank, glanced sideways at Beguchren. The mage was studying the estate and frowning. "What?" Gereint asked, just a little too sharply.

"That pond is empty," Beguchren answered, not appearing to notice the sharpness.

Gereint frowned, too, and followed the direction of the other man's gaze. It was true. He had not noticed at once, but the new pond Eben Amnachudran had recently constructed, nearly filled with water when Gereint had first seen it, now contained only a glaze of dry, cracked mud across the bottom. He looked farther, up the hills, and found that the stream that should have fed the pond was dry as well. "It's late in the summer, now," he said uncertainly. But in his mind, he heard Amnachudran's voice: *My house is at the base of some low hills, where a stream comes down year-round.*

Beguchren shook his head. "Not that late. And there should be plenty of rain here and in those mountains"— he nodded toward the gray-lavender shapes of the far mountains—"no matter how late the season."

"The griffins are interfering with the rain?" Gereint asked him.

Beguchren only shook his head again and nudged his mare forward at a gentle walk.

Gereint followed reluctantly. He imagined riding into the courtyard and one of the hostlers coming forward to take their horses; he could all but hear the man's friendly *Ah, Gereint, back for a visit?* and Beguchren's raised eyebrows. The mage might be distracted by thoughts of griffins and dry streams and lack of proper rainfall, but he could hardly be so distracted as to miss anything of the sort.

It wouldn't have to be a hostler. One of the maids could say something, one of the men-at-arms who had come south with Sicheir and returned. Eben Amnachudran himself, if Tehre's letters had gone astray: *Why, Gereint, back from Breidechboden! Didn't you get on with Tehre after all, then? And who is your friend?*

He should have sent a letter himself—he should have

hired a fast courier to carry it. He and the king's mage might have outridden Tehre's letter if she'd sent hers with some slow, heavy-laden merchant or tradesman. Why hadn't he *asked* how she'd sent the letters?

But the man-at-arms at the gate was not one Gereint recognized, and the hostlers who came to take their horses were equally unfamiliar. The man-at-arms took their names with a kind of grim satisfaction that suggested the recent presence of griffins even before he spoke. "We are very glad to bid you welcome, lord mage!" he said to Beguchren. "We have been much troubled of late. Please allow me to guide you—I will send at once to the honored Eben Amnachudran, master of this house—I assure you, lord mage, he will be very glad to welcome you."

The man-at-arms sent servants running, himself leading them to a library, a warm, comfortable, crowded room lit by round porcelain lamps and heavy with the dusty smell of old books. Half a dozen chairs were arranged in a small group near the room's one window. They had elaborately carved legs and backs, but their cushions were thick and soft and the rug beneath them was large and likewise soft. Gereint was too nervous to sit down, but he pointedly shifted a chair a little out from the others for Beguchren. The mage gave Gereint an ironic look, but settled into the chair without comment.

Eben Amnachudran came to them there, a very few minutes later. Gereint stared urgently into his face, trying to ask without words, *Did you get the letters, do you know what happened?* Trying to command soundlessly, *Don't know me, don't recognize me.*

Amnachudran did not even glance at Gereint. His smile was welcoming and appeared perfectly guileless, but he focused entirely on Beguchren. Gereint felt the knots of tension in his neck and back begin, very slowly, to relax.

"Lord mage!" Eben Amnachudran said to Beguchren, bowing swiftly. "Welcome, my lord, to my house and to the northern mountains, and may I be so bold as to say you're very welcome indeed? We have had a challenging few days. I hope that is why you have come?"

"Yes," Beguchren began, but paused as Lady Emre came in. She was carrying a large platter with tea things and cakes. She nodded, smiling, and said warmly, "My lord mage."

To Gereint's well-concealed—he hoped—surprise, Beguchren rose, walked forward, and took her hands. He was almost exactly her height. He said, "Emre. How long has it been?"

"Too long, truly. Please, sit. May I offer you tea? I believe you take honey and milk in your tea? Have a cake, do. Our cook would be the envy of many a great house in Breidechboden, so perhaps it's as well we dwell so far removed, though it means we see our friends too seldom."

Eben Amnachudran watched this cordial meeting between his wife and the king's mage with no sign of surprise. He had known, Gereint surmised, that they were friends. Or at least warm acquaintances. Well, his wife was one of *those* Tanshans; small surprise she should have at least some acquaintance with a court mage. And, being herself, any acquaintance would naturally be a warm one. That was good, surely.

And, better still, Emre Tanshan, like her husband, glanced at Gereint with not even the smallest flicker of recognition. "And your associate?" she said to Beguchren. She turned to Gereint with the exact polite smile she would, no doubt, have given any stranger arriving in a friend's company. "Would you care for tea, honored sir?"

There was tea all around, and cakes. The cakes were made with chopped apples and coarsely ground walnuts and had been generously glazed with honey. Eben Amnachudran took a chair near his wife and let her carry the conversation, which she did effortlessly, staying to safe subjects: painting and poetry and court gossip, but nothing unkind or even ungenerous. Neither Emre nor Beguchren mentioned griffins.

Amnachudran sipped tea and said very little, but his gaze was shrewd and knowing. He glanced once, unobtrusively but not quite covertly, at Gereint. Then he offered him a plate of cakes and a smile. "You are a mage yourself, honored sir?" he asked courteously.

"An associate," Beguchren answered for Gereint, smoothly, while Gereint was still wondering how to answer. "Honored sir, perhaps you and your lady wife will describe for me now the events of, as you say, your 'challenging' days? You have, perhaps, seen griffins flying overhead? Perhaps repeatedly crossing your sky?"

Eben Amnachudran and his wife shared a wordless glance. Then Amnachudran turned back to Beguchren. "My lord, as you say. Not today, as happens, but I set one of the boys to counting: We have had griffins pass overhead thirty-seven times, beginning nine days ago and continuing through the day before yesterday, at intervals from three to fourteen hours, averaging nine hours. We have seen three to seven griffins at a time, with the modal number of griffins being three."

Gereint was mildly amused. How like a scholar to calculate intervals between flights and numbers of griffins.
He glanced at Beguchren, wondering if the mage found
these numbers useful. Beguchren showed nothing but
impenetrably polite attention.

"The track of their flight," Amnachudran was continuing, "has shown a steady trend...If you would be so kind,
my dear..." His wife brought a scroll from a rack and
helped her husband unroll a map across the widest table
in the room. Everyone leaned forward to look.

"You see, the first flight we saw curved along here,
above the hills." Amnachudran traced a curving line north
of his home with the tip of a finger. "I did not begin to
chart as early as I should have, but by noon of the second
day, the line was here, parallel to the original line, you
see, but almost directly above the house. And by that
evening, here." They could all see the progression of that
line from north to south. The last flight Amnachudran
drew for them had been along a line well south of the
estate.

"Extrapolating from this trend...and in the clear
understanding that trends usually do not continue indefi-
nitely...nevertheless, I calculate that these overflights
probably began to cross over Tashen four or five days
ago."

"Yes," murmured Beguchren.

"That is a concern, my lord, because..." Amnachudran
hesitated. "It might be better to show you..."

"Please tell me," Beguchren said quietly.

Amnachudran opened his hands, a gesture of conces-
sion. "At first it was only red dust," he said. "And sand,
and a hot wind. That wind still blows every morning. Or

not this morning, did it?" He glanced at his wife for confirmation, and she nodded. He went on. "But for the past several days. It comes off the mountains, so it should be a cool wind, but... and it's not merely a hot wind, it's a wind allied to fire, as Beremnan Anweierchen describes in his *Countries Near and Far*. Are you familiar—?"

"Yes, I understand. And after the dust?"

Emre Tanshan leaned forward anxiously, her hands clasped in her lap. "We sent word south, Lord Beguchren. So they would have warning. First came the red dust, carried on a hot wind. And the sun began to come up... different. Fiercer. Then..." her voice trailed off.

"We sent men upriver and down," Amnachudran said, picking up the tale once more. "After our stream failed. It's not only our stream and our pond. The river, the upper Teschanken, where it comes down out of the mountains, it's run dry. Not merely low. The men who went upriver tell me that the desert has cut across the river's channel and claimed all the mountains along there—" His wave indicated the general extent of the desert, north and much too far to the east. "Now, you may know, my lord, that Gestechan Wanastich describes finding, in his history of Meridanium, an immense lake high in the mountains. A lake that feeds the Teschanken and, so Wanastich had it, the Nerintsan River as well. I always wanted to follow the river north and find that lake," he added tangentially, his didactic tone going wistful on this thought. "It must be a splendid sight: a lake as great as a sea, cupped in the mountains between earth and sky... Well." He recollected himself. "But whether the lake itself has been encompassed by the desert and has actually gone dry, and what an immense undertaking it must be to destroy so great a lake—but, that is to say, whether the griffins have destroyed the lake or merely cut across the Teschanken south of the lake, we've no way of knowing."

There was a little silence. Gereint thought about the Teschanken and Nerintsan Rivers, which not only linked north to south but also watered all of Meridanium and the whole eastern half of Casmantium. If the whole lower Teschanken ran dry—not merely low, but dry, as Amnachudran said—he said in a low voice, "Casmantium can't exist without the river."

"Not as it is presently constituted, no," agreed Emre Tanshan.

"Without the rivers, a good part of the north will turn to desert," put in her husband. "Not necessarily to a country of fire, but to a country where men cannot easily live. Our rain rides the cool winds off the mountains: If the griffin's lay their desert across those mountains, none of our northern towns will survive. Tashen, Metichteran, Pamnarichtan—and over in Meridanium, Alend and Taub, Manich and Streitgan and Raichboden—everyone will have to flee south, as the people of Melentser did."

"Dislocation enough to have the folk of Melentser displaced. But if the whole north empties, we will have nowhere to go," Lady Emre said in a low voice.

"The river sustains Dachsichten as well," murmured Gereint, not really speaking *to* anyone, but merely speaking aloud because his mind had leaped ahead and presented him with images too grim to contain in silence. "And Breidechboden. Geierand will do well enough, and Wanenboden, and Abreichan. Or they would, if not for northern refugees. But there will be so many refugees." He could imagine, far too vividly, the flood of desperate folk from north to south, hopelessly in excess of the numbers the south could sustain.

Peaceful towns like Geierand would simply be overrun and destroyed, as surely as though a plague of locusts had come down on the land, and far more thoroughly. But Breidechboden and Abreichan—he knew that the great cities of the south would arm against the mass of northern refugees—they would have no choice—he tried not to imagine soldiers in their shining ranks drawn up against the ragged multitude of refugees, but the images were vividly compelling and he could not put them out of his mind. He said, his tone hushed with horror, "Casmantium will be destroyed. It can't sustain this blow. Something will survive, but…I think it won't be a country any of us will recognize. It will be something small and poor and weak and well practiced in brutality…"

Beguchren settled back in his chair, tented his hands, and gazed at Gereint over the tips of his fingers. "Destroying Casmantium is, I believe, the griffins' whole intention," he agreed.

"How can they dare? However strong they are—however few cold mages we have—how many griffins can there *be*? A few thousand? They must know we will spend however many men and mages we have to stop this—"

"Due to a slight miscalculation on our part, and a tremendous stroke of good fortune on theirs, the griffins at this time possess an immense advantage that we may not, in fact, be able to overcome." Beguchren's quiet, uninflected voice concealed, barely, a horror that, Gereint was beginning to suspect, equaled his own.

Everyone gazed at the frost-haired mage, waiting. For

a moment, Gereint thought he was not going to answer their unspoken question. But he said eventually, "I should think you had word of the, ah, the broad outline of events in Feierabiand."

"Well, yes, an outline, at least," Lady Emre said sympathetically. "I was very sorry to hear of your loss, Beguchren."

"Yes," the mage said, and paused. For the first time, Gereint wondered exactly how many cold mages had died in Feierabiand: all of them, he knew, except Beguchren. Half a dozen? A dozen? And how many of those mages had been Beguchren's personal friends? He had understood the tactical problems that arose from the lack of cold mages—or at least, he had understood that tactical problems did arise from that lack—but now, for the first time, he flinched from the question of how it would feel to be the only surviving mage.

"But you—" began Amnachudran, but stopped.

"But, Beguchren," protested Lady Emre, bolder than her husband, "you're only one man, after all, however powerful—"

"I can effectively oppose fire. I am alone, but so is the remaining griffin mage, I believe." Beguchren's voice had gone taut. "He is very powerful, but I can challenge him. If it were only he and I, I would challenge him and win. But there is now a fire mage in the high desert who was born human, whose nature is not quite the nature of a griffin. Had you heard so? Well, it is true. She lends the griffins an advantage I—we—cannot well answer.

"We hadn't thought the griffins bent on our destruction. They seemed otherwise inclined, and we didn't understand that they might use Melentser as a bridgehead to support an attack on all of Casmantium. Or, as you might guess, we would have tried much harder to prevent them taking Melentser. But we failed of imagination, to our great cost. Now, with that human fire mage to support them, a few thousand griffins may well match all the men and mages we can possibly bring to this...conflict." He did not quite say "war."

"But..." Gereint protested, but then, under Beguchren's level gaze, did not know what to say and fell silent once more.

"I have one method in mind that may hold some promise." Beguchren turned his gaze toward Eben Amnachudran. "I will wish to see the desert. I also wish my associate Gereint Enseichen to see the desert."

Gereint kept his expression placid, refusing to be drawn.

Beguchren finished quietly, "Then I will need a day or two to arrange...certain matters. I will have instructions for you, I believe. And then...we shall see what can be done."

"If you believe anything can be done, my lord," Eben Amnachudran said fervently, "I assure you, my household and all my resources are entirely at your service."

Beguchren inclined his head in courteous, unsurprised acceptance of this offer. But his glance at Gereint questioned whether Gereint too might be willing to place everything he owned and all his resources at his service.

"I understand why you want me to see this," Gereint said to him a little later, as they made ready to ride up into the hills and look at the desert that, they were assured, lay hardly any distance from the estate. "But I've seen it before. It hardly seems necessary to ride out to the desert on my account. What if there are griffins there? Their mage, the one you say opposes you, what if he is there now, today, waiting for you?"

"He is not. He is the last of the great griffin mages; he will be too wise to risk himself against me when he has no need. He will not face me directly unless I can manage to force a confrontation."

"Can you?"

Beguchren lifted an ironic eyebrow. "The griffin mage thinks not, I suspect. He is mistaken. I will force him to face me, Gereint, but not today, and not until I have arranged circumstances to my liking."

Gereint shrugged noncommittal acceptance of this assurance, took the reins of both the horses a hostler had led out for them—not the black mares, which had been turned out to rest, but a pair of Amnachudran's horses that he had loaned them for the afternoon—and without comment turned to assist Beguchren to mount. Equally without comment, the small mage set his foot in the cupped hands Gereint offered. Straightening, Gereint tossed him up into his saddle without effort. He said, "An easy ride up into the hills, an easy ride back in time for supper: That's the idea, is it?"

Beguchren gathered up his reins, gazing down at Gereint with a wry look in his pale eyes. "Just so."

"We don't intend to do anything more than look at the desert this afternoon."

"Just so," Beguchren repeated.

Gereint shook his head, asked rhetorically, "Why do I doubt that assurance?"

"You needn't. It's quite true."

"I've seen the griffin's desert before," Gereint repeated.

"Then this afternoon you can see it again. Or will you balk?"

"Now? No. Maybe later. Now, it's either too late to shy away, or too early." Gereint swung up into the saddle of the other horse, a sturdy bay gelding with the height to carry a man his size, and gave Beguchren an ironic little nod.

The mage didn't flinch from that irony, but only led the way out of the courtyard and through the near orchard without hesitation, heading straight north as though he knew exactly where he was going.

He probably did, Gereint reflected. Probably he could feel the precise border where the country of earth gave way to the country of fire; probably it was like an ordinary man watching a storm approach across the southern plains, or the line of a swift brush fire pass through a woodland. Something obvious, powerful, and potentially dangerous.

There was no red dust riding a hot wind today; Beguchren's doing, Gereint suspected. But the orchards showed the effects of the past few days: The leaves of the apple trees had gone dry and brown around the edges, and the green was leaching away to browns and yellows as though the season had already turned. Ripe and near-ripe fruit had been picked, but the unripe apples still on the trees were shriveling on the branches.

They passed the empty pond and rode up along the dry bed of the stream that should have fed it, topped the hill and headed up again at an angle along the slope of the next hill. Then they crested that hill and looked down across the slope that fell away from them toward the next, higher, rank of hills, leading to the mountains beyond.

The edge of the desert lay directly over the crest of the hill less than a mile to the west from Eben Amnach-udran's estate. Gereint had expected to find the border close at hand, but never so close as this. He drew his horse to a halt, staring, appalled, at that boundary. "How can it have come this far?" he whispered. "They've brought their desert all the way across the river. How can they have done this?"

"When we gave them Melentser, we gave them a hold they have used to claw their way across all this country," Beguchren answered. "Let us go down to it." Gereint could read no expression in the mage's fine-boned face.

Gereint had forgotten the strange, terrible, profoundly foreign power of the griffins' desert. He had forgotten the ferocity of its sun, the hard metallic glint of its sky, the savage knife-edged red cliffs that sliced the hot wind into ribbons. Flames flickered among the red sands, dying away again like water ebbing on a beach, leaping up without tinder and burning without fuel. No griffins were in sight; not riding the fiery wind nor lounging upon the red cliffs. But near at hand, two of the scimitar-horned fire deer flung up their heads in alarm at the glimpse of men and horses and fled across the desert in long low bounds, flames leaping up where they disturbed the sand.

Gereint feared that Beguchren might cross the intangible boundary between earth and fire and set foot on the red sand, under that fierce sun. He did not know what he expected might happen then—a hundred griffin's coming down, outraged, out of that empty sky? The griffin's own mage pouring himself out of the burning wind? Or that other mage who had once been human flickering out of the hot wind to meet the cold mage, perhaps. But Beguchren drew his horse to a halt a little on the earth side of the border and merely gazed into the country of fire, his gray eyes impenetrably remote.

Gereint nudged his own horse up beside the other and asked in a hushed tone, "You mean to challenge...all this? Alone?"

"Not alone," Beguchren murmured.

Gereint stared at him, incredulous. "You should have brought every mage in Casmantium with you. Some must remain. If not cold mages, at least ordinary earth mages." He tried not to allow his voice to rise to a shout, but found he could not match Beguchren's composure. "What does the Arobern think he's about, sending you alone? If you need makers—if you need makers who can leap right through vocation and gift and power and remake themselves into mages to serve you, then you should have brought every maker in Breidechboden here! And you only brought me?"

Beguchren returned a calm gaze. "The Arobern wanted to give me an army. I persuaded him to give me a free hand, instead. Ordinary mages would not understand what they saw here: They would see"—he nodded toward the desert ahead of them—"*all this*, as you say, and they would lose all capacity for balanced thought. They would only wish to argue with me. Nor do I need every maker in Breidechboden—or if I do, then nothing will suffice. If I am right, I will in fact need only one maker."

"You can't...How can I possibly...What is it you intend to do?"

"Let us go back a little way." Beguchren reined his

horse away from the desert's edge and toward a tumble of flat gray stones set amid a patch of tough, wiry-stemmed bindweed, its graceful heart-shaped leaves and perfumed white flowers as yet untroubled by the encroaching desert. Beguchren slid down from his horse and waded through the tangled vines to sit on one of the stones, gesturing to Gereint to join him. "Let it go," he said, of Gereint's bay gelding. "They won't wander far."

"Unless a griffin comes."

"None will, today. Sit down. I'll tell you a story."

"Will you? About this past summer?" Gereint slipped his horse's bit, twisted the reins around the pommel, and picked his way through the weeds to join Beguchren. His horse dropped its head, untroubled by the burning desert not a hundred feet away, and began nipping leaves off the bindweed.

"Yes. But my story begins earlier than that." The white-haired mage tucked one foot up, laced his fingers around his knee, and watched the horses. His expression was closed and ironic; Gereint suspected that he was not seeing the horses or the bindweed or the stones or even, perhaps, the desert beyond. Beguchren said, his tone perfectly level, "This was my fault, you know. Or the fault of all the cold mages, if you like, but only I remain to take the blame for our mistake. That is only just. It was my mistake as much as anyone's. How shall I put this? We saw an opportunity to use the king's ambition to destroy the griffins once and for all, and we took it."

Gereint didn't think that he made any sound or movement, but the mage's fine-boned face turned to him as though he had exclaimed aloud. Ice-pale eyes met his, remote as winter.

"We didn't think of it in quite that way, of course," said the mage. "The king was ambitious for a new conquest, and we, well, we longed to rid Casmantium of the threat of fire. Someone thought of a plan. I hardly know, now, whose idea it was, in the beginning. But I favored it as strongly as anyone." He was silent for a moment.

Gereint did not speak; he hardly breathed.

"We thought we would drive the griffins out of their desert and across the mountains into Feierabiand," Beguchren went on at last. "We thought we would send them before us, a storm of fire and wind, and that, coming behind them, we would find Feierabiand distracted and weakened. Then the king could have his new province—or if he failed of that ambition, we did not care. We thought we and the mages of Feierabiand would, in the end, join against any few remaining griffins and destroy them utterly. Then the country of earth would in time overwhelm the country of fire." He paused again.

After a moment, when the mage did not continue, Gereint said quietly, "Everyone knows something went wrong. But I never heard anything but guesses as to exactly what happened."

Beguchren's mouth crooked; his smile held irony rather than humor. He said, "Nothing went wrong, at first. We came into the desert swiftly and quietly and came upon the griffins in the dark. We drew upon the long, slow memories of the sleeping earth. We smothered fire with the weight of earth and laid a killing cold down before us and around us, and they could not withstand us. In those first moments, we destroyed almost all of the griffin mages: all but one. Anasakuse Sipiike Kairaithin, greatest of the griffin mages. But even he could not hold against our concerted effort. The griffins fled west and south, just as we had intended, and we spun a net of frost across the sand behind them to hold their fire from rising again...

"It was not an effortless victory. We lost Leide. She had hair like a drift of snow, eyes black as a midwinter night, and a cold, clean power like the heart of winter. We lost Ambreigan, who was eldest of us all: He was too proud, and tried to stand alone against three griffin mages. But there were seven of us who lived to see the dawn, and likely it was a gentler dawn than that country had ever seen. Though we grieved, we counted our battle a victory and we declared our war as good as won." He stopped.

This time Gereint did not prompt him. But after a moment, the mage went on, starkly. "Then the griffins found in Feierabiand a weapon none of us had expected. A human girl, a girl right on the edge of waking into her power as a mage. Kes, daughter of...some Feierabianden peasant, I suppose. We don't know her birth, but it doesn't matter. Sipiike Kairaithin found her and took her and poured fire into her. He corrupted the magecraft in her before it could wake."

Gereint exclaimed, "He made her into a *griffin*?" and then, afraid Beguchren might stop, leaned back and pressed his lips together, trying to pretend he had not spoken.

But the mage barely seemed to have heard him. Though he glanced at Gereint, he did not really seem to see him. He spoke quietly, almost as though to himself: "He made a fire mage of her. He made a weapon of her. Or, not exactly a weapon. He made her into, not a sword, but a shield. He made her into something no griffin could be: a healer of fire. We did not realize at once what he had done. He made it impossible for men to do battle with griffins, for that girl would heal them as swiftly as they were struck down. We did not understand this quickly enough. By the time we discovered it, we had already lost everything. We were too confident."

Beguchren meant himself and his fellows, Gereint realized: He meant the cold mages. He was not thinking of the Arobern or the ordinary soldiers at all. He spoke with a kind of calm desolation that was very hard to listen to.

"While soldiers battled, Sipiike Kairaithin hunted us down and killed us," Beguchren said, still with that terrible calmness. "We did not understand quickly enough...and then we found the King of Feierabiand had made a terrible bargain with the griffins and allied his country with fire. And so we were defeated. And at first we"—now he meant himself and the Arobern, Gereint guessed—"at first we thought that was the end of it." He bowed his head for a moment, then seemed to recollect himself out of memory. He turned back to Gereint, smiling his wry, imperturbable smile. Gereint found he had preferred it when he had not known what depths of loss and grief lay behind that smile.

"We expected a little political maneuvering, a temporary embarrassment, shall we say? But it is clear now that the griffins intend to force their way to a stronger, more decisive victory than we imagined. I think, now, that they intended this from the first." The mage nodded toward the desert, where golden flames flickered across red sand and the fierce sun glared down out of a metallic sky. "We gave them Melentser and the surrounding country. The griffins said they did not desire vengeance, that they would be content to have Melentser as their indemnity. But they are treacherous creatures. We did not expect—how could we?—that the griffins would drive their desert so far east, or use their new foothold in our country to strike against Casmantium's very life. It did not occur to us that they could, or perhaps it did not occur to us—even to me, though *I*, of us all, should have suspected it—that they would realize their own advantage and press it home."

"So you came here," Gereint said quietly. "You alone. Except for me."

Beguchren moved his shoulders, not quite a shrug. "I would do anything to redeem our mistake." He glanced up, meeting Gereint's eyes. "I would certainly sacrifice one maker. One skilled, strongly gifted maker; the sort of maker who already has a thread of magecraft running unrecognized through his mind and soul and gift. That sort of maker might do for me what must be done." He paused. Then he went on, deliberately, "It was not your mistake, Gereint. But I am compelled to ask you to help me repair it."

Gereint met his eyes. "But you can't force me to help you," he said. It was not quite a question.

Beguchren bowed his head again. "If the *geas*, if any part of magecraft, could force you to answer my need, I would use it. As it happens, nothing I know can compel you to the...immolation and remaking of the self that is necessary."

"Save voluntary self-abnegation." Gereint tried to keep to the same deliberate tone, with how much success he could not tell.

Beguchren inclined his head. "Just so. But not today." He rose, glanced once more across the hillside to the burning sands of the desert, and then stepped instead toward his horse.

Gereint also got to his feet, took one step across the mat of tangled flowers, and called after him, "Why not today?"

The mage stopped and swung around. For nearly the first time in Gereint's experience, he seemed surprised. He began to speak, hesitated, and said at last, visibly choosing his words, "The, ah, appropriate circumstances are not yet properly arranged. I dare not act until I have done everything possible to ensure success. But hold to this image"—he nodded toward the desert, beautiful and terrible and utterly foreign to the country of men—"and when the day comes at last down to the hour, I hope you will ask that question again."

The ride back to Eben Amnachudran's house was very silent and not nearly long enough to suit Gereint, who would have liked a good deal more time to think through everything Beguchren had told him. They had seemed to Gereint to stay a long time looking at the desert, to sit a long time on the gray rocks. But the sun was still high above the western horizon when they came back through the orchard and into the courtyard. Here in the country of men, the sun seemed only a little too large and too fierce as it dropped slowly toward the western horizon. Clouds stretched in crimson bands across a deep azure sky; the tawny hills rolled out below, with the distant mountains a ruddy gold above. It was beautiful. But both hills and mountains should have been green with late summer, not tawny and gold with autumn.

Hostlers came to take the horses, darting anxious glances up at Beguchren and only slightly less anxious ones toward Gereint. He thought he recognized one of the men. But the hostler gave no sign that the recognition was mutual. He only gave a respectful little nod and wordlessly took the bay gelding away to the stables.

They found Eben Amnachudran in the room that was both his office and his wife's music room; or Beguchren found him there. Gereint only followed, silent and self-effacing.

The spinet was the same, the floor harp, the racks of scrolls. But the books were all neatly put away on the shelves. Gereint recognized some of the ones Amnachudran had brought from his friend's house, set now in their own places on those shelves; gold lettering embossed on rich brown cloth, or silver on red silk, or powdered opal on black leather: Maskeirien's eclogues, Deigantich's allegory about the white eagle and the black wolf, Hrelern's four great epics, Fenesheiren's *Analects*...They made Gereint think of the quiet days he'd spent cataloging philosophers' theories of materials for Tehre in the Breidechboden townhouse. He wished, with a sense as of something long ago and now forever unobtainable, that he might someday finish that work and see what use she might make of it.

"A beautiful library," Beguchren said to Eben Amnachudran, and with a slight shock Gereint recognized the faint wistfulness of his tone. The mage went to the shelves, touched one embossed leather binding and another. He turned to give Amnachudran a nod of wry self-deprecation. "One does not expect to find a collection of this quality outside the capital—or I had not. It's a lesson for me. You must have gone to great trouble to build this collection."

"Some of the choicest volumes I inherited after the loss of Melentser," Amnachudran said. "Unfortunately." He had risen respectfully to greet the lord mage, and now paused. Then he added, with a glance that took in the contents of the room, "Perhaps I had better send these south, lest some scholar inherit them from me a little sooner than I'd anticipated." His glance, sharpening, returned to Beguchren. "Perhaps you might advise me in that regard, my lord."

"The precaution might not go amiss," Beguchren said softly. He lifted a hand toward a set of chairs near the desk. "You will have a day or two to do so, if you wish. Let us sit and discuss what we shall do."

"You have instructions for me?" Amnachudran moved toward the chairs but waited for the mage to sit first. "I had hoped for that, but I did not know whether to expect it. If you have something useful for me to do, my lord mage, I would be delighted, I promise you."

Beguchren took the largest and most luxurious of the chairs and then, to Gereint's surprise, produced the purple-dyed token of a king's agent. He turned this token over in his slim fingers. It multiplied in his hand, bone clicking softly against bone, one elaborately carved token becoming two, and then four, and then eight...The mage cast the handful of tokens across Amnachudran's desk, where they rattled like dice: half came up with the Arobern spear-and-shield uppermost and the rest with the tree-and-falcon.

Beguchren said in his coolest, most precise tone, "Send to Tashen, to Metichteran, Pamnarichtan, Raichboden,

Streitgan, Manich, Taub, and Alend. All towns of any size where fewer than three days' fast travel will allow your messengers to reach the town and for men, returning, to reach this house. I will require men-at-arms from each of those towns. Each governor must send me no fewer than fifty men, even if he must arm tradesmen and farmers to fill out the numbers." He added, at Amnachudran's slightly stunned look, "They will bring their own supplies. Their own weapons, rations...tents. They do not need horses; we will not take horses up to the country of fire. You will write the orders; put in what you like. You will not be required to furnish anything but space to keep them."

"But, my lord—" Amnachudran began, then stopped.

Gereint, not so inhibited after days on the road with the mage, asked bluntly, "If you wanted an army, why strip these little northern towns of their half-practiced men? Why not take the professional army the Arobern tried to give you?"

"But I don't want an army," Beguchren said softly. He did not look directly at either of them, but only gazed with remote and rather terrible detachment into the air. The lines of his fine, ascetic face seemed to shift before Gereint: now familiar, now cold and strange. "I don't want officers who will insist on describing military options. There are no sound military options, now. I don't need soldiers who will march into the desert and die bravely. No, I don't want an army. I want a diversion."

"A..." Amnachudran began, but once again stopped. He glanced at Gereint, took a breath. Let it out. Looked back at the mage. "My lord mage...I will send to the towns, just as you command. But may I ask: a diversion for what? It will make a difference, perhaps"—he added apologetically—"for what the men are to bring, and for what, ah, other arrangements must be made."

"You are asking whether I mean to send these men to their deaths? There is some risk. But, I hope, not a dire hazard. If the diversion does not work swiftly, it will not work at all."

"But you'll sacrifice them if you must," Gereint said. Not a question.

"Oh, yes." Beguchren turned his ice-pale gaze to Gereint, no less remote for that sudden, intense focus. "I will draw Sipiike Kairaithin and his human fire mage to this place; I will compel them to face me...in the country of earth, if I can. In the country of fire, if I must. If I am able to destroy Kairaithin, that would be as well. But it is utterly crucial that the human fire mage be destroyed. Only that is vital. Her death can and will shift the balance from deep defeat to decisive victory. If this one objective is achieved, it matters little what happens to the griffin mage or to me. I will certainly sacrifice all those men to achieve that aim if I must. But I think that particular sacrifice need not be made."

There was a small, profound silence.

Then Beguchren said to Amnachudran, in a perfectly matter-of-fact tone, "Three days to gather, shall we say? But once the men are here, I believe events will move very swiftly." His glance moved, opaque, unreadable, to catch and hold Gereint's eyes. He moved his hand, a tiny gesture toward the north, indicating the desert. "And if we do not achieve victory swiftly, we will surely be defeated."

"Yes," Gereint said, a touch impatiently. "You needn't keep on. I understand."

Beguchren did not quite smile. "Yes. Very well." He glanced at Amnachudran. "You are clear on what you will do?"

Eben Amnachudran hesitated, his round face creased with worry, but he nodded.

"Within reasonable bounds, Gereint Enseichen will be able to answer any concerns you may have," the mage stated, optimistically, in Gereint's opinion. He gripped the arms of his chair, rose, and sent a remote glance from one of them to the other. "It is early, I know. However, I believe I shall retire. Gereint—"

Gereint's now-practiced eye found the subtle evidence of incipient exhaustion in Beguchren's very stillness, a stillness that was meant to conceal the tremors of sudden weakness. "Shall we—are there griffins near at hand?"

"I am holding clear the boundaries of earth," the mage murmured in absent assurance. "They do try me. But I hold the boundaries." His glance sharpened, moved to catch Amnachudran's eyes. He added, "They will wait to see what I mean to do before they set their strength against me, and what they think they see will please them—but in the end dismay them utterly. If all men play their parts with passionate sincerity."

Amnachudran's eyebrows drew together in a kind of bewildered resolution. "We'll see that all men do, then."

And if Beguchren did not lie down soon, his part would be a collapse that would dismay him and frighten everyone who wanted to depend on him, was Gereint's opinion. He confined this thought to a sharp-toned, "I'll bring up your things myself. Permit me to escort you." He took the long stride necessary to bring him to the mage's side, ready to offer covert support if necessary.

"I'll have someone show you," murmured Amnach-udran, his eyes narrowed with concern. Yes, Gereint well remembered the scholar's perceptiveness; Amnachudran had missed nothing. But he only went to the door and called for servants. "Tehre's room, for the lord mage," he told the women who came in answer to his call. "And the brown room for the honored Gereint Enseichen."

"You're very kind, honored sir," murmured Gereint, with a wry, ironic inflection that he trusted only Amnachudran caught.

The scholar moved his shoulders in a minimal shrug. "If you have a moment later, honored Gereint, perhaps you might indeed answer the concerns I do have? Within, to be sure, reasonable bounds?"

"In only a moment," Gereint assured him, and accompanied the frost-haired mage down the hall, ready to catch him if he went down. For the moment, Beguchren was concealing his weakness well enough…If it was not too far…

The room was not far. "You'll be well enough?" Gereint asked, watching the mage all but vanish into the embrace of a large and well-cushioned chair. The line between reasonable concern and hovering seemed difficult to tread, at the moment. "I'll send for tea—"

"Of course you will." Beguchren's tone was reassuringly dry. "I am quite well, Gereint. You do not need to stay so close. Go, if you wish."

Gereint gave a noncommittal shrug. "If you say so. I don't understand. You say no griffins are overhead. It's nearly dusk. If you're"—*so weak*—"experiencing such difficulty now, how can you possibly face this powerful griffin mage you say is your enemy, not to mention the human fire mage he made?"

Beguchren half smiled, leaning his head back against the headboard of his chair. "Physical strength matters less than you might think in a challenge of this sort. Besides, Gereint, when it comes at last to that challenge, I won't be alone."

Gereint looked at him for a moment. Then he said merely, "All right." He rose, turned to go out.

"Gereint," Beguchren called after him, and he turned back, surprised. But the mage did not speak again, only looked at him with uncharacteristic irresolution.

After a moment, Gereint shook his head. "It will be well enough," he said quietly. "In three days, and certainly tonight. Rest. The servant will be along soon with tea. And anything else you need, I'm sure. I'll see you in the morning. I assure you I will." He went to the door, glanced back at the mage. Beguchren was sitting quietly, watching him, his expression unreadable, his fine features shadowed by the winged headboard of the chair. Gereint hesitated another moment. Then he left him there like that, sitting alone in the dark.

Eben Amnachudran was still waiting in the library-study-music room when Gereint made his way back to it. He was alone, absently turning the pages of a book so large it barely fit on the desk. The book was bound in black leather...Erichstreibarn's *Law of Stone and Fire*, he saw.

"Topical," he commented.

"Hah." Amnachudran rose quickly and came to take his hands, looking searchingly into his face. "I have received the most incredible series of letters, fortunately in time to expect you and the lord mage. Are you well? How was Tehre when you left her? Did you know she is coming here? In company with a lord of Feierabiand, apparently."

"She's coming here?" Gereint repeated. And, "With *whom*?"

"I've sent men by every conceivable path she might take, to stop her on the way and warn her not to come. Half the folk on the road must be mine: I sent nearly all my people south days ago, after I understood the progression of the desert's edge. Including nearly everyone who would know you by sight, by the way. Someone will find her, I'm sure. I don't want her to come around the last curve of the road and find sand and fire where her home used to be...She's worried about her mother and me. And you, I believe, though she didn't quite say so. You must have suited one another rather well, or so I gather, reading between the words." He moved to sit down, waving Gereint toward a second chair. "Tell me everything."

This was difficult to do without terrifying Amnachudran over things that might have happened, but Gereint tried. The scholar listened without questions or interruptions, but his mouth tightened twice as he caught back an exclamation only with an effort. At the end, his face was pale and set. When Gereint had done, he asked only, "Do you truly think the king meant what he said to you as a threat against my daughter?" and, when Gereint had no answer, "He can't blame her for Lord Fellesteden's death. At least, he'll find little sympathy for that judgment if he tries: a young noblewoman defending herself and her household against attack the only way she could, with the only weapon to her hand?"

"You know people, I'm sure. If he tries, you must

make sure the tale that whips around Breidechboden blames me, not her."

"Yes, Tehre told me what tale you suggested for her. Though she left out...never mind. It was clever of you to recast, ah, events as you did. And generous." Amnach-udran moved restlessly, rising to light a lamp that hung over his desk; the dusk had crept down from the hills and across the house and Gereint had not noticed. The flick-ering light of the lamp sent shadows wavering through the room, made it into a small haven of human warmth beneath the crouching darkness.

The scholar went on, coming back to resume his seat: "But the king himself knows the truth about what hap-pened at my daughter's house, does he not? Nearly all the truth. So no false tale can be put about now. Perhaps it's just as well. I do know various people, and my lady wife has a great many friends, and the Tanshans would hardly want a daughter of Emre's dragged down into the mud. No...no. The king won't make good that threat. He has no reason to move against Tehre anyway. You are here, after all."

Gereint opened his hands in a gesture like a shrug. "I think you needn't concern yourself. Either the lord mage will succeed and the Arobern will be happy, or he will fail, and the Arobern will have much more important concerns than how Perech Fellesteden died, and by whose hand or will. Though, unfortunately, so will everyone else."

Amnachudran gave Gereint a sharp look. "*Will* he succeed? What is this weakness? Or did I mistake what I thought I saw?"

That took a moment. At last Gereint said carefully, "It's an intrinsic weakness, I believe, but exacerbated by the close presence of griffins. And possibly by the desert itself. I don't quite...I expect going out to look at the desert might have brought it on, or maybe working to keep the edge where it is and the griffins from pressing into our country...He doesn't like people to notice it."

Amnachudran nodded. "I could see that, too. He hid it...fairly well, I suppose."

"He does, usually. He says physical strength will matter little in the conflict he means to provoke."

"Really."

"And he reminds me that he will not face the fire mages alone."

Amnachudran looked down at his clasped hands. Then he said, "Ensemarichtan Temand disagrees with Warichteier and Anweierchen about the fundamental distinction between magecraft and ordinary magic. I gather that Beguchren Teshrichten agrees with Temand."

"He went into my mind," Gereint said slowly. "Right after he...after the Arobern gave me to him. And then he said I would suit his purposes and...began to set me tests, though I don't...I didn't understand at once what he was doing. I suppose I must have passed them. Enough of them. I haven't read Temand. But I know Beguchren means to make me into a mage. Or, no. He means me to do that to myself."

"Yes." Amnachudran tapped his fingers restlessly on the arms of his chair. He rose again, went to his shelves, and came back with a heavy volume bound in plain leather. He brought this back to his chair, absently propped a foot on the upholstered seat, rested the volume on his knee, and flipped it open, not quite at random. "Magecraft...mages...magic and the gift. Yes. Temand

says, *The making of a mage thus depends on a definition of the self and on the power to bend that definition;
magecraft does not blend with the ordinary gift, but in
that definition can lie the link between mage and ordinary
man, for every man defines himself*... And then he goes
on about, hmm, this and that." The scholar closed the
book, his shrewd eyes meeting Gereint's.

"Yes. The lord mage said that about definition of the
self. Or the making of the self, which I gather is the same
thing."

"Yes, did he? Gereint, he will make you into a mage,
but for what? What help can a brand-new, utterly inexpe-
rienced, entirely untrained mage possibly *be* to the king's
own mage? He means to betray you: bring you into power
and then rob you of that power. That is how he will find
the strength to overcome this weakness of his, defeat the
griffin mage who is his enemy, and destroy this human
fire mage he so greatly fears."

Gereint was silent for a moment. Then he asked, "Is it
betrayal if you see it coming?"

Amnachudran's eyebrows rose.

"He told me, *I will do anything.* Before you made your
guess, I made mine, and with a good deal more evidence.
He told me flatly he means to sacrifice me in this. But
what am I to do, knowing that?" Gereint went to the window, looked out into the dark. Nodded toward the north
where the desert lay hardly a spear throw from the house.
He said, "He will sacrifice me, and those men you'll call
up, and himself. Well, what else is he to do?"

Amnachudran began to speak.

Gereint shook his head, stopping him. "I could let

him drag me to the edge of the desert, but clench my eyes shut and refuse to look at it, like a child refusing to look at something that frightens him. Let the griffins' fire burn the rivers dry and plunge Casmantium into disaster: Beguchren would try to stop them by himself, I expect. He would die. Then I would be truly free." He stopped, lifted an eyebrow at Amnachudran.

The scholar looked very sober. "You won't do that."

"No. How could I?"

The pause spun out in the room to meet the greater silence waiting outside the house.

"Three days," Amnachudran said softly.

"They say waiting's the hardest part."

"They do say that. I'm sure it's sometimes true."

Gereint smiled, a touch grimly.

"Well." Amnachudran smiled in return, with some evident effort. "I'm sure supper is waiting for us, and Emre hates waiting supper. Come down with me. You can tell us about Breidechboden, and about the things Tehre's been working on, if you understood them." *And not about fire or the desert or anything to do with griffins*, he did not say. But Gereint understood that, too.

CHAPTER 12

The three days swept by in a hurried blur, which was strange because every separate moment seemed to linger as it passed. Messengers arrived; the swift little Nerintsan River had gone dry as old bone, and in Meridanium Province the desert had come down the mountains almost to the northernmost town of Alend. All the people had fled the threatened town, pressing south to Manich or Raichboden. None of the refugees had gone west from Alend to Tashen, not merely because Tashen was not a Meridanian town but also because, the messengers said, everyone thought Tashen was too far north.

"And what does that say about us?" Eben Amnach-udran said wryly, meaning that they were well north of Tashen themselves. He had sent almost all the rest of his household south as well—not merely to Pamnarichtan or Raichboden, but all the way south to Breidechboden. "And lucky we have a house there to receive them," Lady Emre said, no doubt thinking of the thousands of displaced northerners who did not have southern property or relatives.

But the estate was far from deserted. Men gathered at Amnachudran's home. A town of tents bloomed amid the orchards and pastures, red and blue, or orange and gold for the men from the Meridanian towns. Every governor had sent the required contingent, or near enough. They were not, in general, soldiers. Virtually all of the men carried spears and many had bows slung over their backs, but only about one in five had at their sides, in plain, worn scabbards, swords that had belonged to their fathers or grandfathers.

Steel flashed in the sunlight as their officers tried, cursing, to shape men-at-arms from a dozen towns, mixed with a generous number of unpracticed tradesmen and farmers, into coherent companies. But Beguchren, looking down at them from a wide window, did not seem dismayed by their disorder.

"Tashen is short," Amnachudran commented. It was the morning of the third day. He had brought a wide map and pinned it open on the largest table in the house, which was in the library. There was plenty of room for it there, as nearly all the books had been sent to the greater safety of the Breidechboden townhouse.

Amnachudran stood deferentially by Beguchren's chair as the mage settled into it and leaned forward to examine the map. Gereint wondered whether the mage had guessed that the chair, the tallest in the house, was not a normal accoutrement of the library but had been provided especially so he would not have to stand. Lady Emre was, he suspected, the subtle force behind the tall chairs that always happened to be in any room frequented by the mage and the frequency with which girls came around to offer tea with honey and milk, or bread with sharp golden cheese and apple butter, or tarts made with tart apples or buttery pears. Eben Amnachudran had tried to send his wife south along with his library and the household. But she had refused to go.

If Beguchren realized he was being cosseted, he did not object. Nor had his strength failed again during these days...so far as Gereint could tell. Now the mage turned a cool, neutral expression toward Amnachudran.

"You can't actually blame Tashen for sending a short count," the scholar went on. "I'd be amazed if they had fifty sound men left in the whole city. Everyone with sense must have headed south days ago."

"One might say the same for Metichteran," murmured Beguchren. "It's half the size, if that, and yet the governor of Metichteran managed to find fifty. All men-at-arms, too, and I think a quarter or more of the men from Tashen are shopkeepers and farmers. I rather believe the governor of Tashen has kept his own personal men-at-arms for his own personal protection."

"Is this of practical importance?" asked Lady Emre, her eyes dark with thought and worry. "There is still time to send a firmer command to Warach if we must." Warach Beichtan was the governor of Tashen. "But it would be faster to fill out the count ourselves. We could do it, if we call up every man remaining to our household. As long as you don't need them to do more than wave a spear right-end up. We, too, have few men left save the odd farmer and orchardist."

Beguchren slanted a warm look up at the woman. "Thank you, Emre, but I think that will not be necessary.

But when Warach Beichtan disregards my command, he disregards the command of the king. And when he reserves his men for his own protection, he offends against the responsibility he holds to guard his people." He paused, his gray eyes now cool and thoughtful. "Make a note of this," he said to Amnachudran. "You are one of the Arobern's judges, yes? If appropriate, later, you will send word in that capacity to the king of Beichtan's dereliction."

He meant, *If we win the victory but I am dead.* And he meant it for an order. Eben Amnachudran bent his head obediently, acknowledging the command.

"No," Beguchren continued, now speaking to them all. "We have nearly four hundred men in all. That will suffice. So long as, as you say, they all wave their spears right-end up." He glanced up at Gereint. "We will go up toward the desert at...shall we say, at the fifth hour past noon? Our little army will brandish their spears and put on a show, but we shall hope they need not be put to the test of battle."

"If they are?" Amnachudran asked him. "We have no real general to lead them; they have barely had a chance to train; they are unfamiliar to one another and under officers they do not know. They will be slaughtered to a man..."

"If it comes to battle," Beguchren said softly, "then it will not matter whether they are slaughtered in these hills or die later in their own homes or on the road south or at the gates of a southern city that will not let them in."

There was a moment of silence. Then Amnachudran said steadily, "If you permit me, my lord, I will lead those men myself. I do not claim to be any kind of general. But at least I have studied military history, and most of those men know me."

Gereint, standing behind Beguchren, swallowed a sharp protest and watched Emre Tanshan do the same. Beguchren leaned back in his chair and regarded Amnachudran with close attention. He said at last, "Honored Amnachudran...I am willing to leave these men in your hands. You are clear on the role I mean for them to play?"

"We must make a show. You intend the griffins to come down to do battle, so we must seem to offer them one. Then they will bring this fire-healer of theirs into your reach. Then you will do...what you will do, and all will fall out as it will."

"Just so." Beguchren paused. Then he said decisively, "It would indeed be well to have those men led by a commander who understands clearly what I require. You may arrange matters in that regard as you see fit." He tapped his hand gently on the widespread map. "I had hoped to avoid it, but I think we will need to enter the desert. We will go up here or here. Those are sensible lines of attack that suggest a reasonable objective. We will appear to wish to press the griffins away from the northern reaches of the river, perhaps freeing the waters to come down, if indeed Wanastich's lake is still there and only the rivers dry."

"They will believe we might attempt such an ambitious objective?"

"Desperation might reasonably drive us to this strategy. And then...I will be with you."

"Ah." Amnachudran gazed down at the map, his expression thoughtful. Then he looked at the mage. "But we will not be able to depend on you. Yes?"

"When fighting begins, if it begins, I will not be able to help you. Save by procuring a swift victory through, as it were, a back door. That will be my intention. Once their human fire mage has been destroyed, the griffins will—must—reconsider their aggressive intent."

The scholar nodded. He looked at his wife. Emre Tan-shan gazed back at him, her face set and pale. She said, answering the question he had not asked aloud, "I will wait here. If you are victorious, you will probably need a place to bring the wounded, and people to care for them, and a strongly gifted healer. And...and if the day goes otherwise, you will need someone to organize a retreat."

Amnachudran looked as though he wanted to object, as though he longed to command his wife to flee for the south now, this moment. He also looked like a man who knows he can't give any such order, or that if he does, it won't be obeyed. He said nothing, but went to her and touched her face. She lifted her hand, covered his hand with her own. Neither of them spoke.

Beguchren said merely, "Good." And then, "The fifth hour past noon. So we must prepare for that." It was a dismissal, and Amnachudran and his wife took it so. They went out together, her hand tucked in the crook of his arm.

Gereint crossed his arms over his chest, leaned his hip against the edge of the table, glanced down at the map, and then looked up deliberately to meet the mage's pale eyes. He said nothing.

"You will stay close to me," Beguchren told him. "We dare not act too quickly, and yet when we come to act, we must do so decisively. Sipiike Kairaithin must not be allowed to guess what we intend."

Gereint appreciated that "we," delivered without a trace of irony. He nodded.

"Gereint—"

Gereint held up a hand. "Don't say it. It's not necessary, and I would take it as a slur."

Frost-pale eyebrows rose over eyes the color of a winter dawn. But the mage only bowed his head a little, accepting this.

"And you?" Gereint saw the faint puzzlement in the mage's eyes and elaborated, "*You* are well enough?"

"I shall do very well," Beguchren said, blandly unemphatic. He rose. If he was suffering now from any weakness, he concealed it with admirable thoroughness.

The hills seemed steeper when one walked up them instead of rode. The mountains were not so far away; they rode through the foothills even now, close beside the Teschanken River. Or, more precisely, beside the bed where the Teschanken ought to have run. The riverbed was dust-dry now, the rounded stones exposed to view. Before them rose the sharp teeth of the mountains. Close at hand, three peaks rose hard against the sky, high granite faces shining in the late afternoon sun, dark forest cloaking their lower slopes. Two more mountains loomed to their left, on the other side of the river, seeming so close the company might walk between them by dusk.

Only Beguchren and Eben Amnachudran rode: Amnachudran because he needed to ride from one end of the marching column to the other, and the cold mage putatively because of his rank but really, Gereint suspected, to spare his strength. But also, quite deliberately, to make a show.

Beguchren was riding one of Amnachudran's horses, a gray gelding with powerful quarters and an amenable nature. The cold mage did not carry bow or spear or any weapon more dangerous than a small belt knife, but, not much to Gereint's surprise, he had somewhere found blue ribbons to braid into his horse's mane and tail. He was sitting up very straight in the saddle, with his shoulders back and his head high. He wore fine white clothing that he must have brought all the way from Breidechboden for this exact purpose: Tiny white pearls gleamed on his belt and on the cuffs of his low boots, and there was a single blue ribbon braided into his white hair. With his pale coloring and silver eyes, he looked very much as though he had been sculpted out of ice. The whole intention was to make a show, and so he did: he might have been a parade all by himself.

There were reasons to limit the number of horses. No one, not even Beguchren, would actually take a horse into the desert. This was not Feierabiand, where horse-callers might have held the animals docile and obedient even under a rain of fire. Horses would be nothing but a liability when—if—the griffins came down, and everyone knew it.

The afternoon was a fine one, though unseasonably warm. But it seemed far grimmer when one walked in company with four hundred men who all thought they were marching to battle. The men trusted Eben Amnachudran: Gereint saw how they looked to the scholar and saw that they all knew him, or knew of him, and that they were glad to have them lead them. He had not guessed that Amnachudran was so well known. He remembered him saying, *Having to run down to Tashen every time we wanted a judge was so inconvenient. Everyone seems to prefer to simply come to me.* Gereint had not, at the time, quite understood how broadly that "everyone" applied.

And they trusted Beguchren. Not as they trusted Amnachudran, but they trusted his power and skill. The officers, Gereint suspected, probably mostly guessed that Beguchren meant to sacrifice their company—any who were not fools must at least wonder. But Amnachudran had at least persuaded them that the mage meant to do it to some purpose. Thus they went forward with purpose and faith.

A sweet breeze came from the south, across the hills, smelling pleasantly of autumn grasses. The sun lay low in the west, but its light was an ordinary light and its warmth no more than pleasant in the afternoon. The hills might lie dry and golden with the too early autumn forced on them by the pressure of the griffins' approaching desert, but they were beautiful and peaceful in the quiet, and there was not a trace of red dust in the air.

Then they came over the crest of the hills and looked down upon the country of fire. To either side, the hills were sweet with autumnal gold; to either side, the mountains were still green with forest just beginning to turn red and gold; their high, wind-polished faces glittered with ice. But straight before them, running north and west, the desert shimmered with fire all the way out to the far horizon.

All the men stopped, as though by shouted command. They halted high on the summit of the hills and gazed down at the burning sands. There were no griffins in sight, but the desert itself seemed threat enough, and there cannot have been a single man of their number who did not think of simply dropping his spear and walking away, south. They were not, after all, soldiers.

Then Eben Amnachudran rode his horse out in front of the little company, turned to face the men, and declared in a clear, loud voice, "Beguchren Teshrichten, the king's own mage, is here to stop that country of sand and fire from coming down across all our homes. He did not bring an army from the south, because he does not need one. What he needs is the honest courage and resolution of ordinary men of the north, and he knew he would find that waiting here for him. And so he has." Then, in the great silence he had created, he turned, deliberately, toward the silver-eyed mage. "My lord, what will you have of us?"

"Courage and resolution," Beguchren answered, just as loudly and clearly. "We will go down into the desert, and when we are finished here, it will be once again a country of earth."

"As you command, my lord," Amnachudran said formally. He was not carrying a spear, but he lifted his arm and pointed forward, and the officers took up the command in their sharp, carrying voices, and they all went down the hill, along the ripple in the red sand that marked the bed of the dry Teschanken, and into the griffins' desert. At the edge of the desert, Amnachudran swung off his horse and stripped the saddle and bridle from it and let it go, and Beguchren did the same. And then they went down into the country of fire.

Little flames flickered amid the sands, and the towering sharp-edged cliffs stood hard against the fierce, brazen light that lay heavily across the desert, nothing like the ordinary sunlight in even the hottest southern summer.

Gereint vividly remembered the brutal hammering power
of the desert sun. He closed his eyes, swallowing, as he
walked beside Beguchren, across the boundary, and out
of the country of earth. But though he could tell when he
crossed the boundary, the heat did not come down from
the molten sky nor strike up from the fiery sands with
anything of the ferocity he recalled, and he opened his
eyes again in astonishment.

The fires died away as Beguchren walked across
the desert, and the red sand somehow took on a softer
look, as though it might lie thinly over ordinary soil.
As all the men followed him, the desert itself gave way
beneath them and around them, yielding to his power, and
although the light pounded down upon the surrounding
desert, it lay on them gently, and a sharp wind followed
them from the south, bringing the scents of earth and
water and growing things into the country of fire.

Gereint looked sharply at Beguchren. The mage's face
was calm, but his eyes were narrowed and his mouth set
hard with strain. Gereint wanted to ask, *How long can
you keep earth under our feet and a natural light over our
heads?* But if he asked, everyone who heard would know
there was a question about it. So he did not ask.

"We will go this way," Beguchren said quietly, and
walked straight forward into the stark desert, between the
high mountains, which now seemed much farther away,
half hidden by—well, not by dust nor by haze but seemingly by some quality of the air itself. Amnachudran nodded in return and waved to his captains, and the company
strode straight ahead almost without hesitation.

Before them, the fire died down under the sand;
above them, the sky softened from its terrible metallic

ferocity; to either side of their line of march, the sunlight lay gently on the desert. Gereint understood, now, why Beguchren had been so certain that the griffins would come down to meet them. This was not a challenge that could be let pass.

And on that thought, the griffins came. They came from the west, out of the blaze of the lowering sun, slicing across the face of the mountains alone or in small groups, cutting paths of stark beauty through the empty sky. Gereint first thought there might be about a hundred of them all together, but more came, and more after those, and he saw, appalled, that there actually were many more griffins than they had brought men.

Even in those first moments, when they were still distant, no one could have mistaken the griffins for hawks or eagles or any bird; the light that struck off their wings was too harsh and their beaks flashed like metal. They cried out in high, fierce shrieks like hunting eagles, and the sky behind them turned red with the violence of wind-driven sand; fire scattered down across the sand from the wind of their wings.

"We will hold them here," Beguchren declared, in a sharp, loud voice meant to carry. "As long as we hold firm, they will not be able to come down as they wish. Remember what we are about, do you hear? Hold, hold, and I shall protect you. Do you understand?"

They had discussed this, but it was not the same when one actually watched the griffins come sweeping across the wind. Eben Amnachudran had gone dead pale, but he nodded and turned to the men. Beguchren did not watch him, but gripped Gereint's arm and nodded aside, to where the red desert mounted up a rugged hill. Gereint thought he merely meant to take a place up on that hill where he could be seen, like a talisman. Then he saw the frost that spangled the sand where the mage set each foot, spreading outward from where he walked, and realized that a cold wind had risen and was blowing with increasing force past them from the south. After that, it occurred to him that Beguchren meant to teach him this power, and then he was truly frightened, because the glittering ice that challenged this desert was nothing he understood at all.

They did not go far, but when they turned, the griffins were almost upon them. They looked enormous; he had not realized they were so large: the size of lions, he thought first, but they had not even yet arrived and grew still larger in the vast sky; the size of ponies, and then heavy cart horses, and then at last they came down, with appalling speed: splendid and terrible creatures of bronze and copper and gold and jet, with ferocious talons and brilliant inhuman eyes. But the fire they brought with them only spattered harmlessly against Beguchren's cold wind, and the men held firm, their spear points glittering like chips of ice in the sunlight; arrows whistled into the sky, very few at first and then more: Most of the men had been too stunned to shoot at once. Watching the arrows rise, Gereint said, without thinking, "I should have made those arrows—or some of them—"

"There wasn't time," Beguchren answered. "I put my name and intent into them. That isn't quite the same as making them for this exact purpose, but it will serve."

Rather than striking down through the arrows and into the waiting spears, the griffins spun away to every side and climbed swiftly back into the heights of the air. They were not shrieking now: They were silent. But Gereint could hear the wind rushing through their great wings, with a sound like stiff cloth in a high wind or, to a sufficiently attuned imagination, like the roaring of a fire. The arrows did not reach them but began to fall back to the ground. Every one of them burst into flames before it struck the sand.

"We turned them," Gereint said to Beguchren, and he found that his voice was shaking, and he was not even ashamed of that. And then, with perhaps more accuracy: "You turned them."

The cold mage barely seemed to hear him. His head was back at a sharp angle: He stared upward with an almost frightening intensity. "He is not here," he said, not so much to Gereint as to himself. "*She* is not here; that is why they turn aside. Where are they? Do they think I am not serious in my challenge?"

Gereint did not know how to answer.

"They *will* answer me, if I must turn every grain of sand to good earth and every rising flame to a chip of ice," the mage declared. He waved sharply at Amnachudran, and the scholar called out to his captains, and the little company began to make its way along the dry path of the river, west and north, up the rising slope of the foothills. Their spear points dipped and rose as they marched, in series, like flashing ripples rolling across a lake. They did not call out or shout; even the commands of the officers seemed muted. As though commanded to review before their lord, every row of men turned to look up at the cold mage as they passed his position. For reassurance, Gereint knew. From his deliberate hauteur, Beguchren knew it too.

The griffins wheeled in a great circle, now very high aloft, now so low the long feathers of their wing tips brushed the sand. But they did not come within bowshot of the company. They were glorious and terrible. Their feathers might have been beaten out of bronze and then traced with copper or gold; powerful muscles rippled under lion haunches as golden as the purest metal. Their beaks and talons flashed like knives and their fierce eyes were flaming gold or coal black or brilliant copper. One griffin was pure white, the white of the hottest flame at the fiercest forge; another nearly as pure a black, but with gold barring the long feathers of its wings and dappling its haunches; a third, black flecked with crimson and copper. But they did not close against the men, but only swept up and around and down again in their great circling path.

"They're waiting," Gereint said suddenly, realizing this must be true.

"Yes," Beguchren answered, but absently, as though he barely heard. "For their human fire mage who can keep them whole. They will not come down against our arrows and spears until she is here. She *must* come. They cannot possibly mean to permit our incursion, and they will not attack without her. Maybe they are waiting for Kairaithin—maybe *she* is waiting for Kairaithin. Ah!"

This last exclamation marked the appearance of another griffin. It did not soar in from the deep desert as the others had; it did not come down from the heights or out of the crimson sunset in the west as the sun slid down on its slow path beyond the mountains. The griffin was simply there, balancing on the fiery wind, out of bowshot but close enough to make out clearly.

The new griffin was slim and graceful; large, to be sure, yet smaller than most of the other griffins. It was a rich dark brown, the feathers of its wings barred with gold. On its back, as on a horse, perched a small human form.

The pair spiraled around and slid down across the wind, and as they approached, Gereint saw that the rider was a girl. Only she wasn't really a girl. Gereint stared, trying to understand where the difference lay. It was a little like looking at a very fine statue of a woman: It might mimic the form of a woman very, very well...but no one could possibly mistake the carved stone for a living woman. This girl was living, but it was immediately obvious that she was somehow not human. Her fine hair blew around her face like gossamer thread spun out of white-gold flame; her skin seemed translucent, as though almost-visible light burned through it; her face was alight with a terrifying inhuman exultation. Her hands were buried in the feathers of the brown griffin's neck. She was laughing. Gereint flinched from the sound of her laughter; he could not understand where the difference lay, but it was not the laughter of a human woman.

"There," said Beguchren, his voice urgent and tense. He swung to face Gereint, his fine face set hard, his ice-pale eyes intent. His small hands locked around Gereint's broad wrists. "And their mage is not even here. There will never be a better time! Do it now!"

Beguchren had refused to explain in detail how Gereint was to remake himself into a mage, saying that a maker had to find his own way to any making. Gereint had accepted this vague instruction at the time, turning over in his mind possible methods by which the "self" might be "remade." He'd thought he understood, in principle, how it might be done. But all this vague advice and subsequent thought seemed a good deal less helpful now. He had intended to make himself into a mage for Beguchren; he had come into the country of burning sands to do precisely that; he knew perfectly well that the lives of everyone in the company depended on his ability to do it. But now it came to the moment, he had no idea how it might be done.

Beguchren saw his helplessness, but the cold mage only shook his head. "I cannot help you. If you do not find the way, it was all for nothing and we will all die here: Our bones will burn to ash and blow away in the wind and the desert will lie across our rivers forever—"

"I know!" Gereint exclaimed.

Beguchren gave him a tense nod, let him go, and turned to stare down at the company of men. It was not yet quite besieged; the griffins, welcoming their human fire mage, had raised their burning wind and come at last down upon the men. But arrows flickered out into that savage wind, and spears tilted and rose, and Beguchren drove up, from the now-distant country of earth, a stinging wind that glittered with ice crystals, and so the griffins did not, as yet, close to battle.

If we do not achieve victory swiftly, we will surely be defeated, Beguchren had said, and Gereint had understood exactly how he was expected to contribute to that victory. Now, staring instead down the sweep of the desert straight into defeat, it occurred to him for the first time that Beguchren might have meant the little company of men not only serve as a feint against the griffins, but also to drive *him* forward: *We will all die here, our bones will burn to ash and blow away in the wind*... Yes, the cold mage had brought them deliberately into peril and set all their lives in Gereint's hands. Anger drove him, and despair. He dropped to his knees on the sand, burying his hands in it.

The sand was, in a strange way, living—not as good garden soil was living, but alive with fire. It was unalterably opposed to everything he loved; it would destroy anything of earth that it touched... The magic of earth ran through him: He knew it, tried to feel it; the effort was like trying to feel the flow of blood in his veins. It was impossible to truly feel something so integral to his body and to life.

Except that the power of earth was at such odds with the power of fire, and in the conflict that blazed between the two he almost thought he could perceive both... Rising, acting on nothing like a thought, merely on impulse borne out of terror and desperation, he reached out, jerked the knife off Beguchren's belt, tossed the sheath aside, caught the mage's wrist in a hard grip, gave Beguchren one instant to see his intention, and flicked the tip of the knife sharply against the palm of the mage's hand. Then his own, and he closed his hand hard around Beguchren's small hand, palm against palm.

It was not any kind of technique he'd ever read about or thought of, nothing that would have been useful when working with wood or stone or metal or any normal material. But he shut his eyes and defined blood as symbolic of self; Beguchren's a cold mage's self and his a maker's, and he did something with their mingled blood he could never have described but more or less seemed to recognize. And then he followed the pattern he had made, or completed, or perceived. It was not a pattern he understood, but he followed it anyway, and felt his blood, or mind, or self, slide with surprising ease into that shared pattern and then follow a half-forgotten intention at last into the pattern of magecraft.

Doing so, he died. It was like death. He had not understood what it would be like: like a shattering of memory and identity, like the flowing out of his heart's blood. He would have fought this loss if he had understood how to fight it, but it was already too late to undo it. He struggled, but it was like the struggle of a drowning man against the ripping current of a river; there was no firm ground beneath him and the air was closed away from him, unreachable...He was drowning, not in water but in a wild tide that he recognized, dimly, as magecraft. Something integral to everything he had been cracked across, and something else rose in its place, as though one building had been torn down to make room for another.

Gereint drew a hard, shuddering breath and...opened his eyes. He had not been aware of closing them.

The desert had changed. It was still starkly beautiful, stretched out under the bloody sky, reflecting the last fire of the setting sun. But it had become not merely terrible but dreadful. He shuddered uncontrollably, looking out at it: It *pressed* at him with suffocating force. It would kill him if it could, and burn his bones to ash that would blow away on the wind. It *wanted* him to die. He had felt this before, but now the sense was a hundred times stronger and somehow more personal, as though the desert almost had an actual *self* of its own that was utterly opposed to everything natural and human.

Like the desert, the griffins had become dreadful. He

remembered clearly that he had found them beautiful. But now he saw that they were profoundly inimical, in a way he'd previously completely failed to understand. And the brown griffin and the once-human girl were far the worst. They appalled him. He choked on revulsion against them...

A strong, small hand closed on his shoulder and he looked up, swaying because the desert underfoot seemed to shift with anger; he thought it would burst into flame beneath him and spun a web of frozen quiet across the sand to hold it quiescent.

Then Beguchren moved to face him, set a hand on his other shoulder as well, and met Gereint's eyes. His silver eyes were filled with ice and intensity. Without hesitation, with a skill and power that Gereint could not understand, could barely recognize, Beguchren stripped the new power from his blood and mind and self, turned, and sent a glittering net of ice and power flashing through the hot wind toward the girl and her griffin companion.

Gereint folded down to the sand, unable to brace himself up even on hands and knees. He felt not merely weakened but half blinded and deafened and all but disembodied by the loss of power; worse, he felt somehow that the world itself had been stripped of presence and reality, that what remained was nothing but an attenuated echo of the world that had surrounded him a moment earlier.

But the brown griffin staggered in the air, crying out in a high harsh voice as the icy net closed around it. The girl cried out as well, her voice high and sweet and not at all human.

And a massive griffin, black as charcoal, touched

with red the color of smoldering embers, blazed out of
the wind between Beguchren and the brown griffin, and
Beguchren's net shattered into shards of ice that dissolved into the fiery light of the desert sunset.

Gereint thought he shouted, but his voice was only a
thin gasp.

Beside him, Beguchren made no sound at all, but
turned to face the dark griffin, his expression strained
and tense, his eyes filled with a pure and frozen blaze of
power that had nothing to do with desert fire.

In the west, the sky burned with a crimson light as the
sun sank at last beyond the fiery horizon. Then the light
died, and the hard desert night crashed down around
them. Yet the darkness was broken by a bloody light
that seemed to emanate from the fiery wind or from the
griffins themselves, and from a frosted silvery radiance
that surrounded the cold mage. By that light, Gereint
could see the great black griffin stoop down across the
sky toward Beguchren, and he saw Beguchren take a
small step backward, and it occurred to him, for the first
time as a serious possibility, that the cold mage might,
despite everything, simply find himself overmatched in
this challenge. But Gereint did not have enough strength
remaining to be afraid. The darkness closed in upon
him, a greater darkness than even the desert night could
impose, and his awareness spiraled down into the dark,
and dissolved in it, and was gone.

CHAPTER 13

The road between Dachsichten and Breidechboden was much too good, Tehre decided. Even if you weren't in a great hurry, your carriage would travel smoothly and swiftly, and if you *were* in a hurry, well, you could travel very quickly indeed. Even with the very best roads, however, no one but a courier or a king's agent could cover the whole distance from Dachsichten to Breidechboden in one day. Which was just as well, Tehre thought.

Sicheir rode his own horse, not too near Detreir Enteirich. Though Meierin rode with Tehre in the carriage, the girl was silent and pale. She sat with her hands folded primly in her lap like a child, and her gaze fixed on her hands. She evaded Tehre's eye and said very little. Tehre was aware she should reassure the girl, but did not know what she might say. She would have liked to send her out to ride with Sicheir so that she could speak privately with Lord Bertaud, but of course that was impossible. Lord Bertaud had turned his carriage south without apparent hesitation, but his eyes were secretive and bleak, and Tehre knew his grim mood had nothing to do with fears of the Arobern's anger.

She said at last, speaking straight across Meierin since there was no choice, "Will you go all the way back to Breidechboden?"

Lord Bertaud lifted his eyes to meet hers, but he did not answer.

"You needn't," Tehre said firmly. "Did I make that clear? But you need to tell me what *I* should do."

"Lady—" Meierin said tentatively.

"Hush," Tehre told her. She hadn't looked away from Lord Bertaud. "You know, if you simply turned about and headed north again, there wouldn't be anything at all the Arobern's agent could do to prevent you."

"He could prevent you, however," Lord Bertaud said, frowning.

"Not necessarily, if I were with you. If he had to set himself against you, honored lord, I don't know what he'd do. The Arobern's agents have wide authority. But they have to use it with discretion. It would even be an act of war to raise a hand against you. Wouldn't it?"

"And an act of treason for you to defy him. Isn't that so?"

"Lady!" Meierin exclaimed.

"Hush!" Tehre said, more firmly this time. "Meierin, hush. Not even Fereine will blame you for anything I do, you know."

"Yes, she will—"

"Well, tell her I said she mustn't." Tehre turned once more to Lord Bertaud. "Well?"

The Feierabianden lord said nothing for a long moment.

His expression had become abstracted, but some of the bleakness had gone from it. Tehre said nothing, did not move, tried not even to breathe obtrusively. She heard his voice in her memory: *I think it may be worse than even your king suspects. I have a suspicion about this.*

At last Lord Bertaud lifted his gaze to meet Tehre's. He said, "What you did with language...I said you must be a mage. You said you are not. Tell me, lady, are you in truth a mage as well as a maker?"

"No," Tehre said, surprised. "No, I'm a maker, and maybe something of an engineer, but not a mage. I'm sorry—if you need a mage, I'm afraid there aren't any more—"

Lord Bertaud dismissed this concern with a wave of his hand. "The one remains. The king's mage. The cold mage. Beguchren."

"Beguchren Teshrichten," Tehre agreed, mystified. "Yes."

"He went north."

"Yes?" Tehre couldn't see where the foreign lord was heading with this. She tried to wait patiently for him to explain.

"Mages of earth and fire..." Lord Bertaud began, and stopped.

"There is an antipathy," Tehre said cautiously. "All the philosophers agree there is an antipathy."

"Yes." Lord Bertaud's mouth tightened. His gaze had turned inward. Whatever he was seeing, Tehre thought, it was not the interior of the carriage or the neat fields that lined the road. He turned to her with sudden decision. "You're very powerful. But you are not a mage."

Tehre nodded to each statement, baffled.

"Your king should have sent you north. Not his mage, but you. And me, perhaps. Well, we shall see what this Detreir Enteirich does with his authority and his discretion," Lord Bertaud declared, and leaned forward to speak to his driver.

Detreir Enteirich appeared beside the carriage almost before it had completed its turn. "Stop!" he ordered the driver. But the driver was one of Lord Bertaud's retainers and not Casmantian at all, and he did not stop, but instead clucked to the horses and made them trot more briskly than ever. Northward.

"Lord Bertaud!" the king's agent said, falling back to ride alongside the carriage so he could speak to them through the window.

"I said I would escort the lady wherever she might wish to go," Lord Bertaud said blandly. "It appears she wishes to go north."

The agent digested this for a moment. Then he leaned down a little in the saddle, peering past Lord Bertaud to Tehre. "Lady Tehre—"

"Yes, I know," said Tehre.

"This defiance is treason, lady—"

Yes, Tehre began to repeat. But agreeing made it seem more real, and she found herself flinching from the word. She said instead, almost pleadingly, "But the Arobern gave me the wrong command. He's given me the wrong command twice! I don't *want* to defy the king, truly, but he should have told me to go north. We have in Lord Bertaud someone who's even allied to the griffins, and the Arobern won't listen to him, either!"

Detreir Enteirich's mouth tightened. "Lady Tehre Amnachudran Tanshan, is that what you will tell the king?"

"No!" cried Sicheir, from the agent's other side. "Tehre—"

"*You'd* better go to Breidechboden," Tehre said sharply. "One of us needs to, if that Fellesteden heir is going to make trouble."

"Tehre—"

"I can't!" Tehre said. "Sicheir, I can't! I have to know what's happening in the north! Don't you see I have to?" Before her brother could answer, she closed her eyes, clenched her hands into fists, and broke the solid roadway behind and to either side of the carriage. She didn't understand exactly what she did. It was a little like getting that sword to shatter, when Fellesteden's thug had tried to cut Fareine; it was a little like exploiting a weakness in a mechanism such as a catapult so that it would break. But it was not exactly like either of those things. There was a deep-set maker's virtue in the road, so that no matter the weather, it would not erode or crack or grow muddy. But Tehre broke it anyway. Beside them and behind them, all the mounted riders fell away, shouting.

"But you are not a mage," Lord Bertaud said seriously, peering out the window of the carriage.

Tehre didn't know whether to laugh or cry. "No! I didn't know I could do that. But it wasn't magecraft, anyway. More like making, only backward. Can you stop the carriage?"

Lord Bertaud's expression grew even more serious. "You have changed your mind? You wish to go back?" He hesitated. "It is a grave matter to defy your king."

"No!" repeated Tehre. "I mean, yes, it is, but no, I haven't changed my mind! Only we need to let Meierin out." She looked at the girl, sitting stiff and horrified beside her. "Meierin, tell them...I don't know. Anything you like. Tell them I'm sorry, but I know there's something terribly wrong in the north and I'm going, and Lord Bertaud is, and you tried to stop me but I wouldn't listen. That's all true, so you ought to be able to sound very sincere."

"Lady Tehre—honored lady—"

"Go on," Tehre said inexorably, and reached past the girl to open the carriage door. "And tell them not to bother coming after us! Not even the Arobern's agent has any right to stop Lord Bertaud, and they should think carefully about whether they want to offend him by trying to make me go back. And I won't, anyway. Remind them about the road!"

"I think I won't need to," Meierin said shakily. "I think you're right; I think the lord mage should have asked *you* to go with him, maybe the honored Gereint too, but he should have asked *you*. If you think you should go now, then I think so, too. Honored lady—good fortune go before you and beside you! I'll tell them just what you said. Only, if something is so terribly wrong in the north, fix it; please fix it! *My* family's in the north, too, you know!"

Tehre did know this once Meierin reminded her, and blushed because she had needed the reminder. She nodded wordlessly, and the girl stepped back—carefully, because the road was rough and broken where she stepped. And Lord Bertaud leaned forward and rapped hard on the back of the driver's high seat, and the driver lifted the reins again, and the horses strode forward. Not running. Merely at a collected trot. Because they were not running from anybody, because if they had to run they had already lost their ability to assert their own independent action.

But they did not have to run. No one, not even Lord Bertaud's other retainers and servants, came after them.

It was nearly dusk when they stopped, neither at a farmhouse nor at a campsite, but simply drawing off the road behind a small copse of oaks and hickories. Not out of fear of pursuit, Tehre knew. Merely because Lord Bertaud had no inclination to seek out any kind of company. Neither did she.

Tehre had barely noticed the change in the light. She had been thinking about making, and magecraft, and risk, and treason, and had not really noticed time passing at all. She walked the stiffness out of her bones while the driver saw to the horses and Lord Bertaud made up a fire. None of them spoke much. The driver modestly produced bread and hard sausage from his personal supplies, and they toasted these rough provisions over the fire.

"I can rest in the carriage, I suppose," Tehre said, a little doubtfully, as the last glimmering glow of the sun sank low in the west. She had not had to think about such practicalities herself for a long time. Ever, really. "But I don't know...maybe we should have found a house to stop at, after all—"

"We won't need a house," Lord Bertaud said abruptly, and stood up.

The fire had burned down to low embers; the flames now were sparse, flickering low amid ashen coals. Lord Bertaud stood close by the fire, a featureless black shape against its ruddy light. Tehre couldn't see his expression. But his voice was grim.

A man flickered into existence by the fire, shaping

himself out of the rising night wind and the glow of the
fire, and Tehre stared. So did the driver. So did Lord Bertaud, but there was something different in his startlement,
as though he *was* surprised, but not at the same thing that
had startled Tehre or the driver. Tehre rather thought he
had been startled by the man's sudden appearance, but
only by the suddenness, not by the appearance itself.

The newcomer was cloaked in black, but the firelight
picked out a crimson gleam at his throat and wrist—the
shimmer of fine cloth. His hair was black as the night;
blacker, for the silvery moonlight could have relieved
any ordinary darkness, but it barely seemed to touch this
man. The firelight showed a face that was spare, strong
boned, haughty; deep-set eyes; an arrogant tilt of the
head. And the man's shadow, Tehre saw with a dawning
sense of amazement and dismay—his shadow, pulled
into shape by the light of fire and moon, billowed out
huge and strange, not dark at all, but fiery in the dimness.
It was not at all the shadow of a man. Feathers of flame
lifted and fluttered around the shadow's head and its long
graceful neck; its eyes were black as the coals at the heart
of a fire.

But then, she realized, nothing about the man, save the
shape he wore like a cloak, was actually human.

Lord Bertaud stepped forward to greet the stranger,
and Tehre was bewildered by what she saw in his face:
gladness and relief and anger and an odd kind of dread—a
strange and complex blend of emotions that should have
been contradictory and yet seemed all of a piece. But
amazement, she thought, was notably lacking. He said
sharply, heatedly, as though answering a challenge or
continuing an argument, "I did *not* call you!"

"You called me in your dreams," the man answered. "I heard my name in your dreams. You called me with your intentions." His voice was exactly as Tehre might have expected: harsh, angry, edged with challenge. "I came so that you would not need to call me aloud. Why are you here so far from your own country, man, if not to stand between men and the People of Fire and Wind?"

The Feierabianden lord did not answer.

The griffin mage—clearly he was a griffin, and if he wore the shape of a man and pulled himself out of the wind he must surely be a mage—this man who was nothing like a man waited a long, stretched moment. Then he said, "Why else are you on this road but to come up to the new desert we have made? And what do you mean to do there? What has the Casmantian king offered you to persuade you to ally with him against us despite all your oaths?"

"I am *not*—" Lord Bertaud began, sounding outraged, but then stopped himself, his breath coming hard. He said instead, "What are your people *doing* in the north?"

"We are breaking Casmantium's power," the griffin mage said harshly. "Should we wait for another cohort of cold mages to be raised up? For Casmantium to strike again into our desert and kill us as it pleases? Should we yield all the country of fire to the soft wind, to the dim, pale sun, to the steel plow and the growing grain, the stone walls and roads of men? I think not.

"Our fiery wind will sing through the northern hills; we are bringing our country east below the high lake. We will turn Casmantium's great rivers to dry dust; its tame fields will crack and wither. The Arobern flung ice and earth against us; we will return wind and fire. Let him send ten thousand soldiers against us: He will discover we have become impervious to even the coldest steel. Thus all men will see the people of fire are strong and dangerous to offend."

Tehre could see at once what would happen to Casmantium if the Teschanken River went dry; withered fields were only the beginning of it. Light-headed with horror, she swayed and put a hand out, but there was nothing to support herself with but air. The griffin mage turned his head, a sharp birdlike movement. His fierce eyes caught her out of the darkness, and she stood frozen under that black, contemptuous stare, as a mouse frozen under the fierce gaze of a hunting falcon, unable to look away or move.

"No!" Lord Bertaud said sharply. He came swiftly to her side and put a protective hand on her arm, turning to stand beside her.

Tehre, somehow freed by his touch or voice, blinked and shuddered. The Feierabianden lord seemed nearly as horrified by the griffin mage's words as she had been, but *he* was not shaking. His grip on her arm was almost painful—she would be bruised, later—but she put her hands over his and clung.

Despite the griffin's brutal speech, there was a strange edge to his ruthlessness and arrogance, as though he were waiting. As though he expected...something...Tehre could not imagine what. His stare, when his eyes met hers, was indifferent. Pitiless. But there was something else in his face when he met Lord Bertaud's eyes. But Tehre could neither recognize nor understand what she saw, just as she could not recognize or understand what she saw in the face of the Feierabianden lord.

"You agreed with this plan?" Lord Bertaud asked in a low voice. "I thought your people were content simply to take back the city of Melentser. And instead, you do *this*? Without even telling me? This is a wind you agreed to ride? Or was this Tastairiane and Esterikiu Anahai-kuuanse?" The flowing griffin names came to his tongue much more easily than Casmantian names had, which seemed ironic. He went on: "You've shown before, if you have to, you can bring your king around to your opinion—"

The griffin mage held up a hand, a sharp gesture that cut Lord Bertaud off nearly in midword. "Eskainiane Escaile Sehaikiu was sometimes my ally and yours, man. Now that he is gone, the Lord of Fire and Air has little patience with moderation. Taking Melentser might have pleased some of us. But once we claimed Melentser and perceived the strength its return brought us, then we saw what other wind had risen up to call us to fly. Then we discovered what more we might do. I will admit," he added harshly, "I did not expect *you* to present any opposing argument. Certainly not personally. This is nothing to do with Feierabiand. A weakened Casmantium is even to your benefit. Is it not?"

Tehre didn't understand why the griffins cared what argument Lord Bertaud might make—it must have to do with his role in the summer's war, and earth and iron, what *had* his role *been*? But to her dismay, Lord Bertaud did not immediately refute the griffin mage's suggestion. She said urgently, "If the lower Teschanken goes dry, Casmantium won't only be weakened. We'll be destroyed! They can't do this, can they? Can they? If we send ten thousand men, surely they couldn't really defeat us?"

But Lord Bertaud looked as though he thought they could, and Tehre stopped, horrified. She cried, "If the griffins will listen to you—if this Lord of Fire and Air will listen to you—you mustn't let them do what he says they mean to do!"

"Woman, do you think any man of earth may instruct the people of fire as to which wind to ride, or whether to call up fire or let it die?" demanded the griffin mage, directing the hot force of his attention on Tehre for the first time.

Flinching under that stare, she nevertheless made herself meet his eyes; she even managed to speak. "No, but you said—you implied—" But she could not manage any sort of coherence, stuttered to a halt, tried to collect her wits, and appealed instead to Lord Bertaud. "Your country is allied with the griffins now, isn't it? Your king is an ally of their king, isn't that right? You're an agent of the Safiad. Don't you speak with his voice? Isn't there something you can do? Are you certain there's nothing you can do?"

Lord Bertaud gently freed his wrists from her grasp, but then he took and pressed her hand in reassurance. He said to the griffin mage, "Kairaithin..."

"Hush!" said the griffin mage, lifting his head suddenly, as though he had heard a shout. Tehre listened, but she heard nothing at all—nothing save the breeze in the oaks. But the griffin mage took a swift step back away from the fire. He said, his eyes on Lord Bertaud, "I must go."

The Feierabianden lord hesitated, glancing at Tehre. Then his mouth firmed as he made a decision and he let go of Tehre's hand, took a step forward, and said to

Kairaithin, "Take me with you." His tone was midway between a command and a plea. "Take me with you. Us. Take us with you."

"There will be nothing you can do," the griffin mage said harshly. "Except one thing. And will you do that, man?"

Lord Bertaud hesitated and then shook his head. He answered in a low voice, "No. I won't. I don't want to." He lifted his head, then, and stared into Kairaithin's black, unhuman eyes. "If you were presented now with the same choice you were given at Minas Ford, how would you choose?"

The griffin mage did not answer.

Tehre stared from one of them to the other, aware that she did not understand everything that either of them meant. She hardly understood anything, and that was a dangerous ignorance if the griffins truly meant to destroy Casmantium and had the power to do it. As both Lord Bertaud and Kairaithin seemed to believe.

"I *must* go," Kairaithin said suddenly, sharply. "Beguchren Teshrichten has struck into our desert. Man, I must go."

"Beguchren?" Tehre said, startled and intensely relieved. "Oh, maybe it will be all right, then—he's not *alone*, is he?" She thought of Gereint. And of her father. Maybe her mother had fled south? Maybe everyone had; except what if Beguchren Teshrichten had needed help of some kind, any kind? Her father would have stayed to help the king's mage if he thought he could be any use. And Gereint had gone north *with* Beguchren, which was all very well. He was a strongly gifted maker, but she knew without any need for false modesty that he wasn't as broadly gifted as she was—she said, "I *have* to be there!" and stared in appeal at Lord Bertaud, who clearly had some strange influence with the griffin mage.

"We shall all go," Lord Bertaud agreed. He put his arm around Tehre's shoulders and said to Kairaithin, "We'll all go."

The griffin mage did not argue; he did not, Tehre supposed, much care whether a couple of human folk trailed after him or not. Probably he was sure there was nothing they could do to interfere with the griffins' plans; probably he was right. But she knew she had to go if she could. Though she did not know exactly why Lord Bertaud felt *he* had to go into danger and terror in the north, when Casmantium wasn't even his country. But she wasn't going to argue. She put her hand over his where he gripped her shoulder, lest he try at the last moment to leave her behind.

Before them, Kairaithin stretched out, expanding, his shadow seemed somehow to close around him and then open violently outward. Great black wings narrowly barred with ember red stretched and opened; black feathers ran down from his fierce eagle's head and neck, ruffled like a mane around his shoulders and chest, and melded to a powerfully muscled lion rear. His eyes were the same: black and pitiless.

Tehre had seen illustrations of griffins, of course she had, but the sheer ferocious power that radiated from the griffin mage was nothing she had ever imagined. She tried, quite involuntarily, to back away; only Lord Bertaud's arm stopped her. She realized she had stopped breathing; it was a surprising shock to start again. She did not look at Lord Bertaud; she could not look away from the griffin.

Then the black wings came down, and either the red barring across the feathers caught light from the glowing embers of the fires or else flames actually flickered to life amid those feathers—Tehre couldn't tell which—and the griffin lunged forward and up. The wind from the downbeat of his great wings struck across them, furnace hot and dry, and Tehre, staggering, realized they were now standing within a night that was utterly different from the gentler night they had left behind.

The stars overhead were diamond bright and hard, very different from the delicate flickering stars of the country of earth. The lay of the land here was much steeper than the farmland between Dachsichten and Breidechboden, tall mountains rearing hard against sky, visible by the stars they blocked from sight. Sand shifted dangerously underfoot, heat rising from it almost as though they stood on banked coals. They did, in a way, Tehre understood suddenly: She could feel, with her maker's sense of materials, the slow shifting heave of molten rock below the sand—not so far below.

A wind netted with fire came down upon them, so that she cried out, brushing futilely at sparks that came down across her hair and shoulders. Lord Bertaud patted out tiny smoldering fires on her back and in her hair, and Tehre quickly did the same for him, standing on her toes to brush urgently at a small blaze eating its way across his shoulder toward his neck.

Then a different wind rose, utterly foreign to this burning country, stinging with ice, and all the fire above and below them died.

Somewhere close at hand, a griffin shrieked like a hunting falcon. Tehre flinched and stared toward the

sound. She could not find the griffin that had cried out
above them, but for the first time she realized she *could*
see, a little. Not by the light of the stars, though each
seemed to shed a tiny trace of heat and light, but by a
burning glow that seemed to emanate from the griffins
that slipped past high overhead and from the wind that
they rode, and by the cold light that flung itself out in
defiance from a nearby hillside. The source of that light
was Beguchren Teshrichten, of course, who shone with
silvery radiance. Near the cold mage crouched another,
much larger man: Gereint, Tehre assumed. Above them,
between them and the high, deadly forms of the soaring
griffins, soared the dark shape of Kairaithin; the fiery
wind from his wings met Beguchren's cold wind and
matched it, and drove it back toward the mage.

And below them, far down the hill, below Tehre and
Lord Bertaud, was clustered a small number of soldiers in
leather and bits of mail, bright spear points rising above
them, griffins spiraling through the air above them like
so many falcons circling above mice, waiting only for
Kairaithin's strength to overmatch Beguchren's before
they came down to kill as they chose.

"He'll hold them," Tehre said, to herself more than
to Lord Bertaud; she only realized she'd spoken aloud
when she heard her own voice, fragile in the vastness of
the desert.

"I don't think so," the foreigner answered grimly.
He took a step up the hill, toward the cold mage, then
hesitated and looked instead down the slope toward the
threatened company.

"No, this way," Tehre said. She caught his hand and
tugged him uphill. When he still hesitated, she added

urgently, "If Beguchren falls, everyone will fall! Everything turns on him: If we can help him, that's where we should be!"

This was logical and obvious, and Lord Bertaud yielded. They ran up the hill together, hand-in-hand like lovers, steadying each other when the fire-laced desert wind gusted down upon them from one direction or the ice-laden cold wind came battering from the other. Neither Kairaithin nor Beguchren seemed to notice them, either to help or hinder. They struggled at last to Beguchren's position. The cold mage still did not notice them, and Lord Bertaud hesitated, staring first at the mage and then upward toward the dark griffin he fought.

Tehre, crouching low to keep her balance under the violent winds, went instead to Gereint. She had known it had to be him, here on this hillside with Beguchren Teshrichten. Who else would it be? And it was. But he seemed barely conscious. He was not injured. When she looked as a maker, Tehre could find no weak or broken place in the structure of his body. But he seemed dazed with horror or exhaustion. He was kneeling, sitting back on his heels, his head bowed and his hands pressed over his eyes as though in denial of the desert and the fiery wind and the griffins and everything to do with any of them. That didn't seem like him at all. She patted his shoulder and then his face, but though he lowered his hands, he did not seem to recognize her. Indeed, there was barely even a flicker of awareness in his eyes. And he moved as though he had to shift the weight of the world to move even a finger.

Baffled, Tehre twisted about and tucked herself down on the ground beside him, watching Beguchren instead.

The king's mage was battling Kairaithin, that was obvious. The griffin mage had come down to the desert and now stood facing Beguchren, his massive wings half spread amid blowing sand and leaping flames. Hardly anything farther away than the griffin mage remained visible: Though she tried to see the company of men, the night and the desert wind hid them from view.

Kairaithin lifted a feathered forelimb as though to stride forward, but then he replaced his taloned foot in precisely the same location from which he'd lifted it. Tehre thought the griffin mage had tried to move toward them and that Beguchren had stopped him. The cold mage was leaning slightly forward, frowning, his face masklike in the strange light, his eyes opaque and white as the ice of a deep northern winter. He was holding Kairaithin back; that, too, was obvious.

But Tehre saw several less obvious things as well. She saw that, though Beguchren was battling the griffin mage, his attention was really elsewhere. His strange icy eyes hardly turned toward the griffin; he was searching instead through the roiling, dust-laden sky for something else. Or someone else. A different griffin? Tehre guessed. Another griffin mage? Or something else?

And Lord Bertaud also seemed distracted or worried— well, anybody would be *worried*, yes, but in fact anybody would be terrified, and he did not seem terrified at all. He was not crouching under the violence of the winds, as she was. He was standing, his hands at his sides, his head back, watching Kairaithin. Sometimes he stared up at another griffin as it passed more closely than usual, flashing into view and then disappearing again into the fiery winds; the only time Tehre saw him flinch was at

the swift approach of a gleaming white griffin, so pure
a white that it might have been carved out of alabaster
and then brought to burning life. It slashed all along the
hillside, so low the long feathers of its wing tips might
have brushed the sand if it had stroked downward. But
its wings tilted before it touched the sand, and it angled
sharply up and away—actually, feathers must be made
of a peculiarly strong and flexible material or they would
surely break against the force of the air when any feathered creature turned like that—

Tehre was recalled to the moment as pillars of twisted
rock forced their way abruptly through the sand behind
Kairaithin, and to either side; the desert trembled and
rumbled as the stone tore its way free from the sand and
out into the violent wind, which shrieked and moaned as
it was cut by the sharp edges of the rock. She could feel
the grinding movement of those contorted pillars where
she sat—no, she realized: She could feel the movement
of the pillars that were rising behind them. The griffin
mage was building a circle of twisted pillars to enclose
them all. That could not be good. She stared at Gereint
for an instant; he seemed no better. Beguchren did not
seem able to keep Kairaithin from making the pillars.
Tehre got unsteadily to her feet and made her way over
to Bertaud's side, catching his arm to steady herself as the
ground shook again.

"Do you understand this?" she asked him when he
glanced distractedly down at her. She had to half shout
to be heard over the battling winds and grinding stone.
"You—in Feierabiand—did you—did they—"

The foreigner put an arm around her to steady her as
the ground shuddered. He shook his head. "Nothing like

this happened in Feierabiand! Not that I saw! Kairaithin killed a lot of cold mages, he said, but I didn't see it!"

"Beguchren was always the strongest of our cold mages!" Tehre peered through the veiling sand and dust that obscured the desert. "I don't understand what he's doing—I don't understand what he did to Gereint—it looks like he's battling Kairaithin, but I'd take oath half his attention's on something else, only I don't know what!"

"He's searching for Kes," Bertaud said, grimly, but almost too low for her to make out his words. "He's searching for Kes!" he repeated, when she shook her head. "A girl—one of ours—he made her into a fire mage, a fire-healer; she's why the griffins don't have to fear ten thousand soldiers—if your king had sent so many, and I saw only a few hundred down there, I think!"

The griffins had made a human girl into a fire mage? Tehre stared at Bertaud, but he seemed perfectly serious.

The desert cracked open at their feet, knife-edged stone ripping free of the sand to slice the dust-laden wind into shrieking ribbons; both Tehre and Lord Bertaud staggered backward. Tehre would have fallen except Bertaud caught her, and then he slipped and might have fallen himself except she braced her whole strength to support him, and with one accord they flung themselves, stumbling, toward Beguchren. They knelt down there in the relative calm behind the cold mage, beside Gereint, where the ground was steadier and where they might be protected from the worst of the violent winds. The mage did not pay them any heed—neither, more disturbingly, did Gereint.

She asked Bertaud, "He made her into a fire mage? A

human girl? He made a creature of earth into a creature of fire? Didn't it hurt her terribly? Didn't she *mind*?"

Bertaud, hunkering down to one knee between Tehre and the scattered sparks that came down the wind, shook his head. "Not after it was done, I believe. You have to understand... once you're a creature of fire, once you understand fire and take it into your heart, the country of fire is very beautiful."

She supposed that might even be true, though at the moment the desert seemed anything but beautiful— fierce, worse than fierce—savage, even murderous. But if you were a creature of fire, she supposed it might seem different.

"Your Beguchren is trying to find Kes, I think," Bertaud said, while Tehre was still trying to understand how a human woman might be made into a creature of fire. "He wants to kill her, I suppose! He might want to kill Kairaithin, but that isn't important—but it would change everything, if the griffins didn't have Kes—if they didn't have her, I expect your king would send ten thousand soldiers to destroy them all—he'd want to destroy the country of fire entirely and reclaim not only Melentser for his own, but all the northern desert—he's ambitious, is the Arobern—"

Tehre supposed this was true. At the moment, destroying all the griffins and reclaiming this burning desert for earth seemed a fine idea to her, but Lord Bertaud sounded terribly grim. His face had gone tight and hard, and the expression in his eyes was bleak. He said something else, too low for Tehre to understand. Then he glanced at her and said more clearly, "Everything depends on your Beguchren's strength, and Kairaithin's—Kairaithin told me once that in the desert, he was stronger than Beguchren—"

"Oh," Tehre said, surprised. Pieces of a puzzle she'd barely glimpsed in outline fell suddenly into place. She said with conviction, "Beguchren's made Gereint into a mage, and now he's using Gereint's strength to support his own. Gereint would have had plenty of strength to give, I expect—"

Bertaud was shaking his head. "Wait, wait, he did what?"

"As Kairaithin made your Feierabianden girl into a fire mage," Tehre said patiently, surprised he hadn't grasped this at once. "It's not quite the same thing—in fact, it should be much easier. I wonder if it takes a maker who's already got a little magecraft woven through his gift? Or if any maker can be made into a mage? I wonder if *I*..." She stopped. It was a disquieting idea.

Another griffin came slanting out of the fire-streaked wind and landed neatly on the sand by Kairaithin, and another after that. The first was large, not as massive as Kairaithin, but heavy and muscular: a powerful griffin with golden eyes and bronze feathers; the feathers of his wings were bronze streaked with copper and gold and his lion rear a dark bronze gold. The second, smaller, griffin was a rich gold-stippled brown.

On the back of the smaller griffin perched a human girl, only even without Bertaud's explanation, Tehre would never have mistaken her for anything human. She was fine boned, small, pretty—but she looked even less human than Kairaithin had when he'd taken human form. She seemed spun out of white gold and fire; her eyes were filled with fire; bright little tongues of fire flickered in her pale hair and ran down her bare arms. She was smiling, a dangerous expression that was also somehow joyous. She slipped down from the brown griffin's back to stand between it and Kairaithin, but she left a hand buried in the feathers of its neck.

Beguchren, frowning, took one step forward. Ice rimed his white eyes and his hands; ice glittered on the sand where he'd set his feet and sparkled in the air around him; near him, the dark of the desert night was lit by a pearly light that sparkled with frost. He took another step.

Kairaithin folded his heavy black wings, a gesture that somehow seemed contemptuous, and tilted his head downward so that his savage beak pointed at the burning sand under his feet. The other griffins swayed forward, their wings still half spread; the bronze one snaked its head out low and hissed. Kes tossed her head, dropped her hand away from the brown griffin's neck, and stood straight, smiling.

Behind them and to either side, a net of fire spun itself between one stone pillar and the next, and the next, and the next after that: a tight-woven web of fire wound itself around the griffin mages and Beguchren, and around Tehre and Bertaud where they knelt beside Gereint. All around the circle flames sprang up, burning tall and smokeless, white and gold and blood crimson, columns and sheets of fire that towered straight up toward the sky in a sudden, shocking absence of wind.

Beguchren took one more step forward, and a broad, nebulous bolt of mist and frost speared out toward—not Kairaithin, Bertaud had been right—toward Kes.

The girl did not move. But she did not need to. The attack never touched her. Fire rose up and swallowed the cold mist and absorbed it, and then burned higher, reaching out to engulf Kes entirely. Any normal human girl would have burned alive in that fire. Kes stood amid the flames, her smile never faltering, her body blurring into fire and then reshaping itself out of fire once more.

"They're all mages," Bertaud said quietly, to himself as much as to Tehre. "Kairaithin's brought some of his young students into their power—including Kes. I don't think your Beguchren can match them, however much power he's taken from your friend."

Tehre shook her head, wanting to deny this, but actually she thought he was right. The frost surrounding Beguchren had closed in around him, and she doubted the mage was contracting his power of his own accord. His face was taut and strained. He bowed his head and lifted his hands, but the spear of ice he shaped out of his need flung itself only halfway toward the human fire mage before the fierce heat of the surrounding fire trapped it and it dissolved back into the air.

Beguchren made a low sound, lifting his head again. In his frost-white eyes was frustration and anger and the terrible knowledge of failure, and Tehre found herself holding her breath in sympathy—she leaped to her feet and ran to him, in her mind a confused idea of telling him to make her into a mage, to use her power, she was ready to argue, *I have more strength than you'd think. Use it. Use me.* But the thought came too late and she had no chance to make the offer: Even as she reached Beguchren, his eyes rolled back and he folded slowly to his knees and then to the sand. She caught him, went down with him, supported his head on her knee, setting her hand against his face as she tried to determine whether he'd actually died or only collapsed—he was cold, cold as ice to the touch, but she found a weak pulse beating against the fine skin of his throat.

But she already knew it didn't matter: If the mage still lived, he wouldn't for long. She could feel the ferocity of the surrounding desert without even looking up.

Then she looked up.

The fire woven between the stones had begun to die—or, not die, but ebb slowly back into the sand and the wind. The stone pillars stood like plinths of hot emptiness against the sky; far above, an unseen griffin cried out, a high, wild shriek, fierce and exultant. The sound sent icy prickles down Tehre's spine. Kairaithin and his companions, lit by their own fire, were still visible, and that was worse than the unseen griffins in the air above.

Kes was laughing, delight in her eyes, in her face. She said to Kairaithin in a light, fierce voice that was nothing like the voice of a human woman, "This was a night for victory and the living fire!"

And we shall finish the victory, lest we dishonor the night that has given it to us, agreed the griffin mage, his voice slicing not quite painfully around the edges of Tehre's mind.

Kes shook off fire as an ordinary woman might shake drops of water off her hands. Then she flung herself onto the back of the brown griffin, which dipped its wings to make room for her to mount. The griffin was laughing too, not aloud, but joy blazed from every line of its slender body. It hurled itself aloft, the girl bending low over its neck, and the fiery wind blazed around them both, the darkness opening to let them through.

The bronze griffin said to Kairaithin, its voice

terrifyingly eager, *Shall we end this?* It swayed forward
a step, its wings flaring, the rising wind hissing through
the feathers with a deadly sound. Tehre thought it might
simply bite Beguchren's head off and she crouched
defensively down over the mage. Though probably that
would simply prompt the griffin to bite *her* head off
instead...

"No," said Lord Bertaud. He stood up, walked quietly
to stand beside Tehre, dropped a hand to touch her shoulder. But he did not look at her. He was looking only at
Kairaithin. He said flatly, as though he really thought the
griffin would care what he said, "It's not acceptable to
Feierabiand that Casmantium be destroyed."

*Is it acceptable to you that the country of fire be
destroyed?* asked the griffin mage, his voice terrible with
contained anger. *Is it acceptable to you that the People of
Fire and Air be destroyed?*

"No," said Bertaud. "Find another way."

Kairaithin's wings flared; he flung his head up, his terrible beak snapping shut with a horrifying, deadly sound.
If there is no other way?

"There must be," Lord Bertaud insisted, but to Tehre
he looked grim and ill, as though he thought maybe there
was not.

The griffin mage caught fire from the wind, drew fire
from the sand, sent fire running in a thin loop around
the circle of pillars. He was going to kill them all, Tehre
thought; whatever alliance existed between the griffins
and Feierabiand, he was going to burn them all to ash,
she and Lord Bertaud and Gereint, and below them all
those men with their useless spears, and then the griffins
were going to ruin the rivers on which all of southern

Casmantium depended and laugh as the country of earth
withered...She said, "No," and stood up, lowering Beguchren gently to the sand. Everyone was staring at her, but
she barely noticed. All her attention was on Gereint, who
was unchanged, tucked down against the sand, not quite
unconscious, but certainly not aware. Alone of them all,
he had noticed neither battle nor defeat and was now
innocent of their imminent death.

His strength had been taken by Beguchren. But he
hadn't been injured. He was only weak. If he regained his
strength, he'd be a mage, probably. Untrained, of course.
That hadn't mattered to Beguchren. The king's mage
might even have found it an advantage. It wouldn't be
an advantage now. But still...Tehre knelt beside Gereint,
laid a hand on his shoulder, and spun off some of her
own strength, feeding it to him as a healer might support
an injured man. She'd watched her mother do this, and
although she'd never done it before herself, it seemed
easy enough. She had told Beguchren the truth: She was
stronger than she looked; she could draw strength from
her gift, plenty to spare.

Under her hand, Gereint's shoulder tensed. His head
came up. Awareness came into his eyes. He looked first
up into her face. He was pleased to see her: that, first.
Then surprised. Then frightened, as memory and thought
came back to him. He looked past her, then to Lord Bertaud, whom he did not know. He dismissed him, looked
farther. Saw Beguchren, lying abandoned and insensible
on the sand. The fear was replaced by anger, and then, as
he turned his attention instead toward Kairaithin and the
other griffin, by grim revulsion. Tehre stared at him. She
had understood the surprise, the fear, the anger. But the

depth of loathing she saw in Gereint's eyes astonished her. Or, no. Hadn't somebody...probably Andreikan Warichteier...said something about a violent antipathy between mages of earth and mages of fire? And Gereint was a mage now.

Not taking his eyes off of Kairaithin, he got to his feet, and Tehre jumped up and backed away, suddenly not certain whom, or what, she'd woken from an exhausted stupor and brought back into the desert night.

CHAPTER 14

Gereint was aware first only of Tehre's presence, which for an instant seemed ordinary, expected, part of the natural order of the world. Then he remembered that he'd left her in Breidechboden, and although he didn't yet recall where he was now, he knew it wasn't the capital. So then he wondered, How she had come to this place? Puzzled, he looked past her. But he did not understand at once what he saw: a man he did not recognize, and a hillside that fell away into the darkness; sand and fire; pillars of twisted stone standing black against the dark sky—inimical fire linking one pillar to the next in a thin circle; crushing heat rising from the sand underfoot and pressing down from above. He remembered the desert at last, and looked for Beguchren. Found him: collapsed and unconscious. He was immediately angry: why had no one helped the mage? Couldn't they see he needed attention, care? He began to push himself up.

Then he finally saw the griffins, and the anger he'd

felt on Beguchren's behalf flared into a cold white fury laced with loathing. Memory crashed back with an almost physical shock, and he found himself on his feet, glaring toward the creatures, outraged by their very existence. If he'd known how to attack them, he would have done it then. Though, an instant later, it occurred to him that Beguchren *had* known how to fight them and *he* was lying helpless on the sand. And if the king's own mage had been defeated, what chance did an ignorant, untrained new-made mage have in any battle? He hesitated, caught between furious antipathy and an awareness of his own helplessness.

Then Tehre caught his hand.

Startled out of his anger, Gereint stared down at her. She was tiny, covered with red dust, her hair singed and her hands blistered from the fire that scattered from the wind. Her mouth was set in determination, her eyes snapping with forceful thought. She did not seem frightened at all. She looked exactly as she always did when absorbed by a difficult problem: intense and absorbed and distracted. She said quickly, "Either the griffins will destroy Casmantium, or we'll destroy them, and we don't have the strength to stop them, but there's another way, there really is—as long as you'll help me, are you a maker at all, anymore?"

"I—" began Gereint. He meant to say, *I'm a stranger to myself. I don't know what I am.* Only Tehre did not wait for him to say anything at all.

She put her other hand on Gereint's arm, whether to steady herself or to somehow balance her gift against his unskilled mage power or to take back some of the strength she'd given him or even to give him more of her strength; he couldn't tell.

But what happened was nothing he'd thought of. Instead, the pillars nearest at hand shattered. Shards of knife-edged stone whirled into the night. Then the farther pillars broke, and the ones after that, all around the circle. Tiny fragments flew like arrows, large pieces fell to the sand with massive, dull impacts. The fire between them died; the griffins were gone—no, the smaller one was gone; the massive black one had merely shifted back a short way. It called up a fiery wind; the desert trembled; stone shifted underfoot.

"I'll break the desert itself," Tehre warned breathlessly. "I'll make a crack right across this hillside, a crack that goes down so far the molten fire under the sand drains down into the darkness under the mountains. I can do it. I can do it, so back away! Get your people away! Gereint, the mountains, I can feel them looming over there, all that stone; raw stone is just waiting to be shaped into masonry, don't the stonecarvers say that?"

That was all the warning she gave him before she broke the mountains.

It should have been impossible. It was certainly a feat beyond any maker Gereint had ever heard of, yet completely unrelated to anything he could imagine doing with magecraft. But Tehre had certainly done it *somehow*. Though the mountains were far away and invisible in the darkness, he heard them go: the three on the right and the two on the left, and maybe others more distant still; a heavy grinding roar so immense it went beyond any measurement of sound and became a physical presence in the night. It went on and on, fathomless: a huge booming roar of stone falling, pounding against more stone, grinding inexorably downhill.

"Help me make a wall," Tehre ordered breathlessly, standing on her toes to shout into Gereint's ear. "They're falling, but they're not falling *right*, I can tell, the pieces are scattering all down the hillsides, they need to be a *wall*—"

No, it wasn't a wall she had made, not yet. It was an avalanche, and it was huge. Gereint tried to use his maker's sense of materials to track what Tehre had done, but he couldn't. He reached after his gift for making, after the familiar awareness of materials that waited to be shaped, but that awareness was gone; there was nothing left. The loss was like the loss of a hand, of his eyes, but in place of the maker's awareness was something else, a more direct awareness of power and force and strength, an awareness of movement and the chance that something would go one way and not another.

Not just the near mountains, Gereint thought. Tehre had pulled down half the mountain range, by the sound and the feel of it. She had broken free the granite at the heart of the mountains and called the stone down from the heights toward the dry track of the great river— toward them all. He shouted back to Tehre, over the roar of approaching stone, "You should have *warned* me—"

"How long do you think I should have waited?" Tehre had closed her eyes, letting her maker's awareness guide her. She said urgently, her eyes still closed, "I can break the pieces into blocks as they come, but I can't get the blocks to fall where they need to go. There're too many and they're too heavy and coming too fast—"

Everything was *too heavy and coming too fast*. Gereint shut his eyes and tried to think about being a pivot in the world, a point of focus where forces balanced. It was surprisingly easy to think of himself that way. He could *feel* the grounded power of the hundreds of men below the hill, surprisingly steady, like springs of water welling up through the sand. He could feel the deep strength of earth and stone, behind or beyond the quick, foreign balance of fire; it underlay the new desert and rose, he thought, somehow *through* the men.

And beyond desert and fire and men and earth, he perceived the rushing stone and earth of the avalanche. He felt the shattered, thundering stone as a gathering rush of power—not a maker's sense at all, not something he could touch or hold, not something that spoke to him of potential shape and form, but *something*.

Something suddenly caught up all the strength of earth Gereint could perceive, power right at the edge of his perception, stripped that power out of the men who had dared the desert, and through them pulled strength right out of the earth beneath the fiery sands and set it loose in an unfocused whirlwind.

Gereint, stunned, nevertheless caught up the freed power and bent its path. He let it slam through the world not as it wished to run, a wild and uncontrolled outflow across all the hills, but channeled into a narrow strip— was dimly aware of another focal point in the world that balanced against his, that supported him—the avalanche tore its way through the desert sand and piled itself up all along the western shore of the dry river, stretching north to south and then bending away to the west in a wide strip of... blocks, he realized at last. Not raw stone mixed with gravel and dirt and desert sand, but huge rough-edged granite blocks that Tehre had shaped out of the mountains, without chisel or mallet or the thousand years of labor it should have taken her. He opened his eyes, looking for her.

Tehre was sitting now at his feet, near the limp shape of Beguchren. She had one hand on the fallen mage's shoulder, but her head was bowed over her drawn-up knees and her eyes were closed. She was not looking at Beguchren, Gereint knew. She was watching the cracking stone with her inward maker's eyes, encouraging it to break along the lines she wanted, with something greater than the skill of any ordinary builder or engineer. Coaxing the blocks to fall into position even far to the west, supported by the enormous power Gereint had caught and made, in turn, available for her.

Gereint glanced over at the stranger, who was standing, oddly, beside the black griffin mage. Down by the dry river, he could dimly make out Amnachudran's company—not with his eyes, he realized eventually, but with some new strange sense. He thought the men still lived...He was not certain. The griffins had not destroyed them. The dimness was a function of what he had done himself, was still doing. He thought they had not died when magecraft had suddenly seized on their strength and through them on the strength of the earth. But he was not certain.

The griffins were gone out of the wind, out of sight... He was aware of them, a tug against his attention, flame-edged monsters with no proper shape, pulling the natural strength of earth in thoroughly unnatural directions...but high, distant, not at the moment dangerous. Save for the griffin mage. He stared that way, torn, hesitating to go down toward the wall Tehre was building because he did not want to have the griffin at his back, knowing he did not have the skill or experience to do proper battle—

"Go on," shouted the stranger over the gradually lessening crash and rumble and roar of the avalanche. "Go! Kairaithin won't fight you!" His Prechen was fluent, not exactly accented, but with a foreign touch to it: He was Feierabianden, Gereint realized, and guessed that he might actually be able to speak for the griffin—and he had come with Tehre, and she had not seemed to think of him as an enemy. And now he said the griffin mage would not fight? If he had the strength and training and the *time* to fight the griffin, Gereint would never have trusted that assurance. But he could feel the wall still crashing into place far to the west, and there was no time.

He took a step down toward the riverbed, paused impatiently, and moved himself through a fold of space to stand beside the great wall. Above him and all along the wall, he could feel blocks break free, roll and crash down from the stony heights, pirouette, and slam into their proper positions. That was Tehre's task.

But a deep steady vein of magecraft ran through him now, and he had a task of his own. He laid his hand against the rough face of the wall and made it heavily itself, made the block of stone more thoroughly stone, anchored it solidly to the rock that underlay the new desert and to the blocks that surrounded it. There was no moisture in the air. But the griffins' desert was too new to have burned the memory of water out of the land. The river at his back, dry as it was, remembered water, remembered the rushing, unpredictable force of the spring flood and the slow, deep, easy wash of the summer. He let that memory bend around him, flow from memory into the moment, laid the memory of water and ice into the stone under his hands and between that block and the next and the next. He turned, trailing the tips of his fingers across the stone, walked slowly upriver, setting the memory of living water and the solidity of the earth deeply into the wall as he walked.

He did not know how long he walked. He was not only walking but letting himself blur through distance, moving higher and higher into the mountains, the dry Teschanken to his right and the wall to his left. He became aware, gradually, of a presence paralleling his path on the other side of the wall. It was a fiery presence, powerful... It laid fire and the memory of fire into the wall on its other side. Gereint's first impulse was to fight that foreign magecrafting, but... the memory and training of a maker could not help but understand the balance and symmetry implicit in that working. Earth and water on this side of the wall, fire on that; it would be, he thought, a wall that would forever lock the country of fire away from the country of earth.

At least so far as the wall reached. He wondered how far it ran, how many mountains Tehre had shattered, how many blocks she had coaxed into shape and position... *That* was not any simple gift. No. *I'm something of a maker, a builder, an engineer, a scholar*, she had said. She had not said, *And something of a mage*. But Beguchren had wanted Gereint because he'd seen a streak of hidden magecraft in his gift; Gereint understood that now, because he had seen the same touch of magecraft in Tehre, only clearer and stronger, he suspected, than his had ever been while he was a maker.

The wall trailed off at last, high in the mountains. The

blocks here were smaller and narrower, and then smaller still, until there was only ordinary unshaped stone underfoot and the clear sky of afternoon overhead, and nothing to balance and anchor and layer with memories of earth and water and ice... Gereint pulled his awareness slowly out of the stone. It took him a moment to remember his own shape, to remember he was not granite. Then he found he stood by the shore of a lake so immense that he could not see the other side. Curious, he tried to span the lake with his new awareness of space and movement... Even then, he could not find its opposite shore, only mist and glittering frost that reached from the surface of the water to the clouds above. The wall held any touch of fire back from it and from the rivers it fed, and at his right hand the Teschanken poured in an icy cataract down from the infinite bowl of the lake and away toward the country of men.

"This is not a place for the People of Fire," said a hard, austere, weary voice, enunciating clearly to cut over the noise from the river. The griffin mage came around the low end of the wall to stand on the shore of the lake. He wore the shape of a man. But Gereint would never have mistaken him, even for an instant, for a man. He was horrified the creature should have come here, to this place, where the magic of earth and water lay so close to the ordinary world that one might almost waver between them. It was a terrible place for a creature of fire.

He shifted back a wary step, groping after magecraft, after memories of ice.

"Be still, man. Peace," said the griffin. His tone, though weary, was also sardonic and edged with dislike.

"You do not wish to do battle against me, even here in this place of water and earth."

This was true. Gereint could feel the appalling force of the griffin mage flaring barely out of sight behind the shape he wore. The griffin *felt* old: ageless in the same way that Beguchren had seemed ageless. Gereint did not doubt the depth of the griffin's skill, or his strength. He most definitely did not want to fight him. He knew he would lose. He said nothing.

"The Safiad's man, the representative of Feierabi-and...he argued the wisdom of sealing this wall from both directions," the griffin said. "I agreed, and reached after a new wind, and called it down from the heights. The great wind that shatters stone...Your little maker has surprising strength. You lent a great deal to the effort. But not enough to build a wall along all the border between our two countries."

Gereint groped after coherence. "You...helped her? *You* helped us?" It seemed too ridiculous a suggestion even to put into words.

"I helped you," agreed the griffin, drily mocking. "Were you not aware? To build the wall, and then to seal the wall from our side as you did from yours. Walls are not a thing of my people. But this one...this one may serve us. Perhaps the man of Feierabiand had the right of it. A wall may serve better than war. I am told that Feierabiand would turn against the people of fire, raise up its mages and arm its soldiers with cold metal and ice, did we bring Casmantium to ruin. I am told that even Linularinum would enter the war that would result."

This was a new thought, but, "It would," Gereint answered the griffin mage's sardonic tone. "I hadn't thought...but of course it would. Feierabiand would have to renounce its alliance with your people, and Linularinum would have to support Feierabiand. We all..." He did not quite know how to phrase the thought.

"Belong to the country of earth; just so," agreed the griffin. "And we do not. A truth my people had perhaps not sufficiently considered. Thus, I decided it would be best to ride this new wind all the way to its end. Especially as I saw no other alternative." He turned, gestured back along the long endless structure of the wall. "This remains unsealed along half its length." He considered briefly and then added, harshly amused, "More than half."

Gereint didn't answer. He had a strong feeling that the griffin was concealing something, or at least failing to mention something important. That the reason the griffin mage had chosen to set his strength alongside Gereint's on the far side of the wall...was complex and dangerous and either inexplicable in human terms or else something the creature had no intention of explaining. But he could also see that the griffin was right about the wall: It was unfinished. The task needed to be seen through all the way to the end. And for whatever reason, the griffin meant to complete it. But he was appalled by the idea of doing over again the labor they had just completed.

"Though, if you lack the strength—" the griffin mage began, his tone edged with contempt.

Shaken by loathing, Gereint said sharply, "I'll manage my side. See you do the same!" And he flung himself away from the lake, with its mysterious shores hidden by its shifting mists, and back through a fold in the world, to the place where he had started the work of sealing the wall. It was easy: as easy and natural as making had once been for him; a step and the world tilted and swung around him, and another step and he stood again by the river, below the hillside where Beguchren had challenged the griffins. The hills were empty now. Neither men nor griffins remained. But water ran clear and sweet in its rugged channel, finding its way around the odd, twisted red cliff that had blocked its old path. Delicate green shoots were already poking up along the river's new channel, from good earth only lightly disguised by a thin covering of red sand.

Now, in daylight, Gereint could see the broken mountains. Some of the broken mountains. He could see where the three closest mountains had stood. The earth was nearly level there now, the broken and torn ground between the more distant mountains and the wall showing where the avalanche of stone had come down. Gereint shook his head, looking at the miles-wide trail of devastation that marked the path of the avalanche through the stark emptiness of the desert. If there had been forest or pasture left there, the avalanche would have destroyed it as certainly as the desert had done. And if he had looked over the wall, he knew he would find similar destruction. How many mountains must be leveled to build a hundred miles of wall? Two hundred miles? All the closest mountains, he concluded, and probably some of the more distant mountains had been hauled down as well... Tehre would never have had the strength to do this, not even with the power he had found for her. More than ever, Gereint was aware that he did not want to fight the griffin mage. He was unwillingly, bitterly, grateful to the Feierabianden lord for persuading the griffin to throw his immense strength behind Tehre's effort, and now behind his own.

He knew the griffin was there now. On the other side of the wall. Waiting. He could almost feel the creature's fierce, patient scorn. *If you lack the strength* . . . Gereint set his teeth and turned back to the wall.

CHAPTER 15

At dawn, a night and a day and another night after Gereint and Eben Amnachudran and four hundred men had followed Beguchren Teshrichten into the country of fire, Gereint stumbled suddenly out of hard blocks of granite laced with hornblende and dark, rich hematite and found himself standing, blinking and dazed, amid the jagged crags of great, toothed mountains. Their polished granite faces shone in the sun while darkness still lay in the valleys between the peaks. He realized slowly that these were not the smaller and more comfortable mountains that held the vast, mist-wreathed lake north of Meridanium. These mountains were taller and altogether wilder, their faces glittering with ice that flung back the early light of the rising sun. These were the mountains that raked down along the border between Casmantium and Feierabiand. They rose and rose before him in serried ranks, rose-pink cloud shredding around the naked teeth that sliced up into the sky.

Behind him, he knew without turning, ran a hundred miles of wall. Two hundred miles. More, maybe. Blocks of stone a spear-cast wide and three high wound along a path all across northern Casmantium. On the far side lived fire and the hot wind, the merciless sun and burning sands...The griffin mage was there, opposite Gereint, a fierce presence that blazed and flickered with fire. But, though Gereint tried to gather the remnants of his strength to meet the challenge he half expected, the griffin did not intrude into the country of earth.

On this side, the mountain was glazed with ice. Mist condensed in the cold that radiated from the wall, curling in wisps and streamers along the powerful earth. The ice and the heavy earth denied fire, resisted any incursion of fire. But, though any ordinary griffin might be held by the wall, Gereint suspected it would not stop the griffin mage if he bent his strength against it. Though surely this dawn had found the griffin as exhausted and worn as Gereint...

Perhaps it did, for suddenly Gereint could tell that the griffin mage was gone. Away into the brilliant inimical desert, to rest amid the red sands and burning winds—he was welcome to them. Gereint longed for his own place of rest and silence. He rested his hands on the frozen wall, bowed his head, stretched his awareness wearily back along the long, long span of stone, and let the world fold itself around him. And found himself standing, for the third time, in the courtyard outside Eben Amnachudran's house, surrounded by the scents of cut hay and horses, apples, and, somewhere close at hand, warm bread fresh from the oven. The familiar, homey scents, the ordinary bustle of men and women about their ordinary business,

the natural warmth of an ordinary autumn dawn, were all
suddenly overwhelming after the desert and the griffin
and the wall. Gereint folded up his knees and sat down
right where he stood, on the very doorstep of Amnachudran's house, lacking even the strength to look for the
fragrant bread.

Amnachudran found him there. He did not speak: only
Gereint's name. He put a hand under Gereint's elbow,
urged him wordlessly to his feet, and brought him to a
room paneled in pine and oak. Lady Emre, her face shadowed with worry, brought him bread dripping with butter
and honey. Gereint ate three bites of the bread and then
found enough strength and awareness to ask, "Tehre?"

Amnachudran and his wife exchanged a glance. "She's
fine. She's here," Lady Emre assured him. "She'll be glad
to know you are—you are here. Shall I send for her?"

Gereint shook his head. "Later." He set the bread down
on its plate, leaned his head against the back of the chair,
and was instantly asleep.

He woke early in the morning on the next day, having
slept around an entire day and night. He knew exactly
how much time had passed; a deep awareness of time and
place seemed an odd and unexpected offshoot of magecraft, more welcome than some. And he woke rested, and
clear-headed, altogether a better awakening than his last
in this house...Eben Amnachudran sat in a high-armed
chair by the room's window, gazing out at his orchards.
His expression was quiet, thoughtful, still touched with
the weariness and strain of the past days. His elbows
were propped on the windowsill and his chin rested on
his laced fingers; in one hand he held a quill pen, its

feather brushing his mouth and cheek. On a table by his elbow rested a large leather-bound book, laid open to a map of northern Casmantium, with notations in black and red ink fitted into its margins. Also on the table, of more immediate interest, rested a plate of honey cakes and a platter with tea things.

Gereint cleared his throat. "That's a copy of Berusent, isn't it? You're not getting honey on the pages, I trust?"

Amnachudran swung around, smiling. "Gereint. Good morning! We were beginning to fear you might never wake on your own—I half wanted to try to bring you back to 'this hither shore of dreams' myself, you know, but Emre was adamant that you should be let sleep till you woke. How are you? Can you sit up? Can you hold a cup? The pot's a good one; it keeps tea hot and fresh for hours. I don't know how you usually drink it, but I thought it best to put plenty of honey in this." Rising, he poured steaming tea and brought the cup and the plate of cakes to the bedside table.

Gereint propped himself up against the pillows. He found himself smiling. "I always seem to be waking up in your house..."

"After prodigious feats deserving of the very best tea." Amnachudran handed him the cup, watching to be sure he could hold it without spilling the scalding liquid.

Gereint drank the tea all at once, like medicine, and allowed the scholar to take back the cup and pour it full again. The tea was indeed very sweet, much sweeter than he ordinarily took it, but this morning he welcomed the rich sweetness. He ate a cake, licked honey off his fingers, and asked suddenly, "Tehre?"

"Perfectly well. Asking for you. She argued, along

with me, that we should try to wake you, but Emre over-
ruled us both, no doubt wisely. She was worried about
you. She said you hadn't anything like your ordinary
strength to start—and we all could see what you'd done
to the wall. Tehre's friend Lord Bertaud insists it runs the
entire length of the griffins' desert?"

"From the great lake high in the north, along the
Teschanken, and then west along the border right to the
western mountains. Lord Bertaud? That is the Feierabianden lord?"

"Yes. A very useful sort of friend for Tehre to have
made, I gather."

Gereint shuddered at the memory of the griffin mage,
but he said, to be fair, "The griffin said the Feierabianden
lord persuaded him to seal the wall with fire on his side."

"Yes, so I understand." Amnachudran poured a cup of
tea for himself and sipped it slowly. "We are very fortunate Lord Bertaud was sufficiently concerned to insist on
coming north. And very fortunate my daughter insisted
on accompanying him. I'd never have thought—well,
parents are the worst judges of their children's skill, as
they say. But among you all, we managed to claim something very like victory. I'd not have imagined that, watching the griffins ride that burning wind of theirs toward us.
But I admit, I didn't believe the wall could run all the way
to the western mountains."

"I didn't exactly use my own strength to seal it. I used
mine, but also the deep strength of earth." Gereint paused,
looked more closely at Amnachudran's face. "And the
strength of your men. Isn't that right? Your strength...
but you seem well enough..." He could not quite bring
himself to ask the question he wanted to ask.

"Hardly anyone actually died," the scholar answered, not needing to hear the question. "Fortunately, once the desert withdrew, Emre brought nearly everyone remaining in the household to find us and bring us home."

Gereint imagined the lingering death that would otherwise likely have claimed the men whose strength he'd so ruthlessly used. He swallowed.

"What you did was necessary. You saved us all," Amnachudran said gently, watching his face. "You and Tehre. And Beguchren Teshrichten. And even that griffin mage, once the Feierabianden lord persuaded him to help rather than hinder..."

"Beguchren tried to explain to me about making earth more...I don't know. More itself. The earth holds so much power...I could never have done it with only my own strength." Gereint paused, then added, "It's true about the griffin. He used his own strength, but he also channeled the fierce strength of fire. He said he helped Tehre build the wall...He helped me seal it." Though it was hard to believe a creature of fire would speak any sort of truth. "Maybe Beguchren—" He paused. Put the cup he held down on the bedside table. Asked, trepidation running through him like ice, "Beguchren?"

Amnachudran hesitated. "Asleep," he said finally. "We think."

The cold mage was asleep. But asleep in a way that worried Gereint enormously. He seemed shrunken among the bedclothes, lost amid the blankets and pillows. He had never been anything but slight, but now the flesh seemed to have melted away from his body. The fine bones of his face stood in stark prominence; his eyes had sunk into shadowed hollows; he was deathly pale. Gereint thought he looked far closer to death than to waking.

Lady Emre sat in a high-backed chair close beside the bed, her hand resting lightly on the blankets close by Beguchren's face. She looked drained and weary, and she had lost a good deal of the comfortable plumpness Gereint remembered. But her smile, as she sprang to her feet and came to greet him, had all of its accustomed, lively warmth. "Gereint!" she exclaimed. "Back among us! You see, I told Eben to let you sleep, and here you are! You look quite wonderful! Though you need feeding up, I can see. You're still far too thin. Eben, you must remember to tell the cook—oh, he's not back yet, that's right. Well, then, let's remember to tell whoever's in the kitchen to make something fortifying for noon."

Gereint smiled back at her and forbore to mention her own strained look. She had not asked anything about the battle or the griffins or the wall, for which he was grateful. He cast an inquiring look at the still figure on the bed.

"Yes, poor man," Lady Emre agreed. She moved back to the bedside and frowned down at the small figure of the mage. "I don't know. I thought he would wake, but as you see, he hasn't."

"Which didn't reassure us about you," put in Amnachudran.

Tehre came in hurriedly, catching herself on the door frame when she stumbled in her haste. "Gereint! I thought I heard your voice." She came to him unselfconsciously and took his hands, tilting her head back to gaze up at his face. "You look good. More at home in your mind and heart than I thought you'd be. I was worried about you.

But you've adjusted to the magecraft you enfolded within your self, haven't you? That's splendid. Did you run that ice and mist all the way to the western mountains, then? I told my father there'd be no point to sealing that wall along only half its length."

It was so like her, Gereint thought, to make an instant and correct judgment about him, mention and dismiss it in the same breath, and shift at once to a technical question. He smiled down at her. "I can't believe you broke half a mountain range and built a wall *two hundred miles* long. Do you know, the blocks right up in the western mountains are just as big and well-formed, and just as neatly placed, as the ones over here by the river? I don't see how magecraft could do anything like that, so I guess you're truly a maker and not a mage, but I've also never heard of any feat of building that could even *begin* to touch that wall."

Tehre blushed and looked down, suddenly shy. "Oh, well...I'd never have had the strength to run the blocks so far without the power you found for me. And actually I think it might have been Kairaithin who did the last bit, up by the western mountains. I don't think I did that. And maybe Beguchren..." She glanced uneasily over at the small, still, pale form tucked into the middle of the bed. "I think maybe he helped. Mages might not be makers, but I think he put his strength into getting the blocks to land right. I think he gave me the strength of the earth. I think..." She hesitated, then finished in a rush: "I think that's what happened to him: I think he used himself up by making himself a channel between the deep magic of the earth and me."

Gereint followed her gaze. "Yes. I think that's right.

Someone pulled the power of earth up through the men, and I don't think it was I…I thought I knew why he wanted those men to come with us. Maybe I guessed right, but I didn't guess everything. I would never have thought it was even *possible* to do that."

"It was evidently as hard on him as on any of us," Amnachudran said.

Gereint continued to gaze at the still, small form of the mage. "Oh, yes."

"You recovered," Lady Emre said optimistically. "Perhaps he will, too. All of you collapsed except Tehre." She gave her daughter a proud glance.

"It didn't take *strength* to actually bring down the mountains, you know," Tehre explained modestly. "Just an understanding of how things break." She turned to Gereint. "You know, I figured something out up there when I was helping the mountains break into proper blocks." She leaned forward, her eyes lighting now with enthusiasm, her voice rising as her tone gained intensity. "If you take the force with which a material is pulled under tension, call that the stress to which you subject the material, and how far the material is stretched by that tension, call that the strain, then the ratio of stress to strain gives you a very simple measure of the material's stiffness, do you see?"

"Yes…" Gereint thought he might, more or less.

"Well, it turns out that when you run a thin crack through a material, what happens is there's a tremendous increase in the stress right at the tip of the crack because the stress has to go around the crack and it just piles up at the tip. And the finer the crack, the greater the increase, do you see? You can calculate it—it's the stress times a factor, I think the factor must be something like double the square root of the length of the crack divided by the radius of the tip of the crack. If you calculate it like that, you can see right away why a crack through any stiff material would have a critical length and after that length, the crack would run, and *that's* why stiff materials like stone can't take any tension to speak of, do you see?"

"Well, I'll just leave you children alone, then," said Lady Emre, casting her gaze upward. But she was laughing at the same time, though wryly. "I'll go find your Lord Bertaud, Tehre, my dear, and let him know our friend Gereint's awakened. You can find me in the library, probably, in the unlikely event you want me." She dropped a fond kiss on the back of Tehre's neck, patted Gereint's arm, and went out.

Gereint nodded absently, but he was too delighted by Tehre to really notice her mother's departure. "Fascinating," he told Tehre, sincerely. "And *useful*. I can visualize what you mean, more or less, I think. You figured that out right there, with fire scattering in the wind and wrapping around that circle of pillars? Tehre, you amaze me."

Tehre blushed and glanced down. "Oh, well...I ought to have worked it out long before. Only I didn't until I started breaking the pillars..."

"So you reached up to the mountains, started tiny cracks in the stone, and then applied tension."

"It took hardly any tension," Tehre said earnestly. "That's the whole point. But applied in the right directions. And a *lot* of cracks, of course."

Gereint couldn't stop smiling. "Of course."

"I'll show you—" But she stopped, her enthusiasm fading.

"It's all right," Gereint said gently. "Beguchren was right, though for reasons I don't think he anticipated. It's all right."

"You don't mind?" But Tehre saw or guessed the answer to that question and went on immediately so he wouldn't have to answer it: "You can't undo it? Make yourself over again, in reverse?"

"No," Gereint said. "A maker can remake himself. But a mage's skill isn't in making. It's like shattering a sword or breaking a mountain into blocks: You can't change your mind later and put the material back the way it was to start."

"No," Tehre agreed in a small voice.

"That's true for everything of importance," Eben Amnachudran said quietly. He laid his hands on his daughter's shoulders and looked over her head at Gereint.

Uncomfortable, Gereint turned away and went to stand by the bed, gazing down at Beguchren. He asked, not looking up, "Your lady wife couldn't help him?"

Amnachudran came to stand beside him, Tehre moving up on his other side. The scholar said, "We all collapsed at the end, of course, but that was just a matter of rest. Tauban was torn up by a blow from a griffin—almost the only real casualty we suffered—though, if that counts, Ansant managed to catch a spear in the thigh, somewhere in the most confused part of the..." He paused. "Exercise. Beguchren Teshrichten protected us, exactly as he said he would."

By the scholar's tone, he'd believed they would all die. Gereint nodded, without comment.

"Emre could handle all that. But this"—Amnachudran gestured to the still figure amid the pillows—"this she couldn't touch, and rest doesn't seem to be doing it, either. I thought I might; I thought it might be some sort of symbolic injury—to the will, perhaps, or the heart or the self. But..." His voice trailed off.

Gereint stared down at the small form of the mage. Then he glanced sideways at Tehre. "You were right. He caught the strength of the deep earth and bent it around his own strength and handed it off to you and me. I don't think he's injured. Not even symbolically. But I think he emptied himself down to the very dregs of his will and heart and self..." He laid one hand gently on Beguchren's arm. It was painfully thin.

Closing his eyes, Gereint sent his mind groping after the mage's awareness and memory and self. He found nothing but emptiness...But within that emptiness, the deep magic of earth and stone, which filled the world, so that actually there was no emptiness anywhere. Beyond that deep magic lay an aching cold, as familiar to him as his own hands and mind...He glimpsed years scrolling out endlessly, faces and voices he remembered...He realized only slowly that they were not faces or voices *he* remembered. This cold magic was not something familiar to *him*. And at the beginning, the blank drifting emptiness had not been *his*.

So he reached out to find that sense of emptiness, and into it he poured all the memories he'd caught out of the dark. He tried to fill it with the essential, intrinsic aware-ness of earth and stone and cold and mist...that slid away from him, but his mind caught eagerly at memory. No. Not *his* mind. A woman's face, fair and smiling; a man's face, dark and angry. A voice that spoke his name. Not *his* name, but...It was hard to tell which name was his by right, which heart, which mind, which self... The music of a spinet, winding through a familiar house; the music of a harp, notes drifting up to the sky...

Gereint pulled himself painfully free of memory, up into that measureless, empty sky, and found himself blinking and dazed, in a small, warm room with the warm autumn breeze blowing the curtains at the window, with Tehre on one side and her father on the other. He remembered Tehre at once, but it took a moment for him to recall Eben Amnachudran's name.

On the bed before them, Beguchren drew a breath and opened his eyes.

Beside Gereint, Amnachudran made a small sound. Tehre didn't. She backed quietly away and ran out into the hall. Gereint knew she'd gone to summon her mother and fetch tea, and since Beguchren needed both, that was eminently practical.

The mage's white brows drew together. His eyes were no longer ice pale. They were the powerful dark gray of pewter, of storm clouds, of the last beat of dusk before full dark... Gereint blinked, realizing at precisely the same moment as Beguchren himself that the man was no longer a mage. He felt Beguchren's shock reverberate through his own mind. That deep awareness of earth, the awareness that Gereint had learned in the desert while fire fell out of the dark wind and the wild cries of griffins echoed overhead—*He* still held that awareness, like an extra sense, like an extension of his very *self*. But Beguchren did not. It had not been merely weakened. It was gone. Burned out by fire, used up by merciless need...

He did not say anything. There seemed nothing to say. Except he did not let Beguchren fall back into the

waiting emptiness, which for a moment he was afraid he
might try to do. He made him sit up instead, arranging the
pillows behind him, took the tea Tehre had brought, and
himself held the cup to Beguchren's lips.

"Is he well, now?" Amnachudran asked nervously—
asking Gereint and not Beguchren. He leaned around
Gereint, reached to take Beguchren's thin wrist in his
hand, set his thumb over the beating pulse, and paused.
He was, Gereint surmised, enough of a mage to understand, if belatedly, what had happened.

"He's perfectly fine," Gereint said flatly, his tone dar-
ing Beguchren to contradict him even in the privacy of
his own mind.

Beguchren's storm-gray eyes closed. But his mouth
crooked. He said nothing, but lifted a hand to demand,
wordlessly but stubbornly, that Gereint give him the cup.

Equally wordless, Gereint set it into his hand.

Beguchren lifted the cup, sipped, and lowered it again
with determined steadiness.

Gereint took it just as the other man's hand began to
tremble. He said quietly, "There is a wall stretching from
the cold lake above the Teschanken down along the river,
and then west all the way to the far mountains. It is sealed
with ice and earth on this side, and with fire on the other.
The rivers are flowing with clean water again, and the
country of fire won't overreach itself again."

Beguchren nodded, very faintly. He whispered, "I'll
sleep now."

"A little more tea first," Gereint said gently, and folded
Beguchren's smaller hand around the cup, steadying it for
him to lift and then lower once more.

Lady Emre hurried in with a plate of cakes, Tehre's

Lord Bertaud trailing diffidently behind her. Gereint did
not appreciate the crowd, but he took the cup away again,
broke the cake, and put a sticky fragment in Beguchren's
hand. "Eat that," he said. "Eat it, and then you can sleep.
But promise me you'll wake." He paused and added, with
a measure of ruthlessness that surprised even himself,
"You owe me that."

Beguchren's brows drew together, but he did not deny
it. He nodded again, very slightly, and fell asleep sitting
up, with the bit of cake dissolving on his tongue.

Very much as Gereint had done, Beguchren slept through
the day and then the whole of the following night. And
very much as Gereint had, he woke in far better command
of himself. No one had to bully or coax him into eating
honey cakes, and then porridge and eggs and cold sliced
beef. He spoke to Gereint for a long while—or Gereint
spoke to him: Beguchren wanted to know everything that
had happened after his own collapse. Gereint could not,
of course, tell him anything about most of that. Tehre
filled in the part she knew, and her father described,
though only in very restrained terms, the confusion and
terror that had beset the company down by the river.

"Until the mountains broke, and the great stone blocks
came spilling down from the heights, and the wall built
itself all along the river," he said, his eyes dark and amazed
with memory. "And we all fell, then, just fell where we
stood—that was you, my lord, of course. Emre says she
found us there at dawn. She and the other women carried us all out of a desert that was, she tells me, already
trying to be good, ordinary earth, through breezes that
carried the scents of warm grass and damp leaves. Before

they'd got us two miles, the river came pouring down its bed... It's not quite the same bed," he added as an aside to Gereint. "I've been to look at it. The nearer mountains were so broken and leveled, it's a wider, shallower river now when it reaches this country. Where the water strikes the wall, do you know, it freezes? Cold mists roll over its surface... I don't know. It's no river you'd think to fish from, now."

"Farther south, it will seem more familiar," Beguchren said quietly.

"Well, lord, I'm sure that's true, and probably just as well. I'm not sure anyone would want to put a boat out in the river amid that mist."

Beguchren nodded, his storm-gray eyes unreadable. "And this Feierabianden lord? Lord Bertaud, yes?"

"Bertaud son of Boudan," Tehre put in quickly. "He helped us, helped me..."

"Yes?"

"The griffin mage told me he helped build and seal the wall because of Lord Bertaud's influence," Gereint added.

Beguchren's expression became even more inscrutable.

Tehre traded a glance with her father, which Gereint found impossible to decipher. "I'll find him, ask him to speak with you," she suggested.

"Please do," Beguchren said softly, and sent everyone else away so that he might speak to the foreign lord alone.

"Though I don't know why," Tehre told Gereint later. "Bertaud said he only asked perfectly normal, straightforward things. Just what happened."

Bertaud? Gereint thought. Tehre was so informal

with the foreign lord? She called him by name like that, without even thinking? But he said only, "Perhaps he was simply tired of being attended by a crowd, and I don't blame him."

"Perhaps that's so," Tehre agreed, and began absently to sketch equations containing the square root of the ratio of crack length over the radius of crack tip, or so Gereint supposed. She was, she'd said, trying to work out whether you indeed simply doubled that value in her stress calculations, or whether the multiplicative factor merely *approximated* two. And she thought there was some small additive factor as well... Gereint left her to it. At least any Feierabianden lords who happened to wander by would probably find the calculations even more impenetrable than he did himself.

The day after that, Beguchren got up from his bed and made his way through the halls and out into the courtyard, speaking to no one save for a polite murmur of acknowledgment to an astonished man-at-arms at the front gate. The man-at-arms hurried to tell Eben Amnachudran, and Amnachudran told Gereint, and Gereint found Beguchren sitting, pale and exhausted, underneath a big old apple tree. He was leaning against its knotted trunk, his face tipped back toward the leafy branches, his eyes closed, looking so ethereal it seemed strange the light breeze did not carry him away.

The tree had recovered well from the brief encroachment of the desert wind. Sweet golden apples hung thickly overhead. Their fragrance drifted in the quiet air. Amid the grasses, windfall apples buzzed with wasps too busy to notice or resent the intrusion of men.

"You don't need to fetch your own, you know,"

Gereint said, sitting down beside Beguchren. "The children brought plenty right into the kitchens."

The smaller man smiled wryly, not opening his eyes. After a moment, he said, "It's just as well. I think I could neither climb the tree for the hanging fruit, nor chase away the wasps from the fallen."

"You're stronger. You think you can walk back to the house from here?"

"Oh, yes. In a little while. After I sit here for a few moments..."

"Shall I leave?"

"It doesn't matter. Stay, if you wish."

They sat in companionable silence for a time. Eventually, Gereint ventured, "The Arobern will value you anyway, you know," and then flushed, immediately realizing how stupid that sounded.

Beguchren mercifully didn't even open his eyes, much less respond.

After a while, Gereint gathered his nerve and tried again, more simply and directly. "I'm sorry. I'd give it back to you, if I could. I suppose you can't make yourself back into a mage as I did? Recover magecraft through the side door, as it were?"

"No. I'm not a maker." Beguchren paused, and then added, "We both lost what we valued, I suppose. It's fair enough. It's not that different from what I did to you. In reverse."

"It worked."

"Not in anything like the manner I'd intended. Nor at the price I'd prepared to pay. Not even in the same *coin* I'd prepared to pay." He suddenly sounded exhausted. "Thus the world teaches us humility."

"But it still worked."

"...true." There was a small silence. Beguchren said, "I suppose I'll become accustomed to it, in time."

In much the same way that a man might become accustomed to being blind and deaf. Just so. Gereint did not answer. He stood up after a moment, reaching high into the branches for a couple of apples. He had a belt knife, but it was too large and clumsy a thing to peel apples with. If he'd still been a maker, he could have coaxed the knife to exceed its design, encouraged it to hold the sort of edge such delicate work demanded... He cut each apple in quarters, cored them, and handed half the pieces to Beguchren without trying to peel them. They sat under the tree and ate the apples, surrounded by the quiet autumn sunlight and the buzzing of wasps. In the distance voices called, indistinct but cheerful.

"I believe I can probably walk back to the house now," Beguchren said. He glanced at Gereint, half smiling. "And if I can't..."

"I'm sure that won't be necessary." Gereint got to his feet and offered the other man a hand up.

Beguchren made it back to the house on his own feet. But once they were back in the house, he shook his head quietly as Gereint turned toward his room. "I'll speak to Eben Amnachudran. And Lady Emre."

Gereint said, puzzled, "You can do that from your bed—"

"No," said Beguchren. Quietly but definitely.

By which Gereint understood that Beguchren did not want to *chat* with Amnachudran or his wife. He wanted to talk to them in some more formal place than a bedroom, in some more formal capacity than that of their guest.

And since he was no longer a mage, that most likely meant he wanted to speak to them as a king's agent. "Likely they'll be in Amnachudran's office," he guessed, and hailed a passing servant with the query.

Both Eben Amnachudran and his wife were in the office-music room. Amnachudran was, of course, at his desk and surrounded by books, but somewhat to Gereint's surprise, Lord Bertaud was also leaning over the desk. Both men were poring over a large open book bound in pale linen and illustrated all around the text with dragons and griffins in gold and red and black ink. Tehre was a few steps away, gazing down at a sketch of a bridge and absently rolling a quill pen between her fingers. Lady Emre was seated, as she had been the first time Gereint had seen her, at her spinet. This time she was playing, her expression abstracted. The music was a northern children's song, very simple and plain. In Lady Emre's hands, it recovered the charm that too great familiarity might have stolen from it and became not merely plain, but elegant.

But she lifted her hands from the keys, turning with everyone else when Gereint and Beguchren came in. Amnachudran moved hastily to pull chairs around for them. Beguchren sank into his with a slight nod, but Gereint merely drifted a step away to lean his hip against the edge of the big desk, watching curiously.

"I'll leave tomorrow morning," Beguchren began. "So if I may trouble you, honored sir, for the loan of a carriage and driver? Thank you." He paused and surveyed them all. The cool authority of his tone and manner could be estimated, Gereint thought, by the lack of overt protest at the idea of his traveling. The effort that matter-of-fact coolness cost him was less easy to estimate.

"I am grateful for all your efforts over the past days," Beguchren continued. "On my behalf, and in the Arobern's voice, I thank you. We can only imagine how else events might have unfolded. With, to be sure, the most profound gratitude that we need imagination to view those events." He gave them each a slight nod and said to Lord Bertaud, "I am quite certain the king will wish to thank you personally for your assistance. I hope you will accompany me back to the court in Breidechboden?" He accepted the Feierabianden lord's murmured assurance with another nod.

Then Beguchren leaned back in his chair, took a breath, turned his storm-gray eyes to Eben Amnachudran, and added, "The only question that remains to be settled before my departure, then, is this: Was it you yourself who removed Gereint Enseichen's brand? Or was it your lady wife?"

There was a deep, deep silence. Gereint hadn't seen that coming at all. But, he gradually realized, Amnachudran had. The scholar looked shocked by the question, but he did not, somehow, look *surprised*. He stood with his palms flat on his desk, his head slightly bowed, not looking at any of them. After a moment he lifted his head and glanced at his wife. Lady Emre looked stricken. Her eyes were on Beguchren, not on her husband; she shook her head very slightly in a motion that might have been disbelief or might have been a plea, and either way was probably involuntary. But she did not say anything or make any overt gesture.

Amnachudran said at last to Beguchren, "My lord, it was I."

Beguchren inclined his head. "Then I will have to ask you, also, to accompany me tomorrow."

"Of course," said Amnachudran, just a little stiffly.

No one else said a word. Tehre opened her mouth, but her mother half lifted a hand and shook her head quickly, and, to Gereint's surprise, Tehre closed her mouth again without making a sound. Her eyes snapped with anger, but then narrowed, and Gereint knew she was thinking hard. He wished he knew what conclusion she might come to. He himself felt torn between wanting to exclaim to Beguchren, in outrage, *How can you?* and at the same time wanting to plead with Amnachudran and the rest, *He's the king's agent; what else can he do?* He said nothing at all.

CHAPTER 16

The Arobern received them, two days after their return to Breidechboden, in an intimidating room large enough for thirty men to gather, a room that held enough large, heavy, ornately carved chairs to accommodate all thirty as well as a single massive and ornate desk. The king had heard the whole account from Beguchren, or so Gereint surmised. Certainly Beguchren had gone to him at once on arriving in the city. No one else had; no one else had been invited to.

Gereint had stayed, of course, at the Amnachudran townhouse, with Tehre and her father, and Sicheir, who, he gathered, had gone on to Breidechboden with the king's agent after Tehre had defied the agent to go north. The other party to that defiance, Lord Bertaud, alone among them presumably not at personal risk of the king's displeasure, had returned to whatever apartment within the palace was allotted for his use. Tehre had received two messages from the Feierabianden lord, one each day, and returned three of her own, which was only natural. Gereint set his teeth against any ill-considered comment he might have made about this correspondence.

There had been no word from either Beguchren or the king until at last, and to everyone's unspoken relief, the command to appear for an audience had been brought by an extremely elegant royal chamberlain. The waiting had been difficult for Eben Amnachudran and his children, Gereint knew. But if any of them had said a word about their nervousness, it had not been to Gereint.

The king was not seated at the desk, nor in the room at all, when the chamberlain ushered them within. This was not a surprise; he would hardly have arrived early to wait for suppliants to come before him. No; they had been sent for and had come, and now would wait the king's pleasure. Nothing rested on the desk save an elegant gold-and-crystal four-hour sand timer, turned recently, so that perhaps half the sand had run through to the bottom glass. Gereint hoped the sand did not mark the wait they were expected to endure: Two hours might not realistically be long to wait for a royal audience, but at the moment it seemed an intolerable span of time.

Though the room was not without interest. Blue-and-teal abstract mosaics rippled all along three of the walls, high up, near the ceiling, which was painted pale blue with flying larks. The remaining wall held only a large painting framed with long velvet hangings of blue and violet, showing Breidechboden from above as a lark might see it. The light that poured across the painted city possessed a crystalline clarity, as though the city had been created in just the instant the painting captured and had not yet begun to age. It occurred to Gereint, for the first time but with a curious sense of inevitability, that the artist was certainly Beguchren Teshrichten himself.

Gereint found the room, as a whole, rather alarming. And yet... it might have been far worse. It might have been a formal audience hall, all porphyry columns and vaulted, echoing marble, with a chill to it that bit worse than any northern midwinter. This room, though it fairly radiated authority, was not nearly so formal, and the chamberlain who guided them invited them all to enter with an expansive gesture that suggested welcome rather than command. It was not the sort of reception they might have expected from an angry king. But it was a little hard to estimate what sort of reception it actually *was*.

Lord Bertaud was already present. Gereint could not decide whether the foreigner's earlier arrival was accidental or meant to indicate something, or, if it was deliberate, what it was meant to indicate. Probably he was reading too much into mere happenstance.

Tehre went at once to greet the Feierabianden lord, Gereint and Eben Amnachudran and Sicheir following more slowly. Tehre's father had been very quiet and inward for the days of the journey from his house to Breidechboden, and after their arrival in the capital he had become quieter still. But there was a new quality to his silence now. Gereint understood that, or thought he did. He believed the Arobern would forgive any of them anything, as well he ought to—he *believed* that—but the king was well known to despise corruption or vice or any dishonesty in his appointed judges. So Gereint did not know, none of them knew, exactly what the king would do.

The Feierabianden lord had a smile for Tehre; rather

too warm a smile for any foreigner to direct toward a Casmantian lady, was Gereint's impression. The nod of greeting he himself gave the man was perhaps a little stiff. Neither of them spoke; it did not seem a place or moment for idle conversation, and what could they possibly say? But the foreigner offered in return a gesture that seemed oddly poised midway between a nod and a bow, and the same to Eben Amnachudran. Amnachudran inclined his head in response, glanced briefly at his daughter, and drew breath as though he might speak. But then he said nothing.

"You may all sit," the chamberlain told them, arranging chairs in a loose semicircle by the desk. "You, honored sir—you, sir—you, sir—Lady Tehre, if you wish—over here, my lord, if you would be so kind."

No one ventured to protest these arrangements, which placed Lord Bertaud a little away from the rest and in a distinctly more ornate chair. Gereint's chair was close enough to Tehre's that he might have held her hand, and he was tempted to, save any such gesture would have been thoroughly inappropriate under the circumstances. Not to mention the eye of her father.

The entrance of the king interrupted Gereint's thoughts, which was perhaps as well.

The Arobern, as was his widely reputed habit, was not wearing court dress. He was dressed only a little more elaborately than a soldier, in black, except his belt was sapphire blue and his buttons, probably, were sapphire in truth. He wore around his throat the thick gold chain of the Casmantian kings, and around his left wrist a wide-linked chain of black iron.

Beguchren Teshrichten walked not behind the king,

like a servant, but beside him, like a friend. Beguchren
might, next to the dark bulk of the Arobern and with the
smooth fineness of his face, have looked rather like an
elegant, wealthy, arrogant child. But despite the strain
and weariness that still clung to him, there was too
much authority in the tilt of his fine head to support that
illusion, and far too many years in his storm-dark eyes.
Those eyes met Gereint's, unfathomable as ever, but he
did not even nod, far less speak.

Everyone rose hastily, even the Feierabianden lord, but
the Arobern turned a big hand palm upward to signal that
no one need kneel, and then turned the gesture to a casual
little wave that invited them all to resume their seats. The
courtesy made Gereint uncomfortable.

Beguchren settled quietly into a particularly ornate
chair set next to the heavy desk, rested his hands on the
arms of the chair, and gazed at them with impenetrable
calm.

The Arobern did not sit but leaned his hip against
the polished edge of the desk, crossed his arms over his
chest, and surveyed them all. When his forceful, dark
gaze crossed Gereint's, Gereint wanted to flinch and drop
his eyes; a slave's impulse, or the deference any Casmantian owed his king, or the impulse of a guilty man? It felt
oddly like guilt, though he knew very well he had nothing
for which to atone. He set his jaw and stared back.

"I believe," the Arobern said, in his deep, guttural
voice, "that I have the tale plain and clear. Does anyone
believe it necessary to add to the account my agent Beguchren Teshrichten has given to me?"

No one appeared to, though Gereint could not stop
himself from glancing at Amnachudran.

"So," said the Arobern. He turned to the Feierabianden lord, inclining his heavy head. "Lord Bertaud, you spoke for Casmantium before the representative of the griffins. Their mage, yes? It was your word that caused the griffin mage to align his power with ours in the building of that wall. That is so, yes?"

Lord Bertaud hesitated for a long moment. At last he said quietly, "It was a little more complicated than that. Sipiike Kairaithin himself favored the solution Lady Tehre devised. I know he set himself against the will of his own king to support the building of that wall. We—you owe him a debt, which I doubt you will ever have an opportunity to repay. But I hope you'll keep in mind, Lord King, that at the end, not every griffin strove for the destruction of your country."

The Arobern paid the foreign lord careful attention. When the foreigner had finished speaking, he answered, "As you say so, Lord Bertaud, I will remember it. I know well your people, and you particularly, have forged a much greater understanding with the griffins than Casmantium has ever managed, despite all our long experience."

Lord Bertaud inclined his head. "Perhaps it's our lack of violent history that allows Feierabiand to approach the People of Fire and Air more, ah—"

"More productively," suggested Beguchren, quietly. "I think it's clear that earth mages, particularly cold mages, should not determine policy when dealing with the... People of Air and Fire. Certainly the counsel of mages is suspect in that regard, and so I've advised my lord king."

Lord Bertaud looked startled and satisfied in approximately equal measure. He said after a moment, "I'm...

that is, I think perhaps you may be correct, Lord Beguchren, and I'm very much hopeful that this, ah, caution,
may lead to a better outcome along the border between
earth and fire. If, ah…"

"If the wall should fail," Beguchren completed the
thought. He turned his head, regarding Gereint, one pale
brow lifting. He said, not quite a question, "As it should
not, however."

Gereint shook his head uncertainly. "I don't think
so, my lord. I don't—I can't well judge, but I don't
think so."

"It should last for a long time," Tehre put in earnestly.
"Quite a long time, really. It's structurally very sound.
Because of how wide it is, you know. Width and weight
always stabilize a wall—"

The Arobern smoothly interrupted what might have
become a detailed digression on the nature and stability
of walls. "Lady Tehre," he said formally, "Casmantium
is amazed by your skill and prowess as a builder and an
engineer. Casmantium and I are grateful for your insight
and your skill, laid down at great risk and in despite of
my command." His manner became less formal and more
expansive. "Which, hah, I think I might forgive! My agent
Detreir Enteirich was most alarmed at your defiance and
the defiance of Lord Bertaud, but I have assured him that,
under the circumstances, he need not be concerned at his
failure to complete the charge I gave him."

From her air of startlement, Gereint rather thought
Tehre might have genuinely forgotten about this incident
herself. Lord Bertaud's mouth crooked in a wry smile.

The king, too, looked amused, as though he also suspected Tehre had forgotten. "I think I will send you west,

with your honored brother and with Lord Bertaud if he
will agree, to where my engineers and builders are working on my new road," he told her. "I think you have ideas
for bridges and roadwork. And more than ideas, I think!
You are not any ordinary maker, hah? My friend Beguchren tells me that we need a new word to describe what
you are: not a mage, but not exactly a maker. You and he
can decide. But I will send you west, and send my agent
Detreir Enteirich with you, to ensure my engineers know
to regard your views with respect."

Tehre had flushed, but her face was alight with enthusiasm. "Oh, yes! I have this wonderful idea for a new
kind of bridge; it has—well." Surprising Gereint, she cut
herself off and said merely, "I'm sure it will work. Nearly
sure." But then she frowned, suddenly cautious. "Oh!
But the Fellesteden heir, what *is* his name? I don't know,
maybe he—it's possible he might—"

"I think Casnerach Fellesteden will not further trouble
you or your family," the king assured her, smiling affably
and somehow almost as fiercely as a griffin. "So you will
go west. That is good." He turned at last to Gereint. "And
you, Gereint Enseichen. What should I say to you?"

Gereint knew he had flushed. He truly had no idea how
to respond. The king's gaze was uncomfortably intense
when it was aimed precisely at him, Gereint found.

The Arobern said, "So we gain at very least a respite,
maybe for years, maybe for our generation. Maybe for an
age. And you did this for us."

This was unanswerable. Gereint managed a small nod.

"I am very satisfied with your work in the service of my
friend Beguchren Teshrichten, and of Casmantium—that
is, my service. Beguchren hoped you would do well for

him. Neither of us, I think, understood how well you might do. Or under what circumstances. Or at what cost."

Gereint shook his head. "The cost wasn't mine. Not really. Not in the end." His eyes met Beguchren's, and he looked away again at once. He said to the Arobern, "It wasn't any of my doing that put me in a position to stumble into a way to be useful. I know that very well. I'm grateful Lord Beguchren's foresight and courage brought us all through that night of fire." He met Beguchren's eyes again, this time deliberately. "If not quite as we expected, still we came through to the dawn."

"As you say," the Arobern said, as gently as his gravelly voice permitted.

Beguchren bowed his head a little, and there was a pause.

Then the Arobern said, turning to the last of them, "Eben Amnachudran, your role, also, I have heard described. I commend your decisiveness and your steady courage in those days of fire. And through that last night. And your kindness to my friend Beguchren, among all the men who fell under your care."

Amnachudran, rather pale, bowed his head. He began to speak, but stopped.

The Arobern's heavy brows lifted. He asked, "What penalty should attend a judge of mine who interferes with a proper *geas* in defiance of my law and then conceals that interference? And what difference should it make if that same judge should comport himself creditably during a crisis in the days following that crime?"

Tehre sat frozen, her hand touching her mouth. Lord Bertaud looked quietly aside, not to intrude on this Casmantian matter. Beguchren was, as always, calmly inscrutable. Gereint didn't know what he showed—nothing, he hoped. Yet, at least. It took an effort to say nothing, to leave Eben Amnachudran to answer that accusation alone.

Amnachudran lifted his head. "No difference, of course. The law is very clear that one honorable act does not clear dishonor from an earlier act. As I knew very well." He got to his feet, took one step forward, and sank to his knees. "Lord King, when I chose to break your law, I should have resigned my judgeship. Instead, yes, I tried to hide what I had done. I ask for mercy."

"Do you so? Now?"

Amnachudran flinched just a little, but visibly. "Lord King, you'll say I should have come to you then if I would ask for mercy. That to plead for clemency only after one is caught is nothing honorable. That's true. Of course I should. And I'm aware, as Touchan Dachbraden points out, that any judge renowned for mercy must also be renowned, in precisely equal measure, for injustice. I know it. I don't argue it."

The Arobern went around the massive desk, took a velvet pouch from a drawer, and poured out into his broad hand two familiar silver *geas* rings. They chimed together as they slid into the king's hand, delicate and horrifying. The king stirred them with one blunt finger and they chimed again, more quietly. With his new mage's awareness, Gereint found he could actually *see* the cold magecraft woven into the rings, like a filigree of frost laid over the silver.

The king said to Amnachudran, "Justice might be to set the *geas* on the man who unlawfully interfered with its binding on another. What say you, my judge?"

Amnachudran had gone dead white. He began to answer, and stopped as Gereint's hand closed hard on his shoulder. Tehre, with a self-control that amazed Gereint, still said nothing at all, but waited to see what he would do and what the king would do. Her eyes were brilliant with anger and fear.

Gereint had found himself on his feet and beside Amnachudran without thinking. Now he took an instant for thought, reached the same conclusion the back of his mind seemed to have made first, and said sharply, allowing himself the sharpness, "If I served Beguchren Teshrichten, I should have those rings. You said I might melt them down or throw them in the river, whatever I chose. You said that. But there are other rings, I suppose. I'll beg you not to use them, Lord King. If I am owed anything at all, I'll beg you for mercy for my friend."

Tehre leaped to her feet and said fiercely, "If *I* am owed anything, then *I* will beg for mercy for my father. And I *am* owed, Lord King! You said you were grateful! And you should be!"

The Arobern considered her, bright and intense and tiny, with the light shining gold in her hair and her eyes snapping with passion. His expression was hard to read. He drew breath to respond.

Before the king could speak, Beguchren rose, effortlessly drawing all eyes. His manner impeccably elegant and formal, he went over to where Eben Amnachudran knelt and stood for a moment looking down at him.

Then Beguchren turned to face the king, standing on Amnachudran's other side, his small hand resting on the kneeling man's shoulder in an echo of Gereint's gesture. When Beguchren looked at the king, it was with a confidence no one else could possibly share; even, perhaps, with a trace of humor. He said gently, "Lord King…I, too, beg you for mercy for this man. Not for justice, for one need not plead for justice from a just king. But for clemency for a man who has served you; for the father of a lady who has served you well; for the friend of my student Gereint Enseichen, who has served you well. And for my sake, because I ask you."

Student? Gereint thought, startled. He glanced side-long at Beguchren's face, but there was, of course, nothing to read there.

"Well," said the Arobern, a little blankly. And then, "I meant to offer clemency, you know, my friend."

"I would have thought so," answered Beguchren, smiling his slight, impenetrable smile. "But as I am the architect of this moment, I wished to be quite certain of the resulting…"

"Edifice?" suggested the Arobern. "Or artwork, hah?"

"If you like." Beguchren glanced down again at the kneeling Amnachudran. "I'm grateful for your assistance," he said to him softly. "And your kindness, and that of your lady wife. On my own behalf, not the behalf of Casmantium entire."

Eben Amnachudran lowered his head in quiet gratitude and then lifted his gaze once more to the king's face. He did not speak.

"A king who is renowned for mercy," said the Arobern, with heavy irony, "must also be renowned in equal measure for injustice." He paused. No one moved. The king said, "Eben Amnachudran, no judge of mine may disregard my law with impunity. I therefore declare that you are no longer a judge."

Amnachudran's mouth flinched slightly, but he nodded.

"However, yes, I think the *geas* would not be a suitable punishment for you, and anyway, I have said I would be clement." He dropped the silver rings carelessly to the polished surface of the desk and went on: "You dislike the *geas,* I think. Not only for yourself; you dislike it generally. I think it serves its purpose. But recently it has occurred to me that sometimes it may be too harsh a penalty for one man or another, or applied under questionable circumstances. It has occurred to me that I might appoint an agent of mine to investigate possible abuses of the *geas*. To determine whether there may be some men—and women—who might have been bound unjustly, or who might reasonably apply"—his mouth twisted slightly—"for clemency. But this work would take a long time, yes? I do not have an agent I can spare to this work." He paused.

Then he took a carved bone disk from the same pouch that had held the *geas* rings. Unusually, the token was dyed in two tones: sapphire on the spear-and-shield face, rich purple on the tree-and-falcon side. The king tossed the token upward and caught it without looking. He said to Amnachudran, "You might undertake this work for me, do you think so? It would take you away from your home, from your family; it would require you to travel widely and spend prodigious effort. So this is not a reward I give you. But it is clemency, I think, yes?"

"Yes," Amnachudran whispered. He cleared his throat and said more loudly, "Yes, Lord King. I thank you for your generosity."

"Hah." The Arobern tossed the disk upward once

more, caught it. Held it out to Amnachudran. "Take it," he commanded.

Gereint put a hand unobtrusively under the older man's elbow to help him to his feet, but once he was up, Amnachudran walked forward on his own, steadily, to take the dyed token from the king's hand. The king tipped it into his palm, closed a powerful hand around Amnachudran's fist as he took it, and said sternly, "The task will require a man of careful judgment. That is important. Not too merciful, not too harsh. Yes?"

Amnachudran bowed his head. He did not answer hastily, but only after a moment, and in a low, serious tone, "My Lord King, I will try to be worthy of your trust."

"I think you will be," said the Arobern, and let him go. Then he scooped up the *geas* rings with a sudden motion and held them out to Gereint, who took them. The rings burned in his palm with an odd cold life, not quite like anything he had ever perceived.

"They are yours," the king said gravely. "Did I not say they would be?"

"I believe I might be able to teach you how to unweave the magecrafting," Beguchren said, equally serious. "It would be a useful exercise."

Gereint crushed the first response that came onto his tongue into a polite and restrained, "I'm sure there will be other exercises that will prove as useful." He, in his turn, tossed the rings to Tehre.

She caught them out of the air as neatly as though she had known from the first precisely what he would do. She was smiling. It was a brilliant smile, edged with irony. "Silver's not the same as stone," she told him. "I don't think the same calculations exactly apply."

"Do you need them?"

"No," Tehre said. "There's another equation for metals; I've just now worked it out." And she tossed the rings into the air. The light glittered on the silver, and on the frost that wove like lace across the metal... and, with a delicate shivering music like the shattering of tiny bells, the rings dissolved into a glittering dust that scattered across the Arobern's polished desk.

The destruction of the symbols of slavery was, in a strange way, more dramatic than freedom itself had been. Gereint felt his mouth curving into an involuntary smile, probably, he suspected, with an edge of concentrated lunacy beneath it. "You'll have to teach me that equation."

Tehre gazed back at him with cautious, pleased surprise that only barely overlay the intensity beneath. "I'll teach you *all* the equations. If you like."

Gereint could not stop smiling. He wondered how long it might take to erase that caution from her eyes. Not so long, perhaps, with some dedicated effort. He said, "All of them? I'm sure that will take a long time. Years, I expect. But I can't think of a better way to spend years." And he crossed to her side and, as he had wanted to do almost from the beginning, folded her small hand in his large one and looked down into her eyes.

Tehre flushed, and laughed, and glanced at her father and the king... but then she tilted her face up to gaze at Gereint, put her other small hand halfway around his—all it would reach—and said, teasing, but serious as well, "It might take forever. Because when you've learned all of them, I'll invent more."

"The philosophers say numbers are infinite," Gereint

said with deep satisfaction. "So there's no reason we should ever run out."

"Go away," the Arobern said, amused. "Enjoy your infinite equations, and if some of them apply to the building of mountain roads and high bridges, all the better." He gestured dismissal to them all.

Gereint lingered to give Beguchren a long look, afraid he might well feel himself abandoned. Beguchren smiled. This time, to Gereint, the smile did not seem entirely inscrutable, but amused and even pleased; avoiding bitterness, he suspected, with a deliberate effort. Gereint nodded to Beguchren, then turned to Eben Amnachudran with an apologetic little tilt of his head that said, *I know I should have asked you first*, but was not very sincere about the apology. There was nothing but approval and relief in the smile the king's newest agent returned. And at last Gereint spared the Feierabianden Lord Bertaud a glance of acknowledgment that he tried not to let be smug, and received in return a quiet, sincere nod that almost made him repent the smugness, not that he could restrain it.

But he didn't speak to any of them. He only said, "Bridges," to Tehre, and she, trying not to smile and failing spectacularly, nodded with a pretense of solemnity that fooled no one and answered, "Bridges. We definitely need to study bridges," and pulled him with her out of the room and the palace and the court entirely, back into the brilliant light of the world.

acknowledgments

Thanks to my agent, Caitlin Blasdell, whose insightful comments about my manuscripts always help me fix weaknesses that I should have spotted but missed; and to my editor, Devi Pillai, who not only tells me I'm "awesome," but also talked me into writing a trilogy when that wasn't initially what I had in mind.

extras

orbit

meet the author

Rachel Neumeier started writing fiction to relax when she was a graduate student and needed a hobby unrelated to her research. Prior to selling her first fantasy novel, she had published only a few articles, in venues such as *The American Journal of Botany*. However, finding that her interests did not lie in research, Rachel left academia and began to let her hobbies take over her life instead. She now gardens, cooks, raises and shows dogs, and occasionally finds time to read. She works part time for a tutoring program, though she tutors far more students in math and chemistry than in English composition. Find out more about Rachel Neumeier at www.rachelneumeier.com.

introducing

If you enjoyed LAND OF THE BURNING SANDS,

look out for

LAW OF THE BROKEN EARTH

THE GRIFFIN MAGE TRILOGY: BOOK THREE

by Rachel Neumeier

Mienthe did not remember her mother, and she was frightened of her father—a cold, harsh-voiced man with a scathing turn of phrase when his children displeased him. He favored his son, already almost a young man when Mienthe was born, and left Mienthe largely to the care of a succession of nurses—a succession because servants rarely stayed long in that house. If Mienthe had had no one but the nurses, her childhood might have been bleak indeed. But she had Tef.

Tef was the gardener and a man of general work. He had been a soldier for many years and lost a foot in a long-ago dispute with Casmantium. Tef was no longer young and he walked with a crutch, but he had never in his life been afraid of any man save, long ago, his sergeant. Certainly he was not afraid of Mienthe's father. He was as constant a feature of the gardens as the great trees. It never crossed Mienthe's mind that *he* might give notice.

Despite the lack of a foot, Tef carried Mienthe through the gardens on his shoulders. He also let her eat her lunches with him in the kitchen, showed her how to cut flowers so they would stay fresh longer, and gave her a kitten that grew into an enormous slit-eyed gray cat. Tef could speak to cats and so there were always cats about the garden and his cottage, but none of them were as huge or as dignified as the gray cat he gave Mienthe. She named the cat Dusk. The cat slept on Mienthe's pillow until a nurse, horrified by the shed hairs and the dead mice that turned up in the corners of the room, took him away. Tef told Mienthe he'd found him a comfortable home at a dairy far away where he wouldn't bother the nurse at all, and that he had plenty of mice to chase and cream to drink. Mienthe believed this implicitly.

But she also deliberately spilled a bowl of soup at supper and dropped a glass the next evening, and after that deliberately tripped and knocked hard against the table, spilling all the vases of flowers. Mienthe merely waited stoically through her father's tirades about clumsiness and *Why cannot an adult woman teach a child a graceful air? Is my daughter to grow up to be a pig herder or may she someday be allowed in polite society?* But the cold sarcasm terrified the nurse, who had hysterics on the third night and gave notice.

When Mienthe was seven, one of her nurses started teaching her letters. But that nurse had only barely shown her how to form each letter and spell her own name before Mienthe's father raged at her about *Good paper left out in the weather* and *When are you going to teach that child to keep in mind what she is about? A sight more valuable than teaching a mere girl how to spell*, and the nurse gave him notice and Mienthe a tearful farewell. After that, Tef got out a tattered old gardener's compendium and taught Mienthe her letters himself. Mienthe could spell Tef's name before her own, and she could spell "bittersweet" and "catbriar" and even "quaking grass" long before she could spell her father's name. As her father did not notice she had learned to write at all, this did not offend him.

Mienthe's nurses never stayed long enough to teach her much, although one, hardier than the others, taught her a little about sewing and a little about how to stand gracefully. Tef could not teach Mienthe embroidery or deportment, but he used a boy's bow to teach her to shoot, and he taught her to make simple soldier's medicines out of herbs. He also taught Mienthe to ride by putting her up on her brother's outgrown pony and letting her fall off until she learned to stay on, which fortunately her brother never discovered, and he taught her to imitate the purring call of a contented gray jay and the rippling coo of a dove and the friendly little chirp of a sparrow so well she could often coax one bird or another to take seeds or crumbs out of her hand.

"It's good you can keep the cats from eating the birds," Mienthe told Tef earnestly. "But do you mind?" People who could speak to an animal, she knew, never liked constraining the natural desires of that animal.

"I don't mind," said Tef, smiling down at her. He was sitting perfectly still so he wouldn't frighten the purple-shouldered finch perched on Mienthe's finger. "The cats can catch voles and rabbits. That's much more useful than birds. I wonder if you'll find yourself speaking to some of the little birds one day? That'd be pretty and charming."

Mienthe gazed down at the finch on her finger and smiled. But she said, "It wouldn't be very useful. Not like speaking to cats is to you."

"You're Lord Beraod's daughter," said Tef. "You don't need to worry about being *useful*. Anyway, your father would probably be better pleased with an animal that was pretty and charming than one that's only useful."

This was true. Mienthe wished she were pretty and charming herself, like a finch. Maybe then her father...But she moved her hand too suddenly, then, and the bird flew away with a flash of buff and purple, and she forgot her half-recognized thought.

When Mienthe was nine, a terrible storm came pounding out of the sea into the Delta. The storm uprooted trees, tore the roofs off houses, flooded fields, and drowned dozens of people who happened to be in the path of its greatest fury. Among those who died were Mienthe's brother and, trying to rescue him from the racing flood, her father.

Mienthe was her father's sole heir. Tef explained this to her. He explained why five uncles and four cousins—none of whom Mienthe knew, but all with young sons—suddenly appeared and began to quarrel over which of them might best give her a home. Mienthe tried to understand what Tef told her, but she was frightened and everything was suddenly so noisy and confusing. The quarrel had something to do with the sons, and with her. "I'm...to go live with one of them? Somewhere else?" she asked anxiously. "Can't you come, too?"

"No, Mie," Tef said, stroking her hair with his big hand as though she were a kitten herself. "No, I can't. Not one of your uncles or cousins would permit that. But you'll do well, do you see? I'm sure you'll like living with your Uncle Talenes." Tef thought it was Uncle Talenes who was going to win the quarrel. "You'll have his sons to play with, and a nurse who will stay longer than a season, and an aunt to be fond of you."

Tef was right about one thing: In the end, it was Uncle Talenes who vanquished the rest of the uncles and cousins. Uncle Talenes was one of the half-uncles, Mienthe knew: one of the sons of Grandfather Berdoen's second wife. Uncle Talenes finally resorted to the simple expedient of using his thirty men-at-arms—no one else had brought so many—to appropriate Mienthe and carry her away, leaving the rest to continue their suddenly pointless argument without her.

But Tef was wrong about everything else.

Uncle Talenes lived several days' journey from Kames, where Mienthe's father's house was, in a large, high-walled house outside Tiefenauer. Uncle Talenes's house had mosaic floors and colored glass in the windows and a beautiful fountain in the courtyard. All around the fountain were flowers, vivid blooms tumbling over the edges of their beds. Three great oaks in the courtyard held cages of fluttering, sweet-voiced birds. Mienthe was not allowed to splash in the fountain no matter how hot the weather. Nor was she allowed to walk on the mosaic floors in case she should get them muddy. She was allowed to sit on the raked gravel under the trees as long as she was careful not to tear her clothing, but she could not listen to the birds without being sorry for the cages.

Aunt Eren was not fond of Mienthe. She was not fond of children generally, but her sons did not much regard their mother's temper. Mienthe did not know what she could safely disregard and what she must take care for. She wanted to please her aunt, only she was too careless and not clever enough and could not seem to learn when Aunt Eren wanted her to come forward and speak up and when she wanted her to stay out of the way and be quiet as a moth.

Nor did Aunt Eren hire a nurse for Mienthe. She said Mienthe was too old to need a nurse and should have a proper maid instead, but then she did not hire one. Two of Aunt Eren's own maids took it in turns to look after Mienthe instead, but she could see they did not like to. Mienthe tried to be quiet and give them no bother.

Mienthe's half-cousins—Terre was twelve and Karre fourteen—had pursuits and friends of their own. They were not in the least interested in the little girl so suddenly thrust into their family. Usually they went their own way, but sometimes Aunt Eren made them include Mienthe in one activity or another. That was worse, because when Mienthe was with them the boys made a point of speaking only to each other, deliberately over her head.

Nor, aside from the courtyard, were there any gardens. The wild Delta marshes began almost directly outside the gate and ran from the house all the way to the sea. The tough salt-grasses would cut your fingers if you swung your hand through them, and mosquitoes whined in the heavy shade of the mangroves.

"Stay out of the marsh," Aunt Eren warned Mienthe. "There are snakes and poisonous frogs and quicksand if you put a foot wrong. Snakes, do you hear? Stay close to the house. *Close to the house.* Do you understand me?" That was how she usually spoke to Mienthe: as though Mienthe were too young and stupid to understand anything unless it was very simple and emphatically repeated. Nor did Aunt Eren understand how a girl of nine could have so little ability with a needle. What *had* her nurses been teaching her? And she was appalled at Mienthe's letters, which were clear enough but *not at all* the graceful looping letters a girl should write.

Uncle Talenes was worse than either Aunt Eren or the boys. Mienthe had learned very young how to be quiet and not bring herself to her father's attention, but Uncle Talenes seemed to notice her no matter how quiet she was, and never to her credit. He had a sharp, whining voice that made her think of the mosquitoes, and he was dismayed, *dismayed*, to find her awkward and inarticulate in front of him and in front of the guests to whom he wanted to show her off. Was Mienthe perhaps not very clever? Then it was certainly a shame she was not prettier, wasn't it? How fortunate for her that her future was safe in his hands...

When she could, Mienthe fled out to the courtyard and hid behind the hanging moss that draped the largest of the oaks. The little birds fluttered in their cages when she disturbed them, their wings flashing yellow and blue and green, but when she tucked herself down close to the trunk and held still, they calmed. Sometimes they would sing. One of the birds, bright gold, had a clear and delicate song that seemed to Mienthe to be the very voice of grief. She often looked at the wires that held the birds trapped away from the sky and wished that she had wings herself, and no cage to keep her pinned close. She wanted to open the cage, all the cages, let all the birds go...but she did not dare.

Most of all Mienthe missed Tef. She tried to think about him working in the gardens, patiently teasing the roots of new flowers apart or carefully pruning the shrubs. But the images she called up seemed faint and distant and not very persuasive, even quite soon after she moved to Uncle Talenes's house. She thought perhaps Tef was no longer the gardener at her father's house. But she did not know how else to imagine him.

Mienthe also wondered who was living in *her* house now, who walked in her gardens? But in her mind, everything seemed empty—waiting for her father, who would never come back. She felt she would never go back to that house herself, even though her uncle said it was still hers. Her memories of the house, too, seemed strangely distant.

But her uncle's house seemed much too real.

Those three years were the worst of Mienthe's life. She could never please Aunt Eren, not even after she had learned to embroider neatly and write prettily. Uncle Talenes was worse: Mienthe sometimes felt her uncle did not see her at all, but only a kind of large doll he had won by a feat of cleverness and kept now as a trophy. And as an investment for the future. She understood that, eventually. But she had nothing in common with her cousins, nor did they care for her—no more than they cared for a new servant or a new table. They were interested in horses and hunting and swordwork. Neither of them was in the least interested in a *cousin*, even a half-cousin, no matter how much an heiress. Anyway, Karre already had his eye on the pretty daughter of one of Tiefenauer's wealthier merchants. Terre accepted with resignation his father's decision that he would eventually marry Mienthe, but he did not like the idea. He told Mienthe, matter-of-factly, that she was too pale and skinny and her eyes were too close together.

Then, when Mienthe was twelve, her cousin Bertaud came back to the Delta from the royal court. For days no one spoke of anything else. Mienthe gathered that this was a full cousin, that his father and hers had been full brothers, but that he was much older than she was. He had grown up in the Delta, but he had gone away and no one had thought he would come back. Only recently something had happened, something violent and dangerous, and now he seemed to have come back to stay. Mienthe wondered why her cousin had left the Delta, but she wondered even more why he had returned. She thought that if *she* ever left the Delta, she would never come back.

But her cousin Bertaud even took up his inheritance as Lord of the Delta. This seemed to shock and offend Uncle Talenes, though Mienthe was not quite sure why, if it was his right inheritance. He took over the great house in Tiefenauer, sending Mienthe's uncle Bodoranes back to his estate in Annand, and he dismissed all the staff. His dismissal of the staff seemed to shock and offend Aunt Eren as much as his mere return had Uncle Talenes. Both agreed that Bertaud must be high-handed and arrogant and vicious. Yes, it was vicious, uprooting poor Bodoranes like that after all his years and *years* of service while Bertaud had lived high in the court and ignored the Delta. Why, Bertaud was nearly foreign; as good as let someone from Tiearanan itself come and try to hold the Delta! What would Boudan have thought of his wild son? And flinging out all those people into the cold! But, well, yes, he *was* by blood Lord of the Delta, and perhaps there were ways to make the best of it... One might even have to note that Bodoranes had been regrettably obstinate in some respects...

Since it was full summer and sweltering, Mienthe wondered what her aunt could mean about flinging people into the cold.

And how exactly did Uncle Talenes mean to "make the best" of the new lord's arrival?

"We need to see him, see what he's like," Uncle Talenes explained to his elder son, now seventeen and even more interested in girls than he had been at fourteen, as long as they weren't Mienthe. "He's Lord of the Delta, for good or ill, and we need to get an idea of him. And we need to be polite. Very, very polite. If he's clever, he'll see how much to everyone's advantage raising the tariffs on Linularinan glass would be"—Uncle Talenes was heavily invested in Delta glass and ceramics—"and if he's less clever, then maybe he could use someone cleverer to point out these things."

Karre nodded, puffed up with importance because his father was explaining this to him. Mienthe, tucked forgotten in a chair in the corner—she had been looking at an illustrated herbal—understood finally that her uncle meant to bully or bribe the new Lord of the Delta if he could. She thought he probably could. Uncle Talenes almost always got his own way.

And Uncle Talenes seemed likely to get his own way this time, too. Not many days after he'd returned to the Delta, Lord Bertaud wrote accepting Talenes's invitation to dine and expressing a hope that two days hence would be convenient, if he were to call.

Aunt Eren stood over the servants while they scrubbed the mosaic floors and put flowers in every room and raked the gravel smooth in the drive. Uncle Talenes made sure his sons and Mienthe were well turned out and that Aunt Eren was wearing her most expensive jewelry, and he prepared detailed charts showing just how additions and increases to the current schedule of tariffs would benefit the whole Delta. He also explained several times to the whole household, in ever more vivid terms, how important it was to impress Lord Bertaud.

And precisely at noon on the day arranged, Lord Bertaud arrived.